PRAISE FOR SUSAN KEARNEY

"Kearney is a master storyteller."
—Virginia Henley, *New York Times* bestselling author

"Susan Kearney is a gifted storyteller with carefully woven plots and refreshing characterization. Her style is crisp and keeps her readers hungrily turning the pages."   —*The Tampa Tribune*

"From the first page, Kearney captures the reader."
—*Affaire de Coeur*

PRAISE FOR *THE CHALLENGE*

"Looking for something different? A futuristic romance: Susan Kearney's *The Challenge* gave me a new perspective . . . love and sex in the future!"
—Carly Phillips, *New York Times* bestselling author of the Chandler Brothers series

PRAISE FOR *THE DARE*

"Out of this world love scenes, pulse-pounding action, and characters who come right off the page."
—Suzanne Forster, *USA Today* bestselling author

"A desperate gamble leads to high-voltage action and sensuality in Ms. Kearney's newest page-turner. One of Ms. Kearney's strengths is her deft use of characterization which instantly vests readers in the perilous quest."   —*Romantic Times BOOKreviews*

TOR ROMANCE BOOKS BY SUSAN KEARNEY

Solar Heat

SUSAN KEARNEY

tor paranormal romance

A TOM DOHERTY ASSOCIATES BOOK
NEW YORK

SOLAR HEAT

A Tor Book
Published by Tom Doherty Associates, LLC
175 Fifth Avenue
New York, NY 10010

www.tor.com

Tor® is a registered trademark of Tom Doherty Associates, LLC.

ISBN-13: 978-0-7653-5844-8
ISBN-10: 0-7653-5844-1

First Edition: February 2008

Printed in the United States of America

0 9 8 7 6 5 4 3 2 1

This book is dedicated to my daughter, Tara Kearney. It's not every mom who is lucky enough to have a daughter as wonderful as Tara, especially a daughter talented enough to shoot *Solar Heat*'s cover models, design her mom's press kits, update her Web site, and act in her trailers. But most of all, thanks for putting up with me. I love you.

Acknowledgments

So many people help put out a book that it's impossible to name and thank them all. But my thanks have to begin with Tor for letting me write the books I love; my creative and supportive editor, Anna Genoese; Seth Lerner in the art department for his marvelous cover design; Leslie Henkel in publicity; and then there's the wonderful production, sales, and marketing teams, plus probably other departments I know nothing about.

I'd like to thank Charlotte Douglas and Jeanie London for reading the book and making suggestions. All mistakes are my own.

Also, I owe thanks to my publicist, Shannon Aviles, for pushing me to get the word out there about my books, and to the booksellers who so often hand-sell futuristic romances to readers. And I'd like to thank my fans who read and recommend my books to their friends.

1

Talk about unlucky missions. Everything that could go wrong *had*. One moment Azsla and her crew of four "fugitive" slaves had been on course for Zor, the next the starboard stabilizer had malfunctioned, damaging the hull. The spaceship had jolted, and engine failure had turned their systems inside out, and slammed her crew into unconsciousness. The cosmic whammy had dealt them one hell of a beating, and she thanked Holy *Vigo* for the lifelong supply of salt that had given her strength and enabled her to remain alert.

The ship was currently powerless and drifting toward the portal that was supposed to have transported them to Zor and freedom. The lights flickered. With the snap of a toggle, Azsla cut the blaring alarm. She didn't need a news flash to know that unless she altered her damaged ship's course, the forces sucking them into the black maw would squash them flatter than a neutron particle.

By now, the backup system should have come on line automatically. Azsla initiated emergency procedures and flipped open the auxiliary engine panel. Twisting the manual override, she thrust the handle to starboard. But the reboot mechanism was also on the fritz. When no lights or controls lit up, licks of alarm shot down Azsla's back. Mother of Salt—a double cosmic whammy.

Keep it together. She'd drilled for emergency situations. Only this was no drill. They were in trouble. Bad trouble. And fear ignited in the pit of her gut like a retrorocket on nitro.

She checked her watch, then estimated the triple threat of time, distance, and mass. At the inescapable result—certain death—her scalp broke into a sweat. As a First of Rama, Azsla had been entitled to a life of privilege and all the strength-building salt she could swallow. But what should have been a life of luxury on Rama had been destroyed by a slave rebellion that had led to hundreds of thousands of slaves escaping from Rama to Zor, a planet in another solar system. To prevent further uprisings and retaliation from the slaves, she'd agreed to go to Zor as a spy. She'd always known her mission would require sacrifice and she'd accepted the danger of pretending to be an underfirst, a lowly slave, in order to assess what kind of weapons Zor was developing against Rama. But to succeed, she had to get to Zor.

Right now, that didn't seem likely. Or even possible. She glanced around at her still unconscious crew. She'd always thought she'd understood the risk of covert operations. When her superiors had cooked up this mission, she'd volunteered. The decision hadn't been a hard one.

Fifteen years ago when she'd been in her early teens, a slave uprising on Rama had killed her parents and ruined her home. Some 200,000 slaves had escaped her world and resettled on the planet Zor. Eventually the Firsts had regrouped and regained control, but life as Azsla had known it was over.

After losing everything, her existence had gone from street orphan to ward of the state. When the Corps offered to train her as a weapons specialist and promised her a shot at stopping any chance of another slave rebellion, they hadn't had to ask twice. As a First she'd understood, even as a teenager, that as long as Zor offered safe haven to slaves, all Ramans stood in peril, their way of life threatened. And it had been surprisingly easy to leave behind her regimented, friendless existence where no one would miss her.

But to become an effective spy, Azsla had been asked to accomplish what no other Raman had ever done: suppress her *Quait,* a First's ability to dominate. She'd accepted she might never succeed—but after years of training she had achieved the impossible. Sort of. As long as she kept her emotions in check, her *Quait* didn't take over and Azsla could prevent herself from overpowering the will of her crew and outing herself. By reining herself in tight, she could now pass as one of them.

She'd never considered that engine failure might kill her in this tin can before she'd even landed on Zor.

If her crew ever sniffed out her real role, they'd sabotage the journey to Zor. Slaves might be weak, but they were fanatical. Dangerous. They placed little value on life, even their own. To find out what the Zorans were up to, Azsla had to be just as ruthless. Knowing any one of them would turn on a First to keep her away from Zor reminded her to keep up her guard. Always.

One by one, the systems went down. Getting to Zor, at this point, was secondary to staying alive. Artificial gravity failed. The air grew stale. It was already freezing cold, as if the heat hadn't been on since liftoff three days ago. Azsla gripped the command console to maintain her position at her station and ignored the white vapor puffing from her mouth, the prickly bumps rising over her flesh, her body-racking shivers. Her unconscious crewmen floated away from their stations as the ship lost gravity and she couldn't blow off a spark of sorrow over their plight. But during the long months of training for this mission, she'd come to know her crew, and, to her surprise, respect them. Now, she couldn't remember when she'd stopped thinking of them as slaves and started thinking of them as people.

"Anyone awake?"

None of her crew answered, likely frozen, shocked, and possibly injured. Yet, they weren't dead. Rak, her second in command, drew in choked breaths. Kali, the copilot and chief engineer, flailed on the ceiling, seeking leverage to alter his attitude.

Knowing she had mere moments to divert the ship, Azsla stayed put. If she couldn't change their course, the wormhole would devour the ship, leaving nothing, not even scattered debris, to mark their passing.

"Report," she insisted, her voice lowering an octave

as if ashes filled her mouth, her cold-numbed fingers flicking the damaged control toggles, frantic to restart the engines. Surely Jadlan or Micoo in the sleepers had been jarred awake? Or had they ditched protocol, abandoned their posts, and ejected in their escape pods? Azsla had no way of knowing, not with her instruments off line, but as always, she cut her crew some slack, all too aware that none of them had her superior intellect or physical strength. After all, they were slaves.

Taking stock, she assessed their predicament with as much presence of mind as she could summon. Instant depressurization had collapsed the aft stabilizer. Her damage-weakened ship now spiraled end over end—straight toward hull-crushing forces that would terminate her mission—unless she found some miraculous way to steer clear.

Azsla ripped open the panel's cover to examine the wiring. The reek of burning plastic singed her nostrils. Smoke filtered into the cabin and fear scratched along her skin like claws, ripping and shredding, threatening to tap out her last reserve of *Quait* control. Damn her crew. They should have responded by now.

Not that she was even close to normal. Her fingers trembled and she loathed her own weakness as much as that of the underfirsts who hadn't responded to her plea for information. With her gut doing a slow spin job, she battled fresh panic.

Easy. She was beginning to hate the empty brutality of space. Not that she was bitter. Sweet *Vigo,* people were supposed to live on planets where they didn't have to breathe recycled air, where every little mechanical failure wasn't life threatening, where a stray piece of dust didn't create lethal havoc with her ship's systems.

Trying to buy herself a little relief from pounding panic, Azsla attempted to dial down her emotion. She cornered it, squashed it. Beat it into submission. *Pretend it's just another drill.* After ten years of keeping her cool and suppressing her *Quait,* her spontaneous instinct to dominate should have been under control . . . yet, as the port fuel tank exploded, her natural inclinations to overpower kicked in. Hard. Every cell in her body ached to reach out and make the crew work as one. But if she reverted to instinct and used her *Quait* to save all their lives by forcing them to fix the ship, her crew would then learn that she wasn't one of them. If they didn't kill her, she would wind up returning home in defeat. Sure, mind scrubbers could erase her crew's memories, but the Corps didn't accept failure. Azsla would never get another shot at returning to Zor.

But the aching instinct to survive at any cost began to burn. Sizzle. Her blood boiled with the need to take charge . . . for the sake of self-preservation.

She was about to lose it and take over the will of every underfirst on board. With no time to talk herself down slowly, she popped a *tranq,* swallowing the pill without water. Immediately, the fire eased. The seething boil cut to a manageable simmer. Of course, later, if she lived that long, she'd pay for relying on the *tranq.* If her superiors ever discovered she'd resorted to artificial tactics, it would put them off—enough to shut her down, boot her from the Corps. But with the metal hull groaning, official consequences were the least of her problems.

The portal was sucking them in. Thanks to the *tranq,* her *Quait* settled and the need to dominate abated. Finally, praying to save the ship from annihilation, she struggled to route the last remaining battery power into the bow thrusters.

Her fingers manually keyed in instructions, and she regained her normal tone of voice. "Kali. What's doing?"

Kali groaned, opened his eyes, shoved off the ceiling and buckled into the copilot's seat. He slapped his flickering monitor. "Navigation's a bust. Hyperdrive's nonoperational. Engineering's off line. Life support's nonfunctional. Time to bail?"

Unless she could alter their direction, they'd have to abandon ship or be crushed four ways to summer solstice. However, the portal would draw in the sleeping pods, and, as long as the emergency batteries maintained the pods' shielding, they'd shoot straight through to Zor. Hopefully someone at the other end would pick up an automated distress signal—if not, they would drift in space, frozen. Forever. Not an appealing option, but neither was instant death.

Azsla jerked her thumb toward the escape pods. "Hit the airlock."

Although her crew often disappointed, not quite living up to her standards, they tried hard. And she wasn't cruel enough to dash their hopes and reveal they had little chance of survival, never mind escape. Of course, the Corps never intended for her crew to achieve the freedom they sought. On Zor, they'd be rounded up by other spies and sent back to Rama in chains as an example of what happened to slaves who attempted escape from the mother world.

Kali unsnapped his safety harness, snagged Rak off the ceiling, and swam toward the rear. "Captain, you coming?"

"Just messing with the bow thrusters." She didn't exactly lie. Although she had little hope of cranking out a course alteration with the bow thrusters, she used the excuse to stay at the helm to secretly shoot the logs and a report of the disaster back to Rama, a last-ditch effort to inform the Corps of their predicament. Notifying home was a calculated risk. Her crew believed they'd escaped Rama, when in actuality the government had allowed them to leave in order to insert Azsla into their midst. If any of them caught a whiff of what they'd consider betrayal, there was no telling if she could handle them after swallowing that *tranq*.

"Captain."

At Kali's sharp tone, Azsla stiffened. Had he seen her dispatch the log? Despite the *tranq*, she couldn't conceal the edge to her voice. "Yes?"

"Ship temperature's approaching freezing. The hull's breached. Shields are failing. We need to leave, now."

Relieved her cover remained intact, Azsla skimmed her hands over the keys, robbing the remaining power from every system except the pods. "I'm right behind you."

Kali soared through the control cabin into the ship's bowels. She heard him pop open the pods and the terrified voices of her crew. So the others had awakened. She shouldn't be thinking about them. Slaves were easily replaced. Weak. A waste of salt.

Yet . . . this crew had trained hard. Not as hard as she had. But then they didn't have her abilities. Still, they'd done what they could with what they had.

Finally, she shunted the last of the power into the boosters.

Done. She turned and shields began to go down. The injured hull squealed in agony, the tearing of metal a death knell. Diving for the escape pod, she overshot her mark. Kali snatched her by the ankle, saving her from a painful smack into the bulkhead.

"Thanks." She seized a handhold and righted herself. He'd already stuffed Jadlan, Micoo, and Rak into the pods and ejected them through the airlock.

"Ready to bounce?"

"Absolutely." Totally on board with the plan, she slapped the button to open her sleeper. Kali slid into the last remaining pod.

She tensed her muscles to do the same. Only her pod didn't open. "What the frip?" All hell was about to come down on the ship and she nailed the button mechanism again with her fist.

And got zip. Zero. Zilch. The canopy refused to budge. Her high-pitched gasp shamed her and she hoped Kali put it down to the cold that seemed to have frozen her bones.

This was insane. Surely every freaking system on the ship couldn't fail . . . unless someone had sabotaged the mission. But who? If the slaves had known about her subterfuge, they would have killed her, or died trying.

Not even they would have vandalized the entire ship. And she had no other enemy. The Corps wanted her to succeed.

The delay didn't seem to faze Kali. Instead of ejecting, he moved smoothly, climbing from his pod. "Let me." Picking up a wrench, he slapped the release button.

"It's no good." She pointed to the hull that had caved, crushing her pod, the metal cross brace obstructing the release mechanism from firing properly.

The hull howled like a wild beast, the last of the shields failing. From the ship's bowels, the engines rumbled like a volcano about to erupt. Her ability to issue orders dulled by the *tranq,* she said nothing as Kali picked her up, slipped her into his pod, and closed the canopy with a click of finality. Hit the eject button.

Her last sight of him floored her. He seemed at peace. Eyes closed, his lips moved, and if she hadn't known better, he'd appeared to be praying. At peace with his death.

She shot into space, a rush of emotions flooding over her *tranqed* emotions. Relief. Hope. Astonishment.

Kali had given up his chance to live. For her.

She hadn't even used her *Quait.* She closed her fingers into fists. Kali had meant nothing to her. Slaves were easily replaceable. Unworthy. Yet, she'd spent enough time with her second in command to know Kali's life had meant everything to him. He'd planned to begin anew on Zor. Marry. Have children. His dreams would never have happened because of her mission . . . but Kali hadn't known that.

Turning, she watched the ship implode and vanish

into the portal. Kali was dead, his body relegated to tactonic dust.

She shouldn't have cared. Cold from the sleep capsule spread over her skin like guilt. She told herself slaves died every day. So what?

But if Kali's selfless sacrifice didn't matter, then why was her vision blurred? Why were tears freezing on her cheeks?

2

✵

Derrek Archer tunneled through his sash drawer in search of sleek and elegant, finding rumpled silk instead. Apparently disheveled was the current fashion. While the sash looked frumpy and silly to him, he didn't keep up with planetside fashions.

He didn't need to.

Before Derrek's ship, *Beta Five,* hit Zor's gravity well, his tailor Egan had downloaded the current style statement to his com system in the aft section of Derrek's new spaceship. She'd worked him up this jazzy new wardrobe and the tech knew her stuff. When Derrick debarked, he'd be good to meet or retreat with businessmen and manufacturers or to smartly hover off to sporting games. While he'd never been the least concerned with his appearance, he'd learned that dressing the part allowed him to win more concessions for his workers, tax breaks they badly needed in order to continue to bring the precious salt back to Zor. After his visit planetside was done, he'd happily give up making fashion statements and return to his home in the asteroid salt mines, which couldn't be soon enough for his taste.

His com unit vibrated. "Derrek here."

"Hi, boss. Sir, is this a good time?" Haywar, one of Derrek's five assistants back home on Alpha One, spoke warmly, his voice crisp and clear, as if he stood alongside Derrek in the ship's master cabin, not hundreds of thousands of miles away in the asteroid belt.

"What's doing?" Derrek always made time for Haywar. The man stayed on top of things and he appreciated not only his efficiency but his loyalty.

In preparation for landing on Zor, Derrek armed up. He slid a knife into the band at his ankle, a stunner into the holster at the small of his back and hid extra credit chips in a pocket in his belt. Not that he expected trouble, but he never went out without arms. A decade of salt had strengthened all the former slaves' *Quait,* but with their new strengths came new problems. Occasionally they settled disagreements with violence. As a wealthy spacer, Derrek was a target. It was all too likely he might link up with some nut job who'd injected more salt into his system than his legal allotment. Most slaves wanted nothing to do with the powers salt could give them—a power to dominate others who'd ingested less salt. But a few renegades were on a power trip and had yet to realize it wasn't right to dominate others simply because one could.

"Is *Beta Five* tricked up the way you wanted, boss?"

Oh, yeah. Double, yeah. This latest prototype had

given him one sweet ride. Derrek hadn't been so hyped about a new project in years. This ship's technology would give his people more options, letting them explore farther for precious salt than ever before. "The ship's moves are smooth, but navigation needs an upgrade."

"Just don't get lost," Haywar teased.

"You won't get rid of me that easy. Besides, if I let anything happen to Taylo's new design, he'd jettison my hide out the nearest airlock."

Beta Five might need tweaking but she was a thing of pure beauty. Now she could really go fast. Really far. Maybe buy all Zorans freedom from the ever-present fear of recapture from their former masters who lived back on planet Rama. And it was all thanks to Taylo Misa, a brilliant engineer Derrek had hired.

Five years ago Taylo had discovered a way to open a portal for sound waves, allowing for instant intersolar communication. Derrek had paid Taylo a small fortune to give up tinkering in his garage to work for him. He'd tricked out a lab with the latest and most esoteric equipment he could buy. The payoff had been worth the enormous expense. Taylo had taken the same sound wave principles he'd discovered and applied them to moving mass through space—inventing the hyperdrive for Derrek's newest spaceship. But Derrek wouldn't say more over an open com. Not when he didn't trust his scrambler to keep his business private. Not when he didn't know who might be spying this close to Zor's atmosphere.

Last time he'd been dirtside, some grifter had planted a bug on his com unit, broadcasting Derrek's conversations to the highest bidder. He wouldn't get nailed again. As a target he had to stay one step ahead of the pack nipping at his heels. That meant planning. Using his head. Never taking anyone or anything for granted. He owed it to Taylo and his team to make sure their hard work wasn't stolen.

Currently Derrek's company ferried salt through a stationary portal, but the journey still required expensive fuel and skilled man hours to transport the salt to and from the portal. The mind-blowing possibility of using Taylo's technology to open a portal whenever and wherever it was needed, of shooting salt directly through hyperspace with no spaceship required, had Derrek charged. Soon there might be enough salt to increase the planetary population threefold. The beauty of a point-to-point delivery system was an idea he couldn't let drop—even if the research cost him a fortune in salt. Success would open up space travel like never before possible. And it would ensure their children, who wouldn't have to spend months in space, grew up with strong bones and muscles as well as clever minds.

"Sir, can you hear me?"

"Like you're planetside." The question drew Derrek from his plans back to this awesome ship. Once he'd mined enough light metal to mass produce the craft, her sweet design would revolutionize space travel for the masses. Well, maybe not the masses but for the salt miners and the military and the unstable Zoran government. Not even the home planet of Rama had this kind of technology. And with the Zorans gaining technological superiority, they could remain free. Finally he could make a lick of difference. A fleet of these ships could be the answer to freeing the rest of the slaves on Rama—especially if the spaceships came blasting through hyperspace with high-tactonic weapons.

Knowing Haywar wouldn't have linked just to chat about *Beta Five,* Derrek asked again, "What's up?"

"The drill bit on Asa Major cranked out. Until we replace the *diamondite* heads, we're shut down."

Derrek's eyes narrowed. Any stoppage in the salt supply had serious consequences attached. He wasn't just thinking about company profits, but the strength and well-being of all Zoran citizens. For them to stay healthy, the salt supply had to remain steady. "When can Vanguard Mining send us a replacement?"

"There's a waiting list."

So what else was new? Resources on Zor were scarce. They needed more labor to keep up with the high demand for manufactured equipment, but Rama refused to release any slaves. And none were escaping—not since the mass revolution a decade ago. Now Rama was locked down tight, preventing the other slaves from leaving. And the birth rate on Zor wasn't growing fast enough, either—due to lack of salt.

Taking advantage of the new technology that could open a window anywhere on the hull's surface, Derrek widened the view port to the planet below. The greenery looked . . . messy. As they hovered, waiting for permission to dock, he zoomed in on his estate, pleased with *Beta Five*'s magnification upgrades. Every blade of grass had been neatly clipped, edged and manicured, but already Derrek missed the sharp edges of home. Green didn't impress him. Space where a man had room to grow was more to his taste. Back home, his house looked out on spectacular vistas of Alpha One's twirling water crystals, and the three blue spectrum moons that revolved and cast an array of changing hues over the pristine *granitite* face of Mount Crion. On Alpha One, the air was filtered and pure, not clogged with the reek of Zor that awaited him below.

He drummed his fingers on the view port. "Simon owes me a favor, I'll look him up after I'm dirtside."

"Thanks, boss. The sooner the better."

"Understood. Make sure to send Simon a case of salt. Use express shuttle."

"Got it. Have fun, boss man."

Like that was going to happen. Derrek didn't do fun. He stuck to what he was good at. Business. And bribes were standard operating procedure. A little extra salt went a long way towards easing a lot of headaches.

Spending most of the last decade building Archer Intersolar Mining from a four-bit operation into a megacorporation that employed thousands had its perks. He spent most of his time where he wished. In space. Yet, business occasionally required Zor-side networking and his personal touch. So he made a trip in-system every few cycles.

Once he landed, he had meetings set up to fill every waking hour. But like a little kid who didn't want to leave his new toy, he wished he could stay aboard, really rag her out and see what she could do. He reminded himself this was a shakedown cruise and he wasn't a test pilot. But Holy *Vigo,* he ached to see what she could do in a flat-out race for the stars. . . .

Truth be told, meetings with government diplomats were more his brother's thing. But with Cade off on a second honeymoon and incommunicado, Derrek couldn't ask him to stand in for him—especially with President Laurie.

He'd best finish dressing or he'd miss the landing. He shot firestone links through his cuffs, a gift to himself on his thirty-fourth birthday last year. He'd mined the precious stones while prospecting for salt and the flashing magenta and sapphire hues reminded him of who he was and how far he'd come—from former slave to salt miner to influential and wealthy entrepreneur. He donned a jacket, its severe style tightly fitted to his chest and shoulders, and suppressed a shrug. It wouldn't kill him to link face-to-face with the current president. As always, he'd keep the visit short.

Derrek didn't belong dirtside. Never had. Civilization and Zor reminded him of . . . Poli, his ex-wife. And his children.

While resigned to the fact that the only family he'd ever loved didn't flipping want him in their lives, he'd nevertheless used his influence to ensure they'd escaped Rama during the first wave of colonization. He'd even allowed the new husband to accompany his family. Reports said they were happy, happy, happy. But their well-being didn't stop the pain of losing his wife and children from stabbing like an ice pick in his heart.

He still resented the fact that they neither needed nor

wanted him. So maybe it was better he was in full-avoidance mode. While his blood pressure still soared during his perusal of the weekly reports about his former family, at least afterwards he no longer had to toss back a whisky to score bunk time. That was progress. Sometimes he even squeaked by with a few hours of sleep. Yeah. He was fine. In another decade or so he might not even care they'd shut him out.

"President Laurie's tough to read." Sauren Kalow, his friend, a straight-shooter and Derrek's VP of Archer Intersolar Mining, ducked through the bulkhead door into his cabin. With his lips curving into a smile, his eyes twinkling, he plucked out of the drawer a wrinkled white sash with tiny sparkles on the edges and offered it up. Sauren, stunted by a severe lack of salt at birth, made up for his diminutive stature with a positive attitude and fierce determination. He knew his way around Derrek's dirtside estate quite well, probably better than Derrek did—since he stayed there more often—but this journey through hyperspace had faded his bronzed skin to a puckish green. Finally, last shift, he'd kicked the nausea and the healthy glow was back. "Any idea what the pres wants from you?"

"He's got his hands full, I'll give him that. I'm guessing he requires money, salt or advice."

Sauren snorted. "Too bad you can't give him some common sense about taxing miners."

Derrek pinned the sash to his shoulder, then ignored the silly flash. Although he'd contributed heavily to Laurie's campaign, Derrek had also funded the other side. He found it valuable to be connected, no matter who was in power. "Our president won't be effective until he stops trying to gain a consensus. He talks out of both sides—"

"He's a politician." Sauren rolled his eyes in disgust. He wouldn't have been Derrek's second in command if he hadn't known how to get things done, and the current political mess annoyed him almost as much as it did Derrek. "Politicians negotiate. That's who they are. What they do."

"They get nothing done." Derrek had no time or patience for the eternal squabbles over how much salt each person should consume. Some slaves argued they should strengthen themselves until they were as strong as the Firsts on Rama. Other recalled that the ability to dominate and steal the will of others had a way of making good people go bad. After thousands of years of slavery, freedom and *Quait* didn't solve every problem. Zorans had real issues to deal with. Hard problems to solve. And most citizens wanted a say in how Zor should be run. So instead of consensus, controversy was the norm . . . and no one decided, never mind accomplished anything. As a result, the planet's defense was a mess. The economy verged on catastrophe. They needed a larger labor force. If only they could free the rest of their people still on Rama these problems would be solved, but since everyone feared incurring the wrath of their former homeworld, the matter had been put off.

The Zoran government lacked balls. They acted as if they believed if they hid from the Firsts on Rama, the Firsts would forget them. But that wouldn't happen.

That's why Derrek was making plans. Long-term plans to free the people still enslaved on Rama. He didn't mind depleting his fortune to construct the hyper-drive engines as well as a self-sufficient city in space—another one of his ongoing and expensive projects—if it would eventually lead to freeing all his people. And he didn't have time for tax debates—

As if reading his thoughts Sauren interrupted. "Not even you can ignore a presidential invite."

"I could if I had the right excuse." Derrek allowed himself a tight smile, then adjusted the sash over his dark emerald suit and slipped his feet into boots of soft leather. Thank-you, *Vigo,* the heels that had been so popular during his last visit were now history.

With that thought, Derrek altered the material's light refraction until the boots' color exactly matched his fitted trousers, tailored jacket, and his deep-set eyes. This moon cycle on Zor, monochromatic color symbolized power and his tailor had smartly capitalized on his assets. More than once, Egan had told him that his eyes were his best feature.

Derrek knew better. Women were attracted to his salt stash. Without his showing an iota of encouragement, women hit on him. Often. But he'd kept his nose in the salt dust, where life was simple. The more salt he mined, the more people he helped. After growing up with nothing, life was . . . good. Excellent, really.

Still . . . he wondered if the pres would be insulted if he didn't accept the invite. Likely—the answer was yes. So although he had a dozen links to make, he went to the bridge to take the president's message, fully expecting that the busy politician might have had to reschedule or cancel the invite to the mansion.

With one last image-check in the mirror, he raked his fingers through his collar-length black hair. Although the most successful salt miner on Rama could get by with eccentric, Derrek had never been interested in merely getting by. After he'd figured out that information was the key to getting ahead, he'd worked on having more information, getting it faster and jumping on it more quickly than anyone else. To acquire that information, he had to network. And to network to best advantage, he had made himself fit in. The formula was simple and one he adhered to religiously since it had always served him well.

Almost always. If one discounted the total memory scrub that had cost him his family.

Shove it.

It had taken one brutal year of pushing himself to the max to learn to walk and talk again. But that determination had helped him to build an empire. Later he'd done as much as any man to help his people free themselves from slavery and salt deprivation. He had friends. Success. For him the payoff for years of hard work had been millions of tons of life-giving salt—and the satisfaction that neither he nor his people would ever be kept down again. This was his life.

It was enough.

He and Sauren stepped through the corridor to the bridge, where Derrek got a bead on his crew. Adain squawked on the com with flight control, but that didn't stop him from whistling when he spied Derrek's new duds. "Damn. If that's the style, I may not get off *Beta Five.*"

"Your choice." Derrek raised a brow. "But I thought you had a hot date?"

Adain flushed and suddenly busied himself with his controls.

Their shipboard computer genius, Benet, was eyeing Derrek with a jealous gleam. The youngest of the crew, he was also the largest. He'd still been a child when he'd left Rama and the extra rations of salt during his growing years had made him taller and stronger than his elders. "Think Egan can make me a set of those—"

"No problem. I'll even advance you the credit." Derrek waved Sauren to a seat at the science station. His crew had worked long and hard on this project and deserved to blow off some steam.

Benet looked up from engineering. "Don't waste the credit, Adain. Clothes ain't fooling the ladies none into thinking you're a dirt lover."

They'd all spent so much time in space that anyone with eyes could tell from their rolling gaits that they were accustomed to low grav. Although the doc required the crew to build muscle in anticipation of landfall, their spaceman stride was unmistakable. Unfortunately for his crew, women wanted men who stayed home with them and the kids, not ones who left for months at a time. Of course, there were a few women who didn't mind the loneliness out in the asteroids and who didn't miss the amenities—but not enough. The chance that these men might find a mate who wanted to live in the asteroid belt was poor, and those few females who were out there . . . tended to be independent. Eccentric.

The crew settled. Benet pivoted back to his electrical

impulse console, reducing feedback from the engines in a never-ending tune-up. Cavin, an average-sized, chestnut-haired man, with excellent skills was busy monitoring nav and life support.

The picture of smooth efficiency and sleek black modern design, *Beta Five* sported crew stations along the perimeter of a circular bridge—with command control at the center console. Above the crews' heads, they all had a 360 degree view outside. But from command, the panorama was nothing short of spectacular.

At the moment, Zor's three continents and four oceans dominated the lower section, and beyond, the ebbing moon cast a soft crescent shadow as it ascended into eclipse. Derek hit the privacy mode to prevent his conversation from distracting his people. Although he and his crew were tight, he was careful by nature. He shared high-level conversations only on a need-to-know basis.

From the Zoran capital below, President Laurie strode toward his own monitor and greeted Derek with a stiff bow. "Good to see you again."

Derek bowed in return. "The pleasure is mine."

"In a hurry to land?" Laurie raised an eyebrow.

"Why do you ask?"

"We spotted something interesting in space. At first we feared Rama had sent a ship through the portal, but instead, we now believe we're picking up several escape pods."

Interesting. Although rumors always abounded that more slaves would follow them to Zor, none ever had. When the portal had opened several years ago, Zorans prepared for attack. They monitored that section of space closely, but no one had ever come through the portal . . . until now. "How many pods?"

"Four."

"Survivors?"

President Laurie didn't answer his question. "I heard you always travel with a doctor."

"Doc Falcon is aboard."

"Perhaps you could check out the pods for us? We don't have a ship in the sector large enough to handle the load of four pods."

More likely there were political implications and Laurie wanted to distance himself from the fallout. Derrek weighed the choice of satisfying his curiosity and possibly saving lives against the nuisance of rescheduling his meetings.

"I'd be happy to do the honors. If we find survivors . . ."

"Do what you wish. We never had this conversation."

Derrek frowned. What the hell was going on? He didn't need to step into secret political crap. "I don't understand."

Laurie eyed him, his eyes pleading. "I'm in a difficult position." Clearly he didn't feel free to say more.

"Fine. You owe me." Maybe he wouldn't have to beg to get rid of the miner's tax.

Laurie nodded. "I'll remember." Then he ended the com with a click.

Weird. The entire conversation had given off deadly vibes. Derrek felt as though he were feeling his way through a mine field, without having a clue to what might trigger a blast.

Derrek punched in the coordinates to Adain. When the numbers hit his console, the pilot shot a piercing look at his captain. A good man, he didn't ask questions, just rerouted *Beta Five* back into space, banking and rolling into a 160-degree turn. "Sir, you want the helm?"

Derrek shook his head. Although his fingers itched to take the controls, he needed his mind free of piloting duties to oversee the op.

"New coordinates laid in, captain." Adain swung around in his swivel chair. "Cavin, get me a nav check."

"Nav check is . . ." Cavin hunched over his screen and frowned.

"I'm picking up four emergency signals," Benet peered at his instrument panel.

"There are four vessels out there."

"Escape pods. Let's pick them up, boys." Derrek leaned forward and upped the magnification. At the same time he peered at the pods, four tiny dots floating in the vastness of space, he switched on the com. "Doctor Falcon, please report to the cargo bay."

DERREK WIPED THE pod's spaceshield free of condensation with a rag and stared at the sleeping woman. She was tall for a slave. But was she too tall? Since the portal had opened three years ago, no one from Rama had come through it. No Firsts. No underfirsts. No one.

Rumors had flown like crazy. Rumors that the Firsts of Rama were waiting to use the portal to stage a full-fledged invasion. Rumors that the portal was haunted and anyone who went through would be cursed for eternity. Rumors that the Firsts had found a way to cloak their ships, that they were already on Zor, fully *tranqed* to disguise their *Quait,* enabling them to spy on the Zorans.

Derrek didn't believe rumors. However, he couldn't discount that rumors were often grounded in truth. And the woman frozen in her pod was tall for a slave.

Salt deprivation during the formative years didn't only stunt *Quait,* it stunted physical growth, strength, and stamina. On Rama the Firsts weren't just taller and stronger, they radiated vitality and arrogance. The privileged Firsts had straighter spines. They held their heads higher, their shoulders were squared. Slaves pretty much were the opposite. Slouched, heads bowed, shoulders sagging, their lives of toil wore them down physically and emotionally.

Since the escape to Zor, the freed slaves had had access to more salt. Although the adults could no longer regain their lost height, their muscles and bones had strengthened. Their *Quait* increased—although it was against the law to ingest enough to be able to dominate the will of others. Obedience was voluntary, with most freed slaves having no wish to turn into the cruel and freakish Firsts they'd left behind.

Anyone caught breaking the law was severely punished.

The three other males were smaller, in poor physical condition, much like Derrek had been after his escape. But for this woman in the pod to display such height spiked Derrek's suspicions as much as his curiosity.

She was an anomaly. As he leaned forward and smoothed away the condensation on the canopy, he read her name on her flight suit. *Azsla*.

A beautiful name for an extraordinary woman. Not only did she appear exceptionally healthy, her skin flawless, her teeth good—at least what he could see of them through her slightly parted lips, she was stunning with silky dark hair that brushed her shoulders in a ragged cut that emphasized the delicacy of her features. Looking at her didn't just make him catch his breath. His breath left his lungs with a taste of wonder. His skin tingled. Blood surged south.

Every primal instinct urged him to pop the canopy. Take her into his arms. Warm her with his own body heat. It was such a ridiculous notion that he had to clutch the pod's spaceshield to remain standing. What was the matter with him? Waking someone from a sleep pod was a delicate process that took careful monitoring of temperature control and if he tried to hasten the process, he could cause her serious damage, even death. Doc Falcon would handle her awakening. But, it was taking every microunit of willpower to step back. And when he could no longer see the woman's face, his sense of loss was nothing short of staggering. His heart beat hard. His chest grew tight and he found himself leaning forward, eager to catch another glimpse.

His reaction was way out of whack.

He liked women. He did. Although, *Vigo* knew he probably hadn't had his share. After his mindwipe, he'd had a dry spell in the female department. He'd spent so much time recuperating, then escaping and establishing a new life, he'd neglected his social life. Actually he didn't have a personal life. Not if he discounted business relationships.

So why were his hands shaking? Why did he feel as if every second it took for the pod to recycle and for Azsla to wake up was an eternity? It made no sense. Deeply disturbed by his unexplainable reaction, he was suspicious as hell.

Had he inhaled some kind of drug on the pod? One that affected him physiologically? Was she some kind of secret weapon? Because she sure as hell didn't look like a Raman slave—unless she was one of the women Firsts used for pleasure. But that couldn't be right, either. Not only was she gorgeous, she was physically fit. And slaves didn't eat enough salt to be in her kind of shape.

So why had he reacted to her as if she'd been created especially for him? His body might be craving her, but his brain told him to back off. Fast.

So what if she was incredibly lovely. This sure wasn't his normal reaction. As a wealthy man, Derrek had women hit on him all the time. Many of them were attractive. Compared feature to feature, some were even more beautiful. But none of them had made his heart beat triple time. None of them had him sexed up as if they were a total package of feminine heat.

What the hell was wrong with him? He shook off the personal interest and glanced at Sauren. He, too, was staring at Azsla but had she affected him the same way? Was she some new kind of First? When Firsts used their *Quait*, they forced slaves to submit to their will. But the slaves remained fully aware of the mental manipulation. The slaves might not want to do a task, but while they had no choice, they understood their muscles obeyed a different master and that knowledge was part of the horror. They knew exactly what they did—but had no control over themselves.

Terror that the Firsts might have learned to manipulate emotions helped beat down his attraction to her. Derrek took a fast step backward from the pod in his cargo bay. "Sauren, is she weirding you out?"

"Huh?" Sauren leaned closer, peering through the canopy. Then he straightened and joined Derrek. "What's wrong?"

Like he was going to admit that the sleeping woman had set his heart racing? Just because he'd looked at her? Such a strong physical reaction to her didn't make sense. He needed to know if she affected other people that way . . . or just him. "Sauren. Think hard. What were your exact thoughts when you looked into her face?"

"Pity at what she must have suffered." Sauren shot him a puzzled look. "Frustration over the sad fact that all our people still aren't free. Relief that she made it. Hope that more slaves will arrive soon."

Sauren didn't mention lust. Or even attraction. And that made Derrek even more suspicions. "What about her looks?"

"She's well formed."

Well formed? Could he have been more insulting? She was fripping awesome. Before Derrek realized his mind had ordered his feet forward, he was back at her pod, staring into her face. As the unit warmed, color returned to her cheeks, turning them a soft golden hue. Her full lips turned pink.

Damn, she looked good. Too good.

Even as his palms turned damp and his pulse raced, he recognized his attraction to her as dangerous. While he had no idea what was going on, he did know his reaction wasn't normal. As her lungs expanded, she began to breathe, her chest rising and falling in an enticing rhythm. He didn't think he'd ever seen anything so beautiful.

He was losing his mind.

Or she was influencing him in a way he didn't understand. Derrek didn't pretend to like or understand his reaction. Since he wasn't a man to turn his back and run, he leaned closer, annoyed that she could put him off-kilter. Angry the Firsts of Rama might be tricking him.

He might be jacked up about her. But he wasn't stupid. And if talking to her meant getting answers, then that was exactly what he would do. Derrek was good at plans. He was about to put this one into action.

"Wake her up, Doc."

Doctor Falcon looked up from the pod's instrument panel. "She'll be groggy if I wake her now."

Groggy was good. Derrek allowed himself a small grunt that almost sounded like a snarl. "Groggy works for me. Do it."

3

✦

Azsla blinked open her eyes, then blinked again, breathing in dry air with a slight scent of oil. She was lying in her pod, the shield open, inside an enormous cargo bay alongside crates and barrels and pallet racks. Weak artificial gravity told her she was still in space.

While she'd been out, a relentless chill had sneaked through her insulated flight suit. Mind sluggish from the cold, her flesh icy, the chill from space had set up shop in her bones and numbed her thoughts. Her mouth tasted dry and bitter.

Her lethargic thoughts accelerated into survival mode. Where was she? How long had she slept? The fuzzy quality of time was as blurry as her predicament. A glance at her pod chronometer told her she'd only slept for six days. But who had found her?

Her heart was going off like a jackhammer. And still she couldn't stop shivering. Thanks to years of difficult training, she had an array of emotional experiences to call on. The training had put her through hell. Mental pain. Physical agony, terrible depths of loneliness. Even helplessness. Whatever happened next, she'd had to be ready. At least the *tranq* had had time to wear off or she wouldn't be able to adapt to her new situation. That's why she'd trained so hard to learn to suppress her *Quait* without the use of a drug. *Tranqed* Firsts could only obey orders. And their usefulness in the field was extremely limited.

Azsla should be able to do better. She would get past the loss of the ship and the leftover cold from the sleeping pod, the light gravity, and the odd scent of oil that reminded her that this was not training. This was real. And failure held consequences that upped the stakes and set her teeth chattering.

Maybe it wasn't the mission's high-test stakes so much as the unfamiliar surroundings that were responsible for the ice in her core. She'd expected the slave world and their spaceships to be rough and sturdy. Not elegant. Not superior to anything she'd seen on Rama. From the curve of the craft's graceful bulkhead beside her to the indirect lighting overhead, this ship was all clean lines and spiffy black. Masculine.

She tried to sit up, but couldn't move, as if her body was a block of ice. She looked down and saw straps. A sleeping web held her firmly in place. A cuff on her arm sprouted wires hooked to an array of instruments that beeped and chattered.

A dark-haired man loomed over her, his face stoic as if his feelings were locked so tight, he wouldn't permit a stray emotion to escape. She tried to force her numbed fingers to release the straps from the sleeping web and unhook the cuff, but she couldn't. Her hands were too cold.

So she glanced back to the man above her. From the confident set of his broad shoulders to his narrowed gaze, he looked too purposeful to be a doctor. While Firsts rarely required doctors, slaves often did, falling prey to sickness due to their weak constitutions and inferior biology. Only he looked like no doctor she'd ever seen.

For one, he was staring at her as if displeased she'd awakened. For another he was a lot of man. Intense. Rough and tough with calloused hands and scraped knuckles as if accustomed to hard physical labor. As his intelligent eyes drilled hers, with attitude to spare, she pegged him as more curious than hostile.

Folding his arms across his chest, he cocked his head, his eyes narrowing, a muscle in his jaw tensing. "Why did you have a *tranq* in your system?"

She sucked back a sarcastic response. Who was this guy? No friendly *hello*? No *how are you*? And so it began. The interrogation. Proving she was one of them—when she wasn't. Azsla would have preferred to meet him eye-to-eye, or at least on her feet, but she was stiff, her body not yet warmed enough to move.

After his question . . . he'd said nothing. Simply waited. Let the silence stretch as if to derail her.

Uh-oh. The big guy wasn't just hunky, he had brains. And he had one hell of a bedside manner.

All those years of training would allow her to adapt to her current circumstances, to think clearly as a First should—while keeping her *Quait* a secret to avoid detection.

"Who are you?" She ducked around his power play. Still chilled from the sleep pod, her voice eked out weakly. She went with helpless and injured, buying time to get a clue to what was going on, doing nothing to stop her shaking. How dare he treat her so rudely? He hadn't even lifted a hand to help her sit up and climb from the pod.

Her anger at his lack of manners warmed her. But she couldn't afford the luxury of anger.

With her emotions jacked up, her *Quait* spiraled to the surface. Holy Mother of *Vigo*. What was she thinking? She couldn't indulge in feelings. She couldn't do indignant and hostile. She couldn't let loose. Couldn't dive into an emotional tailspin. Discipline kicked in.

She jerked back her *Quait*. Sat on it. As much as she wanted to force her will on this man to make him release her from the pod—it was imperative she keep her First status hidden.

As an escaped slave, she had no *Quait*.

She had no *Quait*.

She had no *Quait*.

She couldn't allow one wisp to escape. She pursed her lips. Bit the inside of her mouth. Tightened her hands into fists. And battled down the wild urge to slam the big guy.

She fought. She coaxed. She folded the emotions in on themselves and stuffed them down. Flattened them, hammering her *Quait*. Until she once again leveled at neutral.

However, at the realization of how close she'd come to exposing her true self, sweat broke out on her scalp. She reminded herself that the years of training had paid off and ignored the throb at her temples. Accepted that her head would soon be hurting. Yet, she almost welcomed the pain since it would remind her how critical it was to stay in control.

"Why is there a *tranq* in your system?" he repeated.

Finding his tactic off-putting, again she ignored his question. Ignored the command in his tone. Ignored the attitude that demanded an answer.

She cranked her head around, searching the parts of the cargo bay she could see from her prone position on her back. "Where's my crew? Are they—"

"They're fine." He spoke in a clipped fashion but she caught a tiny flash of approval before he shut it down.

Still, at his words, the tension in her shoulders eased. She told herself it was because she'd asked the right question, as if she was one of them—not because she cared about slaves—or gave a fripping neutron about his personal reaction. Although her cover demanded she play a role, she couldn't ever let herself forget who she really was. Or her real reason for risking her life. The faces of her parents swam before her eyes. She recalled them the way she always did, their faces bloody, their bodies broken—after rebellious slaves had murdered them while they slept.

She looked at her cuff and the webbing in her pod and hardened her tone until it set like cement. "Why am I strapped down?"

"A safety precaution only. Your body needs time to recuperate. To warm slowly."

"Okay." She heard and accepted the truth. Although her body temperature was rising, she was too weak to sit up yet. And his statement verified what her own mission specialists had told her—that after using an escape pod, after awakening, recovery took time. So she forced patience.

His eyes softened as if he understood how difficult it was to lie there helpless, at the mercy of strangers. "I'll free you as soon as it's safe. We don't believe in locking up free people."

As if he couldn't stop himself, he placed a gentle fingertip under her ear, along her jaw. He urged her head around until she stared him in the eyes, but although his touch insisted, it also warmed. A flush came over her body, as if someone had trussed her on a spit, shoved her in an oven, and switched the dial to high. Could he see her discomfort? Could he see through her outer layer of cool to how his glint of interest had sliced right through her? Or was he like most people, who never saw past the surface?

"Please answer my question about the *tranq*." Although he phrased his words politely, his tone remaining easy, she understood his question was not a simple request. He was in charge.

And his soft whisper held an undertone of power she didn't quite understand. He was no First. Probably, he was from Zor. But he was like no slave she'd ever met. He held his head high, his demeanor confident and calm. Although he had no reason that she knew of to be suspicious of her motives, he was clearly wary. Did he have a clue who she really was? Or was he, by nature, cautious of strangers?

If the other escaped slaves were like him, it was no wonder the Firsts feared these people. Fifteen years of freedom had changed him from subservient slave to her equal. She shuddered. Never her *real* equal. After all, she could dominate at will. But he certainly appeared superior to the slave woman she pretended to be.

Even as she admired his tactics, she didn't like how he'd separated her from the others. Had he isolated her to see if her story would match theirs? Or had the *tranq* in her system set him on edge? If it had, that meant he'd heard about *tranqed* Firsts on Zor and suspected she might be one of them. But according to her preflight briefing the Zorans didn't know about *tranqed* Firsts. Yet his suspicion indicated otherwise.

Azsla relied on her training and stuck to her story. The truth. She just didn't tell him all of it. "Our starboard stabilizer malfunctioned. The systems went down one by one. So I popped a *tranq* to calm my nerves."

He peered at her, his focus intense. "Have things changed so much on Rama? Last we heard, the Firsts regained control. So where would a slave get a *tranq*?"

His eyes fixed on hers. She expected to see suspicion. Wariness.

Not heat. Not male interest.

Whoa. She sucked in a breath. If she hadn't known better, she'd have thought the big guy was coming on to her. Just like that. Although slaves were often into casual relationships, she and this man were strangers. It made no sense. Yet the spark was there. Out there for her to catch. Was the interest another tactic? Like asking about the *tranq* before she'd recovered from the cold?

She'd recognized the moment he'd switched gears, the moment his suspicion had turned from wariness and curiosity to . . . something else. Was he faking that banked interest? Could he manufacture a gleam in his eyes? Was this some kind of test? A trap? Or was his reaction a true one, something she could use to transform his distrust?

"Answer me."

What had he asked? She was having difficulty keeping a train of thought when her emotions kept jumping off track. *Think, woman.* Oh, yeah, he'd asked about the *tranq.*

She closed her eyes, needing to escape his direct look until she could dial in a convincing performance. Finally she reopened them. "I found a *tranq* supply on the ship."

"The others didn't have any in their blood."

She shot him her best sheepish look. "I didn't share. I was going to . . . it's just I thought we were all going to die. The ship's systems went down so fast. It was like a terrible nightmare. Only worse . . . because it was real. We had to abandon ship. One of the pods was damaged. My pod."

He frowned down at her pod. "I see no damage."

"Kali was in his own, ready to eject when he saw what was going down. He hauled himself out, put me in his pod, giving up his shot at life."

"I'm sorry."

Her head throbbed. "I didn't even thank him."

"You must have been in shock."

"I've never known anyone so brave. He had little. No possessions, of course. No family. He'd had only his life. And he gave that up . . . for me." Unbidden tears flooded her eyes. One or two may have escaped, but her flesh was too cold to feel them.

"Kali must have thought you were worth it." He held out his hand and clasped her forearm, but ended the brief touch as if he found the gesture painful. "I'm Derrek Archer."

"Azsla." She didn't give a last name. Slaves had them of course, but they didn't use them.

"Can I see . . ." She wasn't faking. She found herself actually aching to see Rak, Micoo, and Jadlan, to see with her own eyes that they were okay. While it was part of her cover to pretend she cared about slaves . . . she needed to tell them about Kali's death. About his selfless sacrifice. So he would live on in their memories.

"How did you escape?" Derrek pulled up a chair, placed a sipping tube into her mouth. Although he seemed sociable enough, she wasn't fooled. He was still suspicious. Wary. Careful. This man planned every move and she could only hope he wasn't four steps ahead of her.

She sipped her water, enjoying the lack of aftertaste. Cool, clean, and as crisp as the air in the ship, she swallowed greedily, her parched throat sucking in moisture. This part of her story had been rehearsed so it was easier to deliver as if it were true. "We'd planned our escape for a long time. Months. Over a year. It seemed like forever as we waited for the right moment. We knew we'd only get one shot."

"You stole the ship?" he guessed.

She nodded. "My First worked in the military. At night, to impress the ladies, he held liaisons aboard ship. It was against regulations." She shrugged, aware her shoulders had moved a bit. Progress. "Anyway, he used to bring me along as a servant. One night, after he drank too much, we heisted the ship. The patrols assumed the First was captaining his lady friends as usual and didn't think to question us. We slipped right by."

"You learned how to fly?" His mouth compressed into a tight slash, reminding her this was no friendly conversation but an interrogation.

Did Derrek think she had only half a brain? "I'd flown many times with the First. I watched what he did."

"You make it sound easy. Yet since the rebellion and the portal's opening, no one else has escaped Rama or come through that portal."

She was relieved to learn that he seemed to have no knowledge of the second portal on the back side of his world. A portal the *tranqed* Firsts used for communication with the homeworld and also to come and go in secret.

"We were lucky, I guess," she continued. "The most difficult part of our escape was learning the portal's coordinates. Jadlan stole those. You can ask him the details."

Of course the Firsts who'd planned her covert op had made certain that Jadlan had had access to those plans. They hadn't made it easy for him. So he still believed he'd been an integral part of the escape. Her story would hold. She sucked more water from the sipping tube and lay back, sapped out.

"For a slave you are tall and fit." He didn't bother to hide the accusation in his eyes. Although prepared, she hadn't expected his suspicion level to be so high or his sharp assessment to make her so uncomfortable.

But what exactly was he accusing her of? Stealing salt? Or did he suspect she wasn't a slave?

"My salt ration was increased because my job might require strength."

"And your job was . . . ?"

"Protecting the children in the household." Azsla forced normal breaths into and out of her lungs and met his scrutinizing look with an even one. His suspicion whirled around her, like a tornado, but she remained centered, refusing to let his emotions touch her. She would no more cave to his pressure than resort to using her *Quait*.

When she sensed she'd held his gaze long enough that he wouldn't think her changing the subject was suspicious, she spoke again. "Where are you taking us?"

"To Zor."

She sucked in an awkward breath. She'd done it. The insert part of her mission was about to be accomplished as soon as they landed on the slave world.

It was a triumph and should have elated her. It didn't. Not in the least. Celebrating felt wrong after the sacrifice Kali had made. Especially when she knew her contacts on Zor, fully *tranqed* Firsts, had orders to round up Rak, Jadlan, and Micoo. Her crew would be sent home and executed in front of millions to show what happened to slaves who risked all for freedom.

Her spurt of adrenaline at finding herself in a new world suddenly wore off. The throbbing in her head intensified. Suddenly too weary to keep her eyes open, too lethargic to force her lids back open, she allowed exhaustion to suck her into sleep.

She thought Derrek's hand smoothed away a tear on her cheek. But it must have been a dream. When she awakened, Derrek was glaring at her again.

4

What's wrong?" Azsla stretched, released the wrist cuff and the web straps, then climbed from the pod. The chill in her bones had disappeared along with her exhaustion. While she had no idea how long she'd crashed this time, she felt solid, juiced up even. Oddly, Derrek had nasty circles under his eyes, a dark dusting of hair on his lower face which emphasized the stubborn tilt of his jaw and which indicated he might have been standing there since she'd fallen asleep.

"Where are you from?" he snapped, his eyes flashing, his voice raspy.

"Rama."

He looked twitchy, as if crawling insects were biting his flesh, yet he was stubbornly refusing to acknowledge or brush them away. Folding his arms over his chest, he towered over her, the muscles in his bronzed forearms tense. "Which province?"

"Divonia."

"Which First did you work for?"

Her stomach growled loud enough for him to hear.

"Would you mind if we had this discussion . . . over a meal?"

"Fine." He gestured toward a door-sized hatch but his body language told her he was nowhere close to finished. His tone was ripe with suspicion he didn't bother to hide, his muscles tensing with a raw energy that did a number on her nerves. If possible, he now seemed even more steamed up than the first time they'd talked.

While she'd slept, had the other rescued slaves said or done something to cause his hostile attitude? Or was he naturally difficult? The man was wound down tight. And not much was leaking through to clue her in.

They exited the cargo bay into a corridor. Indirect lighting softened the bulkhead colors, muting the gray-silk tones into a space of beauty. Beneath her feet, plush rubberized deck provided traction and did double duty as an insulator. She couldn't hear the engines thrum or even feel the drive vibrations beneath her feet. "This is the most beautiful ship."

"So you've been on many?"

"I didn't say that."

"You haven't said much at all."

She heard the quiet accusation in his tone and stopped in the middle of the empty corridor, uncertain just what he was accusing her of. "I'm sorry if I've done something wrong. Are the customs here different? Have I said something to offend you? Because if so, it was done out of ignorance, not malice."

"Did you leave family behind?" he asked, ignoring her question and firing one of his own.

What she'd assumed was a discussion was still an interrogation. At first, she'd tried to placate him by simply answering. But no sooner did she give one response than he challenged her again. Since his animosity meter was beating a steady increase no matter what she said, she might as well give it right back at him.

"Are your questions official or personal?" she countered, her voice controlled as she pretended not to notice his annoyance. Or was it irritation? "Do you work for the government?"

"I'm too much the rebel for that." Derrek threw back his head and laughed, his mood change lightning fast, but natural, almost charming. His full-blooded chuckles shot a sparkle into his eyes and his face lit up and chased away all suggestions of his previous negativity and suspicion. "I'm an asteroid miner."

A miner? In the asteroids? She'd heard of such men, of course. But since she'd never expected to meet one of them, she hadn't studied the subject. Reminding herself no real slave would know anything at all about Zor, she chose her words with care. "You picked us up when you heard our distress call?"

"Actually the government picked up your signals and asked us to investigate." He didn't sound concerned and his demeanor remained casual.

Still, she worked over his response and found the situation odd. She'd assumed the government would want to take charge. "Zor has no military spaceships?"

"They do, although not like *Beta Five*. However, the current powers in charge like to distance themselves from controversy."

"What's controversial about a few escaped slaves?" Her stomach rumbled again. She really wanted to eat. But she wanted to understand even more. "I'm a nobody."

"Spoken like a true slave."

"I am a slave." She stopped and lifted her chin. "Correction. I *was* a slave. Never again." She faked a shudder. It wasn't hard. All she had to do was recall the humiliation from her training. Of course, it had been harder for her than for a slave born to that station to submit to such lowly work. And it had almost been fripping impossible to learn to control her *Quait*.

That she'd had a choice, that she'd had the ability to quit at any time, had made her life more difficult. Every day, every hour, she'd asked herself if her goal of stopping another rebellion was worth what she'd had to bear. While a slave born to obedience had never known freedom and couldn't miss what they'd never known, Azsla still remembered her wonderful childhood, when she had all the toys she wanted, playmates who let her win every game. Any food she'd requested had been cooked and brought to her by loving attendants.

Later she'd learned those attendants hadn't been loving at all. They'd looted her home. Murdered her parents. She'd sucked down many hard lessons that terrible day.

Her words must have convinced Derrek of her status. He finally seemed to put away the last of his suspicion. "Come into the galley. I'll rustle you up some food and try to explain a little about Zor."

She followed him into the efficiently designed but

actually cozy space. Like the other parts of *Beta Five* that she'd seen, the layout was sleek, compact and utilitarian, yet beautiful, with a huge view port that allowed starlight to enter the room. Several holo pics of the crew were set in frames on shelves. A vase of yellow and magenta flowers lent a sweet fragrance to the air. A polished black stone table was set with condiments. And in the middle, like a *diamondite* among sand, perched a shaker of salt. Right out in the open.

She stopped. Stared. Was he testing her honesty?

Never in her life had she seen so much salt in one place. It had to be worth a fortune. She swallowed hard, glancing from the salt to Derrek. He removed a pan from a cabinet and set it on the stove, looking comfortable as he rolled up his sleeves, then took eggs from the coolster.

"You the ship's cook?"

"Sometimes." He grinned easily.

She sensed he might be toying with her, but his tone stayed even, almost playful. If any of his previous hostility was still there, he'd buried it so deep she could no longer discern it. So either he was much better at hiding his feelings than she'd assumed, or he'd faked the previous anger, or he'd put whatever had been bothering him behind him. She didn't know him well enough to venture a guess. "What's your job when you aren't the cook?"

"Most of the time . . . I'm the captain."

"Oh." What was going on here? Ships' captains didn't cook. But as astonishing as his willingness to cook was, it didn't explain that fortune in salt sitting out as if it were no more valuable than the *pepperite* beside it. "Forgive me if my question is awkward or personal."

"It's all right. You're free now. Ask whatever you like."

"It's just that I don't know your customs and don't wish to insult."

"What do you wish to know?"

She really wanted to know why he'd been so angry with her before, but didn't dare ask for fear she might annoy him all over again. And she much preferred this casual conversation and his easy smile to his snapping questions at her while he glared. "How come you don't consider cooking beneath your status?"

He shrugged and broke the eggs into a bowl. "Cooking's honest work. No different than mining salt. Or captaining this ship."

She recalled the calluses on his hands and considered the hard labor he must still do. "I don't understand."

"I'm not sure I can explain." He beat the eggs in the bowl. Poured in milk. "Zor is different from Rama. We didn't come here to be free only to succumb to the same social stratification. Work is work. Who is to say what kind of work is more meaningful or valuable? The important thing is to do a task as well as one can. Mining salt for our people doesn't only provide a good living, it allows me to help our people. But I also like to cook. I really like the idea of cooking your first meal as a free woman."

"Thank you." Her gaze returned to the salt. He must have caught a glimpse of her staring. His voice actually turned gentle. "Salt is still precious to us. Like the air we need to breathe. And the water that we drink."

"Anything I can do to help?" she asked.

"Relax."

She slid into a seat at the table. "Salt is so common that you don't have to lock it up?"

"We didn't find much salt on Zor itself. But the asteroids have plenty."

"Getting it to Zor must be difficult."

"Working in space can be a challenge. However, the planet is a gravity well. We shove the salt loads in the right direction and gravity does the rest until the braking systems kick in."

"So you live on this ship?"

"I nest on Alpha One." He poured the eggs into a hot greased pan. "Onions and cheese?"

"Yes, please."

"The onions we grow in hydroponics are sweeter than those from Rama." He diced them and sprinkled cheese on top.

"What's Alpha One?"

"It's the asteroid where I first found salt. The mine gave out years ago and I turned the caves into my house. Filed a homestead on Zor and have a century lease." While he spoke warmly about Alpha One, he'd said *house*. Not *home*. The subtle difference in meaning warned her she might be on a touchy subject. So did the pride and isolation rising around him. He sprinkled salt and *pepperite* on the eggs, then flipped them over. "Alpha One has a spectacular view of Mount Crion." He gestured to a holo pic of a stark landscape amid a backdrop of stars. The imposing mountain sparkled with silver and green iridescence, with not a plant or structure in sight.

She suppressed a shiver. "You live there alone?"

As if he'd read her thoughts, he spoke gently. "Not too many women like the idea of having to clear an airlock before going outside. So the boys and I journey down-gravity to Zor for socializing."

"And saving me and my crew shortened your party time?" The scent of the onions frying made her mouth water. He set a glass of yellow juice in front of her, then waited expectantly for her to taste it. She picked it up and sniffed. The crisp scent of citrus had her eager for a sip. Lifting the glass, she swirled it, then took a swallow and enjoyed the burst of flavor on her tongue. "Delicious."

He grinned. "We've found lots of new food and drinks on Zor. The variety keeps the farmers busy. However, it was tough at first. If not for our alliance with Earth, we might not have survived. They sent seeds and tools through the portal—until Rama shut it down."

She knew her history—at least from the Raman viewpoint. After the slave revolt, Rama's Firsts blasted apart the portal that the slaves had used to escape to Zor, preventing all other slaves from trying to follow. Shortly thereafter, they'd closed the Earth–Zor portal, too. But even during the short time the planet-to-planet portals had been open, the slaves had only been able to take with them to the new world what they could carry in their hands.

If Raman spies hadn't sent back secret reports, she would have expected a primitive planet. But Earth must have helped them a lot. Clearly, Rama's most industrious slaves had escaped and they'd thrived on Zor. They'd built cities. A spaceport. If they weren't a threat to her home, she might have been proud of their accomplishments.

But they'd founded this world on the blood of her parents. And too many others like them. As long as Zor survived, a tempting source of freedom, other slaves would try to revolt and follow. Six days before she'd left Rama, before another uprising could be quelled, the slaves had massacred ten Firsts. Such violence could not be tolerated.

Now these slaves had more precious salt than their former masters. No First she'd ever known had displayed salt on a table. If they had that kind of wealth, they locked it up in a vault. So despite her attempt not to gawk, the salt attracted her gaze like *magnetite*. And she eased into the next topic, careful not to reveal more knowledge than a Raman slave would have.

"I heard a rumor that if we increase our salt intake, we actually develop *Quait*."

"It's true."

At his admission, she pretended surprise. Her mission would be easier if she could get him to reveal things she already knew but wasn't supposed to know. There would be less chance of her slipping up that way. Less chance of someone questioning how she'd come by her knowledge.

He turned his head from the stove and met her gaze, his mood serious. "But you'll never have the power to rival a First."

Little did he know. But she hid the thought down deep. "Why not?"

"Lack of proper nutrients during childhood stunted

us for life. But you must also understand that although we can develop some *Quait,* we also have laws that limit our salt intake."

"You do?" She frowned at him. "Why? If salt is plentiful, why not eat as much as you want? Become as strong as you can?"

"Because we don't want to become like them." Venom and horror and viciousness colored his tone. As if being a First committed one to monsterdom.

She didn't have to fake widening her eyes. She'd assumed all escaped slaves would want *Quait,* to be as powerful as Firsts, and here was another clue that her training might not have been as complete as her instructors had believed. "You've never dreamed what it would be like to dominate others with your will?"

He flipped the eggs onto her plate. His eyes burned as bright as the sun. His voice remained whispery soft. Dangerous. His tone strong and true without a hint of deception. "No one should have that kind of power over another."

She chose her words with care, wanting his take, but careful not to reveal her own. "Rama would fall apart without their slaves."

He shot her a you-know-better look, but his tone remained mild. "Oh, I think not. It's human instinct to survive. If all the slaves on Rama left, the Firsts would have to do their own labor. Or pay others to do it."

She hoped to God that never happened. If the slaves revolted *en masse,* she doubted they'd leave any survivors behind. And even if the Firsts lived, she didn't believe they would adapt very easily—if at all. After her normal childhood, her life had been hard. Adjusting had been difficult. If instead, she'd been a pampered adult thrown into a slave's life, adjusting wouldn't have been just miserable, but impossible. It had been hard enough to adapt as a teenager but as an adult . . . no, she couldn't even imagine it.

She returned to his earlier statement, another that required explanation. "So no one on Zor eats enough salt to develop their *Quait*?"

"With one exception."

How interesting. Her training had so many gaps. She raised an eyebrow. "Really?"

"My brother had to eat enough salt to open the portal from Earth to Zor. His *Quait* developed to a higher level than the law allows but our government has given him amnesty."

Her eyes widened. "Your brother's Cade Archer?"

"You've heard of him?"

"He's a legend on Rama." And all Firsts cursed him for freeing the slaves. "Mothers tell their children stories of his courage, of his daring. Of his great feats." If she could hand over Cade Archer to the authorities, she'd become a legend, too. However, becoming famous had never been her goal. She'd settle for justice. "But we were told that he'd died from eating too much salt."

"That's a lie. He's fine. In fact, he's touring the unexplored third continent on Zor with his wife, on a second honeymoon."

"With the Earth woman?"

"Her name is Shara." Admiration warmed his tone.

He handed her a fork, a napkin, and pushed the salt toward her. "Eat."

She lifted the salt shaker, holding it with reverence. She peered at the eight tiny holes at the top that would release the grains of salt. "Suppose too much comes out? If I eat too much and break your laws . . . what would happen to me?"

"Banishment to the second continent. But don't worry about it. Your body's been deprived for so long you couldn't possibly go over your legal allotment in just a few meals. It takes a great deal of salt over many days to affect *Quait*."

Her gaze zinged from him to the salt and back. "Still . . . I cannot pay—"

"You are a guest. Eat before your eggs grow cold."

With a trembling hand, she turned the shaker upside down and shook. "What of my crew?"

"They weren't as strong as you and are still recovering. Doctor Falcon is monitoring them in our sick ward."

Very carefully, she placed the salt shaker back in the middle of the table and used the *pepperite*. "After I eat, I'd like permission to check on them."

"Certainly."

He had made no eggs for himself, and she hesitated as she lifted the fork to her mouth, needing to make sure they had plenty of food aboard and she wasn't ingesting his ration. "Aren't you going to eat?"

"I ate before you awakened. We have plenty, if that's what is worrying you. Please, our rules here are simple. Eat while it's hot."

"But you didn't sleep, did you?"

"No."

"How come?" She scooped egg onto her utensil, lifted the food toward her lips. And inhaled. The delicious scent made her stomach growl and she placed the first bite between her lips. A delicate flavor of egg, salt, and *pepperite* tingled on her tongue. "Mmm. This is so good."

"Your pod's chronometer said you slept in suspended life for six days. So of course, you're hungry. Did I make enough or will you require more?" He placed a basket of fresh bread and a choice of either a reddish jam or rich butter before her. And by her left hand, he set a hot cup of *whai* tea, the pungent aroma immediately recognizable.

"This is plenty. Thank you." She filled her belly, surprised that when they lapsed into silence, it was no longer awkward or tense. While most people liked to chat during a meal, she didn't. Taking a breather allowed her to savor her food and relax. After she'd emptied her plate and sipped the last of the *whai,* he cleared the dishes and placed them into an autoclean.

"You were going to tell me more about Zor," she reminded him.

"Why don't we talk and walk at the same time. You wanted to see your crew?"

"Yes, please." When she stood and waited for him to lead the way, his com link chimed.

He raised his wrist toward his mouth. "Derrek here."

"Boss man, we got company," a male voice hit the airways.

"What kind of company, Sauren?"

"Adain's been unable to identify them. The two ships are running silent and won't answer his hail."

"Cavin, what's their heading?"

"Straight at us."

"ETA?"

"Two micronbits. It's like they burst out of hyperspace right on top of us and are spoiling for a fight."

"Benet, juice up the engines."

"I'm already on it. But we need eight micronbits to reach max power."

"Understood. I'll be on the bridge in two." Derrek changed direction and fired a thoughtful look her way. "Any chance you were followed?"

The idea startled her. The Firsts had intended for her to escape, so what would have been the point? But she pretended not to know that and to think over his question, even as her nerves rewound into knots. "No one was around when we abandoned ship. But even if the Ramans picked up our distress signal, I hardly think they'd bother tailing us. We just aren't that important."

"Of course, you are," he disagreed. "If you made it, other slaves will try to follow. I'm thinking they want you back. To prove escape is impossible."

His guess was more correct than she could say. While her mission was to appear to be a fugitive slave and escape to Zor, it seemed a waste of life and effort that *tranqed* Firsts would round up her crew, send them back to Rama, and execute them as a political statement.

She understood the logic but the idea of Firsts bringing Rak, Micoo, and Jadlan back in chains, possibly executing their innocent families alongside them, made her sick. Her crew mistakenly believed they had no families. They'd told her so. Because if they'd had family, they wouldn't have risked the escape.

To discourage escape attempts, Firsts didn't just execute the guilty slave—they used their *Quait* to force the slaves to kill every surviving family member. The practice was rarely enforced and the severity of the consequences kept the peace.

Except—all of her crew had family members they didn't know about. Half brothers and sisters. A father. Even a daughter. After birth slaves were sent to crèches run by the state. So they had no way of knowing if they had family—except from official records—which had been altered.

According to Azsla's mission plan, her escaped crew was going nowhere. *Tranqed* Firsts had orders to round up her crew and send them back to Rama in chains, reunite the family members—who didn't even know one another—and then make her crew kill them before they themselves died a painful death.

This just couldn't be happening. Not now. Not this quick. When she'd sent that report back to Rama that they'd had to abandon ship, the military must have intercepted her message to the Corps and sent ships to investigate. Now that the Raman military had spied *Beta Five,* neither side could afford to let the other return to their home base with information. Likely the Corps hadn't informed the military about Azsla's mission. In fact, her mission was so secret other members of the Corps weren't kept in the loop. So the First military no doubt thought she was an escaped slave and wouldn't hesitate to fire on them. The military's ruthless reputation stabbed a sliver of fear into her heart.

A male voice shot through the com link at Derrek's wrist. "Captain, we just received an ultimatum."

"From whom?"

"I'm not sure."

"What's the message?"

"A First by the name of Tomar is demanding we turn over the Ramans to them . . . or die."

Tomar? Azsla recalled the name, the stories about him. Although they'd never met, she hated him for his needless cruelty. "I've heard of him."

"Anything useful?"

"He's vicious. And incredibly tenacious." He'd applied to the Corps but had been refused admission because of his inability to follow orders. The man had a reputation for cruel and ruthless behavior, and the Corps psych analysts hadn't believed he'd ever learn to control his emotions and *Quait,* never mind suppress them. But their military had happily accepted him and he'd quickly moved up through the ranks. "Tomar's family was especially brutal—even for a First. During the revolt, slaves responded in kind. He was badly burned and his face remains scarred. It's said that even his own children fear him."

"Arm forward weapons," Derrek ordered.

"Aye, sir."

Derrek's voice remained calm, as if imminent attack from the cruel commander was an everyday occurrence. "Can we outrun them?"

"I don't know," Adain said. "Our aft weapons aren't

on line yet. This was supposed to be a shakedown cruise, remember?"

"Yeah. Well, we're about to see what she's got." Derrek broke into a grin and she couldn't help thinking that he'd never sounded happier—like a child with a new toy. She followed, her heart whacking out, praying that the beautiful *Beta Five* could protect these people who were willing to risk their lives for her and her crew. She wished they could outrun the other ships and avoid a confrontation. She didn't want Derrek's people to die in a fight that wasn't theirs. But her crew didn't deserve what awaited them if they surrendered, either. They didn't. Their escape had hurt no one. And surely Rama could lose a handful of slaves without missing their minor contribution, couldn't they?

Holy *Vigo*. What was she thinking? She was no traitor. She wasn't.

5

❂

Derrek positioned himself at command, noting that Azsla had followed him to the bridge. She stayed out of the way by the entrance, remaining quiet, her face pale. Clearly shaken by the possibility of recapture, she'd shot him one flash of panic before she'd gone stoic.

Despite the emergency, Derrek had to admire her self-control. When she'd heard Tomar was after them, she'd trembled, all too aware that if Tomar and the Raman ship seized her and her crew, it meant certain death. A very painful and humiliating death. Yet, Azsla was keeping herself together just as well as his trained crew.

Too bad they couldn't make a run for Zor. But not only wouldn't he lead Tomar into the spaceport and risk the lives of the civilian population below, if Derrek turned tail and ran, they'd have to rely on their speed and shielding to survive—because their aft weapons were still off line.

On screen at max magnification, the two alien ships separated and changed shape. Previously, they'd appeared silver and tubular. But one sprouted wings while the other began to shimmer. How strange. It was almost as if the ships had been designed with different purposes in mind. But what? Even stranger, Derrek expected a coordinated attack from different vectors, but the shimmering one held back. The puzzling tactic worried him. He couldn't anticipate what he didn't know about and apparently the Ramans had made technological advances in the last decade.

Wary and puzzled by the new ship configuration, he leaned forward. "What the hell is going on? Anybody?"

Sauren peered at the monitors of his science station. Creative and intelligent, the man could toss out killer ideas faster than a gunner spat bullets. And it was a measure of his self-confidence that he never feared being wrong. "Maybe they're holding one ship back to appear nonthreatening."

The least confrontational senior officer, Cavin, tended

to go with the flow. He hated showdowns—especially the personal kind. Cavin agreed, his broad shoulders shrugging. "Nonthreatening works for me."

"After Tomar issued an ultimatum?" Derrek shook his head. "I'm not buying it."

Paycon, *Beta Five*'s weapons engineer, looked up from his scanners. At about fifty, he didn't talk much. Never about his past. However, Derrek had heard part of his history from a credible source. As a boy, he'd been forced to watch a First rape his mother and shoot his father. He'd never married. Never had children. He and his brother lived quiet lives. He sent most of his income to widows and orphans. A steady worker, he kept to himself and had made no close friends among the crew. Yet, he was liked and respected. "Sensors indicate a large power source is ramping up on one of those Raman ships."

"Which ship?" Derrek asked.

He rechecked his panel. "The shimmering one in the rear."

Benet reported on their own status. "Four micronbits to full weapons power."

"Adain, anything more on the com?" Derrek asked.

"Same old ultimatum. Nothing else."

Sauren jerked his thumb at Azsla, clearly uncertain about her status. "Boss man, should she be here?"

"I'll leave," she retreated a step, then paused as if uncertain where to go.

"Stay." Derrek ordered and she froze—responding just like a slave. Only she didn't quite personify a recently escaped slave. Perhaps it was her healthy looks and the increased ration of salt that made her fit. Whatever. He had no time for her history right now. "If you can contribute, feel free to speak up."

Her eyes widened and shot him a do-you-really-mean-that stare. A stare of awe and hope that made his heart ache. He remembered the day all too clearly when *he'd* realized he was finally free of tyranny. He'd been peering down at a Raman ship, one of the few that had crashed on Zor after the revolution. The pilot hadn't survived. After tossing the First's carcass into the sea, Derrek had stared hard at the ship, thinking about waste. How she'd never fly again.

His brother Cade had been with him and must have seen the yearning in his eyes. "You want to fly, don't you?"

"Yeah. I do." He imagined the freedom of space. The lack of walls. The lack of people. The vastness called to him.

"So go for it."

"Just like that?"

"Exactly." Cade had chuckled. "Your future is yours. You get to make it now."

Until that moment, Derrek had known a bit of nice. An hour to take a walk. To read a book by the shore. To tinker on his engine. To cook a good meal. But until then, he hadn't thought about wonderful. The vast autonomy of space. Daring to explore and maybe make a place for himself in the asteroid belt.

Soaring hope snapped the *Quait* bonds that had chained him physically, then mentally. A squeezing pressure in his chest that he hadn't even known existed loosened, and aspiration surged into his empty chest cavity, freeing him, scaring him, exhilarating him. The realization that his future was really his to mold was a moment he'd never forget. Right then and there, he'd decided to repair that ship and learn to fly her. System by system, he'd built *Beta One* from the decks up. And he'd flown her to the asteroids and beyond. Discovered huge mineral deposits—including salt. The rest was history.

Azsla wasn't quite at nice yet, never mind wonderful. But clearly, she already chafed at the bonds from her past. Was working at throwing off the old thinking patterns. It had taken him months. But then he'd always been a slow starter.

Sauren left his station and headed to Azsla. They were almost in battle mode. Why was he abandoning his post and approaching Azsla? A ripping need to send Sauren back to his station hit Derrek like an unexpected meteor shower. Not only had Sauren left his post, without permission, he was approaching Derrek's guest—

Azsla wasn't *his* guest. Not by a long shot.

Derrek had to stop his hand from resting on his blaster. But his sudden rage wasn't about Sauren leaving his post so much as about his approaching Azsla. Derrek was actually resentful that Sauren was speaking to her, practically shaking with anger over his friend's actions. He clenched his fists against the heightened emotions. And still it welled up his throat.

His complete overreaction confused Derrek. What the hell was going down? His protective response to her in the current situation was so out of control. Yet, he had to fight his muscles that ached to jump between her and Sauren. Grinding his teeth together, he gave them his back.

With the current danger to *Beta Five,* thinking about leaving his post was insanity. Even as Derrek went about his job, his whole body ached to step between them. Barely remaining where he was, he instead keyed in to Sauren's words, which were on-the-surface polite. "The captain is always open to helpful suggestions, but try not to distract him with nonessentials."

Talk about distractions. Derrek yearned to scoop Azsla against his side, slam Sauren back to his post. With his fist.

"Before I left, I heard gossip," she spoke slowly to Sauren as if dredging up a distant memory.

The conversation was innocent. So innocent. Yet, Derrek had to hold onto the console to stop himself from getting in Sauren's face. Sweat broke out on his scalp. Blood heated in his veins. In an attempt to calm himself, he forced air deep into his lungs.

As if sensing the undercurrent, Cavin frowned at Derrek, then Sauren, and without being asked took over the science station the first officer had abandoned. "Captain, the forward ship just shut down part of their own hull's shielding."

"Part? What do you mean by part of the shielding?" Derrek was unaware such technology existed. On *Beta Five* the shields surrounded the entire hull, or they were totally down and vulnerable. A partial shield had yet to be invented. He'd have to start Taylo working on it immediately . . . if they survived.

"That ship is shielded—except where there's an opening for weapons," Paycon explained. "Looks like they're preparing to fire."

Great. As if the Firsts didn't already have enough advantages. Their *Quait*. Thousands of years of civilization. And free labor. Now the Ramans didn't have to lower their shields to attack. And those paltry openings in their shield left only a tight target to aim at.

Sauren leaned into Azsla, prodding her for details. "What rumor?"

As the man leaned in, Derrek bristled. Sweat trickled down his back between his shoulder blades. The hair on his nape stood on end. Adrenaline kicked. And fire roared in his ears. *Vigo* help him, he was jealous. Jealous that another man was talking to a woman he barely knew.

How insane was that?

Recognizing something was way off and that he needed to find a logical explanation for his reactions, Derrek vowed to hit Dr. Falcon up for a physical . . . first chance he got.

Azsla spoke softly. "I heard from a tech that one ship supplies the power. The other grabs the power for weapons."

"What are you suggesting?" Sauren asked.

She hesitated before speaking. "The armed ship is heavily shielded but the ship with the power . . . may not be."

"Thank you." Sauren nodded and pivoted back to his station. "You hear that, boss man?"

As Sauren made distance from Azsla, Derrek's systems calmed, his pounding blood eased and he nodded. "Weapons status?"

Paycon frowned. "If you want full power, we need more time."

"We're about out of time. What can I have now?"

"Enough juice to shoot one ship. Not both," Benet reported. Despite his youth, he kept his tone steady. Derrek had high hopes of turning him into a captain after he gained a few years' experience.

Hoping the current intel would give them an advantage, Derrek ordered, "Shields up. Target the rear ship."

"But it was just a rumor." Azsla's voice trembled. "There might not be any truth to it."

"Your rumor jives with our science station's finding." Derrek flipped an alarm. "All hands brace for impact. Web in."

Sauren led Azsla to an empty station and saw to her safety before his own. A gentlemen, Sauren did nothing improper. Derrek had always been pleased to call the man a friend. Yet, while Sauren was webbing her in, Derrek's muscles twitched. He ached to knock back his friend to prevent him from touching her soft skin, breathing in her feminine scent. Sauren shouldn't even be talking to her.

The rational side of him pounded down his out-of-control reactions. Azsla was not his woman. Sauren had done nothing wrong. But Derrek's body was raging angry. Protective. Ready to fight for what he wanted to claim.

Using all his considerable willpower, he forced his mind back to the crisis at hand, fought down the surging emotions. Now was no time for the distraction of personal issues. If any of his officers had been as agitated as he was now, he would have banished them from the bridge. Yet, he couldn't abandon his crew when they needed him.

Although prepared to fire, he still hoped he might not have to. "Any other communications?"

Cavin shook his head. "Only Tomar's repeated ultimatum. Give up the slaves or die. He must have his hail set on auto loop."

"Maybe," Azsla said quietly, "you should listen and give us back to them, captain."

No fripping way. He'd rather cut off his right hand than turn any person over to these monsters. He'd rather buy into the big Salt Ever After than surrender. "That's not an option I'll ever consider."

Azsla spoke again, her voice firmer. "You should not have to risk your lives for us."

"We don't have to—we want to. Because we are free, we have a choice." He admired her courage but no damn way was he surrendering to those First bastards. Out here in space, over the vast distances, their *Quait* couldn't dominate him. Out here, they were equals. And he'd be damned if he'd give anyone back into slavery without a *diamondite* hard fight—especially Azsla.

"Captain. Sensors indicate they have a lock. If you intend to fire," Benet urged him, "now would be a good time."

Derrek agreed. "Cavin, prepare to get us out of here.

Paycon, fire at will. Adain, send a log home—just in case." In case they didn't make it, at least the Zoran government would know what had happened. For years they'd feared the Ramans would pour through the portal in force. And while two ships could hardly carry an army to Zor, any First who reached Zor would be a class-one threat.

They all understood much too well how a First could disrupt the government by usurping President Laurie's will. A handful of Firsts with their powerful *Quait* could take over the government. Order the military to stand down.

In anticipation of retaliation, the Zorans had placed countermeasures into effect, of course. But no one knew if their safeguards would work, especially since a First had the ability to overpower the will of anyone within their mental reach.

If a group of organized Firsts knew where and how to hit the Zoran leaders, they could force their society back into slavery mode. Maybe not every Zoran citizen. But enough to sabotage their independence. Enough to hurt their fledgling economy. Enough to set them back a decade. The Firsts might be outnumbered but they'd had centuries of practice at commanding obedience and knew exactly how to turn slave against slave. Their sick practices forced men to harm their own loved ones. Derrek had seen fathers crying as their will had been usurped and Firsts had forced them to kill their own children, torture their own wives. No way would he go back to that madness. Better to be dead.

Paycon worked his magic fingers across the console. "Firing now, captain."

Benet's massive engines routed power to the weapons. Lights flickered and, for an instant, life support stalled. Their cannons discharged and the vibration surged up the decks, shivered into the soles of his feet, shimmied into the marrow of his bones. As the cataclysmic cannon blasted electromagnetic energy across space, it left behind the burnt scent of ions permeating the air. He could get used to that smell—especially if it took out a bunch of Firsts.

"We shot our wad, Captain." Paycon peered over his monitors. "So did they. Incoming missile off the bow."

"Full evasive maneuvers." He couldn't wait around to learn if their weapon took out the other ship—not since the enemy had gotten off a missile.

"I'm on it," Cavin said. "Avoiding a hit . . . it'll be close, sir. I'm torquing down the steering. Prepare for high grav."

They could all see the oncoming missile on the screen. "Estimated time to contact?"

"Soon."

The engines whined as the engineer redlined the specs. Then he pushed it up another notch and a higher gravity flattened them all into their seats.

"Time for weapon recharge?" Derrek asked.

"Three micronbits, maybe two."

"Are we breaking their missile lock?" Derrek asked, his chest fighting for air against the high g-force.

"Working on it."

Derrek peered at the monitor and held his breath. *Beta Five* whistled and clicked, then steadied. The missile whooshed by, close enough for him to read the identification numbers.

His crew cheered and broke into smiles. As the ship slowed, the gravity lightened.

So far, so good. They were still here and he risked a deep breath.

But now, he prayed their own weapon would take out the shimmering power source that fed the Raman ship's weaponry or they didn't stand a chance. If the rumor was wrong, if Azsla had heard incorrectly, then this lull was over and the battle would start anew. If their shot missed, the race would be on again to recharge the big guns.

Derrek watched the shot's trajectory on the screen. *Come on, baby. Take them out. Take them out now.*

It looked on target. But distances could be deceiving. And there was always a chance they could disappear down a portal hole or wrench the ship sideways at the last moment. But the Ramans did neither.

Paycon's aim was dead on and his shot struck the shimmering ship's center. For a moment she grew brighter as if sucking in the heat, but then the disruptive energy proved too much. Her hull buckled, cracked, and shredded, the ship dying and taking the crew along with it to Raman hell.

No one cheered. While the sight might have been pretty, Derrek couldn't forget men were dying. He didn't have a shred of sorrow for the Firsts, but Firsts never went anywhere without their personal servants. Innocent slaves had died at the sides of their masters, and for them, he grieved.

All eyes searched the winged ship for any sign of additional missiles being lobbed their way. The starscape appeared empty, a black backdrop dewed with stars.

Derrek had almost allowed himself to relax when an alarm sounded and he tensed once again. Sauren at his science station had spotted the danger first. "The forward ship got off another shot. It's heading right at us off the aft port thruster."

"Hard starboard," Derrek ordered. "Release the chaff." Chaff might teach the Ramans not to screw with them, he hoped. The first attack had come from the wrong direction to employ Taylo's newest invention, which released a comet tail of metal junk behind them. The plan was to confuse the weapon sensors into exploding in their chaff—well before it reached *Beta Five*.

While the theory sounded good, they'd never tested it. But no time like the present. Right now, all their lives rested on Taylo's invention. The bridge was quiet enough for Derrek to hear his own breathing.

Would his life end here? He prayed not. But if so, he was ready to die for his freedom and the freedom of every individual on this ship. At least if the missile struck, they'd die free. They'd die resisting.

"It's changing course. Chaff is working," Benet reported. "Missile's going to miss. But not by much."

An explosion rocked them. The backlash buffeted them. But shields held. Pressure and life support held. Slowly Derrek began to breathe again.

That had been close. Way too close. "Any damage?"

"Hull paint took a burn."

Derrek could live with that.

"Incoming. Two more missiles on the way."

"Damn." Derrek stared at his monitor. They may have knocked off the power station, but the Raman ship had more flipping fire power than a First on a rampage of viciousness. And he had no more chaff. Which left him the option of evasive maneuvers, which wouldn't be good enough. "Come about. Hard to port."

Benet's voice edged with a tight worry. "Looks like we pissed them off. More ships blowing up our tail."

"Hail them," Derrek ordered, greedy to know who else was out here.

Benet frowned but sent out a signal, then his face broke into a sheepish smile. "Sir, they're ours. President Laurie sent them to cover us."

Ah, so Laurie wanted to take credit for their engagement. Not a bad move on his part, hanging back, assessing the enemy, waiting to see if Derrek could handle himself without putting government men and property at risk. Now Laurie could come in and mop up, swipe the glory. But Derrek didn't believe anyone should take credit for something they didn't deserve.

The government ships fired counter missiles at the incoming projectiles. For a moment the heavens erupted in sparks of red and orange. Auto filters shielded their eyes. The shields held, but the winged ship retreated.

Derrek's gaze focused across the bridge to meet Azsla's, but he had difficulty reading her expression. She looked full of sorrow, scared, terrified, and proud—

all at the same time. He again suddenly ached to hold her, to reassure her that she and her crew were safe.

She could see that for herself, of course. But he wanted an excuse, any excuse to take her into his arms. He didn't understand it. He recalled his vow to see Doctor Falcon and moved it up on his to-do list. He'd settle everyone, then pay the doctor a visit.

Meanwhile, he turned to his crew. "You did good, men. Let's bring her home."

"What about the winged ship?" Sauren asked.

Derrek unwebbed from his command seat. "We'll leave the mop-up to Laurie's boys."

"That's not going to happen," Sauren reported.

Derrek turned to the forward screen. A hyperspace portal opened and the Raman winged ship shot through. Escaped. Although Derrek didn't know for certain which ship Tomar had commanded, he suspected a dangerous enemy had just escaped. But as the portal closed, he knew there was nothing more he could do to stop the man from returning to Rama and reporting on what he'd learned.

And he'd learned too much. He'd learned that Zor had spaceships, weapons, and chaff. He'd learned they'd vigorously defend themselves. He'd seen the government fleet. While Derrek hoped those facts would deter the Ramans . . . he knew better. Those relentless bastards would never give up.

However, now he could go to Azsla. "I expect you still want to see your crew?"

"Yes, please." She tilted her head up to look at him. Her eyes sparkled with life. "Thank you. For helping us."

"I would have done the same for anyone," he growled. And he would have. Although he might not have been as pleased by his success if she'd been anyone else. And he wasn't sure why.

6

❂

The day had taken a good turn for Azsla. Derrek's command of his crew had shocked and pleased her. The discipline she'd expected had been there. There had been no question about the chain of command. His men obeyed as efficiently as if they'd been under the direction of a First's *Quait*. But they'd obeyed out of willingness to help, belief in a common mission, not fear.

Because there was no fear, his men had clearly felt free to contribute. She'd felt free to speak up. That freedom had won the day. Azsla hadn't expected to see such purposefulness. Such pride. Such heroics. Kali had given his life for her. Derrek and his crew had been ready to do the same. Their courage humbled her. Saddened her.

These slaves, former slaves, she corrected herself, had conducted themselves like a unit—without giving up their freedom. She'd actually felt part of it. Like part of them. They'd included her without hesitation. Bet their lives on her information. The respect they'd given her had been mutual—unlike her own people.

She hadn't appreciated that at the first sign of trouble, the loss of her ship, the Firsts had obviously altered the original plan. They weren't supposed to recapture her crew until after they'd reached Zor. But after her ship's calamity, before they'd even reached the portal, the Firsts changed the scheme—as if discounting her efforts, as if they no longer believed in her ability to accomplish her mission.

However, that didn't mean *tranqed* Firsts still wouldn't be waiting on Zor to send home her crew. And she'd be damned if she'd let that happen. She wasn't switching sides. She was here to do her duty. She fully intended to infiltrate the Zoran military to learn what weapons they could wield against Rama . . . however, she saw no reason to allow the Corps to execute her crew—just to make a political statement.

Azsla's steps felt light as she accompanied Derrek to the doctor's bay where Derrek assured her Falcon tended her crew. The medical bay made use of every available inch of space. Rak, Jadlan, and Micoo lay webbed into beds set against walls and floors. Instruments hung from the ceiling and were connected by wires to cuffs attached to her crew's wrists.

Dr. Falcon was a frail man with a delicate bone structure. Tall, lean, and gray-haired, he greeted Azsla and Derrek with a warm smile. "Come in. My patients could use a visit."

Azsla peered at their pale faces, closed eyes, and lack of consciousness and had the sudden urge to cuddle Micoo, who looked so young and tiny, hug Jadlan, and smooth back a lock of Rak's hair. They had been through a lot together. They deserved to wake up, go on with their lives. "Shouldn't they be awake by now?"

"Oh, yes. They've awakened, eaten, and gone back to sleep." So they weren't unconscious? Azsla thought. Great. "I was hoping your voice might calm them. They were tossing and turning so much I had to web them in to keep them from pulling off their medical cuffs."

As if to emphasize his words, Rak flailed, throwing out a skinny arm. His monitor beeped and he muttered in his sleep. His distress seemed to set off Jadlan, who tried to roll over, and Micoo, who started twitching.

Azsla placed a hand on Micoo's shoulder, and felt bone bite into her palm. She'd always known that physically he was the weakest, but until she touched him she hadn't realized that his skin stretched over bone, with no subcutaneous fat. "Easy. You're safe. We're all safe. Soon we'll be on Zor where we'll be free." And she would see to it that he had food and salt. She didn't know how, didn't know when these men had become her responsibility—although perhaps it had been when Kali had died in her place—but she would ensure their safety. Somehow. Some way.

"Captain," Sauren called to Derrek over his wrist com. "Sorry to bother you but the government command ship is demanding we dock up. Now."

"Now? What's so important it can't wait until we land?" Derrek asked, his brows knitting.

"They won't say."

Derrek remained calm, but his eyes darkened. "I don't like this. Patch me through to President Laurie."

"I already tried. He's not answering his link."

"Let's just ignore the—"

Sauren swore. "By all that's holy. I don't believe it."

"What?" Derrek punched a monitor to call up a view of the main screen on the bridge.

Azsla peered at it, puzzled by the streak of light across their bow. Her voice rose in confusion. "Did the Zoran government just fire on us?"

"Affirmative. It's a warning shot," Sauren verified, then his tone turned hard with sarcasm. "They seem damn serious about us adhering to their *friendly* request to come aboard."

"We can outrun them, can't we?" Derrek asked. Azsla thought it interesting that the man seemed to consider all options before making his decision. Where most men considered retreat a last resort, to Derrek it appeared merely another choice. Apparently he didn't fear appearances if he was considering running away. Interesting. Was he so confident?

She'd never known a man like him. Firsts ruled because of biological strength and their powers of *Quait*. But on Zor other character traits came into play. She could almost see a checklist of options in Derrek's mind and as he considered them, he crossed off the unacceptable risks, checked down the possibilities that best served his needs.

He was careful, yet unafraid. Confident, without the arrogance that usually piggy-backed a superior intellect. And he ruled by respect. Fear was not his thing and clearly his crew adored him—even enough to tease him. She couldn't help liking him, respecting him.

"Yeah, but what good would running do, boss man?

There'll just be more government issue guys waiting for us at the spaceport."

"It will buy us some time. Do it."

"You sure?"

"Yeah. Something tells me, President Laurie wants our cargo and I'm not talking about the salt."

"He wants *us*?" Azsla guessed. "But why?"

"My guess is publicity. He wants to show the entire Zoran world that he helped slaves escape the Raman Firsts. It will up his popularity and be a show of strength."

"But *he* didn't do anything."

"In politics facts don't count. Appearance is what matters. If he can get the press to say he saved you and your crew, everyone will take the news as truth."

"And this system of government is better that what we had on Rama?" she asked.

"Any system, even an inefficient one, is better than a dictatorship."

"I suppose."

"I'm not saying there aren't flaws. Right now, it's the best government credit can buy."

"Huh?" She didn't understand, but heard his cynical tone. And that surprised her. She wasn't accustomed to anyone openly voicing discontent with the powers that be. Yet another freedom she couldn't help but approve of.

"People with credit . . . can buy influence." He winked at her as if they shared an inside joke.

Interesting. Power here was based on economics— not the power of *Quait*. Clearly, he was a man who didn't even bother trying to hide his connections to power. She rubbed her brow, thinking hard. "What are the consequences for thumbing your nose at the president?"

Beta Five shuddered. Derrek called the bridge through his link. "Status."

"Laurie's boys have caught us in some kind of clutch beam. Heard about it. Guess it works better than predicted," Sauren said.

"Can we break free?"

"Depends on how much hull damage you want to sustain." Sauren's voice turned wry. "You might want to remember we're supposed to be on the same side."

"Tell that to the pres."

"He's your friend, you tell him. You're having cocktails with the great one at nine."

Derrek winced, turned on a memo recorder and spoke softly. "Remind Taylo to work on partial shielding. Also clutch beam. Duplicate it and counter it."

"Captain, what do you want me to do?" Sauren asked.

"Let them dock. But arm all hands."

"Got it."

Azsla cocked her head. "Do you shoot each other on Zor?"

He laughed, but the humor didn't reach his eyes. "Sometimes. Not often. Mostly we get along. However, I've learned to be careful. Especially when the government makes demands."

Once again he impressed her. Although his answer had been brief, he clearly had contingency plans. Backup plans. For any kind of emergency. While she admired his thoroughness, she had to wonder what kind of scars had made him so careful. Why he felt safest constructing his life around plans.

A more fly-by-the-seat-of-her-flight-suit person, she sort of made up her plan as she went along. Circumstances always changed. For example, she could have planned for years and would never have thought she'd actually end up wanting to save her crew of slaves. Not when saving them went against all her beliefs.

But during her life's journey, as she'd learned to suppress her own *Quait,* she must have begun to identify with the slaves on a level she hadn't recognized. And hopefully, if she came up with the right scheme, no one would ever know the part she'd played in saving her crew's lives. If the Ramans invaded Zor, maybe she could keep her crew safe by sending them to work in Derrek's asteroid mines.

Azsla stopped by each member of her crew. She squeezed Jadlan's hand, brushed back a lock of hair from Micoo's forehead, patted Rak's shoulder. Of the three of them, Jadlan was the only one strong enough to speak. He opened his eyes and drilled her with a hard stare. "Kali?"

"I'm sorry. He didn't make it."

Each of them grieved in his own way. Jadlan closed his pain-filled eyes. Micoo let out a sob. Rak turned his head to the wall.

They'd all come to care for Kali. Later she'd tell them of his bravery, but now was not the time.

She'd expected Derrek to leave her side. He didn't. She expected him to deal with his emergency. Instead he stopped his own crewman and made certain he had shoved a blaster into his belt and sheathed a blade down his boot.

His demeanor changed, sharpened. As if every cell in him had charged for action, he tensed, watching her every move . . . almost as if he feared she was about to lead Laurie's men past his defenses. Not that she could or would—even if she wanted to. But he seemed hostile again . . . suspicious. Wary.

And all hard angles. His cheekbones seemed sharp enough to cut glass. His mouth hardened into a tight grimace. A muscle in his jaw throbbed. All his plans didn't seem to relax him. Tense but confident, he radiated menace from his clenched fists to the rough, tough expression in his eyes to his vigilant, warrior-like stance.

When Micoo opened unfocused eyes, Derrek stepped between them as if she needed protecting. Weird. If the doctor's bay had seemed small before, it was positively tiny now. Derrek filled it with his hostility and Micoo flinched.

Azsla stepped around Derrek. "Don't mind him, Micoo. He may look dangerous, but he's on our side. He's already risked his life to save us. For the moment we're safe. We'll soon be free on Zor." She tucked a sipping straw into his mouth and he drew weakly, then closed his eyes once more.

She pivoted to face Derrek. "You didn't need to scare him."

"I didn't say a word," he protested.

"You didn't have to." Dr. Falcon eyed Derrek the way physicians did, taking in his swarthy coloring, yet surprising Azsla that he'd taken her side. "What's up with you? You're as edgy as one of Kendor's glaciers about to calve."

"Yeah." The last thing she expected was for Derrek to admit to unease . . . but he'd done exactly that. "Been meaning to talk to you about that."

Azsla listened to the two men speak as she smoothed the blanket over Micoo, shocked that the captain had admitted that he was anything but calm. Most men considered it a sign of weakness and denied their feelings about fear—even when it was blatant. But he was very open—as if he had nothing to hide. Almost as if this state were normal. But obviously he was far from normal or the doctor wouldn't have brought it up.

Doctor Falcon eyed Derrek, looking concerned. "Talk about what—"

"Docking in two micronbits," Sauren's voice interrupted.

"Understood. I'll meet you in the cargo hold in one." Derrek pivoted back to Doctor Falcon. "There's no time to go into everything right now. But I want a complete chemical and electrical analysis of those pods."

The ones she and her crew had arrived in? Azsla didn't understand what was going on. Apparently, neither did the doctor. What did the pods have to do with Derrek's unease?

Dr. Falcon's angled his chin. "What am I looking for?"

"Anything odd."

"Could you be more specific?"

"A chemical solution. A scent. An electromagnetic

charge. Sonic resonance. Something that alters normal thinking patterns. And emotions."

Before the doctor could say more, an alarm sounded. Derrek's eyes revealed a measure of relief, as if he were reluctant to say more. That he was a tad uncomfortable made her feel better, although she didn't know why. Maybe it made him seem less perfect and that was a good thing. She couldn't afford to become attached. She couldn't afford to trust.

"Later, doc." Derrek sprinted from the bay and Azsla followed, lots of questions running through her mind. Did Derrek suspect something on the pods had affected him? Had made him edgy? Was that why he'd been so curt with her when she'd first awakened?

Did he suspect some kind of trick? But if he had, then why had he risked the lives of everyone aboard *Beta Five* to defend her and her crew? Or maybe the battle had had nothing to do with her. Maybe he'd relished a chance to kill Firsts. However, when that ship had exploded, she'd watched his eyes and hadn't seen triumph—only despair.

She didn't get it. As she ran a step behind him she wondered why she wanted to.

DERREK JOINED A team at the cargo bay where the Zoran military ship would dock. He placed a hand on Azsla's arm. Toned and fit, she had lean, feminine muscles. He whispered into her ear and her fresh scent wafted through his nostrils, drifting into his lungs, circulating through his system . . . jolting him with the realization that any future breaths that lacked her special scent would now seem empty. He tried to shake off the stupid notion that air wouldn't be worth breathing without her scent.

His reaction to her was so off-kilter that it shocked him right down to his space boots. But though his mind told him his responses were uncalled for, ridiculous, and plain crazy, he reveled in one more breath as he tried to reassure her, "No matter what happens, it's going to be okay."

She cocked her head, gave him a sideways glance that drilled down to his bone marrow, and then nodded. Unlike him, she didn't appear the least bit ruffled. Either that or she was an expert at containing her feelings. She stood on the balls of her feet, knees slightly bent, shoulders relaxed, hands by her sides. With her lips parted, she could have been standing in line, waiting for an ordinary hovercraft ride, the standard mode of transportation on Zor.

The government ship sealed with *Beta Five,* the hatches clanging and machines clicking as computers checked to ensure equal pressurization on both sides. A long hiss followed by two short ones signaled the completion of a safe lockdown.

Moments later, the hatch seal cracked open and one commander and four military men boarded Derrek's ship, weapons holstered but their hands clearly twitchy. They wore standard-issue uniforms and, as if the commander had been briefed to know Derrek's appearance and rank, he strode toward him, his gaze sweeping over Derrek, Azsla, his armed crew, as well as the sleek ship.

The commander, a slender man of average height and

superior intelligence shining in his eyes, stopped before Derrek and offered his forearm in greeting. "I'm Commander Gironell. Thanks for inviting us aboard."

"Derrek Archer." He held out his forearm and the men shook, each lightly touching the other's arm at a point just below the elbow. He kept his face smooth and didn't betray for one second that he'd had no choice in allowing the military force aboard.

At least Gironell had the sense not to chuck rudeness in Derrek's face. "This is one sweet ship, captain."

"Thanks. What can we do for you, commander?"

"I've been ordered by President Laurie to pick up the Ramans who came through the portal in escape pods."

"That's odd." Derrek raised an eyebrow.

"How so?"

"Because Laurie asked me to do that, too."

Gironell flushed but kept his tone level. "I protested that decision. The risk was not yours to bear."

The other man's admission and his proud bearing depicted he spoke the truth. Derrek's attitude softened as he recognized that Gironell might be the commander of his ship, but he still had to obey orders. Chain of command sucked, unless one was at the top.

"Right now most of the escaped people are in my doctor's ward. I'm not sure they're strong enough yet to be moved. I'm told awakening from cold sleep is a slow and delicate process and best left to each individual's own time table."

"You said most of them? Can I assume some of the former slaves are ready for transport?"

"That would be me, sir." Azsla stepped forward. "But as I was their captain, I'm sure you can understand that I'm reluctant to leave my crew, especially in their weakened condition."

Gironell's eyes flared with sympathy. "Madam, I assure you, we will take very good care of you *and* your crew. This is," he cleared his throat and shifted his weight from foot to foot, "a matter of procedure."

Derrek held in a snort. "This is politics. Normally I don't mind Laurie's posturing but these slaves have been through a lot." Derrek's career required sizing up men and despite Gironell's orders, he liked the guy. Clearly he was a linear thinker and he struck Derrek as honest, uncomfortable with his orders, caught between duty and what he considered . . . an annoying assignment. Military types didn't like baby sitting civilians— especially weak ones, and Azsla and her crew were no exception.

But Gironell would follow orders. Derrek sensed the man was loyal through and through. "If you ever decide a career change is warranted, look me up," he offered.

Gironell's eyes dilated in surprise but he kept his emotions tucked deep, and his face didn't change expression. "Thank you. I wouldn't mind a stint or two in the asteroids . . . once my contract is up."

Good men were difficult to find and in Gironell, he liked what he'd seen so far. It should have made him feel better about handing over Azsla to the officer. But it didn't. At the idea of losing her, his gut churned like a cement mixer and the hard lumps refused to settle. Chalky dust swirled up his throat and he almost choked on the bitter taste of defeat.

He was going to lose her. Lose her before he figured out what made her so special. Before he learned why he was so taken with her. Before he understood why he was already plotting to see her again.

He *would* see her again. They were all flying to the same city. And Laurie owed him an invite, as well as an explanation for the boarding. But no matter how many times Derrek told himself she would be safe with Gironell, his gut told him differently.

COMMANDER GIRONELL'S PHYSICIAN took over and Azsla and her crew were moved to the military ship. She'd quickly said good-bye and had tried to thank Derrek again, but he'd assured her they were all going to the same city and he'd link up again soon.

As his eyes burned into her back, she strode into the other ship, wondering how she was going to save her crew. If Rama invaded Zor, she needed to find a way to keep them safe, but as she left Derrek and his ship, her idea of sending them to safety in the asteroids looked as if it would never happen. She'd have to think of some other way and tried to tell herself she was sorry to be leaving Derrek—for her crew's sake. But in truth, she'd found him . . . interesting. More than interesting.

Gironell had ordered his men to take her crew to their own doctor's ward. Unlike the luxurious *Beta Five,* this military ship had dull brown corridors, too-bright lights, and bare decks. She'd been given a tiny cabin, which consisted of a single bed with webbing, a functional washroom and a tiny view port, along with a change of clothing—military brown slacks and tan shirt—and told she might have time for a short nap before landing on Zor. Too keyed up to sleep, Azsla made use of the washroom to shower, changed into clean clothes, and paced.

Her mission had exploded into oblivion when they'd had to abandon ship while still on the Raman side of the portal. Could she resurrect it?

What was going on back home? With her ship blown up, she had no way to communicate with the Corps. Would Tomar's return to Rama affect her mission here? Would her superiors eventually learn that she and her crew had survived Tomar's attack? Would her contacts on Zor be aware of her changed circumstances?

Tomar hadn't seen her. And there had been little discussion between the Raman captain and Derrek. Plus, in her favor, Derrek had never admitted the escaped slaves were aboard at all. Which got her to thinking. Whether or not her last message had gotten through, the Corps knew she'd had a major malfunction. They'd investigate and might find debris. Then again, they might not if the debris had been sucked into the portal with the pods. The Corps wouldn't know if she'd lived or died until she reached the planet and made contact with a *tranqed* First. She might even be able to continue with her original mission, especially if her contact on Zor still tried for a meet-up.

The fully *tranqed* First would expect her to hand over her crew to them. But she couldn't do it. Wouldn't do it. She no longer wanted them to die—not that she ever had. Before she'd left she hadn't thought much about that part of her mission. However, in the short time they'd been together, they'd become people to her, people with hopes and dreams, people who laughed, and shared their food. One of them had died for her.

Now she was not about to hand them over to her connection as if they meant nothing. As if their lives didn't count—especially not for some damn political demonstration of power that no one would remember tomorrow.

However, Azsla had to find a way to save them without compromising her own mission. That meant the Ramans couldn't know what she'd done. And neither could the Zorans. Which left her stuck between a falling comet and a gravity well. About to crash.

At least she should have credits, ID, a map and quarters waiting for her on Zor. After she landed in the capital, she could pick up credit at any ATCM, automatic transfer credit machine. But she'd have to be extremely careful. She didn't know anyone and couldn't know who to trust. Even bribes might be reported.

Yet she was determined to find a way to save her crew. But how? If she looked up Derrek on Zor and asked him to hide the slaves, he would want to know what was going on. However, she couldn't give him answers without revealing who she was. Trusting him was not possible.

Yet she found herself wishing she could have told him part of the truth. The man had resources. Besides, he'd already risked his life once to protect them, so she was fairly certain he'd help. She couldn't forget that flash of interest in his eyes, or the way he took charge—while at the same time, encouraging his crew to offer suggestions. The man had impressive inner strength. Self-confidence.

She was getting off track.

Damn. *Think, Azsla.* She needed one of Derrek's plans. A workable idea.

She took three steps, pivoted, took three steps back. At the cabin's view port, the planet Zor loomed ever larger as they orbited in preparation for landing. The three continents seemed tiny in the vast oceans, the world peaceful.

Yet, she knew better. Whatever was down there, whatever the slaves had built, had already been infiltrated by *tranqed* Firsts. They lived and worked among the slaves, taking notes, sending back secret reports, the leading edge of an invasion.

Her mission was only one tiny part of the whole. But it was an important part, because she'd been trained to do what the other First spies could not—control her domination without *tranqs,* drugs that made the other spies unable to do much more than obey orders sent from Rama to Zor through the secret portal. The communication system was awkward and it took time to send reports and wait for orders. Azsla could literally think on her feet with a clear head and that should enable her to bypass the security systems at the Space Ministry and learn their strike capabilities. Before the Corps brought all the escaped Zoran slaves home to Rama, it was Azsla's job to make sure the slaves hadn't developed a terrible weapon to use against the homeworld.

There had always been rumors that slaves might return to Rama with a bioweapon or retaliate by some other means of destruction. The Zorans might have developed and hidden weapons on their military ships or on their moon. There was even a terrible fear that Zorans had developed a weapon that would instantly kill any First who used *Quait*. Once Azsla did her job, her findings would signal the beginning of the end down there.

Ramans would pour through the portal and round up each and every escaped slave. They would all be brought home where they belonged. Except her crew. . . . Maybe she could send them to the third continent. Life would be rough there, but at least they wouldn't be rounded up and executed.

Since the timetable had not yet been set and would be determined by her findings, she hoped to have the time to find a way to save them and had several advantages. As the only fully functional First to set foot on Zor, she should be able to outwit the *tranqed* Firsts who couldn't use their *Quait*, who couldn't think clearly. Sure, they could obey orders, send back reports. Because of the *tranqs*, however, they couldn't think for themselves beyond menial tasks. That might help her find a way to save her crew.

With a clear mind, she could still assess and act. It might be months, years, or decades until the final invasion and regathering of the slaves to bring them back to Rama, but it would happen. While many slaves would be glad to return to Rama where they'd be fed, clothed, and taken care of, she knew her crew thought differently. Although life here couldn't be easy, for them going home meant suffering, humiliation, and execution. She'd spent enough time with Raman slaves to understand how they also longed for freedom and would forego an easy and protected life to make their dreams a reality.

However, Rama's economy needed slaves to make food, clothing, run the factories. It was the way of their world. The way it had always been. The way it would be in the future.

The people she'd met in space couldn't be typical. Neither were her crew . . . a crew that was going to be executed—unless she saved them. Surely she could find a way to free them without compromising her mission.

7

What the frip do you mean, 'they disappeared'?" Derrek stalked over to Sauren's station and glared at the scanners. He'd prayed that distance from Azsla would soften his feelings. That hadn't happened. Talk about temperamental. He was micronbits past edgy, hours past moody. He breathed deeply and reminded himself that none of this, his feelings or Azsla's disappearance, was Sauren's fault. If anyone, President Laurie was to blame. Although Derrek wasn't into presidential assassinations, if the man didn't stop playing political games and come clean, Derrek might not be able to suppress his rage.

Where the hell was she?

Sauren cut him an explanation. "The military ship went dark."

Dark? "As in crashed? Turned off their systems? Or that they're refusing our hails?"

"I don't know. We're checking with our contacts on Zor and in the military as well as those inside President Laurie's staff. We're getting nothing. Not even a hint of a rumor. It's like they landed on Zor and were swallowed."

"Laurie had damn well better cough them up once we link with him." Derrek didn't blame Gironell. President Laurie was behind the mystery, he sensed, and he didn't appreciate the politician's one-upmanship. He didn't approve of Laurie taking credit where none was due, either. And Derrek sure as hell didn't like Azsla and her crew's disappearance.

"Check the news."

"I'm monitoring. There's nothing."

"Get us down there. Fast."

"We're scheduled for—"

"I don't give a slimeworm's ass what we're scheduled for. Fake an emergency. Bribe someone. Or pay the fripping fine. Just get up down there now."

"Yes, sir." Sauren nodded to the pilot, then lowered his voice to a worried murmur until only Derrek could hear. "Has the doc found anything?"

"Damn it. You've been spying on me?"

Sauren rolled his eyes at the ceiling.

"The doc told you?" Derrek's temper was burning on high-test. And he had nowhere to go, until he hit dirt, where he'd tear the capitol building apart with his bare hands if that's what it took to find her. The absolute silence about the first slaves to escape Rama in a decade was huge news. Yet, there was nothing about them—on any transmitter.

Where was she? The question beat in his head like a drum, repeating until the rhythm threatened his mental stability. He felt as if part of him was missing. The intensity of his emotions was far from normal, yet the knowledge couldn't cut the wanting, the yearning, the having to have her back with him.

He was an idiot.

He shouldn't have allowed Laurie to take her. And now just because he was edgy enough to rip the ship's controls from his pilot's hands and fly her down himself, Sauren was questioning him?

Sauren must have sensed his roiling frustration. "I don't spy. No one told me anything. I saw the doctor at the pods taking test samples." Sauren rubbed his jaw. "Maybe old Doc should be checking you out and—"

"I'm fine." Derrek gritted his teeth. While he himself had considered a need for a complete physical, he didn't have time. Doc would hold him up for a day, longer if he had to do a psych test. Thank you, no. Derrek wasn't about to put himself through those again. Not when he knew that finding Azsla would fix him.

"Yeah, you're good to go."

"I'm fine. Really." Derrek paced, stopped, stared at the screen and paced some more. The waiting process unnerved him. He reminded himself no one liked to wait his turn. There were more spaceships in line to land now and he couldn't just wing it.

Adain looked up from communications. "There's a call coming in from Alpha One."

"Record it."

"The mines broke another drill bit," Adain muttered.

"Sauren, you have the bridge." Derrek didn't want to hear about business right now. He had people to take care of details and he paid them well to do their jobs. Instead, he headed to Doc Falcon's ward to find out his test results.

The ward seemed a little larger without the slaves webbed in. Large and empty.

Without Azsla the room seemed colder. More scientific. And instead of her sweet scent, he picked up the reek of meds.

The doctor bent over his scope examining a slide in a slot. "I've got nothing for you."

"You aren't done?" Derrek asked. "Or there's nothing to be found?"

"If there was a contaminant on the pod, it's not there anymore."

Not the answer he wanted to hear. If Doc had found something, they could have countered it with another agent. But how did one fight *nothing*? "Maybe you missed the place I touched—"

"Not possible." Doc swiveled on his stool and selected a bloodsucker, a tiny tube used to collect blood samples. "Let's see if you picked up anything nasty."

Resigned to following through, Derrek held out his arm, wondering if he'd ever know what had been done to him. Because he didn't act like this. The feelings inside him couldn't be his. Mother of Salt. He barely knew Azsla. Yet look at him.

He was all pumped up with overprotective testosterone. Ready to break space laws. Unable to focus on business. Despite his brain telling him to remain calm and detached, rational, his emotions kept sweeping into a place he'd never been. Almost out of control.

His reactions made no sense. And if the doc didn't find something wrong soon, he might start doubting his sanity.

Don't be ridiculous.

Huh? Who'd said that?

A friend.

Great. It wasn't enough that he couldn't control his own emotions, now he had an imaginary friend. "Go away."

"Excuse me?" Doc Falcon pressed the tube to his arm and shot him a suspicious look. Derek couldn't blame the man for asking after having caught him talking to himself. That was smooth. Smooth as gravel. "You okay?"

"Sorry, I was just going over some things. Didn't realize I'd spoken out loud."

Now that's a wimpy excuse if I ever heard one.

Derrek ignored the voice in his head. Surely if he pretended it wasn't there, it would disappear. He'd will it away.

Like you will away your emotions for Azsla?

Damn it. If you're going to stick around, do you have to sound so cheerful?

What's wrong with cheerful? Besides, I'm not the one giving my DNA to a bloodsucker.

Although Derrek couldn't feel the blood being drawn, he still flinched at the hiss. He'd never liked giving blood, giving up a part of his DNA, not when he knew his blood was inferior. Flawed. Because he'd lacked the necessary salt during his early years, the markers in his cells proclaimed to all that he was damaged goods. They all were. At least all the slaves who'd escaped Rama.

Then the mind scrubbers had gone in and whacked him out big time. But he'd thought he'd fully recovered. And now, he had a damn voice talking inside his head.

Don't blame the scrubbers.

"How long until you have results?" Derrek asked, rolling down his sleeve. He was tired. Imagining that voice.

Not.

Doc took the blood and set it into a centrifuge. "It could be micronbits or days. Weeks if I have to grow cultures."

"In other words, you don't know." Derrek stormed out of the ward as the ship's thrusters engaged, bent on exiting the ship the moment they landed. Determined to forget that odd voice in his head, which surely had been just some weirdo aberration, a result of his supercharged emotions, he clenched his jaw and fought down uncertainty.

A long time ago, Cade had asked Derrek if he'd like

to talk to a head doctor, but Derrek didn't want the guy poking old wounds. Cade had accepted his decision but now he wondered if it had been wise. Perhaps one mind could only take so much stress.

Wimpy. Wimpy. Wimpy.

Leave me alone.

As if knowing his plan, Sauren joined Derrek at the cargo bay. "Thought you could use some company."

Maybe he could. Maybe Sauren's presence could drown out the voice in his head. If not, the guy was also handy with a gun. And he had a cool head. Derrek couldn't think of a better companion to have around . . . and yet, a little thought in the back of his mind niggled him. Did Sauren want to go after Azsla for himself?

Derrek hammered the jealous thought into submission. "I'm not even sure where I'm going."

"Doesn't matter." Sauren's solid presence and loyalty made Derrek feel a bit guilty for accusing him of spying on him earlier. Or for questioning his motives a few seconds ago.

"Thanks." Should he tell Sauren that he didn't feel like himself? That he was talking to himself? He trusted Sauren like a brother. Yet he didn't want Sauren second-guessing his every move, worrying over him, pitying him.

"You sure you're okay?" Sauren asked.

"I'm fine." But it was a lie. He wouldn't be fine until he was sure Azsla was safe. Until he saw her again. Part of him wanted to howl in outrage. Shake his fist at the sky and stomp his feet. A more rational part of him knew that wouldn't help. He reminded himself that she couldn't have gone far. With his contacts and a few well-placed bribes, he'd have her location pegged within the hour.

Derrek was fairly certain Doc Falcon was going to find a foreign agent in his blood to explain his aberrant behavior. Maybe even the interior voice would eventually be explained away by an imbalance. Chemical agents could trick the brain into all kinds of weird scenarios. He'd be fine—eventually. However, right now the compulsion to assure himself of her safety was too strong to fight.

The cargo bay opened and Derrek stepped onto the landing pad—a round concrete foundation surrounded by landing lights and other spacecraft, albeit none as sophisticated as his. Officials were hurrying his way, expecting him to head for his private parked hovercraft. Derrek didn't stop and wait or head for his private hangar. Ignoring the weirdness of walking under an open sky without a rebreather or space suit, he didn't stop to ask directions. Moving fast, he wound past forklifts unloading cargo, stepped around mechanics refueling tanks and over a conveyor belt of incoming parts.

The busy spaceport had grown since his last visit dirtside. Mazelike, crowded, the facility was a hive of activity and organization. Thanks to Derrek's vigorous exercise program, neither the higher gravity nor the air that was clogged with pollen slowed him down. He breathed in shallow pants and tried not to think about the fact that air was unfiltered here, that all kinds of nasty pollutants from the smoking stacks of nearby factories were free to enter his lungs.

He reminded himself he'd lived over two thirds of his

life on a planet. And most of those years had been brutal. No wonder the stink in the air reminded him of the past. But for the first time in years, his first thoughts weren't about his ex-wife and the children he'd lost. He wanted to find Azsla, assure himself she was okay, help her settle in. Make sure President Laurie didn't take advantage.

Had his obsession with his past switched to his new obsession, Azsla?

Perhaps he really was crazy. Should he have the head doc check him out?

But surely once he'd assured himself of her safety, he would again be able to go about his business? Ignoring his appointments, he sent a memo to his assistant via his wrist com link to reschedule. He ignored a dozen urgent messages. They could wait. For once he wasn't putting business first.

Damn it. Why hadn't he given her a personal com link of her own? Then he could have tapped her location whenever he wanted. So what if only the wealthiest citizens had them? So what if his crew would have thought he'd lost his mind with such a grand gesture?

He was making her safety his responsibility, and he didn't care who knew it. Or who didn't like it. He reached the taxi bay and flagged down a hovercab, ignoring the spaceport officials who had almost caught up and were signaling him to stop and fill out forms.

"Mr. Archer, I need to stamp your paperwork. The fine for leaving the spaceport without authorize—"

With Sauren on his heels, Derrek slid into the hovercraft and handed the driver a hundred credit note. "Take me to the capitol building in the Granitite District. There's an extra fifty in it for you if you don't stop."

"Sir, the fines—"

"I'll cover them. Go."

Sauren leaned back with an amused twinkle in his eyes and a small grin.

Derrek glared at him. "What's so funny?"

"Never seen you in such a hurry."

AZSLA HAD YET to see one blade of grass, one person, one building on Zor. They'd exited the military ship into some kind of hover vehicle that had no windows in the back where she sat with the crew. The hovercraft had flown right into a huge parking garage that had been empty of any people. From there, uncommunicative guards had escorted them to a holding area where they'd been told to wait for further instructions.

Her crew received medical care from close-lipped physicians who had refused to say where, why, or who was holding them. If this was freedom . . . it sucked. Locked with her crew in a cell no larger than her own room back home, Azsla forced herself to sit.

But she remained tense as a jungle cat on the prowl. If this was the planet of freedom, it sure didn't feel like it. And Zoran hospitality had been downright rude.

Rak placed a hand on her shoulder and gave it a fatherly squeeze. "It'll be okay. They're keeping us from the Zorans just in case we might spread a disease."

"You believe them?" Azsla had heard the same story from one of the medics, only she hadn't bought it. Disease on Rama was rare. And anything they had, this population had already been exposed to. After all, it had only been a decade since the revolt.

"Why would they lie?" Rak's tone was mild and calm. She wondered if a life of slavery had squashed his street instincts, or maybe he hadn't been born with any.

Why would the medics lie? Because they'd been following orders. Because they suspected one of them might not be a slave. Because someone wanted to make use of them for political gain. Because someone had figured out that if slaves had escaped, trouble was brewing and didn't want to upset the general populace.

Azsla forced a nod. "I'm sure you're right. How are you feeling?"

"Hungry. Yet, stronger than I've ever been."

"On the ship, through the cuffs, they boosted salt rations higher than we're accustomed to."

"They did?" Rak's eyebrows rose in surprise before he returned to his placid norm. "How will we pay—"

She smiled and the memory warmed her. "Derrek Archer didn't ask for payment. He saw what we needed and gave us the salt. It was free. A gift."

Rak's eyes watered and he turned away from her, his voice choked up. "We owe him. I was so weak, without that salt, I might not have pulled through."

She gave him a moment to collect himself. Sharing salt freely was something one did for a beloved family member, not a stranger. So Derrek's gesture had touched Rak as much as it had her. For the tenth time, she leaned over Micoo, then Jadlan. Neither moved. Although their even breathing reassured her they would survive, she just barely refrained from shaking them. "I wish they'd wake up."

"The doctors said that their bodies will recuperate in their own time." Rak had more patience than she did. But then he'd spent his life as a slave. Although he'd worked as an engineer and had been highly educated, he lacked initiative. To be fair, she recalled how hard he'd worked to come on this mission. How he'd gone without sleep to make sure his calculations were correct. No one had been pushing him but he'd summoned the good sense to work hard. Perhaps he'd justly feared showing enthusiasm until it had become habit.

Even if she could have divulged to Rak that a *tranqed* First was seeking him out to send back to Rama without breaking her cover, she didn't know if she'd have had the heart to tell him. However, it would have been nice to share the burden. She would have enjoyed talking to him, just to sound out some ideas.

Because none were viable. Until Micoo and Jadlan awakened, she couldn't move them. Even after they awakened, she didn't know how to escape the lockdown. Frustrated, she wondered if the Corps knew she was alive. Where she was. If they did, would they try to break her out?

To contact anyone, she needed to escape this stifling cubicle. She'd even thought about grabbing a sharp implement and attacking one of the doctors, threatening to kill him if the guards outside the door wouldn't free them. But she didn't want to bluff because no way would she kill an innocent.

Plus, she didn't want to reveal her plan to escape with such a feeble scheme. Whatever she did, it had to be well planned. Secret.

When the door opened, her muscles tightened as if in preparation to lunge. But it was only another medical attendant coming to check on Jadlan and Micoo.

Azsla had to control her urge to barge past her in a dash for freedom. Rak seemed content to wait out his fate—he sat against a wall, knees drawn to his chest. But then she caught a gleam in his eyes, a gleam that indicated he too was thinking of making a break. Very slightly, she shook her head, signaling him to remain still.

The attendant, Yawitz, according to her name tag, checked Jadlan and Micoo's wrist cuffs and their machine readouts. "They should wake up soon." Her tone was disinterested, as if she had more important things to do. "I'll send food for all of you."

"Thanks. Why are we being held here?" Azsla asked, not really expecting a response since the other doctors had ignored their questions.

Wide-eyed and clearly puzzled, Yawitz turned to Azsla. "I don't understand."

"When can we leave?"

Her pretty hands fluttered to her neck and then gestured to the door. "Leave whenever you wish."

"But the door's locked. There are guards outside."

"All for your protection."

Protection from whom? Azsla wanted to ask but figured that could wait until after she escaped the room. "Okay, then I'm going to leave with you and help bring back food. All right?"

"Sure."

Yawitz opened the door and spoke with the larger and older guard. "We're going for food and will return shortly."

The big man folded his arms across his chest and scowled. When they slipped past him, he shot a look at his partner. "He'll go with you."

"Why do we need protection?" Azsla asked as she stepped from the room into a long empty corridor. The layout, endless tunnels and bright lights, was utilitarian, and could have shared a designer with the military transport ship. The decor was as different from Derrek's elegant *Beta Five* as she was from a slave.

"It's complicated," the medical attendant lowered her voice. "There are factions that want President Laurie out of office. Anything or anyone who serves to enhance his position can come under attack."

"How will our presence enhance his position?"

"You came through the portal, didn't you? Rumors are flying high and far that Firsts tailed you and will return. Now come along." Bossier than any slave she'd met, Yawitz gestured to Azsla and headed into a cafeteria as if in no doubt she would follow.

When the guard tried to enter the cafeteria, the woman shook her head. "Stay here. I can't have you making the other employees nervous."

What other employees? The cafeteria was empty. Food sat in warming trays under lights. Chairs beside the long tables were empty. A janitor mopped a floor at the far end, but otherwise they had the place to themselves.

As soon as they were out of the guard's hearing range, Yawitz slipped a flat backpack into Azsla's hand. "Hide this."

Startled, Azsla fumbled, then did as she'd been told, slipping it under her shirt. Obviously the woman had told the guard to stay back in order to pass on the information. She could have done it in the room but she obviously hadn't wanted Rak to know about her scheme, either. So who was she? Her contact? A *tranqed* First? But then why hadn't she used the prearranged code?

Had Yawitz found Azsla because Azsla couldn't go to her? To verify the woman's identity in the Corps, she tried to instigate the code herself, uttering the prearranged sequence of words. "What time is the next—"

"Just listen." Yawitz cut her off, her eyes bleak, her tone as cold as hyperspace. "Your contact was killed last week—hopefully before he gave us all up. I don't know the damn codes. My final mission is to hand you that backpack. Now I'm done. And I'm on the next transport back to Rama."

Yawitz referred to the secret portal on the back side of the world that, so far, the Zorans didn't know anything about. So she was an authentic *tranqed* First. Azsla had heard that many Firsts back home had simply wanted to blow up both portals. But that wouldn't get back the Zoran slaves. Nor would it stop the Zorans from opening another portal if they had the technology to do so.

Dozens of questions whirred in Azsla's mind. As they neared the food, she swiped two salt packets, then chose food, an assortment of meats, fruits, and vegetables, many unfamiliar to her. She piled everything on trays to take back to Rak, Micoo, and Jadlan and risked the one question that concerned her the most. "What about my crew?"

"They'll be collected within the hour. They'll get home before I will."

An hour. She only had an hour. Azsla almost dropped the food.

"No more talking."

Azsla had an hour. And no plan. She didn't know where she was. Her only contact had barely spoken to her and was about to abandon her. Worse, Micoo and Jadlan had yet to awaken.

Somehow she had to make this right. She was going to save them. One thing she knew for sure. She had to work fast. Real fast.

8

Azsla slid the backpack from Yawitz into her pocket without looking at the contents. Her training kicked in and she memorized every detail of this place during her walk back to her crew. The cafeteria was a dead end. Ditto this part of the corridor. There were no cross corridors. Lots of closed doors and she'd bet her next paycheck they were locked. No ceiling vents large enough to hide in. No elevators, moving walkways, or windows.

So breaking out had to mean heading the opposite way, in a direction she hadn't yet seen. As she approached her quarters and the remaining guard, she examined the hallway. Cement walls, floors, and ceiling—it could be a basement, a bunker, a prison. The hallway continued for about ten body lengths before T-boning another corridor of similar design.

For all she knew they could be under water. But she saw no other option than to escape, then blindly pound down the pavement as fast as they could go. She'd figure out the rest later. When they had more intel, she'd make more plans.

She entered their cell to find everyone pretty much in the same condition she'd left them in. Rak rose to his feet to help her with the food trays, his expression patient, his tone calm as always. "We have to get out of here."

"Tell me something I don't know."

He glanced at the food. "I'm hungry."

"Good. We eat first."

As the strange scents wafted up to her from the tray and her stomach growled, she reminded herself she too needed nourishment. Taking time for a quick meal, even if it didn't smell familiar, was necessary to keeping up her strength. For one moment she allowed herself a memory of Derrek frying onions and cooking eggs, a delicious meal with fresh bread. He'd been kind and generous.

But he wasn't here now. *Snap out of it, girl.*

She pushed a tray into Rak's hands. "Eat fast. Then we wake up Micoo and Jadlan."

"But they aren't ready and the docs said—"

"I know. We don't have a choice. We're getting out of here," she whispered, hoping her voice was low enough that if a listening device had been planted in the room, her volume was too low to give her away.

"What happened?" Rak was no slouch in the mental department. She suspected he'd spent most of his life hiding his intelligence from his owner. Brilliant slaves didn't live long on Rama, since they often took on the dangerous challenge of a difficult task to break up the boredom of their daily life. Failure meant punishment. Success made others jealous. Both could lead to a short life.

So she kept her lie simple and used part of the truth along with a falsehood. "Yawitz told me we're going to be moved to a more secure prison within the hour." She gestured to the food. "Eat."

"A prison?" He shoveled food into his mouth, the insipid taste not appearing to bother him. "We didn't do anything wrong."

She forced herself to chew and swallow the bland food, knowing she needed to eat to keep up her strength. "It's not about that." Azsla made up a story from the information Derrek had told her. She hoped once they escaped, her words would still make sense and that her crew wouldn't blow her cover. Again she mixed truth with the lies. "There are opposing political forces at work on Zor. Both sides want us. If we don't wish to be used, we must leave while we still can."

"Did you find out where we are?"

"I saw a large cafeteria and a janitor. A long corridor and closed doors. When we break out of here, we go right."

"And then?"

She pushed aside her food. Despite her effort to make herself eat, she couldn't stomach any more. "First, I'll wake up Micoo. You do the same for Jadlan. Expect them to be woozy. So we'll get some salt into them, then food." She handed him one of the tiny salt packets she'd swiped from the cafeteria.

Turning to Micoo, she placed a hand on his shoulder. The skinny kid didn't move. Grabbing his jaw, she opened his mouth and sprinkled precious salt onto his tongue. "Come on, Micoo. It's time to wake up."

Beside her Rak worked on Jadlan . . . who groaned. "We made it?"

"Yeah." Jadlan opened his eyes and then they fluttered shut. "Oh, no you don't," Rak coaxed. "Here. Swallow more salt."

"Micoo. Wake up." His too-pretty lips didn't move. He didn't swallow. Suppose he never woke up? She shivered, a chill breaking out all over her skin. Azsla took some water and flicked it onto his face. Nothing. Perhaps she'd been too gentle. She clapped her hands together, but he didn't even flinch.

Beside her, Jadlan was waking, Rak's efforts paying off. "Eat this and I'll tell you what's happening," Rak offered him food. Jadlan sat up, rubbed his eyes, looking confused but not asking questions. When Rak handed him food, he began eating. Sometimes slave mentality, the instant conditioning to obey orders, came in handy. Now was one of those times. Jadlan's hands trembled but eventually steadied as Rak filled him in with what little they knew about their circumstances beginning with Derrek's rescue of the pods, the Firsts' pursuit through the portal, the Zoran government removing them from Derrek's ship, and their incarceration here.

Jadlan shook his head but kept eating. "You guys have been busy."

Not busy enough, Azsla thought, impatience licking through her. They needed to hurry. "Rak, Micoo isn't responding. Can you please help with him?" Azsla requested.

"Sure." Rak slid behind the other man, eased him up to a half-sitting position and kneaded the other slave's shoulders. "He's so frail. Try giving him more salt."

She should have swiped more. But old habits from training as a slave died hard. Theft of salt on Rama meant immediate memory wipe. There was a zero tolerance policy. While it didn't matter if a thief got caught with a thimbleful or a truckload, the less that was stolen, the less likely it was to be noticed. But she was on Zor now and she wanted to kick herself for not helping herself to more.

"I've only a little left." Hoping it would be enough to revive him, Azsla poured the remaining grains into his mouth.

Micoo sputtered but his eyes never opened. Suppose they never did?

He was much too young to die. He didn't even need to shave. His voice had yet to change. At first she'd been skeptical about taking on such a young man. But they'd needed his computer skills and he hadn't once faltered. Until now. Micoo had to wake up, because she wasn't leaving him behind.

Azsla buried her fear under practicalities. She supposed they could carry him. He was short and didn't weigh much. But that would slow them down, and look weird. She'd hoped they might simply be able to walk out, but carrying an unconscious body would heap all kinds of attention in their direction.

Tension sharpened her tone. "Micoo. We need you. Wake up. Wake up. Wake up and see the new world."

His eyes finally flickered, squinted, and ever so slowly opened. Unlike Jadlan, who'd seemed a bit fuzzy at first, Micoo appeared fully awake all at once. He looked around at his surroundings and cleared his throat. "Did you say new world? This is Zor?"

"Yeah. And we have to get out of here within thirty micronbits. Take five to eat."

While Micoo and Jadlan ate, Azsla opened the backpack Yawitz had given her and slipped out a lock pick, part of the standard gear.

"Where did that come from?" Rak asked.

"I stole a backpack on my food trip," she said, then cut off more questions with a curt, "I need silence."

Very quietly, she went to work, her ear up against the door to hear the clicks. To squelch the sound of the lock giving way, when the lock was about to ping, she slammed her boot into the wall. Micoo jumped at the loud thump and swallowed the last of his food.

"Where did you learn—" Jadlan asked.

Damn it. "Not now." Not ever.

That would be a shocker. Giving away her cover while she was trying to save them. Surely she could accomplish both goals, do her job and save her crew.

She wasn't about to let this mission go down as a complete bust. His questions might make her wonder if she could pull off an escape and question her competence, but she'd trained for this mission, trained for contingencies. Reminding herself that if she failed, she'd have wasted half her life and thrown away the rest, she squared her shoulders.

You know what must be done. Take charge.

"Shh." Placing her finger to her lips, she cracked open the door. Her nose detected the reek of sweat. Two guards were leaning over a vidscreen, watching women take off their clothes. Between the slow striptease and seductive music, apparently they hadn't heard the door open.

That gave her a momentary advantage. But she had to move fast. Not only must she take out the guards before they shouted a warning, she needed to do so before her crew entered the corridor and saw her trained moves—if they did, they'd recognize she had knowledge and training no slave would ever have had.

They'd already questioned her earlier. She couldn't afford to reveal anything else. But it was a risk she had to take.

Her stomach doing a slow churn job, Azsla charged through the door, her focus on the guard looking her way. Shock and fear swirled over his face. The big man's eyes widened and the scent of fear spiked in the corridor. He began to paw for his weapon, but his fingers didn't touch his blaster before she lunged into the air and landed a roundhouse kick to his temple.

Down and out, but not dead, he slumped to the floor, the air going out of his lungs in an oof.

The second guard had faster reactions. Visibly swallowing fresh panic, he pulled the blaster and raised the weapon as he retreated.

Not far enough.

Mind humming like a hard drive, muscles beating in unison, she hit the wall and ricocheted. Thrusting straight at him and blocking his weapon before he'd raised it high enough to shoot, she slammed her elbow into the underside of his chin so hard his teeth clicked. His head snapped back. His eyes clouded. He wobbled, but stayed on his feet. He re-aimed the blaster at her.

Sweet Vigo. Talk about a chin as hard as *diamondite.*

If she hadn't pulled the punch, she would have killed him with one blow. But her intent, to only knock him out, had failed. The stubborn idiot had no idea she was trying to save his life. So he kept fighting. Going on instinct. Refusing to go down.

Heart beating double time, she reminded herself that now was no time to admire bravery and persistence. She had mere seconds before her crew barged through that door and discovered her secret. Azsla down-blocked, the side of her wrist catching his and knocking loose the blaster. The weapon tumbled from his numbed fingers and slid across the floor, metal scraping concrete. She followed through with a knee to the solar plexus. The man gasped and as he retreated, back to the wall, she struck the underside of his jaw with her fist.

Finally, he went down.

Hand hurting, knuckles bruised, she tried to shake away the pain radiating up her arm and regain her breath. Her crew swarmed her and she had no idea how much they'd seen. Jadlan eyed her with serious concern. Micoo whooped with glee.

Rak frowned, suspicion and curiosity in his glance. "How did you—"

"Later." Azsla scooped up the gun. She told herself that she hadn't killed them because they were innocents, like the doctors. But they were soldiers. And killing them or not shouldn't have concerned her—not at all. But she couldn't waste time thinking about it. "Lock them in our quarters. Then let's move."

THE MOMENT DERREK and Sauren shut the hovertaxi door, Derrek's com link beeped an urgent signal. Only a few people had that code, all of them important to him, so instead of shifting it down to message mode, he lifted his wrist near his mouth. "Derrek here."

"Dad?"

Dad? No one called him dad. He might have two kids but they didn't speak to him. He'd been told that long ago when he'd lived with his family they'd had a decent relationship, but Derrek didn't remember it—thanks to the Firsts on Rama who'd wiped his memory as punishment for a crime he hadn't committed.

Since then, he'd had no contact with his children. So the call must be a wrong number. Yet, even after all these years his hope that his family might call him had never totally died.

Tish was just shy of her seventeenth birthday and a slim, blond-haired, violet-eyed beauty. Tad, two and half years younger, had yet to grow into his adult-size body and was at the awkward stage where his hands and feet were too big for the rest of him.

But it had to be a wrong number. Derrek's kids followed his ex-wife's lead and acted as if he didn't exist, with one exception. They cashed his credit wires without so much as a thank-you. As if they deserved whatever he had. As if what he did for them meant nothing.

He wondered if their abandonment pained him less because he couldn't remember their early years when they'd all lived together? If so, he should be grateful, because whenever he thought about his lost family, it was like a fire burning in his gut, the flames agony.

Of course, wanting only the best for his kids, after having been told his history, he'd done his duty sending credits every few cycles. As his income increased, so had his generosity. His family now lived well beyond the means of ordinary Zorans. That knowledge should have been enough.

He should have moved on. In some ways he had. He'd moved offworld to Alpha One and built empire. But he couldn't let go all the way. And he still despised himself for keeping up with his family through reports . . . reports he couldn't stop himself from reading. Those pictures in his files were key to feeling like part of something, part of them—even when he knew they'd prefer him dead. Dead husbands and fathers were less embarrassing than mind-wiped husbands and fathers.

Not even his recent financial success could erase the

stigma of a memory wipe. It didn't matter that he'd been unjustly accused. He'd become a liability and *she* hadn't stuck around to watch the cruel process of him learning to walk and talk again. She'd dumped him. Their years together had apparently meant nothing.

Despite the separation, he didn't think of them as strangers. How could he? He had holo pics of Tish's first day of school. And of Tad's first wobbly steps on Zor. Derrek knew his daughter loved loud music, *carroticle* cake, and had tattoos on her ankle. That his son dreamed of being a top-notch star pilot. Once several years back, Derrek had even interrupted his busy schedule to look them up in person—from a distance, of course. He'd seen ordinary, spoiled kids and he hadn't interfered, knowing if he did, he could turn their ordered lives into chaos.

He'd missed his chance. Instead of bonding with his kids, he'd been in recovery. Those lost years could never be reclaimed and the knowledge chilled him to the bone, a tiny part of him had died when he'd realized it was over.

Still, he had never stopped hoping . . . that one day, Tish or Tad would call. But they never had. So he didn't bother dialing into picture mode to see a kid who wasn't his. "I think you've got the wrong number."

"You're denying that you're Derrek Archer?" the young woman's voice was brassy, bold, yet beneath the fake sass he detected a twang of uncertainty. Vulnerability. "Mom always said you wanted nothing to do with us. Maybe for once she's right."

"Tish?" His throat closed.

He forced his fingers to dial in the picture. Tish. His Tish. With her beautiful lavender eyes and her overdone makeup. She'd twisted her hair into a sophisticated style much too old for her and reminded him of a kid playing dress-up. Derrek might not remember how to raise kids, but even he knew better than to laugh.

"I am . . . your father." At Derrek's words, Sauren's eyebrows rose all the way to his hairline. Then he turned away to give him privacy. Sauren didn't know anything about Derrek's family, but the two men were close. That Sauren didn't know, that Derrek hadn't shared, revealed as easily as a signpost exactly how much the call meant to Derrek.

"Glad to hear you owning up to me." Tish sounded . . . snippy. Rude.

Huh? Some of the warm and wonderful floated away. "What are you talking about?"

"It might have been nice to hear from you on my birthday or on daughter's day. Even once."

"I sent your mother credits every month."

"Did you think you could just pay us off? Abandon your responsibilities?"

Derrek had dreamed many times of a conversation with his daughter. But never had he once imagined the hostility he heard now. And the last thing he wanted to do was to tell Tish that her mother had locked him out of their lives. He wouldn't do that, wouldn't say it, no matter that it was true.

"Why did you call?" he asked, keeping his tone even. No matter what kind of emotional ride he might be on, his instincts kicked in. She wasn't calling out of love or curiosity and disappointment burned through him. He threw dirt on the burn and buried the pain deep underground until he could function.

"I need credits and Mom says you're loaded."

He winced at her crassness. He should have known that was the only reason she'd call . . . she needed credit. And he had only himself to blame. He hadn't been there to help raise her. Give her values. Hadn't been there to help her settle on the new planet. Oh, he'd sure enough arranged for their freedom, hers, her mother's and brother's, but he hadn't been there to support them—except to send credits. Once again he'd failed her.

"How much do you need?" he asked, taking the blame, wishing he had a do-over. That he could go back to a time when he had a tight connection to Tish.

She hesitated as if she were negotiating. "Two thousand."

"Two thousand?" He whistled. "What's a kid like you need two thousand credits for?"

"None of your business," she snapped.

"If you want my money, it is my business," he countered. Guilt and shame and yearning might erode his heart, but what good could come from giving her that kind of credit?

"Dad, I just . . . need it. If you were in my life, you'd trust me. But I guess Mom's right, the memory wipe didn't just take your memories but your feelings."

Her accusation knocked him down, and he had to pick himself off a mental floor and stomp on his emotions because they scared him a little. It was true. He couldn't remember Tish's birth. Couldn't remember feeling happy about her or his son—because he'd been cleaned out. The sons of bitches had taken everything from him. His ability to speak and walk. His skill as a chef. He'd had to learn to read and write all over again. Tie his shoes. Comb his hair. They'd taken away his ability to support his family.

He'd lost . . . his identity. Talk about a total wipeout of essence. They'd left him with no skills—not even the ability to crawl.

Like a baby in a crèche, he'd started over. The re-education process had taken two years. But everything before the memory wipe was still gone. His brother had spent hours telling him stories from his childhood. But to him—they were stories, unconnected to his heart, like a book he'd read about someone else.

He kept his voice gentle. "I'm sorry I wasn't there for you."

"Mom said you'd say that." She spit the words like an accusation. "But it changes nothing."

"However, I can be here for you now."

"Then wire the credits." Tish severed the connection and he felt like she'd cut him back out of her life. Funny, it shouldn't have hurt. But she came from his DNA. His genes flowed through her body. She was his only daughter, and she'd sounded hurt, angry, confused, and scared.

He hadn't a clue what to do.

It would make sense to call her mother, but she wouldn't take his calls. He could pay a surprise visit, but he wasn't welcome in the home he'd paid for. And he couldn't bear to see the new husband, Mavinor. If Mavinor was a decent man, Derrek would be jealous. If

Mavinor was a lousy man, Derrek would be furious. For him, showing up was a lose–lose proposition.

Emotionally he was so ready to wire the credits. His daughter had reached out to him for the first time in her life that he could remember. He couldn't believe he was actually considering not doing it.

And yet, what did a seventeen-year-old need that kind of credit for? She had a roof over her head, food in her belly. Derrek raised his wrist to his mouth and linked to the private investigator who sent him the weekly reports. "Any idea why my daughter wants two thousand credits?"

"Nothing solid."

"So give me a guess."

"I don't do guesses. I have a daughter of my own. At that age, they're all melodramatic. She might want to fly to the capital to see the newest hot band. Or she might want buttock implants."

"What?"

"They're all the rage."

"Buttock implants?" How whacked was that? Every time he came dirtside, the planet's fashions shocked him. He shouldn't have been so surprised that slaves would find the means to make themselves the perfect bodies they'd missed out on through salt deprivation. But butt implants? Sheesh. What would the docs think of next?

"Or she might want to make a down payment on a hovercraft."

Vigo forbid. "She's not old enough for a license."

"Or she might want new threads. You can't believe

what a teenage girl can spend on clothes. Or these stupid hair clips tricked out with *diamondites*."

Derrek looked out the taxi's front shield, unimpressed by the huge skyscrapers that had risen in just a few cycles. Or the many hovercraft blocking their route and adding to the pollution problem. "She sounded . . . desperate."

"She's probably learned the best way to entice credit from a parent is to sound as if all life as she knows it is about to end if she doesn't get the newest whatever it is that she wants."

"See if you can find out how she'd spend the credit if I send it."

"How?"

"Ask one of her friends. Bribe a teacher. I don't care. Just find out." He snapped the link closed.

Derrek had to give Sauren credit. He sat in the taxi beside him and had listened to the entire conversation without raising an eyebrow. He hadn't said a word. Not a question did he ask. A good thing since Derrek was lost in a mental tailspin.

Holy hell. He'd just spoken to his daughter. And she'd been a wave of trouble. A wave so deep and wide she'd swept him off-kilter. He felt as if all the emotions he'd repressed for so many years had just been yanked from his chest, then sliced, shredded, and smashed. And like a secret told and retold, he could never put them back.

It was one thing to deal with a family that he knew through a paper trail, quite another to have to cope with them in real life. He was oh so tempted to just wire the credit. Give Tish what she'd requested. Yet, Derrek hadn't made it to his position without learning about people. And he knew that earning credit was tied to self-respect, being given unearned credit did the reverse. If he became part of his daughter's life, he intended his influence to be a positive one. And handing out freebies might be the wrong way to go.

So Derrek set up the bank wire, so he could transfer the funds. But he held back.

And oddly he didn't worry about what his ex might think of his actions. Instead he thought of the newly escaped slave and wondered how she would have dealt with his spoiled Tish.

The hovercab swooshed into the Granitite District. When the first slaves had landed and seen the natural resources, they'd decided to build their capital here and had taken advantage of the gorgeous *granitite* to build solid structures. Because the best and brightest slaves had escaped along with artisans and craftsmen and tradespeople, the city was a testament to freedom.

Architects and builders worked alongside electricians and stonemasons. Many of them worked harder than they ever had as slaves. But their hearts were light and they slept at night as free men.

But there was also a darker side. New to self-governing, the slaves had created a political system with hitches. Corruption. They had to figure it out. Because if the Ramans returned, the Zorans would need a strong leader.

Perhaps by then, Cade would be willing to run for office. The man would make an excellent leader and with Derrek funding the campaign, he had no doubt his brother would win. However, Derrek had to deal with the here and now. His brother was away on a second honeymoon and Derrek had to deal with President Laurie.

As the hovercab stopped on the steps to Laurie's offices, a group of people hurried around the corner. For a moment, his pulse skidded and skipped as he glimpsed a man and a woman crossing the street, their backs to him. Surely that couldn't be Azsla?

Sweet *Vigo,* he was a mess. First he'd been hearing things. Now he was seeing things.

Still . . . as he exited the hovercab and tipped the driver, he cranked his neck around to catch another look. But the woman and the man were gone.

9

✧

President Laurie kept Derrek cooling his jets for over an hour in the anteroom of black-and-white diamond granitite, with its domed ceiling that let in lots of sunshine and blue sky that did nothing to calm lots of impatient people. Supposedly the pres was in some high-level meeting with oil industry folk. Derrek looked at his chronometer for the tenth time in the past few micronbits. If the pres was trying to make him antsy by the delay, he was succeeding. Derrek was eyeing the guards to the "big office" where Laurie held court, wondering if he could take them out without being shot when a young aide stepped through an arch-way. "Derrek Archer."

Derrek and Sauren followed the young woman past the guards, who gave him the once-over. A second pair dressed in formal whites and ceremonial rifles stood at attention on either side of Laurie's office. One stepped forward. "Sir. Are you carrying any weapons?"

"Of course."

"I'll keep them for you until after the meeting." He held out a white-gloved hand and Derrek would have grinned at the silly gloves if he hadn't been annoyed.

"Suppose I don't want them kept for me?"

Turn over all his weapons? He didn't think so. He might as well walk around naked. Derrek handed over a blaster and the knife up his sleeve and glared menac-ingly at the guard to distract him from asking about what else he might be carrying.

"We've instituted new policies. No one sees President Laurie if they are armed."

Beside him Sauren handed over two blades and a stunner. But following Derrek's example, he kept the one in his boot and the tiny but deadly shooter holstered at the small of his back. Derrek glared harder at the guard. "Have there been any assassination attempts?"

"Death threats. I'm not at liberty to say more."

If Laurie treated his other "friends" like he'd treated Derrek, he could see why the man needed security. Der-rek despised politics and hated politicians even more. And he wanted to turn his brother into one?

Damn it, his people deserved competent leaders, not wishy-washy presidents who had to take a poll before they made a decision. Hiding his thoughts, he smoothed annoyance off his face.

Striding into Laurie's office, he offered the pres his forearm. The room, built to impress with huge marble columns, hand-woven silk rugs, and master-carved furniture with cherry paneling, overshadowed Laurie, who looked haggard. "So sorry to keep you waiting."

Either he was a good actor or he meant it. Derrek no longer gave a damn. Laurie had used him, then abused him. After the ritual shake and the offer of *whai,* which he turned down, Derrek leaned over Laurie's desk. "Why hasn't there been any news of our new friends? You know, the ones I plucked out of space and almost got my ass kicked over?"

"I sent ships to watch your back."

"Ships that could have picked up those escapees just as easily as I did." Derrek eased back and pounded down his tone so he wouldn't growl. "What's going on?"

"I brought the slaves back here to clean them up for a big unveiling."

"You mean you wanted to claim the credit?"

"That, too," Laurie admitted. "My advisors asked me to wait until we planned exactly how to release the news. You have to understand that the political consequences and ramifications are enormous. This is the first contact we've had with Rama since the great escape."

"So?" Derrek didn't care about Laurie's political aspirations. Except when it came to saving his own neck, the man was way too indecisive.

"So once it's common knowledge that slaves escaped

and the Ramans pursued, Zorans will be building bomb shelters."

"What's wrong with that?" Derrek had his own hidey hole, well stocked to ride out a war.

"If our citizens believe we are at war, they may panic and loot the grocery stores."

Derrek snorted his skepticism. "They'll panic because they don't trust you to tell them the truth."

"That's debatable and I don't have time to argue. But consider this—if there's panic, the economy will grind to a halt. I'll have to divert soldiers we need to defend ourselves to keep down unrest."

Maybe Laurie had a point. "So the facts must be presented with care. Why haven't you done it?"

"Because . . ." Laurie squirmed and looked down at a message on his com link.

"You mean you want your spin on it. I get it. What's taking so long?"

"These things take time. Gironell and his men needed to be briefed, then sent on long-term assignment."

Damn. Laurie was covering his tracks. Did he intend to keep the Rama attack secret? "You sent Gironell away so there would be no one around to contradict your story? Is that why we were disarmed at the door? You going to make me disappear next?"

Laurie sighed. "I was hoping for cooperation."

"I've always been cooperative." Derrek's tone suggested that state was about to change. He'd tamped down his anger for what seemed like hours. Laurie had played him. He was still playing him. And he was no closer to finding out what was going on than before. Under normal circumstances, Derrek would have covered his annoyance and asked Cade to see what he could do. His brother was well connected. But Cade was gone. And these circumstances were far from normal. "Too bad I can't say the same in return." He gave Laurie time to feel the bite of his insult, then pressed, "Where are the Raman slaves I saved?"

"I don't know."

Liar. Laurie knew more than he was saying. Derrek could read it in his eyes. No fripping way was he leaving here without answers. Derrek's anger seethed like a volcano that had built up too much pressure. If Laurie had been a smart man, he would have seen the fire in Derrek's eyes, felt the heat radiating off him, heard the rumble of rage that started deep in his bones and blasted outward.

"You don't know where they are or you won't say?" Derrek leaped across the desk, grabbed Laurie by the throat and backed him against the wall. Not exactly a normal reaction for him. Since he'd met Azsla his emotions were over the top. He really needed to get a grip on himself. Two guards entered and Sauren covered them with the shooter he'd hidden behind his back.

"We're fine here." Sweat broke out on Laurie's forehead but he waved the guards back and stared Derrek down. "I don't know where they are."

"What happened?" Although Derrek yearned to slam his head against the wall, he forced himself to loosen his hold, then stepped back.

Laurie rubbed his neck. "I never pegged you for a hothead."

"And I never pegged you for a fool. What happened?"

The guards exited and Sauren put away his weapon. At least Laurie had the good sense not to mention that he wasn't supposed to be armed.

Laurie sighed and pulled up a diagram of the building on his vidscreen. He pointed. "We had them here. In a holding area. They left."

Derrek crossed his arms over his chest. "What do you mean, they left?"

"Apparently we failed to tell them we were waiting for the last two members of their crew to get well so they could all speak with the press."

"And?"

"They came here for freedom and didn't understand we had them under guard for their own protection."

"They didn't understand because you didn't tell them?"

"I'm afraid so."

He and Sauren exchanged a long glance of frustration. "And they escaped?"

"Yes."

Derrek didn't know how anyone who was so stupid had gotten to lead their people. Then again, Laurie probably hadn't handled the slaves personally. One of his people had fripped up. But Derrek believed responsibility came from the top.

"So what are you doing now? You're looking for them?"

"Yes. That was the reason for the delay. I was hoping my people would have found them by the time we met," Laurie admitted.

Derrek swore. Because of Laurie's incompetent leadership, Azsla now had over an hour's head start. The man might appeal to the masses with his paternal face and genuine warmth, but he had no business running a government. He wasn't corrupt or a law breaker, but he did want everyone to love him.

Still, Derrek didn't understand how four slaves could just up and leave. They had no friends, had never set foot on this world, and had no resources. How could they just disappear?

Now that's insane. The damn voice in his head was back.

He would forget about the voice. And he would forget about Azsla.

That won't happen.

He said a quick good-bye to Laurie, and they collected their weapons before heading out of the building. Derrek told himself he was done with Azsla. She wasn't his concern. He had business to—

The voice in his head sighed. *She's more important than business.*

I told you to go away. He couldn't fripping believe his day. Out of the vacuum, his daughter had talked to him. Then Azsla, the first woman to interest him in years, had pulled a disappearing act and now the voice was back in his head, interrupting his own thoughts.

There's no need to swear.

Why fripping not? Derrek challenged. *It's not like you're helping out.*

A low chuckle reverberated through his skull. Not an evil chuckle, but one full of playfulness. For some reason Derrek attached a bright light to the voice. Talk about weird. He probably should be flying back to Doctor Falcon for a full psych checkup. Instead, he and Sauren headed out of the building and down the boulevard, looking for a hovercraft to flag down.

Perhaps you need a glimpse.

A glimpse?

Of what might be.

Great. Now the damn voice had gone cryptic on him. The last thing Derrek needed was another puzzle. He'd had his quota today, thank you.

Derrek and Sauren strode along the crosswalk. And the busy city street disappeared. Whoosh. The road vanished beneath his feet as if he'd changed the vidscreen channel. Sauren was no longer with him. For that matter, all of planet Zor was gone. The mild balmy weather. The government buildings. The hovercrafts zipping along overhead. The entire sky.

In place of Zor was a bluish white ice tunnel. Derrek's warm breath left his mouth and formed white cloudy wisps, and when he took in his next gasp of air, it was cold and crisp. Staggering, he reached out to touch the blue-tinged tunnel wall that let in a limited amount of outside light. Frosty and dry, the wall's temperature was cold enough to cause frostbite and narrow enough to make him feel slightly claustrophobic. He peered up, then down, the tunnel but couldn't see very far. It zigzagged ahead. A wall of ice behind him blocked his back.

There appeared to be only one way out.

Yet he didn't move. He couldn't. Either he had totally flipped off his axis and was truly insane . . . or he was caught in a vision. This ice cave couldn't be real. And yet, it hadn't come from his memories. Rama didn't have ice tunnels. Neither did Zor or the asteroids he'd been on. No way had he been here before.

Derrek closed his eyes, wished himself back to Zor. Offering a short prayer to *Vigo,* he convinced himself when he reopened his eyes he'd be back dirtside. But when he finished the prayer, he was still in the ice cave.

His weight was too light for Zor. Too heavy for Alpha One. Wherever he was, this place had gravity—but not enough for a planet. He guessed it might be a moon.

"Derrek?" A woman called out his name and his heart skittered like oil across a hot pan. For a moment the voice had sounded like Azsla's. But why not? He'd been obsessed with her from the first second he'd seen her. If he was freaking out, why wouldn't she be in his vision?

"Derrek. I'm getting cold."

She didn't sound cold. She sounded tempting and warm and very close by. Derrek glanced over his shoulder once more and checked the dead end behind him. It was still a dead end. Shrugging, he strode forward, thinking he was ready for anything. He wasn't.

He rounded the bend to find Azsla lying naked on top of a bed of furs. Sweet Lord, she was gorgeous and he sucked in a breath, stopped in his tracks, all the blood in his body heading to his *longo.*

Her skin was creamy pink, her breasts rising and falling with every breath, her nipples tight and budded in the icy air. His mouth went dry and like a man with a desert-parched throat, he drank in his fill. He'd always known she was fit, but without clothes, the healthy tone of her muscles emphasized her femininity. Her sleek legs and tight stomach that nipped in her waist were perfection. If she had any flaws, he sure didn't see them.

This was one heck of a vision. In fact, if he was crazy, maybe it wouldn't be so bad. Not bad at all.

Never before had he had a fantasy this good. If he'd drunk or eaten anything while he'd been with Laurie, he would have suspected the man had slipped him a freak-out pill. But Derrek had taken no sustenance for hours.

As he gazed at Azsla, he hungered for much more than food. Something more substantial. Something to fill his soul.

Azsla held out a hand to him and grinned. "Come warm me up."

Derrek kneeled at the edge of the furs. One moment he'd been rational and in control of his emotions, the next, he could think of nothing besides being with her, holding her, tasting her, having her. It was as if he were a river with a huge dam holding him back until the floodgates opened. Only they hadn't just opened, they'd burst and he was being carried away by forces over which he had no control—no wish to control.

His throat turned his words husky. "Do you know how beautiful you are?"

"Tell me later." She tugged off his shirt with impatience, her fingers skimming over his chest and shoulders, and her eagerness shocked him. Azsla had seemed reserved. Even secretive. But she wasn't holding back now. Her hands were tugging, yanking at him. Her eyes were full of laughter and joy.

"Do you know how much I want you?" he asked, his

chest tight, his voice hoarse. This was not happening. He couldn't be in an ice cave. Not with Azsla. And yet her fingers were touching his flesh, creating havoc with his self-control.

This vision was as real as any genuine experience he'd ever had. Perhaps even more real. His senses seemed sharper. Looking at her, he noted the luscious details. Tiny hairs on her nape were encased in goose bumps. Her eyes were already dilated, her eyelashes dark and sassy. And her lips seemed to be calling him as much as her female scent that wafted in the still, chilly air.

Unable to hold back another moment, he reached out, cupped her chin and caught sight of her racing pulse. And when he ran the tip of his thumb over her bottom lip, he enjoyed the soft short intake of her gasp.

His fantasy worked overtime and really did a number on him. No way could she be real. Yet he couldn't find one wrong detail. Usually he didn't even remember his dreams, but when he did, he never recalled the particulars. But now he could feel her hair trailing over his skin and see the tiny quiver of excitement in her lower lip as her tongue caught at the corner of her mouth.

Hell, if he was crazy, he might as well enjoy himself. "Tell me what you want."

"Everything. I want everything." She held out her arms to him. "Kiss me."

"That would be my pleasure."

Her lips welcomed him with a soft caress, then parted. She teased with the tip of her tongue as she traced his upper lip. He groaned into her mouth and she yielded with a surprising strength, pulling him down on top of her, letting him know in quite definite terms that she wanted him as much as he wanted her.

The moment was perfect. Too perfect. But he was past caring. With her scent in his lungs, he had to know more.

She tasted like ambrosia, sweet, with hints of exotic spices, *cinnabari,* maybe *traconia* nectar with a trace of mint. When the tips of her breasts touched his chest, the sensation shot through him like a ravenous craving. He ached to caress every wonderfully delicious portion of her. The muscles beneath her smooth skin added a lovely texture to her softness. And as she moved her hips and opened her legs to cradle his, he felt as if he belonged with her.

Forever.

This was a singular feeling, one he couldn't remember in his faulty memory. He'd never felt this way before, as if all his natural inhibition had been obliterated. Emotions rushed though his systems like a hyperdrive engine, almost too fast to take in or comprehend. He couldn't think past wanting her, having her, needing her.

Azsla was his mate. His life mate. He knew as surely as he needed to breathe oxygen that they were absolutely meant to be together. She was a part of him, his other half. They might have just met, and he might not know her birthday, her history, her parents, or if she liked her salt raw or cooked, but he'd never been so certain of being in love in his life. Azsla was his. *His.* He was certain.

He loved her.

All doubts disappeared.

He loved her absolutely. Unconditionally. Unequivocally.

Loved her with every beat of his heart. Loved her as if she were the best part of himself.

Peace and love slowed down his rocketing rush to have her. He ached to give her pleasure, wanting to ensure this was the best loving she'd ever had. His *longo* might be demanding he thrust into her right now, but he ignored his own needs.

Instead he drew her nipple into his mouth. Pleased when she arched her spine, wound her arms around his neck, and thrust her fingers into his hair, he redoubled his efforts to slow down.

She whimpered. "Don't stop. Please, don't stop."

He laved her nipple with his tongue, appreciating the way she tightened even more under his caresses, his *longo* actually growing bigger and harder. Thankful for the slacks that prevented him from feeling her flesh against his, he used his free hand to lavish more attention on her other breast.

"Yes. Yes. I like that." Her fingers clenched his hair and he smiled, perfectly content to stay exactly where he was. He loved loving this woman.

He shifted a bit to the side and let his hand trail from her breast to her stomach to her hairless *minga*. So smooth, so soft, she opened wider for him, welcoming his touch. He caressed the delicate skin lightly. So lightly.

"That tickles."

He pulled harder on her nipple. Contrasted the deep tug with tiny, light caresses on the lips of her *minga*.

"More." She bucked demandingly and he placed one

leg over hers to hold her steady. Despite the cold air, her skin radiated heat. And he was glad for his pants that held him back. "Please. More."

"You'll have everything you want," he promised. "I'll give you everything I've got."

"I want everything . . . and more."

10

Azsla had never thought she'd find both contentment and excitement with the same man, but Derrek was a giving and creative lover. The man seemed to have intuitive knowledge about what she liked and needed. His kisses had warmed her flesh until she no longer noticed the chilly air of the ice cave.

Soft furs caressed her back—while Derrek took care of her front. And more. The pull of his lips on her nipple, the intimacy of his touch on her *minga* had her crazy with need, squirming with desire. He'd teased and tormented until she could barely think beyond the needs of her flesh.

She was close to the edge. Her cells clenched, her body was oh-so ready. Not just her body. Mentally she ached for release, and resistance seemed impossible when she wanted him so badly. Surely she could have him? Enjoy him? She'd trained so hard, she should be able to squash her *Quait* and have him, too.

But it was as if he'd swirled her *Quait* into a whirlpool of desire that sucked away all her strength to hold back. Emotions began to crack the dam she'd fortified with years of training.

She should push him away. She should be telling him to stop. But for some reason . . . she couldn't say the words.

But neither could she let him learn about her *Quait*. When his finger entered her *minga,* she gasped, the dam springing a leak. Only with the greatest of mental effort could she plug the hole . . . only to spring another.

As his clever fingers and tongue worked over her, she flailed in a rising tide of *Quait*. Up to her neck, she struggled to keep herself level . . . but Derrek was taking over, pushing her to the max.

And while she loved every second of his loving . . . she feared what would happen if she let loose.

At the same time . . . she couldn't hold back. She was going, going, going . . . and she was in trouble. Bad trouble. Her *Quait* was pounding at the dam, trying to rush over the top, trying to seep through the cracks, surging against the wall that was slowly giving way.

Derrek. She clutched him, breathed his male essence deep into her lungs. She hadn't known it would be this good. Hadn't realized that making love could rip her to shreds.

At the very limit of her control, on the brink of orgasm, Azsla felt as if she were falling and suddenly she opened her eyes. She blinked hard. The ice cave seemed to dissolve around her, and she found herself on the street with her crew. Zor. President Laurie. Escape.

What in God's sweet grace had just happened? Her skin still rippled with Derrek's caresses but she was no longer with him. But she had no doubt that she'd been making love to him. Yet how could that be? Some sort of waking dream? And what a dream it had been. He'd been so sweet, so giving, that she still shook with her need for release.

Her crew were acting as if nothing out of the ordinary had happened. And when she checked the time on her com unit, she realized she hadn't been gone at all.

Luckily for Azsla and her crew, no one had tried to stop their exit from President Laurie's building. They'd moved fast, found an outside doorway onto the city sidewalk and blended. That meant walking quickly, but not so quickly they'd attract attention.

She'd been heading outside the building with her crew, and then *wham*. She'd been lying naked on those furs, reaching out to Derrek, words coming from her mouth just like they did in a real dream. Only she hadn't been asleep.

She hadn't.

Could the food Yawitz have given her have been drugged? Now, during the escape, was no time to discuss what had happened to her—not that she'd ever share the details, but she would have liked to have known if her crew had also experienced a waking vision.

As difficult as it was to focus with every unsatisfied nerve cell still tingling, Azsla split their small group into two and tried to ignore the tension thrumming through her body. The vision had ended too soon. And she remained as hyper as a cat on the prowl.

Azsla and Micoo took point. Jadlan and Rak covered their backs. While she knew what to expect better than the others due to her training, she was distracted by the sexual encounter. It was bad enough her body wouldn't cool down, but the burning made keeping her *Quait* under control more difficult than usual. Man, did Derrek know how to kiss.

That thought sobered her and as they walked through the city. She forced her attention to the Zoran capital. Even she was surprised by what the slaves had accomplished here within the span of a decade. They'd built a modern city with glorious architecture, each building a testament to beauty. Maybe the joy of being free led to such magnificent designs.

What an odd thought. She wondered where it had come from? While she'd believed she'd understood how much freedom meant to slaves, she always thought the concept overrated. No one was truly free. She was as tied to her past as any slave. Driven by the memories of her murdered parents. Her days and nights with the Corps hadn't been her own to direct. She'd followed orders every waking micronbit of every long day. The training had been difficult, brutal. After she'd learned to master her *Quait,* she'd pushed her body to extremes, learning hand-to-hand combat that included not only self-defense but innumerable ways to kill. And she'd had to do it all the hard way, by suppressing her *Quait.* Eventually she'd specialized in advanced weaponry, which was one of the reasons the Corps had chosen her for this mission, since she needed to learn the weapons capabilities of the Zorans. If they'd put as much ingenuity into their weaponry as they had into the building of this city, the Ramans had every reason for concern.

If they could create this city, had they somehow engineered her vision of kissing Derrek? She'd never heard of such powers, but if they existed, she could see no reason for the Zorans to do so. What would be the point?

As she thought about that kiss and Derrek, she didn't just recall the physical sensations. Although those were certainly thrilling, it was the emotions she'd experienced during the vision that had staggered her. Shocked her.

She hadn't let herself become attached to anyone—especially romantically—for a very long time. In the process of training for this mission, Azsla had sacrificed her emotions. She'd learned not to dwell on any details beyond the task at hand.

But now that every moment of every waking hour wasn't consumed with training and tactics, now that she was living her mission, there were times she found stray thoughts and emotions seeping to the surface of her mind. And those unfocused ideas were leading her to places she wasn't certain she wanted to go. Sure, she fully intended to save Micoo, Jadlan, and Rak—how could she not after Kali's sacrifice?

And yet, less than seven cycles ago she would have considered saving her crew the actions of a traitor. She had no business hiding these slaves from the *tranqed* Firsts, no business saving their lives or dragging them through the city. Helping them upped the danger of being caught by a factor of ten. And yet . . . she simply could not bring herself to leave them behind for the *tranqed* Firsts to gather up, send back to Rama, and execute.

However, this lapse was going to be her last deviation from her mission. She would get them all to safety and put this incident behind her and forget these aberrations in her nature. They were obviously due to exhaustion and to the soft spot in her heart for Kali. But once her crew was safe, she'd be back on track. She wasn't going to think about her waking vision. No way. There was no rational explanation for that.

And the gorgeous city made for easy distractions. Walking on broad sidewalks, they passed busy shops with overflowing baskets of sweet-smelling flowers, the stores filled with a wide assortment of goods. Chatty shoppers and industrious entrepreneurs went about their business with a happy attitude she couldn't help but notice. Back on Rama, stores were run by slaves and no First ever shopped. The demeanor inside was solemn. No smiles. No forearm shaking. Little talking. Raman slaves waited in long lines with sagging heads and bowed shoulders. Here, there was laughter, chatting, talking, and music systems in many establishments. Children were everywhere and the sight of them playing games with balls and tiny vidscreens in wide grassy medians below the hovercraft grids intrigued her. On Rama, after their birth, slave children lived in crèches until the age of six, when they started to work. The children of Firsts were raised by their nannies and mostly kept out of sight of other adults. So the sight of little ones playing alongside siblings and friends under the watchful eyes of their mothers was one she'd never seen.

These people, so innocent, weren't the least suspicious of strangers. Beyond a few casual glances, no one paid any attention to Azsla and her crew or their government issue clothing, and for that she was grateful. Especially since Micoo was still weak.

Azsla placed an arm around his waist to help support him. He was all skin and bones, but he shrugged away. "I can walk by myself, captain."

"I'm Azsla now." She squeezed his shoulder to take away the sting of her words. "Please, don't use my title again. It might give us away."

"Sorry." Micoo peered over his shoulder. "You think anyone's looking for us?"

Yes. "I don't know. We should get off the streets, but we need help . . . and I might see someone I knew back on Rama." She raised her voice excitedly, hoped Micoo didn't pick up the false tone as she lied. "Stay here and let me see what I can do. If there's trouble, you and the others split."

Micoo might be weak, but his voice was even, determined. "We won't leave you."

His loyalty reminded her of Kali. What was it with her crew? This loyalty to one another, to her, saddened her because she didn't deserve it. If they knew her mission . . . a lump rose in her throat. Nothing was worse than betrayal by those one trusted. She knew that firsthand.

A few years after Azsla had started training, she'd

had a partner. An older man whom she'd idolized. He'd taken her kisses and her lovemaking, and she'd trusted him. At the time, he'd been her entire world. But during a mission, when things got tough, he'd panicked and taken the easy way out—he'd cheated and used his *Quait*. Not only had he failed big time, but he'd attempted to blame Azsla. He'd lied about his error and told the Corps that Azsla had used her *Quait*. But the vidtapes had proven her innocence, otherwise she would have been thrown out of the Corps, not him.

She'd been furious with him for failing, but blaming his failure on her had hurt even more. She'd felt stupid for mistaking a casual pairing during the night for more than it had been. Obviously he'd meant more to her than she had to him. After that, she'd closed herself off, devoted herself fully to her training. And she'd insisted on working alone.

She needed to set Micoo straight. "If I'm caught, you must leave me, because if you're caught too, you won't be free to come back and help me. Understand?"

"Yes, cap . . . Azsla."

"Good. Now, wait here, please." Azsla breezed into a grocery shop as if she belonged. She spent several micronbits walking past an assortment of fruit and grains while she secretly assessed the customers. An older gentleman in a gray coat with a curvy young woman at his side didn't look like a good prospect. Neither did two young teenagers ogling the boy behind the counter. Picking out a matronly woman with a friendly face, she approached with what she hoped was a hesitant smile. "Afternoon."

"Good day to you." The woman squeezed a loaf of bread, then picked it up to sniff.

"I was wondering . . ." Azsla paused, she merely needed to strike up a conversation so that her lie to her crew would be believable.

"Yes?" The woman placed the bread in her basket, then gave Azsla her full attention. Her eyes were sharp, but kind. "What can I do for you?"

"I don't get into the capital often. So I was hoping you could recommend an eating establishment that's not too expensive."

"Certainly." She broke into a wide grin. "My cousin runs a great little diner. It's down one block and over two. Look for the sign that says, *Gourmet on the Cheap*. You can't miss it."

"Thank you." Azsla hugged the woman as if she'd done her an enormous favor. Startled, but going along, the woman hugged her back. Even better, Micoo had caught sight of Azsla's hug and turned away. Perfect. Azsla reached into her backpack and called up a map on the tiny vidscreen Yawitz had given her. Although she didn't like taking her crew to the place where the Firsts had arranged, she had to get them off the street. And they would stay only long enough for her to make other arrangements. It wasn't ideal, but she hoped the Firsts wouldn't ever realize that the missing slaves were with Azsla and would leave her alone to do her job. She was taking a risk, but when the slaves went missing, Yawitz or her replacement would have to report and wait for orders to come back through the portal. By then, Azsla hoped to have found a safer place for her crew. "My sister is letting me stay with her. Could you steer me to her place? I'm a bit lost." She tried on her best sheepish golly-gee-I've-never-been-to-the-big-city look.

"Sweetie, let me see." The woman peered at the vidscreen. "After you eat, go another five blocks northwest. It's right here." She pointed. Azsla thanked her again, slipped the vidscreen back into her pocket, and strode outside to find Micoo, Jadlan, and Rak sitting on a bench. "We lucked out."

"How so?" Rak looked at her, his face blank, his eyes alive and piercing.

"That woman, I thought I'd remembered her. She was a good friend of my mother's. She keeps an extra apartment in the city for her son, who is away visiting his father. We can use it for a few days."

Micoo grinned. "That's wonderful."

Rak clapped her on the back. "You did good."

"Yeah, real good." Jadlan agreed but his tone implied he was suspicious as hell.

And when he came up alongside her, leaving Micoo and Rak together, Azsla's pulse escalated. She'd wanted to say the woman had given them credits so they could purchase food, but Jadlan was clearly already suspicious. So she zipped her lips and waited to see what he'd say.

They walked about a block side-by-side before he spoke. Jadlan was not one to go off without thinking over the ramifications. However, from his stiff posture and the occasional wince she caught out of the corner of her eye, he clearly had something eating at him. Maybe a lot of somethings.

She headed across the street and the hovercrafts droned out any chance for him to talk. A law officer walked by, delaying him again, but finally, when there was little chance of anyone overhearing his words, he muttered, "I'm going to trust you. But I wish you'd trust us."

A dozen replies zinged through her mind. She could play stupid and pretend she had no idea what he was talking about. She could tell him that of course she trusted him. She could accuse him of being delusional. But his simple words had touched her. Damn him. And she didn't want to lie. So she nodded. "Thanks. You won't regret it."

"At least you didn't say I won't live to regret it," he joked. "Since I'm betting our lives on you."

"Kali gave up his pod for me," she blurted. If she couldn't tell him how she was helping them, she wanted him to understand why. "My pod was broken and before I understood what he meant to do, he picked me up, slid me into it, closed the canopy, and ejected me."

Jadlan's shoulders that had been set and stiff eased, as if she'd suddenly added a puzzle piece that made all the rest make sense. "Kali was a good man. Perhaps he knew how much the rest of us needed you."

She would have rolled her eyes at the irony but it seemed disrespectful to Kali's sacrifice. "I didn't say anything before because I thought you would blame me. It happened so fast . . ."

"Cap—Azsla, Rak and I both would have done the same. Micoo might have too if he had the strength."

"Please . . . don't . . ." Sweet *Vigo,* she did not want to hear this. Not from people she'd intended to betray. Her *Quait* rumpled and swirled liked a caged animal eager to escape. Not that she needed her *Quait* to do anything for her. There was no enemy to evade or kill. No defense that was necessary. However, strong emotions unchained the beast, and she couldn't afford the distraction right now.

She locked down the guilt and the sorrow, tied it down so tight, it couldn't draw breath. For a moment she too couldn't breathe, but the door slammed shut, recaging the dangerous emotions. Swallowing down a soft sob of relief, she wondered what Derrek would have thought of her if he'd known she was a First? A spy.

Would he still have kissed her so tenderly? Or would he have killed her himself?

What was she doing? She couldn't afford to confuse reality and fantasy. Derrek had *not* kissed her. She'd had a dream that was too real and unexplainable, but she had to keep things straight in her head.

Perhaps the strain of the last few days was getting to her. Perhaps the cold-sleep medicine had aftereffects. Whatever. She and Derrek had not made love and never would.

From all she'd learned about Derrek Archer, she knew that he saw himself as the protector of his new world. Even when he mocked that world, even when he'd disagreed with its leaders, it had been clear to her he was proud of what they'd built here.

And she understood that pride.

She almost hoped she'd discover a Zoran stash of weapons so terrible that the Corps would change their course of action and decide an invasion wouldn't be worth the cost. That they'd refuse to attack. Perhaps even leave this world alone. After all, no other slaves had escaped Rama in over a decade—and her crew wouldn't have either, not without help. The economy on Rama had readjusted.

The lives lost . . . including her parents . . . could not be brought back. Perhaps it was time to let go of the past. While she couldn't have a relationship with Derrek, it might be time to heal. . . .

She drew up in an abrupt halt. Was this why the Corps had told her breaking one rule led to breaking others? Was saving her crew the first of many steps over the line, ending in betrayal of her own people?

She was no traitor.

If she'd kissed Derrek Archer, she couldn't be blamed. It had only been a very weird dream.

She would do her duty.

She'd forget Derrek's kiss. Forget his hands on her breasts. Forget how aroused she'd been. How much she'd ached for him.

She would complete her mission.

She would.

11

Azsla sensed her crew weakening with every step through the Zoran capital. If she hadn't been so distracted by that strange vision she would have noticed sooner that Micoo was fading fast. She had to get them off the sidewalk, into an eating establishment. Luckily the choices were many. The problem was credit. Although Yawitz had given her plenty, she knew she was pushing credulity to say her mother's friend had loaned her credit as well as the use of an apartment. However, Jadlan had said he trusted her. And with the way Micoo was faltering, she had little choice.

Azsla and Jadlan were practically carrying Micoo. So they stopped, rested, and ate. The food, plentiful and wholesome, gave a whole new meaning to being off Rama. Either this establishment had a master chef, and from the casual atmosphere and low prices she doubted that, or the bland cafeteria food they'd previously eaten didn't represent the food on this world. While Azsla couldn't identify all the savory ingredients, the steaming platter of pasta shells filled with a variety of meats in a hearty sauce filled her belly and satisfied her palate. It didn't hurt that salt had already been liberally sprinkled on their food.

While she ate, she went over her options. Her goal—getting them to the apartment for one night—was her only good choice, but still risky. Since the Firsts had set up Azsla's cover, they knew where she would be staying. Hopefully they had no idea her crew was still with her. But if a *tranqed* First dropped in unannounced and saw that she'd brought her crew to the apartment, she doubted she could explain away her actions.

But without other friends or family here, what other choice did she have? Not only were the *tranqed* Firsts looking for them, the Zoran government probably was, too. She'd landed herself in a fine mess and although she worried over everyone's safety, she felt good about her decision to save them. And if she failed, she wouldn't regret her decision—only that she hadn't found a way to succeed.

So they ate quickly and left. She found the apartment without any difficulty. The single bedroom layout was meant for one person or at most, a pairing. The unit had a tiny kitchen area off a small living room and one fresher, with a sink, shower, and commode. Four of them made the quarters cramped, but her crew was accustomed to tight spaces after working and living within the close confines of the spaceship. Still, no matter how tight the group and how well they got on, Azsla couldn't allow them to stay with her for long.

They needed jobs, new quarters, and new identities to be safe. One thing at a time, she reminded herself.

Micoo had recovered slightly after their meal, but he was so weak that she and Jadlan didn't need to discuss who would get the bed. They placed Micoo there and he grunted as she removed his footwear and covered him with a blanket that smelled new.

Everything in the apartment appeared bright and shiny—just like the city itself. Under different circumstances, she would have enjoyed exploring every nook and cranny, the drawers, the shelves, the sights from the windows, because this was the first space that was hers and hers alone. As a kid, she'd shared a room with her nanny. During her years in the Corps, she'd shared quarters with other trainees. Later, as a slave, they'd bunked down together in groups. Every once in a while during an overnight mission she'd been on her own and had enjoyed the silence, the privacy, the luxury of not having to listen to the constant murmur of voices, of a soft cough, or snores.

Azsla, Rak, and Jadlan convened in the living quarters, which contained a couch, two chairs, and a wooden table set over a soft-fibered floor rug vibrant with colors. While Rak checked the food stores in the well-stocked kitchen, Azsla laid out her plan. The backpack Yawitz had given her included her new job. She intended to report there immediately. Hopefully she could tap into local intel and figure out her next move.

She was most eager to learn about new weapons systems . . . and not just the ones that could be lobbed at Rama. She wanted to know if the Zorans had discovered a way to implant visions. She shuddered at the idea of how that technique could be used against Rama. Suppose instead of a love scene, she'd experienced torture?

The scene with Derrek had been so real it haunted her. All her senses had kicked in. She'd heard him speak and enjoyed the need in his tone, felt his lips and hands skim over her body, tasted his flesh and reveled in his scent. Sleeping dreams shouldn't have been so full-bodied or detailed. Apparently that hadn't been the case with her dream about Derrek.

In every way, making love with him had seemed real. Logic told her that if she hadn't been making love to Derrek, the memory must be fake. And if it was fake, she needed to know how it had gotten inside her head.

"Jadlan. Rak. You two stay here and take care of Micoo. I need to head out—"

"Wait," Rak immediately protested. "Going out alone is dangerous."

Jadlan didn't look surprised that she intended to leave them behind and stepped in to defend her. "They'll probably figure we'll split up into two teams. The last thing the government will expect is for one lone female to be out by herself."

She shot him a grateful look. Rak looked from one to the other of them and frowned. "What aren't you two telling me?"

Jadlan shook his head. "She has told me nothing. But she's gotten us this far. I've chosen to trust her."

"This isn't a question of trust," Rak sputtered. "We expected to be welcomed. We thought our escape would make history. Instead, I'm not sure what happened or what's going on."

"That's why I need to gather information. Let me talk to the women in the shops. They appear to love to gossip here. Did you notice them chatting as they made their purchases?"

"I didn't see—"

"You were too busy watching the hovercraft," Jadlan teased but again defended her. "Besides, you are not a female."

"Exactly. She shouldn't be going alone."

"I'll be fine." Azsla wasn't staying to argue. She headed for the door. "I'll be back as soon as I can."

She'd fully intended to leave before Rak again tried to stop her, but a soft moan from the bedroom had her turning back in concern to see if Micoo was all right. Azsla opened the door to find him thrashing on the bed. The front of his shirt twisted and perspiration soaked through the lightweight material. And either it was a trick of the light or . . .

Micoo wasn't a young man. Azsla saw the curve of a breast beneath the damp material.

Micoo was female.

Stunned, she barely had the presence of mind to walk inside the room and speak to the men over her shoulder. "It's just a nightmare. I'll take care of this."

Azsla shut the door firmly behind her and approached the bed. "Micoo." She shook his shoulder—no, make that *her* shoulder. "Wake up. Micoo. You're having a nightmare."

Azsla prayed the nightmare was simply that and not the kind she'd experienced. She held her breath, waiting to see how Micoo reacted.

Micoo's eyes popped open, terror seizing her into a tight knot as she drew her knees to her chest. Sweat trickled down her face and into her eyes. Azsla smoothed back Micoo's hair and waited for her to calm. Just because

Azsla had had a strange vision didn't mean Micoo had the same problem. She couldn't start jumping to conclusions.

"You're safe now, Micoo. Safe on Zor. We're in an apartment with Jadlan and Rak, and we won't let anyone hurt you."

As Micoo took several deep calming breaths, the terror in her eyes slowly receded. "Give me a micronbit."

Micoo rolled out from under Azsla's touch, and the movement reminded her of other incidents when Micoo had avoided her touch. During the walk here, she'd thought it a young man's embarrassment over his weakness. Now she realized it was more. While it might simply have been that Micoo didn't want anyone to discover that she was female, she hadn't wanted a hand on her waist or shoulder, either.

"Micoo." Azsla sat on the bed. "I know you're female, but I will not reveal your secret."

Micoo hissed on an indrawn breath and her face paled. "Nooo."

Azsla sought to reassure her. "Your secret is safe. I won't tell anyone. Not Rak. Not Jadlan. I just thought if you realized I knew, you would have someone to talk to."

Tears trickled from Micoo's eyes but she didn't seem to notice. Turning her head away from Azsla and to the wall, she spoke, her voice low and anguished. "I don't want to talk."

Azsla sensed Micoo's pain stemmed from something more than a horrible dream, perhaps a real-life terror relived in a nightmare—but not a vision implanted in her head. Her attitude wasn't one of surprise, or confusion, but of trying to get past old memories. Painful memories.

"I understand." Azsla wasn't mouthing platitudes. She knew exactly how Micoo felt. "After my parents died, I didn't want to talk about them either. It hurt too much." The sight of so much blood, the sounds of their dying screams, the stench of their guts spilling out onto the floor and the cruelty of their dismemberment had left her raw, terrified, shocked, and barely able to function. She lifted her hand to squeeze Micoo's, then let it drop to her side, remembering she didn't like touching. "But if you ever change your mind, I'm here. Okay?"

Micoo didn't answer. Her shoulders shook in silent sobs, yet her spine remained stiff, her body turned away, as if her posture could shut Azsla out. Raw pain peeled off layers and each slice revealed more fear, more sorrow.

My God, what had happened to her? Azsla had seen Micoo's file, but nothing in the reports had indicated that she'd led anything but the most ordinary life. Of course, they had no records of her early years in the crèche, where slave children were raised from infancy through the age of five. Only Firsts raised children at home, or rather their nannies raised them. So if Micoo was twenty as her file claimed, then she'd been posing as a young man for at least fifteen years.

Her lack of almost any body fat had hidden her slender curves. Still, now that Azsla knew her secret, she couldn't imagine why she'd never noticed Micoo's girlish high cheekbones, her long eyelashes, and her soft lips. Her dewy eyes had seemed boyish—not feminine. Ditto for her slender frame and frail shoulders. Apparently Azsla hadn't looked carefully enough.

"Micoo? Please, say something. Anything."

When she shook her head, Azsla caught a hint of pure anguish. And then Micoo thrashed, turned over, and sobbed in her arms. The cries came from deep in her chest until her entire body shook with her grief.

Stunned by the sudden outpouring of emotion, Azsla cradled the young woman, totally bewildered as to how to comfort her, helpless to ease her pain. The Corps had trained Azsla to spy, to kill, to be an undercover op. She knew how to assess weapons, kill with her bare hands, and sneak through shadows undetected. But she didn't have a clue about what to do with the young woman crying brokenly in her arms.

Instincts she hadn't known she possessed took over. Protective instincts. She rocked her and murmured to her, sensing the words didn't matter, that Micoo needed to cry out her grief, that within the walls she'd built and hidden behind, Micoo was desperate for human contact. For a friend that Azsla could never be.

Eventually Micoo calmed, finally straightening and blowing her nose into a tissue, her face red and drained. "Sorry to throw all that at you."

Azsla didn't know what to say. Although she sensed the burst of emotion might have been a long time coming and a good thing, she didn't know what to do with all of Micoo's pain.

"I'm solid now. Really." Micoo straightened her shoulders and lifted her chin. "I've actually thought about starting over on Zor as a woman."

Azsla dealt with the statement on a practical level. "If you did, it would help hide you from whoever might come looking."

Micoo flicked her thumb over her cheek and dried the last of her tears. "Yeah. I'm not sure . . ."

"It's your decision. No need to deal with it now. Why don't you rest . . ." Azsla's voice trailed off. She'd felt uncomfortable before, but now she wanted to back out of the room as fast as she could, fearing she'd say the wrong thing. Yet she didn't want to leave if Micoo needed her.

She supposed she should have been curious about why Micoo had chosen to pretend she was male. But Azsla sensed an ugly story—one Micoo didn't seem ready to share. Azsla didn't need any more reasons to sympathize with Micoo or the other slaves. Period. She had a job to do and the more she could keep herself separate from her crew's personal problems, the easier it would be to focus on resolving the situation.

"All right then, I should go." Trying not to run, she headed for the door.

"Azsla."

She slowed and turned. "Yes?"

"Thanks."

"I didn't do anything."

"You were here. You were kind. I won't forget."

Azsla shuddered. She couldn't let down her guard. Not ever.

She shut the door and slammed down on the sadness welling through her chest, an emotion that might cause her *Quait* to raise its nasty head and bite. Sadness was simply another emotion she couldn't afford to feel.

"Micoo's had a terrible nightmare and is resting now," she told the men as she strode through the apartment. They must have heard the edge in her tone. Neither Rak nor Jadlan asked any questions or tried to stop her from leaving the apartment.

Within moments, she was outside. Back on track.

AZSLA HEADED FOR the building where she was supposed to report for work, fully prepared to deny knowledge about her crew's whereabouts if any Firsts came looking to ask her what had happened to them. Since the *tranqed* Firsts had already set up her cover under a new name and identity, she didn't concern herself with worrying whether or not President Laurie could track her down. Her original mission plan had anticipated a huge fuss would be made of the escaped slaves and that Azsla would need a more commonplace identity.

So Azsla had kept her first name, since it was a fairly common one on both Zor and Rama, and now possessed a new last name. At a fantasy store, she'd bought a bottle of instant hair color and her dark black hair was now brunette streaked with blond and red. In addition, she'd colored her irises a nondescript green and punched up her bustline two cup sizes.

Certain that even her own crew wouldn't recognize her after she finished with makeup and a cheek tattoo, she strode into the Zoran Ministry of Weapons, a twenty-story *granitite* building that looked more like a museum than a military establishment, with its beautiful lines and large windows that let in bright sunshine.

She reported to the front desk, expecting to see tight

security, including thumb and iris checks, but the man simply read her pass and jerked his thumb to the elevators. "Third floor."

The gleaming brass elevator opened into a spacious foyer filled with empty chairs, a powered-down vidscreen. She followed a carpet runner, heading to the end of the hallway where a secretary asked her name, then handed her a clipboard and a wad of paperwork. Filling out the myriad of forms took most of the afternoon and she was grateful for her training, which allowed her to answer the questions in a consistent and thorough pattern that went all the way back to her birth.

Azsla had her fake background down pat. Instead of the first child of two Firsts that she really was, she was supposed to be the second child of two Firsts, which would help explain her height, fitness, and superior health. On Rama anyone who wasn't a firstborn sired by a male First was of lower intelligence, possessed slower physical reactions, a weaker immune system, poorer reflexes and muscle control, and had no mind control abilities whatsoever. No *Quait*.

To keep the population stable, male Firsts sired one firstborn with their wife and were allowed to sire one other child with anyone else they chose. These children were raised by the First wife and rarely knew their biological mothers. Theoretically, any accidental and subsequent children of two Firsts became slaves—but no accidents had happened in thousands of years.

Azsla was supposed to have escaped Rama ten years ago and her cover story said she'd lived on a Zoran farm and attended a nearby college. Overly qualified for her position as a weapons specialist and covert ops, she expected a low-level position from which she could work her way up through the ranks until she found a way to hack into the systems or was trusted with the information she needed.

After spending hours filling out the damn forms, she handed them to a woman who tossed them in a basket without looking at them. Azsla frowned, her annoyance rising, but the woman didn't even look up from her paperwork, simply jerked her thumb toward another office.

Easy. Annoyance led to anger. Anger could lead to trouble. Azsla stomped down on the emotion and headed to yet another office. However, when she again was handed more paperwork to fill out, she had more difficulty taming her annoyance. At least these papers weren't about her background. They were simple tax forms.

Although she was in a hurry to hear the latest intel about the slaves who'd escaped from Rama, she hadn't yet made it past the secretaries who guarded the inner sanctums. And every hour of delay placed her crew in additional danger of being found.

But she could do nothing to speed the process. After completing the paperwork, she went to wardrobe where they fitted her for a uniform. And then they sent her home with orders to return tomorrow morning early.

Azsla went to the fresher to calm her irritation and think over her plans. She'd wasted most of the day and had learned nothing. The longer her crew stayed in her apartment, the higher the risk they'd be caught by a *tranqed* First contact.

But Azsla had nowhere safe to move them. She needed intel, access to the government computer systems to see what kind of search was being conducted. And she wanted to find out if that vision she'd experienced was a weapon. Should she risk snooping around? As it was her first day here, if she were caught in the wrong place, she could claim she was lost, but she might be fired. And if she blew this job opportunity, it would make her mission to assess the Zoran weapons a total failure.

Perhaps she should wait.

A woman entered the fresher as Azsla washed her hands. With her head down, she looked a bit familiar and when she raised her head, Azsla recognized her contact. Yawitz. The woman who'd handed her credits and instructions back at the capital. But she had been heading home to Rama. What was she still doing here?

Had the *tranqed* Firsts learned Azsla had helped her crew escape? Were they even now being rounded up and sent back for execution?

Despite her surprise and worry, she chose her words with care, reminding herself that if her contact had shown up here, she probably hadn't gone to the apartment. "I thought everyone was going home?"

"Change of plans." Yawitz took the sink next to Azsla, turned on the water and handed her a key. "Apparently, *we're* working through the night."

We're? The slight emphasis told Azsla she was to work through the night—even though the secretary had told her to go home. Apparently, the Corps needed that intel as soon as possible. Great. Azsla hadn't even had time to scope out the building yet. Sure, she knew the schematics but she'd already learned that her old intel was often outdated.

But she was eager to begin and slipped the key into her pocket. She was also pleased Yawitz hadn't questioned her about her crew, which likely meant the Firsts had no reason to think she knew of their whereabouts. "Actually, I was just heading home," Azsla murmured in case anyone was listening and eased back into the hallway and toward the stairwell. Classified information was on the tenth floor. Hopefully she could walk right inside the inner sanctum since the *tranqed* Firsts had paved the way for her by entering her into the computer's security systems. And now she had a master key for the doors.

What she worried about were human guards. This moment had come much sooner than she'd expected, but it was the one she'd trained for. No one knew about her *Quait* and of course, she wouldn't use the ultimate weapon unless she must—especially since doing so would blow her cover. But now, she didn't just have herself to worry about. If she was caught, the *tranqed* Firsts would track down her crew.

However, security would still be tight. And it was unlikely she could single-handedly take out all the guards.

Damn. If only she could have sent her crew someplace safe before she'd had to complete her mission.

But she had no choice. She had to proceed upstairs. Rama needed to know the weapons capability of this world. While she didn't understand what the emergency was, she suspected Yawitz did.

Why hadn't her contact told her what was going on? Had she feared they'd be overheard? Surely she could have slipped her a coded note like she had the key.

Why had the timetable been so drastically moved up? She was supposed to accomplish her mission over weeks, months, possibly years. What could have happened to alter the careful plan? She didn't like being kept in the dark. She didn't like the change that wouldn't allow her to establish a decent cover before having to break into the Space Ministry.

But she had to follow orders.

Yet this was extreme. Now they wanted her to get the information on her very first day? What was going on?

DERREK HAD GONE straight to Archer Intersolar Mining's headquarters on Zor. Here he had access to communications and computer systems—some of the best equipment and minds on the planet. However, he wasn't about to put the techs on the problem of his vision. For one thing, he'd lose credibility. It didn't look good for the boss to admit he heard voices in his head or that he thought he was having sex with a woman he'd just met when in reality he was walking down the street.

His miners were a down-to-dirt unruly lot. But they were practical men who believed mostly in what they could see and feel. Engineers asked for proof. Geologists demanded it. Spaceship pilots had their own superstitions but if rumors of his vision got out, they'd all think he'd gone off the deep end of Alpha One's Mount Crion.

So Derrek kept the knowledge of the voice inside his head, along with his lovemaking fantasy, to himself—even if the conference room, which could hold fifty, was almost empty. He stood at one end of the giant table with its ten sweet leather chairs on both sides. Right now, only Sauren and Derrek, and several stellar-IQ computer techs, were there with him, along with computer systems and lots of untouched food.

Derrek kept his tone casual. "All right, people. Let's assume we can't find the Raman escapees because they've taken on new identities."

Well, duh.

The voice in Derrek's head was back and he didn't like it, not at all. Once was an aberration he could explain away. Three times meant . . . he'd lost it. He was insane. Crazy.

You aren't crazy. I'm real. Just as real as you are.

Then how come no one else can hear you?

Because I don't want them to.

Derrek shook his head, as if that would stop the voice of the being inside his head. He text messaged Dr. Falcon, his note short and abrupt: *Find anything?*

Zip. You're clean, came the text message reply.

The being in his head even had a know-it-all tone. *I told you there was nothing wrong with you.*

"We have no idea what their new identities might be," Sauren told him from across the conference room, oblivious to the byplay but accustomed to Derrek's multitasking.

Derrek tried not to let frustration override his sense of urgency. He'd canceled many of his meetings, certain his compulsion to find Azsla had to be important. Derrek trusted his instincts and right now his gut told him this woman was vital to his future—although after that dream he was no longer certain that his cravings weren't now just as much physical as mental.

The vision had ended way too soon. Neither of them had reached satisfaction. And since he hadn't taken care of those needs in a long time, he was having difficulty settling down. Even now he was partially aroused, not enough for others to notice but he found the lack of control . . . disturbing.

Yet Azsla had captured his total interest—to the point that he was neglecting the rest of his life. To say he was shocked by his own behavior had to be the understatement of the century. Derrek didn't do lust. He didn't allow himself to be swept away by powerful urges he didn't comprehend.

Yet, like the *salmenda* who swam upstream to spawn, he felt driven, compelled to find her. To be near her. To love her.

Damn it. He could not love her. He didn't know her.

But he did. He loved her with his whole heart. His entire being.

His feelings made no sense. And that irritated him all the more.

Back when he'd been a slave on Rama, Firsts had controlled his will. He'd been fully aware when he'd worked as a chef that he wasn't free to disobey orders. No slave could. The horror of the mental enslavement was that he'd understood every act he'd committed—but couldn't control his own muscles. He'd risked his life for freedom and didn't appreciate being enslaved to emotions he didn't want and hadn't encouraged.

Yet he couldn't save himself. He couldn't stop himself from loving her. From wanting her in his arms, in his bed.

Although it bothered him that he didn't understand why he felt this powerful attraction, he'd figure that part out later. Never in his life had he felt so compelled to do something irrational—except perhaps when he'd been determined to make *Beta One* fly. That project had turned out well—he hoped this one would too.

But they'd hit one dead end after another, and his frustration level had increased. So he'd scratched his schedule and his business meetings to find new equipment and lock up a new contract. For once he'd delegate the business side and go after what he wanted. Azsla.

Where the hell was she? A dream about her was not enough. And he now wanted to know if she'd been responsible for that episode in his head. Had the Firsts sent her as some kind of secret weapon? Because if that vision of her hit every man on the planet at the same time, Holy *Vigo,* look out. He didn't imagine any of them would resist—leaving Zor wide open to invasion.

Starting from zip, placing himself in the position of the slaves, he tried to think through the difficulties Azsla and her crew had faced since their arrival on Zor. Laurie had locked them up. They'd escaped. He didn't have much more to go on. Still, they were people. People always had basic needs. "If you're new on this world, you'd need a place to stay."

A tech said, "We've already checked hotels and—"

"Check every new lease. Each new home sale. All new job applications. These people just got here and need the necessities. Food, shelter, work. Let's start there."

"You know," Sauren said slowly, "maybe we haven't found them because President Laurie still has them."

Derrek never ceased to be amazed by some of Sauren's wild ideas. It's why he liked the man. He thought in directions no one else took. "You boys hack into the government files, too. See what's doing with Laurie."

"How wide do you want the parameters, boss man?" asked one of the techs.

"Cast wide and deep. Let's see what's going on."

Two hours later, they had found an oddity in the election voting system, four bribes to the press, an encrypted data system within the Space Ministry, and massive funds diverted to a secret project, but nothing on Azsla and her crew.

"They can't have vanished. Not without help," Derrek muttered, his frustration making his head pound.

"So let's assume they got help," Sauren theorized. "After all, they are the first escapees in a decade. Maybe they have resources on Zor that we don't know about."

"Like what?" Derrek challenged Sauren's theory. While he liked to encourage ingenuity and outrageous ideas, his job was to search for the best one among the dozens of suggestions that Sauren threw his way.

"*Like whom* might be the better question. If Laurie

isn't helping them or jailing them, maybe one of his enemies is. Or the military. Or that new religious group of reborn *Vigo* worshippers."

Derrek knew these fringe associations were understaffed and underfunded. "None have the resources to have linked up with Azsla's group so quickly."

"Maybe that's why the Space Ministry encrypted their files. Maybe they have resources we can't imagine," Sauren suggested. "There's certainly been a massive infusion of funds in that direction in the last few weeks."

Derrek turned to his techs. "How long until you break the encryption?"

"It could be micronbits. Or days."

"Keep on it." Derrek moved down the list. "What about Laurie's enemies."

"None of them operate in the open. They don't dare. And because they have to stay underground, I can't even name them, never mind find them."

Derrek motioned for Sauren to come with him. "You're with me."

Sauren nodded, his eyes grave. "Where are we going?"

"To the Space Ministry. I want to know what they're hiding."

Now there's an idea.

Shut up.

Anything you say, boss man.

12

❊

Azsla didn't dare wait another moment to confront Yawitz. If she gave her contact enough time to leave the building and she followed, she might not be able to get back in. So she nabbed Yawitz by the elbow just outside the double elevators and escorted the *tranqed* First into the stairwell. Stunned and trained not to bring attention to herself, Yawitz didn't protest until the door slammed behind them and they were alone.

"What are you doing?" she hissed, her voice indignant, her eyes wide with apparent fear and anger.

Azsla leaned against the door, blocking a quick escape in case she decided to bolt. "Why was my mission speeded up?"

"Huh?"

"You told me to go in tonight. But I haven't even seen the layout, yet. It's dangerous."

"It's your job."

"And this kind of rushing lowers my chances of success."

"You're trained for—"

"If I blow my cover due to the grand rush, all the effort to get me here will result in failure." Hoping the woman knew a whole lot more than she'd revealed, Azsla didn't let up her interrogation. "So why am I going in *tonight*?"

Yawitz evaded her gaze. "I don't know."

Azsla tried another tactic, hoping to fill in the puzzle pieces from a different angle. "Are you still going home?"

"Yeah. All of us are. You, too."

"When?"

"I don't know. Soon."

As much as Azsla would have liked to worm out answers from Yawitz, she suspected the woman was mostly telling the truth. She couldn't answer because she truly didn't know more. Flights back home to Rama left from the third continent, the portal shielded by a cloaking device that took huge amounts of energy. The cloaked portal couldn't be used often because of the vast expense. It made sense that Yawitz wouldn't know details . . . and yet, Azsla sensed she was hiding something.

Because rushing her mission made no sense. Firsts had monitored this world for years. Why would every First suddenly be recalled? "Why are *all* of us going home?"

"I've heard only rumors. Nothing solid."

"And?"

Yawitz looked right, left, as if someone could be hiding out of sight on the stairwell. "Originally slaves and Firsts were all going back to Rama. But the plan changed."

"When?"

"Last week. Now only Firsts get to go home. The slaves stay."

"We're letting the slaves go free?" Even as she said the words, her hopes rose but she knew her suggestion was impossible. Firsts kept what was theirs. And that meant their vidscreens, their clothing, and their slaves.

"We have a secret space weapon. The slaves will all die." Yawitz sounded quite satisfied with the new plan.

Azsla wanted to shake her. The image of those children she'd seen in the streets all dying horrified her. She imagined the ladies in the shops, the shopkeepers, Derrek, her crew . . . all of them dead. It couldn't be possible. And yet . . . the Firsts of Rama must be up to something for all the changes to have worked down the line to Azsla's mission. "What are you talking about?"

"I told you. It's only a rumor. Don't blame me if it makes no sense."

Azsla didn't like the sudden switch. She liked the lack of information even less. Since her mission had begun, nothing had gone right. The ship blowing up. The Zoran government locking them up. Now the big rush. Wishing she could use a com unit to call home wouldn't make it happen. She didn't dare use a signal that could be traced. So she had to make do with the resources available to her—even when they stank like slug slime. "Did you hear anything else?"

"Yeah. Every building will be pulverized. The planet totaled."

Surely the plan had to be more than a mere rumor or the Corps wouldn't have ordered Azsla to go in tonight. But, planet busters? Every slave dead? All the buildings smashed? Rama didn't have that kind of technology. At least they hadn't when she'd left.

Still . . . if they did plan to annihilate this planet . . .

the Ramans would want to know if Zor was capable of retaliation. They could wipe out this world, but the Zorans might have counterstrike abilities—on other moons or in their space fleet. Before they acted, they'd need to know for certain.

My God. The timetable must have been moved up because Rama was really planning to destroy this planet. Azsla couldn't banish the thought of these industrious people, the men, the women, the happy children—all of them dying. The gorgeous buildings smashed to rubble and dust. This planet with its balmy climate wiped out.

What a waste. It was one thing to bring the slaves home. Another to kill them all. The tactic was brutal. Extreme. Sickening.

Especially since there were other worlds where slaves could escape to. The need for freedom seemed to burn within them. She couldn't imagine Derrek working as a slave. The idea made her uncomfortable. She suspected that people like Derrek who wanted to be free, people willing to risk their lives for freedom, would always find a way to escape or die trying.

Killing them all was unimaginable. Vile. Wrong. And yet stunning in its audacity. The idea of taking out an entire world revved her thoughts into an overheated hyperdrive hum. However, she tamped down her *Quait* and fought to keep her feelings from exploding onto her face. "How is that kind of destruction possible?"

Yawitz shot her an I-don't-know-or-care frown. "Just do what you're told, then get off this world. Or you'll die a slave's death."

"What about guards?"

"I've seen to them. No worries."

"Understood." She straightened and began marching upstairs to the tenth floor, determined to find out as much as she could about the Zoran capabilities. Below her Yawitz left the stairwell, headed for the elevators. When the door slammed shut, cutting her off from Yawitz and leaving Azsla alone on her mission to find out if the Zorans could retaliate, she wondered what the hell she was doing.

She told herself the dark stairwell was spooking her out. Each footstep echoed, no matter how softly she tread. The dim lighting cast odd shadows and the steady climb raised her heart rate. But it was the fear that the Raman plan might succeed that had her nerves dancing and her *Quait* buzzing in wariness.

Despite her long day and eagerness to return to her crew, she needed answers. Perhaps her skills in snooping through computer systems might even allow her to find a safer place to move Rak, Micoo, and Jadlan. However, no place would be safe if the entire planet blew.

The idea still boggled the mind. The forces needed to harness such destruction had to be immense. Where could the Raman Firsts even have tested such a weapon? The Raman solar system was stable. If they'd lost a planet, it would have upset the gravitational forces and natural orbit of the home planet, wouldn't it?

Besides, Firsts weren't into space exploration. Why bother going elsewhere when on Rama there were millions of slaves to do a First's bidding? Home had been comfortable. Safe. The Raman civilization was old and established. Those in charge were the fittest, strongest, most intelligent. There had been peace for tens of thousands of years until the rebellion a decade ago.

But here on Zor, with adequate salt, the slaves had grown more powerful. Smarter. Perhaps happier. The latter disturbed her the most.

She'd always believed that the underfirsts needed the Firsts to tell them what to do. To care for them. But obviously that had been a lie. Not only could the former slaves take care of themselves, they seemed happy to do so. The entire Raman society now appeared to her to have been built on a falsehood. Given enough salt, slaves had created a world that worked for them as well if not better than the one on Rama. Plus it was new and shiny. Exciting. Industrious.

She almost yearned to be a part of it. She most certainly didn't want to see it destroyed.

While her own life should have been one of luxury and comfort, in retrospect that lifestyle bored her. She enjoyed challenging her abilities, learning new things.

But sometimes she tired of working alone. And blind. Or close to it. Proceeding ahead to the tenth floor, her information based solely on an outdated three-year-old schematic didn't exactly give her confidence. Neither did Yawitz's assurance of the lack of guards. Long ago she'd learned to trust her own judgment. If a guard surprised her, it was her neck on the line.

Since this building had gone up, walls could have been moved, changes could have been made—including the installation of security systems she didn't know how to disarm. If an unaccounted guard took her by surprise, she'd have to deal with it.

Her entire life—all the years of training and all the hard work of learning to suppress her *Quait*—was leading up to this moment. Turning back wasn't in her makeup. But between the rushed operation with its new timetable and the lack of data, it was natural to feel as though she were about to jump out of an airlock without a space suit. Although adrenaline dashed through her veins, Azsla took measured steps, hoping that when she reached her destination, she'd be fresh and alert.

Finally, she climbed the last of the stairs and reached the tenth floor. Very slowly, she cracked open the door and peered into a hallway. A water cooler cycled on. A com unit beeped. An emergency exit light cast a green glow over a long and empty hallway.

Azsla stepped into the corridor. And immediately noted the motion detector that would set off an alarm if she took another step. Rooting her feet in place, she withdrew an alarm deadener from the backpack Yawitz had given her. After shooting the penlike deadener's laser light at the motion detector, she held her breath until the blinking red light turned yellow—effectively freezing the device and preventing it from sending an alarm announcing her unauthorized intrusion.

When she breathed again, she set her com device for four hours, the amount of time she had before the motion detectors would recycle. Four hours was more than enough time to scout out the layout, log into the Space Ministry's computer system, and hack into what she needed. Moving down the hallway, keeping a wary eye out for guards, she took her time to jam one motion detector after another. Lucky for her, Yawitz really did seem to have pulled off the guards. Azsla saw no one.

Heading straight to the offices at the end of the hall, she triggered the lock with a different light beam. When it clicked open, she stepped into the command center. The dark room lit by computer systems was eerily silent. Dozens of blank consoles hooked into a mainframe. All unmanned. The place was devoid of any life.

She worried over the lack of guards. Either Yawitz had taken them out by mixing up the schedules or these Zorans were way too trusting. Or their world was one of peace . . . where people went home at night to their families and didn't worry over war or invasion or planet-busting weaponry that still seemed like a concoction fabricated out of a terrible nightmare. It also worried her that the guards who should have been here could possibly be either hurt or dead.

She shoved the thought to the back of her mind. Whatever she ultimately decided to do with the information she discovered, she needed facts to form a good decision. In her experience facts were rarely clear-cut.

Look at what had happened to her mind ever since that strange waking hallucination. Although she knew she hadn't made love, it felt as if she had, both physically and emotionally. And she was finding it impossible to ignore that her feelings may have altered somewhat due to a dream. Now that his scent and touch were branded into her mind, she couldn't stop thinking about him. When she did, it was way differently than she had before the vision. If she chose to stay, would they meet again? Would they become lovers?

Stow it. Now was not the time.

Sliding behind a computer terminal so that a wall guarded her back, Azsla placed her weapon within easy reach on the desktop. Another spy had already registered her fingerprint and blood type. Azsla placed her fingertip on the bloodsucker, felt the tiny prick, and waited for the machine to analyze her blood. The machine hummed. She held her breath, waiting for it to find her *tranq* free. Only the fingerprints of someone *tranq* free would be allowed to boot in. This was the safety mechanism that she had trained to bypass.

The whirring continued and Azsla tensed. Had the Zorans set up new safeguards? Would the machine detect some kind of subtle difference in her blood type and identify her as a First?

Finally the machine clicked a *go ahead*. She was in!

No computer specialist, she'd nevertheless been trained to search for encrypted files. Azsla found the disk Yawitz had given her and slipped the "hack" program into the computer and let it do its thing.

While it hummed, automatically searching for Zoran weapon capabilities, she slid to another unit. Although the system had a keyboard, these computers were voice modulated. "Give me a quick list of available jobs and vacant apartments."

Azsla, fearing that *tranqed* Firsts might find Jadlan, Micoo, and Rak in her apartment, needed to move her crew. Her plan to save them by sending them to the back continent wouldn't work if the planet was to be destroyed.

So she returned to her original idea of sending them out to the asteroids. But she had to hide them first. Then contact Derrek to see if he'd help.

"Within how large a distance?" the computer asked, its mechanical voice pleasant, efficient, and too loud.

She turned down the volume. "Search within the capital and average commuting areas."

The computer ran through the data in no time and printed out the results without her asking. She folded and stuffed the list into her pocket for later reading.

"Computer, search for Azsla, Jadlan, Micoo, and Rak."

"What kind of search?"

"I wish to know their current location."

The computer's drives whirred. "I have no knowledge of those people."

All the computers on this world plugged into one giant mainframe which was underground, making her task easier than she'd expected. "Has anyone else plugged those names into your search engines within the last thirty hours?"

"Yes. I have four hits. Three from Archer Intersolar Mining and one from the Space Ministry."

Interesting. Yawitz may have logged in here at the Space Ministry to see if anyone was after Azsla, but would she have also typed in the names of her crew? Unlikely.

Or was Pres Laurie after them? If so, Azsla had done her damnedest to hide their tracks. But who at Archer Intersolar was interested in their activities? That had to be Derrek. At the thought that he was looking for her, a glow of happiness warmed her. Maybe he missed her.

Yeah right.

He was probably suspicious as hell that there had been no announcement about their arrival on Zor. And as much as she would have liked to see him again on a personal level, she couldn't afford to let him know her current whereabouts.

The first computer dinged. "Search complete."

"Where's the printout?" she asked, coming around the desk and moving to the other one, praying that if the Zorans did have weapons capabilities that could retaliate against Rama that she'd recognize them. She'd bet her ride home that if the Zorans had progressed in weaponry at the same rate they had in everything else, the homeworld might be in trouble. And then another thought occurred to her. Had Derrek somehow used a trick to place that vision in her mind? If he had deliberately done so, why had he picked that particular vision? She couldn't think of any reason why. The idea disturbed her. Excited her. And the contradictory emotions confused her.

The computer spoke softly, but with conviction. "There is no printout."

She started to open the paper tray. "You out of paper? Or ink?"

"Negative."

"So where's the report?"

"I have nothing to report. There are no weapons systems that can reach Rama. Would you like me to print out a statement to that effect?"

"No." The search had run without a hiccup. And the results were negative. Zor had no weapons capable of retaliation. That meant Rama was free to employ their planet-annihilating weapons without fear that these people could strike back. The news was good. With her mission over except for the wrap-up details, she should have been elated.

As soon as she reported . . . if she reported what she'd learned . . . this planet and everyone on it would be a goner.

Voice shaky, she ordered. "Erase all evidence of my search."

"Compliance."

"Erase all indication that I ever entered this room."

"Compliance."

She popped out the disk, pressed a destroy charge on the face, then set it down on the floor. A tiny flash indicated the disk's self-destruction. Good. There was now no evidence she'd ever been here or why she'd come. So far, so good. The op was going smoothly but that didn't mean she could relax. She needed to exit the building before she could assume she'd gotten away with the rush job.

Azsla backed out of the hallway slowly, retracing her steps to the stairs. She half expected troops or civil cops to stop her as she exited the building, but apparently she hadn't set off any alarms. Either that or Yawitz had disarmed them before she'd even gone in.

Whatever the reason, Azsla didn't question that, for once, luck seemed to be with her. She'd never expected to go in this soon or accomplish her mission with such ease. Apparently the Zorans had put all their efforts and resources into building this world—not preparing for war.

How could they be so naive? So stupid? As she sneaked down the stairs, her anger engaged. It wasn't as if these slaves didn't know that the Firsts they'd left behind were furious. That they had the capability to come after them. Why hadn't they prepared?

Unless . . . she slowed her frenetic pace . . . unless the Space Ministry didn't have the intel she'd come after. Was it possible these Zorans kept intel on their weapons systems elsewhere? The *tranqed* Firsts might have assumed the weapons would be dirtside, but suppose they were hidden on one of their moons? On another planet in this solar system. Or in the asteroid belt?

Derrek might know. The man was connected. The thought flashed into her mind as she picked up her pace. Was she simply looking for a reason to seek him out again?

Possibly. She couldn't ignore the effects of that weird hallucination.

Was she looking for a reason to stay, instead of returning to Rama? She groaned. The longer she stayed on Zor, the more problematic second-guessing herself was becoming. At home, everything was right or wrong, red or yellow with no shades of orange in between.

But on Zor, life was much more complicated.

She could open the exit door and be shot by President Laurie's troops, or arrested by the Zorans whose military base she'd just infiltrated, or taken into custody by the *tranqed* Firsts who may have discovered she'd hidden her crew from them. Guards might materialize out of nowhere. Or she might have another sexy fantasy vision.

Azsla had never had an easy life, but she'd never been in such a mess. Worst of all, she didn't know her own mind. Should she report her findings? Her suspicions? And if she dared mention the hallucination would anyone believe her report? Surely, they'd question her sanity.

And what of the weapon the Ramans were pointing at this planet? Even if she wanted to warn the Zorans, how could she? They wouldn't believe her. She had no proof, and if she tried, she'd blow her cover. She didn't think anyone on this planet would take kindly to a First in their midst. They'd have no reason to believe a First would want to help.

To think that the lives of hundreds of thousands of people depended on her decision was a burden she'd never expected to carry. And it weighed heavily on her heart. She slowed to slip through the exit door but again encountered no difficulty and hurried down the street.

At night, lovers strolled arm in arm. Several teens walked their dogs. The streets were safe. Several late-night eating establishments remained opened, doing a brisk business in *whai*. The scent steamed out into the air, a pleasant reminder of what these people had accomplished, their industry amazing.

If she lied and reported that she'd found evidence of huge retaliatory weapons, would the Firsts on Rama delay their strike? Even if she could warn the Zorans would it do any good? Could they design defensive weapons and prepare for war? If so, could she live with the consequences that Ramans would die?

Stomach twisting into icy knots, Azsla walked blindly, uncertain of her options. Uncertain of her heart.

HOURS LATER AZSLA had come to no firm conclusion—except that she had to verify her data before sending a report. Exhausted from the decision-making process, she'd headed back to her apartment with the expectation that everyone would be asleep. Instead, every window in her apartment was lit up as bright as a retro-rocket on takeoff. Too bad she couldn't see inside. The panes were turned to one-way. They could see out, but she couldn't see in—a precaution they'd employed to keep their presence from being discovered by a casual observer.

Curious and worried something had gone wrong, she took the back entrance, stopped about five feet shy of the door, and placed her ear to the wall. But she couldn't hear voices or music or any kind of noise to indicate her crew still remained inside.

Of course they were there. Where else would they go?

Azsla used her thumbprint to activate the lock and opened the door. Jadlan, Rak, and Micoo sat together on the couch. At the sight of her, their expressions shot a warning.

Azsla spun and reached for her weapon. But she'd barely touched it before Sauren and Derrek stepped forward. Derrek's hand encircled her wrist and while his touch was gentle, it was firm enough to disarm her. "I'll take that."

Her heart beat I'm-glad-to-see-you's. But from his

tight expression that warned her he suspected she was up to something, her mind screamed *run*. But it was too late. She couldn't help but wonder how he'd found her. And why?

At the danger he and Sauren represented, hcr *Quait* awakened like a startled beast. Her *Quait* wanted to howl. To pounce. To force him to stand back so his musky male scent wouldn't cloud her judgment. It was almost as if her *Quait* had been growing stronger, waiting for the perfect moment to escape.

But now was so not the time to let loose or lose one tiny iota of control. Her *Quait* flexed in anticipation of taking over everyone's wills, of forcing them to do exactly what she wished. It was her nature to dominate. A First's right to make them all obey. The *Quait* rising within her was nature's way of telling her she was superior. Deserving to lead. To pound them all down into subservience.

Years of training tempered her emotions and, like calming a stampeding *gazella,* she reined in the primal streak. Turned it in on itself until it spun in a violent vortex. Then she sucked it inward, squashing every last defiant cell until she had herself back under strict control.

That had been close. And the effort had left her trembling, which Derrek had to notice as she allowed him to ease the weapon from her hand. Reminding herself that trembling was perfectly acceptable, she used the emotion, hoping he'd think she was afraid of him, instead of afraid of taking charge. "What are you doing here?"

He ignored her question as if he had every right to

barge into her private quarters. His intelligent eyes focused on her, really looking deep—like straight to her guilty soul—and suspicion shone through.

"Where have you been?" he questioned.

"At work."

"Under your own name?"

"What business is it of yours?" She crossed her arms over her chest, cocked her head, and glared, allowing him to see only her anger. When his suspicion increased, she figured she was showing too much defiance for a just-freed slave and toned down her emotions another notch. "I'm sorry. Have we done something wrong? Violated one of your laws?"

"President Laurie was upset that he lost his honored guests and a shot at presenting you to the world."

"If he'd wanted us to stick around, maybe he should have treated his *guests* better," Azsla countered, still annoyed by the politician. "And I'm glad you're here."

"Really?" Derrek's gaze locked on her and the heat could have curled her *Quait* if she hadn't blocked it. The man really knew how to slide beneath her barriers. She reminded herself to watch out around him.

Azsla didn't understand why every time they were in the same room she felt this connection, as if they shared things that had been real, things that hadn't been said. And she suspected that he knew she'd deliberately changed the subject.

"I was coming back from the Space Ministry to talk to my crew about some disturbing news I'd heard, but we could use the input of Zorans."

"As much as I'd like to hear what you have to say, we

need to leave immediately." Derrek gestured to the door.
"Unless you want to become Laurie's guest again."

"I'd rather not. Especially since I'm wondering if he
could be conspiring with . . ."

"Conspiring? With whom?"

"Firsts on Zor." She no longer wanted to hold back.
Learning that the Ramans intended to destroy everyone
on Zor made the decision simple. It was one thing to
preserve the Raman way of life, to prevent uprising and
killing. But to wipe out every Zoran horrified her. She
wouldn't condone such an appalling plan.

"What?" His brows furrowed and his mouth tightened
into a hard line. "What are you talking about? There are
no Firsts on Zor." Derrek scowled at her, at her crew, at
Sauren, then back at her again.

"Well, maybe the workers were only teasing me."

"Why would they do that?"

"I'm the new employee. It's not like I have a high-level
job or anything, but I overheard that Firsts are working on
Zor . . . undercover." Azsla saw Rak and Micoo exchange
glances, but Jadlan's eyes followed the conversation and
she could see doubts there. Jadlan didn't believe her but
he'd promised to trust her. She tossed him a don't-betray-
me glance, then focused on Derrek. "Perhaps we should
leave and talk at the same time?"

13

✦

Derrek shepherded Azsla and her crew into two waiting hovercraft. He, Azsla, and Micoo grabbed the first vehicle and Sauren followed with Rak and Jadlan. Azsla seemed especially concerned over Micoo, her eyes darting to him with a frequency that annoyed him. It also bothered him that Micoo and Azsla had apparently been sharing the bedroom.

While he told himself he had no call for jealousy, his mind refused to listen. Images of Azsla and Micoo cuddling and kissing were entirely too difficult to banish. Especially when Derrek recalled how eager Azsla had been in his vision. But that had been a dream. This was real. Even worse, dealing with his jealous emotions was making it difficult to concentrate on anything but taking her back into his arms.

However, worrying about Ramans on Zor was a hell of lot more important than Azsla's sleeping arrangements. Especially if President Laurie was conspiring with Firsts. The implications were staggering.

Still . . . Micoo rested his head on Azsla's shoulder and Derrek clenched his fingers into fists, then forced them to uncurl. He might feel like bashing Micoo in the face just for touching Azsla, but a blow might kill the kid. He really looked washed out.

As the hovercraft shot them through the city and

toward Derrek's Zoran home, he searched Azsla's eyes for any clue to her inner thoughts. She looked different without her dark hair. But the new lighter color became her. In truth any hair color would look good with her high cheekbones and healthy skin tone.

"You expect me to believe Firsts are living on Zor and we don't know about them? That's impossible." Derrek hadn't been under the influence of *Quait* in ten years, but he knew that Firsts used *Quait* like he used his hearing. It wasn't a sense that could be turned on and off like a hyperdrive switch.

"I don't expect anything," Azsla replied softly. "I'm telling you what I heard."

Although her news shook him as it would any escaped slave who feared recapture, he kept his tone even. "You must have heard wrong. If Firsts were here, they'd be using their *Quait,* and we would know."

"Not if they were *tranqed*. But that's not important."

Tranqed Firsts lost their powers. But they couldn't bear to live like that. It was like a man with eyesight volunteering to go blind. It wouldn't happen. Or it wouldn't have happened on Rama. But here? Were the Ramans so desperate to spy on their former slaves they'd resort to *tranqs*? Derrek couldn't dismiss the idea out of hand. He hadn't attained his position in life without realizing that events didn't always go the way he expected. But he couldn't take her word for such a startling notion without evidence. "You heard more?"

"Yeah." She spoke in a soft whisper, with an edge of *diamondite*. "The Firsts are all pulling out because there's going to be an attack on Zor."

"An attack. Where exactly?"

"I don't know." She shrugged and her breasts rose and fell, making his mouth go dry as he recalled tasting the tips, the way her nipples puckered beneath his tongue. "Supposedly the weapon's so big it's going to kill everyone. Smash every building."

"You certainly found out a lot of information on your first *day* at work," he muttered.

She twisted her hands, then stilled. "No one paid much attention to me. I had low-level, go-for-*whai* status. And they spoke as if I didn't have a brain." She had a touch of smugness in her voice that suggested she was telling the truth.

However, such a suggestion was preposterous. He didn't believe a word she'd "overheard." A rumor like this would have raced through the population like wildfire. He suspected the Space Ministry employees had been baiting a new employee.

Cautious by nature and just in case he was wrong, he uplinked to Sauren and held the conversation on speaker so Azsla could listen, too. "Have we picked up any rumor of a Raman weapon that could destroy everyone on Zor?"

"Yes, boss man. There's talk of a weapon that will melt our salt. Another that disintegrates flesh. There are also demons on the third continent ready to devour our souls."

"Anything to worry about?" Derrek asked.

"We're trying to break an inordinate amount of encrypted chatter that's going in and out of the Space Ministry. Nothing solid."

"Keep me informed." He cut the link, annoyed that all his blood was hitting his groin. Shifting uneasily in his seat, he tried to make a little more room in his slacks and turned to Azsla. "You sure you didn't dream this up?"

She tossed her hair out of her eyes. "I don't have *those* kinds of dreams."

Sweet *Vigo*. She had his gut churning, his jaw aching, and now she was throwing hints that made his mind spin. He felt as if he were a warrior that had been punched, stomped on, clubbed, and then tossed aside. And her words implied she might have caused that fantasy dream.

He raised his eyebrow. "What kind of dreams *do* you have?"

He held his breath, waiting for her answer. Her eyes met his, a tentative touch, just the merest hint of knowledge shared in her gaze. Heat blazed across the empty space.

She sucked in her breath and bit her lip. "I dreamed of you . . . in an ice cave."

Her words slapped him like a blow across the face. She'd either caused that fantasy or been caught in it with him. Either that or it was the biggest coincidence this side of Alpha One. Derrek lowered his voice so he wouldn't wake Micoo, who had fallen asleep, his head still against her shoulder. "We were making love?"

"Oh . . . my . . . God." Her eyes widened as she stared at him. "It seemed too real to be a dream. But how could we . . . Where were . . . It's not possible. I was awake and walking down the street and then I was with you. When I returned—"

"No time had passed." He smiled at her, suddenly very certain she hadn't been responsible for the fantasy. And that changed everything. She wasn't trying to deceive him. She'd been caught in the vision, just like he had, and he couldn't forget how she'd responded. Responded hell. She'd invited him to her bed of furs. "I liked kissing you."

"You made that happen?" Her fingers reached for the door, as if she'd forgotten that they hovered many feet above the sidewalks below. Then she jerked back, shock in her eyes, but straightening her back and squaring her shoulders. "How? How could you do that to me?"

"I didn't do anything. I don't know what happened. I actually wondered if I was going crazy from too much space radiation."

"Space radiation? Has this ever—"

"Happened before? No." He didn't mention the talking voice in his head. That wasn't the same as a fantasy. And she already had a troubled look in her eyes. Like she wanted to jump out of the vehicle to get away.

Micoo awakened, lifted his head and put a hand on her shoulder. Derrek had to clench his fists not to brush it away.

"You okay?" Micoo asked Azsla softly.

"I've been better," she muttered, shooting Derrek a dark look. Clearly she didn't believe that he'd had nothing to do with the ice cave scenario. But unless she was a very good actress, she hadn't instigated the incident, either. Which left him with more questions than answers.

If he hadn't the skill or technology to pluck two people out of time and space and neither did she, then who did?

Derrek could think of only one being who might have that kind of power. The one in his head. My God. *You did that to me?*

Silence answered his question. That figured. Now he wanted to speak to the voice in his head but the being didn't want to answer for his mischief. He didn't know which was worse, having an alien being in his head or thinking he'd been going crazy.

"Where are you taking us?" Azsla asked as the hover-craft slowed in the residential area.

"My place."

"Aren't you worried that President Laurie—"

"Not particularly. First, he won't know you're with me. And second, even if he figures it out, he'll hesitate to move against me."

"Why?"

Derrek laughed, pleased with his house and wondering what she'd think of it. "Because this place is a fortress and Laurie's a cautious man."

"You can't hide us forever."

Derrek's grin widened as the hovercraft landed. "Sure I can." He popped open the door. "Welcome to my house."

Micoo whistled. "That's a house? Looks like it'll accommodate an army."

"You own this?" Azsla gazed at the place in open awe.

Derrek had built the two-story mansion to be impressive, finding it a necessary business accessory. He'd bought the site years ago, liking the privacy of the large tract of land within the city limits and recognizing the location could only rise in value. One of Zor's finest architects had set the house on the top of a hill. All white, with sweeping columns and many balconies, the building projected a gracious and welcoming air, yet he still preferred his home on Alpha One.

However, he was glad to be here. With its defensive systems, the building was the safest place on Zor. If Azsla's crazy story about a horrible new weapon had even a hint of truth, they weren't safe anywhere on this world. Derrek fully planned to ask her many more questions about what she'd overheard, but he could see exhaustion in her eyes as she turned to greet Rak, Jadlan, and Sauren as they exited the second hovercraft.

At the sight of the house, Rak's lower jaw dropped.

"I'm not sure we're up to roughing it," Jadlan joked but he had a serious look in his eyes, almost as if he sensed trouble arriving.

"Let's get everyone inside." Sauren ushered them forward. In truth, he was more familiar with the house and staff than Derrek was, since he stayed here more often during his visits dirtside, taking advantage of Derrek's open invite, the com systems, and the good location.

"This mansion is larger than any First's on Rama," Rak said as he stepped through the *granitite* foyer, craning his neck and whistling at the stained glass that bordered the domed ceiling.

"Land isn't as scarce on Zor. We had more room to spread out." Derrek kept his words light. Mostly he was interested in Azsla's response. She'd reacted more strongly to his revelation that they'd shared a sexual fantasy than to his obvious wealth. In fact, as if she had more pressing issues on her mind, she barely seemed to react at all to the beautiful sculptures, the *diamondite* stones in the huge saltwater fish tanks, or even the circular stairway, the elegant centerpiece carved out of one enormous piece of *jadite*.

"Would you care for refreshments?" Derrek asked, playing host.

"No thanks," Azsla said. "But I could sack out for a good ten hours. I need sleep. The last time I slept was on your ship."

Azsla's words eased his mind—perhaps she hadn't slept beside Micoo in the bed in the apartment where he'd found them after all. Admitting to himself that he was so insane about this woman, that he'd allowed himself to become jealous for no reason, irritated him. Azsla wasn't the only one who could use some sleep. After a good night's rest, they would all be better off.

Looking closely, he saw weariness in her eyes, dark circles under them, and chastised himself for not realizing how close to exhaustion she was. She looked ready to keel over, indicating she'd likely been staying awake due to pure adrenaline.

Bendor, the butler, appeared in his uniform, a black shirt, black slacks, and shiny black shoes, as if it wasn't the middle of the night. He bowed his bald head in a quick greeting. "If you'll follow me, I'll show you to your rooms."

Derrek headed for his own and tried not to think about which room Bendor gave to Azsla . . . or if she'd end up in a room adjoining Micoo's. He strode into the master suite, tossed off his shirt and slacks, and headed straight for the walk-in fresher. "Water on."

The water, heated to his favorite setting, splashed down from the ceiling as well as spurted from five jets. The fresher soaked, soaped, and rinsed, without him having to flex a muscle. He leaned back into the jet massaging his neck, closed his eyes and tried to banish the image of Azsla down the hall, sleeping in one of his beds, or worse—standing under a shower like he was, the water teasing her bare flesh, caressing her as he would like to.

But he wouldn't go to her. So right now, he needed a distraction.

Where the hell was the nasty voice in his head? He yearned to confront the being for tormenting him with his fantasy. If the alien hadn't made him go through that vision in the ice tunnel, he wouldn't be suffering now.

You can't blame me.

And here I thought you'd abandoned me. Come back to torture me some more?

You wish.

Actually he did, since he couldn't have the real Azsla. He couldn't even keep the thought of having another Azsla fantasy to himself, the damn alien inside his head knew it. How he was supposed to scheme against the thing in his head when it could read his every thought, he didn't know. It was a problem that probably couldn't be solved. Thinking about it gave him a headache and he suspected the alien had the power to toy with him for as long as it pleased.

I do not toy.

Right.

And what you experienced was no dream.

Excuse me? Derrek turned off the water and dried in puffs of warm air before he padded toward his bed, climbed between the sheets, and laced his hands behind his head. "If that wasn't a fantasy, then what the hell was it? And how come Azsla shared it with me?"

What you saw was a scene from your future.

"Uh-huh." His future? He and Azsla? He warmed all over at the idea, but kept his snort sarcastic, although he suspected he wasn't fooling himself, or the alien, into thinking he didn't find that future vision with her very appealing. However, he'd never seen an ice cave and didn't believe the climate on Zor allowed for it. And it couldn't have been in the asteroids since they hadn't needed air breathers.

There's no point in thinking at you, if you aren't going to believe me.

"You want me to believe you? Then prove that scene was from my future."

Laughter filled his head. Not arrogant laughter. But laughter touched with sympathy. Well, he didn't want the bastard's sympathy.

What you want . . . is her.

"It's your damn fault. No need to sound so smug."

My fault? You give me too much credit. I only showed you what you could have someday.

"Could have? What I could have? That doesn't sound like the future to me. It sounds as if you are uncertain. Like you don't have a clue and are trying to cover your ass." Derrek sighed. "Nix that last thought. You don't even have an ass, do you?"

Not for the past few millennia.

Last few millennia? No wonder the being seemed world weary. "How old are you?"

Old enough to have forgotten the horrors of a corporeal form.

"If you think being like me is so horrible, why don't you shove out of my brain?" When the alien didn't answer, he turned over onto his stomach, not the least bit comforted that the being was older than time. "Don't you miss food and sex?"

You can keep your cravings. I am a pure spirit.

"Pure is not how I would describe you. Instead I'd say you are interfering, bossy, arrogant, and annoying. And if you can see the future, I suspect you are also bored."

Very perceptive. But that's irrelevant. What you need is to stop fighting yourself. Go down the hallway and get to know that woman.

"Why the hell do you care?" He punched his pillow. He would talk to Azsla in the morning when she had recovered from her recent ordeal. To do anything less, no matter how much he wanted to seduce her, violated his sense of fair play. So Derrek had no intention of interrupting her sleep.

She's not sleeping.

"Are you in *her* head, too?" The idea startled him. Could this alien—

My name is Pepko.

"Well, Pepko. I am so not glad to meet you."

Would it hurt you to use some manners?

"I didn't know you had feelings but I'm not inclined to be nice to things—"

Beings—

"Anyone who invades my privacy. And I suspect you're irritating her, too."

I don't converse with her.

"But you know her thoughts?"

I know . . . all.

"Then who the hell are you and why are you in my head?"

That will be revealed at the proper time.

"Are you a First?"

Have you ever met a telepathic First?

"No." He hadn't. In fact, before Pepko, he'd thought telepathy no more possible than his growing himself a pair of wings. "So are you friend or foe?"

Life isn't that simple. You just need to believe in me.

"I for one do not believe you are *Vigo*."

Again laughter suffused his mind. *I am no deity.*

"If you know all, then you must have realized by now, with whatever you use for a brain—"

There's no need to be insulting.

"That I am not going to obey you." He'd never obey anyone again. He'd spent most of his life as a slave, taking orders, being bent to do the will of others. Being accused and punished for things he hadn't done. Never again.

Pepko must have sensed his strong feelings on the matter.

I didn't ask for blind obedience. I told you to do what you wanted—which is to go down the hall and get to know that woman.

The sincerity of Pepko's exasperation convinced Derrek the alien wasn't a First. He might not know who or what he was, but he was willing to believe at least this much.

If Pepko hadn't lied and that vision was from his future, that meant he and Azsla would become lovers. But why did Pepko care? He asked, but Pepko didn't respond, seeming to have once again left him alone. Damn it. He'd wanted to ask about the rumor that Rama might wipe out Zor. After all, Pepko knew all . . . he snorted. Damn Pepko with his interference.

Even if Azsla was his future, knowing what they could be like together made this time apart more difficult, and made him more impatient. Just thinking about her had him aroused. Derrek almost wished he'd never kissed her. Never felt her eager response. It hadn't really happened, yet he couldn't stop thinking about her.

The knowledge of how good they could be together burned within him. Fed his fire and added to his agitation to be with her.

When he heard a soft knock on his door, Derrek slipped on a pair of sleeping pants. With a yank, he knotted a tie at his hips, then flung open the door. "What?"

He had been certain it was Sauren. But Sauren didn't have skin as soft as peach fuzz. Or eyes as wide as a young *gazella*'s. Azsla had showered and wore sleeping pajamas kept in the rooms for guests. Over them she'd thrown on a robe that parted in a V at her neck, where he could see her pulse racing.

Apparently she hadn't gotten the greeting she'd expected. Her hand rose to her mouth, but her eyes took in his bare chest and dilated slightly before she raised her gaze to his eyes. "Sorry. I didn't meant to disturb you."

He stepped back and opened the door, curious to see if she'd hesitate to enter. He should have known better. Any woman brave enough to escape slavery on Rama and risk the hardships of space wouldn't be afraid.

She stepped right up to him, close enough for him to smell her freshly washed hair, and placed a warm hand on his bare arm. "I couldn't sleep and hoped you'd still be awake."

The circles under her eyes had darkened and her skin seemed a bit pale. As happy as he was for her company, clearly now was not the time for amorous advances. Her eyes were bloodshot, her lips pressed into a tight line, and he sensed she was keeping herself upright through pure determination. "You look exhausted."

"Thanks."

"I meant no insult. Clearly you are a beautiful woman, but you need rest."

At his comment, red flushed up her neck as if she were unaccustomed to compliments, and he found that odd. Slaves on Rama had many casual relationships, taking pleasure where they could. Few of them married since the consequences could be disastrous when one didn't have any control over one's fate. He'd been one of the few to risk it, and paid the terrible price after his memory was wiped and he couldn't remember his family.

On Zor, many of the escaped slaves had chosen to commit to one life mate, but Azsla hadn't been here long enough to absorb their customs. However, her blush didn't fit in with the typical Raman slave background of an experienced woman who was accustomed to men partnering with her for her beauty, either.

"I can't sleep until I know my crew will be safe." Her tone was fierce, her eyes grave. When she dropped her hand to her side, he missed her touch.

"No one will harm you here," he spoke gently.

She shook her head. "If the Ramans rain weapons down on Zor, no place on this world will be safe."

If her coworkers had baited Azsla, they'd done a good job. She certainly believed the rumor. Perhaps he shouldn't have blown off her concern. At least, he could look into it further. He'd do so in the morning.

"Would you like me to take you and your crew back with us to the asteroids?" he offered, his hopes soaring. He might be impatient, but if she didn't want to live on Zor, he could have all the time he needed to woo her. While the competition for her attention in space would be fierce because of the huge male-to-female ratio of the population, the idea of a challenge never bothered him—not with such a terrific opportunity.

She nodded. "We're not unskilled. And we all work hard. I know it is much to ask, but—"

"I'll make room for you and your people." He didn't even hesitate. He wanted time to get to know her.

Interrupting his thoughts, an emergency message broke through the link. "Boss man, you aren't going to believe this. You'll want to come down to the basement right away."

14

For a moment, Azsla had feared Derrek wouldn't allow her to accompany him. Then he held out his hand and they left together, her curiosity burning. He led her down a hallway to a private elevator that sank into a basement bunker that almost rivaled the instrumentation at the Space Ministry. Inside, a half dozen men sat in front of computer vidscreens, tracking spacecraft, asteroids, cargo transports, and ore, as well as what she suspected were dozens of military ships.

She arched an eyebrow in a silent question at his obviously illegal spying. From his command center he could watch every spaceship landing at the port, military convoys, and troop movements. He tracked news on every station linkup, ships docked in port, railroad cars, and train schedules. He also intercepted satellite transmissions. No wonder he'd hesitated to bring her here. He had to be breaking dozens of laws.

"I like to know what's happening," Derrek explained without really explaining anything at all.

She said nothing. She had enough on her own conscience without judging him. When Azsla had failed to report her findings to her contact, she'd committed treason. And she'd done so again when she'd told him about the *tranqed* Firsts and about the coming attack on Zor. But there had been no way out of doing so. If she'd reported back, she would have been picked up for immediate transport back to Rama. And to save her crew, she'd had to give Derrek enough information to make her story hold together.

"Boss man." The tech pointed to his screen as Sauren came up and joined them. On seeing her, Sauren gave her a startled look, and she didn't attribute it to her pajamas and robe, but to his surprise that Derrek had let her into his secret enclave. Then the tech began to explain. "I broke the Space Ministry's encryption and the picture isn't pretty."

"Show us," Derrek demanded.

A starscape played on the vidscreen monitor. "Zoom. Five hundred percent."

Azsla saw an object hurtling through space, the ominous mass blocking out stars, and her blood chilled. "What is that?"

Sauren went into lecture mode. "This is an asteroid called Katadama. It's over five miles wide and heading our way."

"Towards Zor?" Derrek asked.

"According to my calculations Katadama will probably strike Zor somewhere in the ocean."

"Probably?" Derrek asked.

"Eighty percent probable," Sauren said, though he looked doubtful.

Sweet Mother of *Vigo*. Katadama was the Raman space weapon Yawitz had told Azsla about back at the Space Ministry. Somehow, they'd found a way to aim it at Zor.

Azsla's mouth was so dry she could barely get out her

question. "An ocean strike is better than hitting land, right?"

"Wrong. After it punctures our atmosphere, it'll penetrate the ocean within a second." Although Sauren didn't sound worried, his cool, crisp and very dry factual explanation sent icy chills through her. "Debris will splash out of our atmosphere, perhaps halfway to the moon. The pieces that fall back will burn hot enough to flash bake the entire planet. No plant life or animals will survive. None."

"Sweet *Vigo*." Azsla reached out to steady herself on a desk. The Ramans had actually figured out a way to lob that asteroid at Zor. "Why are you so uncertain about the trajectory?"

"The object is behaving abnormally."

Derrek leaned forward, his scowl making him look threatening. "What do you mean?"

The tech flicked a few controls and the screen changed. Two lines showed different courses. "This is Katadama's usual orbit." Sauren pointed to a path that missed Zor by a few hundred thousand miles, still close in the vast distances of space, but not catastrophic. "Two months ago, the orbit began to alter."

The second path bisected the planet. "It's almost as if someone deliberately shot that hunk of rock at Zor." Derrek frowned.

She was shaking inside. Her people were aiming that asteroid at Derrek's people, his children, people like her crew who wanted to start a new life. After what her people were about to do to Zor, if he learned she was a First, he'd probably stake her out at ground zero.

"How long until impact?" Derrek asked.

"Less than a week. It depends on how the gravity in our solar system increases the asteroid's speed and I won't know that until we determine the rock's chemical composition."

"All right. Keep working. In the meantime, bring in the best people we've got. Put Taylo Misa in charge of figuring a way to blow up that rock or change its course."

"Do we notify President Laurie?" Sauren asked.

If the president was conspiring with *tranqed* Firsts, he'd already know about Katadama. If he wasn't, then he'd need all the advance warning they could give him, so she wasn't surprised to hear Derrek's decision.

"Inform him, but do it quietly. Maybe the military ships can evacuate some people to the moon bases, but remember, we don't want to panic everyone. Meanwhile, see what we can do to transport as many people as possible from the planet."

He turned to Sauren. "Round up every ship we've got and bring them here."

"Our ships are full of salt. And if we offload—"

"Dump it." He didn't hesitate even though he was about to lose a small fortune and her admiration for him, for his concern for his people, made her wither a little inside. Her people were doing this.

"Those ships aren't meant to transport people."

"So re-outfit them."

"You're asking the impossible. They won't be here for days. Then we have to fit them for air, pressure, heating, and cooling systems."

"Do what we can. Gather all our people and their families first. If they have to, they can travel in space suits. It won't be comfortable but they'll live. Take as many supplies as we can carry. Sauren, you're in charge of evacuation. Spend whatever you need to. Go heavy on generators, hydroponics, medicine, seeds. Whatever we can't manufacture in the asteroid mines has to come with us. It may be years before we can resupply."

"Many ships won't arrive in time to do any good," Sauren checked his personal link. "I'll reroute ships and rent, borrow, and beg what supplies I can."

"Good. Try and keep the news quiet for as long as possible. There's no point in upsetting the population. Maybe we'll come up with a way to prevent the disaster. Meanwhile, I'm going after my kids."

"We need you here," Sauren frowned at him, then shut his lips tight as if he regretted giving his opinion.

"My family needs me, too." Derrek squeezed Sauren's arm. "You'll take care of things at this end as well I would. I'll be back soon."

Sauren nodded. "Of course."

DERREK'S THOUGHTS WORKED at hyperspeed as he left the basement with Azsla. Less than a week until impact meant that the asteroid wasn't far away—not in terms of space distances. If it was already targeted at Zor . . . he had to act now. And to give Azsla credit, she wasn't saying, "I told you so." She looked as shaken as he felt that what she'd overheard was true.

They reached a private sitting area and he gestured for her to sit on the sofa while he paced. "That asteroid is the Raman weapon, isn't it?"

I'm afraid so." She swallowed hard. "How far away are your children?"

"Distance isn't the problem." He hesitated. "My family can be difficult."

He looked her in the eyes and saw something in her posture . . . stiffness. She gnawed on her bottom lip, but met his gaze steadily. "I don't wish to pry, but why is this a problem? Doesn't your wife want to accompany you?"

His wife? Ah, she thought he had a life mate. He studied her curiously, trying to gauge her reaction. Was she at all disappointed? After all, they'd made love—if only in a vision.

"I am not mated—anymore. After the Ramans wiped my memory—"

She sucked in air with a hiss and jumped to her feet, her eyes full of sympathy. "Oh, no. I'm so sorry."

His full recovery was really remarkable. Most mind-wiped adults never learned to read again, never mind run a vast intersolar business. While Firsts rarely carried out the punishment, since it lost them the slave's skills, the threat terrified all who'd seen what it did to a person. Firsts usually saved mindwipes for only the worst of crimes and the most stubborn of slaves. But the punishment was so terrible, this losing of one's entire life, that it kept the slaves in line.

He shrugged. "My wife found another mate. She kept the children, our daughter Tish and son Tad. I couldn't care for any of them. I could barely take care of myself. My brother saw to it that I was one of the first colonists to escape Rama, and I in turn made certain my former mate and my children came to Zor. But until yesterday, I hadn't spoken to any of them."

He got the words out steadily, and although the pain of loss still ached, he managed to share his story. Maybe he would finally move on, let go of the old hurts.

Azsla took his hand, slipped her fingers through his, and led him to the couch. She might be tough, but apparently she had a gentle side, too. "What happened yesterday?"

"Tish hit me up for credit over the com link. It's the first contact we've had since the mindwipe back on Rama."

"I don't understand. Why hasn't there been any contact before now?"

"My ex believed the children would be shamed and humiliated by my mindwipe. After she remarried, she preferred to pretend her time with me never happened."

"So if you haven't seen your children in all this time, how can you be sure the woman asking you for credit was really Tish?"

"I've kept track of them." He didn't admit his obsession. The files. The pictures. The private investigators. "Tish wanted a lot of credit. Too much for a young girl. And she wasn't very pleasant."

"Teenagers tend to be self-absorbed creatures. Most of them grow out of it, eventually."

"Yes. Well, my former wife, Poli, isn't going to just hand over her children to me because I tell her an asteroid might hit Zor."

"Maybe Poli and her new mate—"

"Could join us on Alpha One?" Wouldn't that be cozy. "She suffers from space sickness. No way would she voluntarily board a spacecraft. And I won't force her since she could die from the nausea. She barely survived the trip from Rama to Zor."

"And your children?"

He didn't bother to hide his anguish. "Their mother won't allow them to see me, never mind let them make up their own minds. Poli won't just hand them over to me and let me take them to the dangerous asteroid mines."

"You said you wouldn't force Poli . . . but," her hand tightened on his, "are you going to force your children to come with you?"

"I don't know." His stomach churned. He couldn't believe he was having this conversation with Azsla, a woman he'd just met. He'd told her more than he'd told Sauren during the decade they'd been friends. It was almost as if he had no inhibitions around this woman. He couldn't hold back. Didn't want to hold back.

What was it about her that had him opening up?

"I assume you have the resources to grab them?" She didn't even wait for him to nod, before going on. "But would the government try to stop you?"

They could try. But they wouldn't succeed. Derrek had too many resources, too many connections. But her comments took him aback. Azsla didn't think like any woman he'd met. She was thinking about strong-arm tactics, kidnapping and political consequences, analyzing and assessing, almost as if she'd had military training. He supposed she could have picked up a lot of useful information from the First she'd worked for on Rama.

"I'm worried about uprooting my children from everything they've ever known."

"Seems to me you should present your offer of safety to the entire family. Otherwise, if you save the kids and their parents don't survive, they'll blame you."

She made good points. Several he hadn't thought about. In all these years he'd never walked up to the door of the house he'd paid for and demanded a meeting. The other possibilities were endless. His children might wish to come with him. Or maybe not, as he recalled Tish's behavior with him. Perhaps the new husband would convince them to go.

And if they refused?

He'd leave that decision until later. Right now, he owed Azsla an apology. "I'm sorry I didn't believe you."

"If I heard my world was going to be destroyed I might go into denial, too."

She let him off the hook so easily and without blame. And now he asked the questions he should have asked before. "Can you tell me any more about what you heard at the Space Ministry?"

"I only heard bits and pieces." She shook her head, couldn't meet his gaze. Something about that bothered him.

"Nothing else?"

"I heard the *tranqed* Firsts were leaving soon."

"Who told you?"

"People were standing around a watercooler talking. I assume they want to get their people out before Katadama arrives."

He recalled their last discussion, how distracted he'd been. He hadn't asked her enough questions. He'd been too shocked to hear *tranqed* Firsts were on Zor. "How do Ramans get here and get out? We monitor the portal—"

"Both of them?"

"Both?" He frowned at her, his suspicions rising even as he was drawn to her intelligence. "We only know about one."

"There's another portal. The second one is on the other side of Zor, although I'm not sure where exactly."

A second portal? Sweet *Vigo*. There could be *tranqed* Firsts, spies, everywhere. Even in his own organization. "Why didn't you tell us?"

She shivered and rubbed her arms. "I thought you knew . . . I've known about the other portal since before I left Rama. I didn't realize Zorans had no knowledge of it."

Derrek and Taylo had spoken about cloaked portals but the idea was theoretical. Apparently the Ramans had the jump on them by developing a cloaking device. He didn't allow his face to change expression but his suspicions heightened. Azsla knew too many important details, from gossip about the weapon to knowledge of *tranqed* First on the planet, and now the secret portal. Was it simply due to the importance of the First she'd worked for on Rama? He had questions that needed answers about this woman and feared his strange fascination and attraction to her were clouding his thinking. But if what she'd said about the second portal was true, did President Laurie know? Could an attack be stopped?

Derrek realized it was time to interrupt his brother's second honeymoon. He'd put a call through before morning. And he'd like to hear his brother's take on Azsla's story because something didn't sit right with Derrek. She knew too much.

And yet although he was suspicious as hell, he couldn't stop himself from wanting her. And his inappropriate reactions frightened him. Even now, his blood was hot for her. He didn't want to leave her to go after his family but he must. His need for her was distracting, irritating, consuming. He wanted to take her to bed. But he wouldn't. His family came first. However, that didn't mean he couldn't have a small taste. He stopped pacing, sat beside her and leaned forward. "Lady, you scare me."

She tilted up her head. Her lips inches from his. "I don't know what to say."

"Talking isn't required." He dipped his head and kissed her. Her lips parted. He took more. It didn't matter that he was certain she was hiding things. It didn't matter that he didn't trust her. He only knew he needed to kiss her, to breathe in her scent, to hold her in his arms.

And when she kissed him back, he demanded more. For long micronbits, she clung to him, winding her fingers into his hair, kissing him back with seemingly as much enthusiasm as he felt for her. But when she finally pulled back, her eyes were dilated and filled with regret, her hands shaking, her voice unsteady. "You need to go. To your family."

15

✦

Derrek left Azsla to get some well-needed rest and headed out to find his ex-wife and new husband who lived in Latonia, a suburb of the capital. He flew his private hovercraft, his hands steady on the controls, his speed quick but not dangerous. Although he'd never been here before, he had no difficulty finding the residence and parked in front of a good-sized brick house with a well-kept lawn similar to others in the neighborhood. He might be heading to see the family he hadn't seen in years, but surprisingly his mind was on Azsla's kiss.

A real kiss. Not a vision.

That kiss had stirred his heart, nicked it up a little. And he'd wanted more. In other circumstances, taking over would have been automatic. He would have coaxed her to join him in the privacy of the master suite, and taken his time getting to know her better, and loving her properly.

He hadn't, of course. Time was too short. So, he'd tamped down his swirling desires, and prayed no one had noted his struggle to leave her behind. The world was about to go into crisis. His family was in jeopardy and he had no business thinking about Azsla.

Yet . . . he couldn't seem to stop thinking about her. At least she'd seemed happy to accept his offer to take her back to Alpha One with him. And he looked forward to showing her his home.

As he approached his destination, Derrek's muscles tensed, his eyes narrowed, and his back stiffened. He'd paid for this house. His family lived here. If not for the mindwipe, this could have been his home. His life. Dirtside.

He headed up the sidewalk but didn't make it to the front door. A boy, Tad, his son, who was now fourteen, was lying on his back beneath a hovercycle. Derrek had never met this child since the mindwipe had occurred before Tad's birth. But even if he hadn't recognized him from holo pics, his pulse would have raced at the mere possibility of meeting him.

Tad was his son. They shared DNA. With his legs sticking out of the too-short pants that rode up his ankles, as if he'd recently spurted up in height, he looked skinny and determined. He'd scooted under a hovercycle and hadn't yet seen Derrek from his position on his back, his attention on his work. A smudge of grease stained his hand. He had a dried cut over his eyes and he looked totally happy as he whistled while he torqued his wrench.

"Mom's not home," he said, responding to either the sound of Derrek's footsteps or his shadow.

"Tad."

"Who wants to know?" The kid's music box blared hard dunk and dive music and Derrek refrained from wincing or asking him to turn it down.

Instead, he squatted next to the hoverbike, wondering if he'd ever been like Tad. He had no memories of his childhood and although Cade had filled Derrek in, explaining that he'd loved to tinker, there were huge gaps about which he knew nothing. "Doing a tune-up?"

"I'm retrofitting the engine. I want to juice her up hot enough to win a street race. Don't tell Mom. She doesn't like me getting dirty, okay?"

"No problem." Derrek thought it odd that Tad's mother worried about a little dirt and not the fact the kid could get hurt in a street race, but kept the thought to himself.

Tad pulled out from under the bike, jerked a rag from his back pocket and, his touch loving, he polished the shiny chrome that didn't have a speck of dust. "I built her from scratch out of junk parts."

"Impressive."

Now that he could see the boy's face, he realized that Tad looked a lot like him. He had Derrek's straight nose, the same jutting chin and dark brows. But even better, he had fire in his eyes.

"She'd be more impressive if I had the credit for—" Tad stopped talking and stared at Derrek, his eyes widening and openly hurt. Clearly he recognized his father and his tone hardened with defiance. "You come because Tish called yesterday?"

"Not really." Derrek grinned at Tad, surprised Tish had shared with him and he hoped brother and sister were close. "Did she tell you she called?"

Tad winked. "I have resources."

"So why does she need that kind of credit?"

Tad frowned. "She didn't tell you? She wants to study engineering at the university. Mom doesn't approve."

The charming brat was spying on his sister. Derrek had to hide a grin behind a cough. He thought of his own bunker where he tapped into the world's computer system and broke encrypted code. Like father, like son. In addition, the idea that his daughter was interested in engineering impressed him, but he wondered why she'd never told him why she'd wanted the credits. Derrek didn't bother hiding his own amusement at Tad's spying and openly chuckled. "I suppose there's not much around here you don't know."

"I know you pay the bills and Mom lies about it to us. What I don't know is why you never came around." Hurt and defiance wrenched his thin frame.

Derrek ached to reach out and hug the boy, which shocked him. He didn't have any memories of his birth, his growing up. Until this moment, they'd never spoken, never mind touched. But he felt a protectiveness he'd always known was there . . . and that protectiveness was growing. Something in the kid called out to him. Maybe it was his close resemblance to himself. Maybe it was the mix of boyish hurt and adult intelligence. Maybe he reminded him of what he imagined he might have been like at that age—caught up in things he didn't understand.

"I wanted to see you." Derrek spoke softly, his heart aching.

"Yeah, right." His son backed away but not before Derrek caught sight of tears brimming. "You didn't want us."

"That's mud slime. Do you think I would have paid all the bills for all these years if I didn't want you?"

"Mom said you had your mind wiped. That you'd forgotten us."

"She spoke true about that. I was punished for a crime I didn't do. And Firsts took all my memories. I couldn't walk, or talk. I had to relearn everything—just like a baby does. It took a long time to function again."

Derrek tried to keep his tone easy but couldn't help spitting the word "First" from his mouth like a curse. After all this time, he still hadn't stopped hating all Firsts for ripping apart his life, shredding his family. As he spoke to Tad and realized how much he'd missed—birthdays, schooldays, going fishing, tucking him in at night—a lump rose in his throat.

Derrek forced his voice to be matter of fact, and he tried to maintain his cool for the sake of his son. But no one could put that kind of horror behind them and feel nothing—not and remain human. "My brother Cade, your uncle, stood by me during that difficult time. When I recovered enough to ask my brother about my past, Cade told me about my family. About you and Tish. I wanted to come back, but your mother had moved on with her life. She thought it would be best for you if you never knew me. I respected her wishes."

"Why did you listen to her?" The kid eyed him, clearly upset. Derrek guessed his son was torn between wanting to run from him out of hurt and wanting to stay out of curiosity. "Is Mom smarter than you?"

"She knew you better than I did. I trusted her judgment that she would know what was best for you."

Derrek was careful not to place any blame on his ex. He loved his children so much that he didn't want them to think badly of their mother—no matter how unfairly she'd treated Derrek.

"So why *are* you here?" Tad asked.

A hovercraft roared up the driveway before Derrek could answer. He recognized the occupants from holo pics. Poli, a gorgeous woman, immaculately dressed, stepped out of the vehicle with Tish, his similarly dressed teenage daughter. Slender, and fit, they looked like sisters. Both women were stunning. Well groomed from head to polished nails that they showed off in open-toed shoes, their immaculate clothes didn't have one wrinkle and not only fit, but accentuated their curvy figures to perfection.

"Tad, I told you to throw that hoverbike in the trash." Poli spoke as she handed shopping bags to her husband Mavinor, a tall, thin man who looked washed out in comparison with his glamorous wife and step-daughter. Derrek eyed the man and wondered if he was worthy of taking his place. Was he kind? Did he love Tad and Tish? Did he support their goals and hobbies?

"Mom. We have company." Tad's voice sounded almost joyful, as if the mischievous kid couldn't wait to see his mother's reaction.

"What?" Poli craned her long neck around the hovercraft, took one look at Derrek and screeched, "Tad and Tish! Run. Go inside right now."

Tad folded his arms over his chest. "No."

Derrek got the feeling he said *no* often. Defiance sat comfortably on his mischievous face.

Tish strode around the car and tried to slap Tad across the cheek. As if expecting the attack, he ducked and kicked his older sister in the shin. "Owww. You little slime—"

"Tish, watch your language," her stepfather spoke mildly.

She hopped up and down, her elegance forgotten as she screwed up her face in pain. "I don't give a crap—"

"Tish," her mother ordered and pointed at Tad. "Grab your brother and go."

Tad scooted behind Derrek. "I'm not going anywhere."

"You see what I have to put up with?" Poli rolled her eyes at several neighbors who'd come outside to watch the arguing. Then, as if to show off her purchases, she handed a mountain load of shopping bags to her husband and Derrek wondered if she was teaching their daughter anything other than how to shop. Perhaps that's why Tish hadn't mentioned engineering school, she'd thought he'd disapprove like her mother.

"Poli, dear. Don't upset yourself," her husband spoke up, dropped a few bags, then offered his forearm to Derrek in greeting. "I'm Mavinor Raet."

"Derrek Archer."

Mavinor placed an arm over Poli's shoulder. As she calmed down a bit, Derrek decided the kids were better off with the man around than without.

At least Poli seemed to make some effort to lower her voice. "Don't upset myself? You just dropped my beautiful new clothes and now they'll have wrinkles."

"It's okay, Poli. Calm down," Mavinor spoke soothingly.

"And that man," Poli sniffled and pointed at Derrek, "is trying to steal our children."

Weird how she mentioned the wrinkled clothes before

she expressed concern for her children. And why had she jumped to the conclusion that Derrek wanted the kids? Was she paranoid? Or a mind reader? Since he'd seen holo pics, Derrek hadn't been surprised that Poli was gorgeous. What was shocking to him was that he could have ever been attracted to such a seemingly silly woman. Not that she was stupid. Shrewdness glowed in her eyes when she'd guessed he was there about the kids.

According to the reports, the man doted on his wife and Derrek had to give Mavinor credit. He didn't raise his tone and his voice remained patient. "I hardly think—"

"I don't pay you to think," she snapped, and Mavinor turned bright red at the insult. At her rudeness, Derrek thought, better you than me, buddy. Perhaps he hadn't missed as much as he'd believed all these years, the time spent longing for a woman he disliked wasted.

Unlike Azsla, who was calm and practical, Poli seemed difficult, selfish, and one-dimensional. He couldn't help wondering if she'd always been like this or if she'd changed. And the man he'd spent years resenting, Mavinor, well—Derrek couldn't even understand why the guy stuck around if Poli treated him like this. Talk about a doormat.

He also didn't like it that Tish appeared to be a miniature Poli, but approved of the girl's wanting to study engineering. Maybe her mother hadn't ruined her yet, although after the unpleasant conversation yesterday with his daughter, Derrek's influence might be coming at just the right time.

"We can have this conversation here, with your neighbors watching," Derrek said, his tone mild but firm, his face serious, "or we can go inside. However, we *will* have a conversation. The choice is yours."

Poli spun on her heel. "I'm calling—"

"No one." Derrek encircled her upper arm and led her inside. The others followed, but Tad was the only one with a grin. Tish was a fountain of tears. Mavinor looked resigned.

Inside, the house was filled to bursting with stuff, garish paintings in bright green, reds, and oranges, sculptures of naked men, dried flowers in ceramic and glass vases, knickknacks of glass, metal and wooden carvings. Unlike Derrek's elegant mansion, here holo pics spun, spoke, and crawled along tabletops like banners. He noted a *gazella* collection, assorted mirrors in clashing frames of gold, bronze, and silver, lamps with dozens of shades in assorted colors and sizes, all of it glittery and so overdone, he couldn't find a peaceful place to rest his eyes. Talk about overindulgence. Poli seemed to be more than a shopaholic. This extravagance was a sickness. Yet, with all this wastefulness, she didn't have time, credit, or interest to buy Tad proper fitting pants or see fit to pay for her daughter's education.

Poli pointed to a hallway, her voice shrill. "Children, go to your rooms while the adults talk."

Tad shook his head. "I want to hear what my father has to say."

Poli lowered her voice to a threatening menace. "Young man, do not defy—"

Derrek stuck up for his son. "Let him stay. What I have to say—"

"He does not need to hear."

"Actually, he does," Derrek argued.

"Just because you pay for some things—"

"Some?" Derrek arched his brow.

"—doesn't mean you have the right to come here and tell me what my children—"

"Our children."

"—should hear."

"Either I'll tell them while you are around or I'll find another way . . ." Derrek let the threat hang in the air. "Lives are at stake."

"Yeah . . . right." Poli sank into the sofa as if he'd just announced a weather change instead of a crisis. Her eyes burned with accusation. "I've always feared your business dealings might entice a kidnapper to come after the children. It's not right for one man to corner the market on salt. It's not right for you to have so much when others . . ."

"There's no kidnapper. And that salt business has fed and clothed and housed you for many years."

Mavinor placed his hand on his wife's shoulder, a silent entreaty for her to settle down. "Please tell us why you have come."

Derrek told them about the asteroid threat. He explained in great detail that if the rock struck Zor no one would survive. Tad looked thoughtful and almost excited. Tish turned greenish, as if she was about to be sick. Mavinor held it together. Poli's expression remained unfazed. And when Derrek made the offer to move them to the asteroids, a wide grin broke over Tad's face.

"I want to go. I want to go." He practically leaped up and down with joy.

Poli snorted. "I don't believe you, Derrek. If there's a threat, why haven't we heard anything on the news?"

"The danger isn't common knowledge yet. After Zorans learn about Katadama and the threat to Zor, panic may ensue. It will be dangerous to stay."

"So you claim."

"Mom often goes into denial to get her way," Tad explained with an astuteness too old for his years.

"Don't you be rude, young man," Poli snapped.

"Son, I'm glad you want to come with me." Derrek ruffled the boy's hair. "But the rest of your family may decide to stay."

"I know." The boy lost his smile. "Why can't they see what needs to be done?"

Derrek looked at Tish and tried again, taking the high road and trying not to insult Poli. "Your mother likes it here. It's hard for her to leave."

"It's stupid," Tad frowned at his mother, who was shaking her head as if refusing to believe the threat would make it disappear. "But Tish isn't stupid. She's smart. She just plays dumb so Mom will buy her stuff."

Tish scowled at her brother. "Traitor. I heard you."

"That was a compliment."

Derrek approached Tish. "What about you? What do you want to do?"

"Don't you dare take his side," Poli muttered, her tone snide. "He hasn't given us one shred of proof."

"Mom, why can't we all go?" Tish surprised Derrek. She might be spoiled, she might have been taught to value shallow objects, but Tad was right, she wasn't stupid.

"Because I get space sick," Poli whined. "I almost died on the trip from Rama to Zor. This time I might die from the nausea."

"I've developed a new ship that opens a portal. The journey isn't as long as you think. You could come with us." Derrek made the offer, even as he disliked the idea of taking Poli with them. However, for his children's sake, he had to offer her a ride. But he couldn't help thinking about how many more worthy people could have taken her place, pilots, hydroponics gardeners, mechanics, medics. She seemed trained to do nothing beyond shop.

"How new is your ship? Why haven't I heard about it?" Poli eyed him suspiciously.

"It's a prototype."

"Experimental?"

"We tested it on the journey to Zor and it worked fine with only a few minor problems."

"What kind of minor problems?"

"Who cares?" Tad interrupted with the fearless impatience of a fourteen-year-old. "If we stay here, we die. What's to think about?"

"Don't be rude, young man. I'm still not convinced there's a threat. Besides, have you ever been so sick you couldn't keep down food for weeks?"

"Sick is better than dead," Tad argued.

Despite the grim circumstances, Derrek smiled with pride. "I couldn't have said it better myself."

Poli shook her head. "I don't believe there's any danger. Even I know the chance of an asteroid hitting Zor is very small, with all that empty space. So I'm staying and so is my family."

"Mom—" Tad started to protest. Derrek caught the boy's eye and shook his head to silence him. Tad snapped his mouth closed and headed down the hall. "I'm going to pack."

"You're not going anywhere," Poli yelled. "Your father made up a crisis to take you away from me."

Tad kept walking. Derrek took pride in the fact that for a young boy he certainly had a lot of guts. But then Derrek turned his gaze to his daughter and saw the quiet fear in Tish's eyes as she made her decision. "I won't leave you, Mom."

Derrek's heart went out to her, too. She might be spoiled, but she was loyal . . . to the death, her decision painfully brave even if teenagers didn't really believe they could die. At that age most kids thought themselves indestructible. Displeased and unhappy with the family dynamic and Poli's hold over Tish, he saw there was nothing more he could do. Tish would stay. For now . . . but not for long.

"It's your choice." Derrek stood. "If any of you change your minds, my offer stands and you know how to reach me."

"You're just going to leave?" Poli's eyes narrowed on him. "It's not like you to give up."

Poli was right. Derrek would be back to attack the problem from a different angle. Preferably when he could talk to Tish, alone.

"There's nothing else to be said," Derrek said. "Tad wants to come with me."

"I'll take you to court."

Derrek frowned at her, but didn't bother to answer. He was done. He couldn't say or do any more to convince Poli, Mavinor, and Tish to join them.

"And if the asteroid doesn't hit? Do you plan to bring back Tad?" Poli asked, her question an admission she realized that she couldn't stop Derrek.

"That will be up to Tad." Derrek folded his arms over his chest.

Poli reached for the phone. "If I call the authorities on you now—"

"No one will believe you and my attorneys will make your last days miserable. Is that what you want? If so, make the call." Derrek wasn't bluffing. He let Poli read the determination in his eyes, in the hard set of his tone, in the stubborn set of his shoulders.

Tad bounded into the room, a backpack stuffed with his dearest possessions. From the assorted lumps, Derrek guessed he'd packed more hardware than clothing.

Tad tried to hug Poli but she turned away. "Mom. Mavinor. I'll link up over the com when I can."

The parting was stiff, awkward. The moment Derrek and Tad stepped into the hovercraft, his son turned to him. "So what's the plan to get Tish?"

Derrek looked over his shoulder at his son. "I figured you know the family routine and could help me out with that."

Derrek smiled inwardly. Tad's words renewed his faith that despite the bad example Poli set, the boy had both brains and guts. Tish wouldn't be left behind. Derrek's daughter might have made her own decision but no seventeen-year-old girl should have to choose between living with her father or dying with her mother.

Tad tapped Derrek's arm to get his attention. "I'm wired into their personal links, home security, and computer systems."

Derrek laughed. "That will be useful." He looked at Tad again, his smile fading. "I assume you encrypted the illegal tap to cover your sorry ass?"

Tad looked at him warily. But when he issued no reprimand, the kid seemed to understand that Derrek simply wanted to ensure Tad was smart enough not to get caught. Derrek sighed. He suspected his son broke the rules on a regular basis, but then some rules needed breaking.

Tad didn't appear to be hurting anyone, so once again Derrek kept his opinion to himself. He couldn't help but admire Tad, yet he was reluctant to encourage him. Rule breaking needed to be tempered with judgment.

"Yes, sir. I'm careful." The boy took no offense. In fact, he seemed proud that his father understood the significance of the intel he offered.

Damned if the two of them didn't seem to fit together like two kernels off the same cob. And Derrek couldn't help letting some of his joy reflect in his grin. The kid smiled back, as friendly as a puppy and he ached to give him a hug.

During the ride back, Tad asked dozens of questions about flying and even took a turn at the controls. Derrek's happiness was tempered by all the years he'd missed—

Tad's first smile, his first toy, his first school project. Yet, at the same time, he was determined to enjoy every micronbit of time he had with his marvelous son.

AZSLA HAD SLEPT while Derrek was gone and after she'd awakened, she'd checked in with his science team. She'd even spoken to a brilliant engineer, Taylo Misa, and the two of them had tossed around a few ideas that might prevent the asteroid from striking Zor.

She'd watched Sauren coordinate a mass evacuation and realized that the seats on Derrek's spaceships would bring a premium price. With lives at stake, he could sell those spots for a fortune. Yet, he'd offered them to her and her crew for free. While his generosity heated her almost as much as that passionate kiss they'd shared, Azsla had lived long enough to know nothing came without a price.

When Derrek returned to his home, Azsla met them in the hovercraft's garage, expecting to meet his ex-wife and children. After having slept, the dark circles under Azsla's eyes were gone, and she felt more like her normal self. Although she dreaded meeting Poli, she was curious to meet Derrek's son and daughter. So she was surprised to see only Tad, but she didn't blurt out awkward questions.

Derrek stepped out of the hovercraft and introduced them. "Azsla, meet my son. Tad. Tad, this is Azsla. She's one of the first five slaves to escape Rama since the revolution. She came in just this week. Her status is a high-level secret."

The kid looked at her with awe. "Hi. I won't tell."

"Thanks."

"Do you work for my dad?" he asked.

Azsla didn't say anything, preferring to let Derrek clarify their relationship. Apparently Derrek had the same idea, wanting her to define their situation. The silence grew and soaked up tension.

"Damn." Tad looked from his father to her. "I stuck my foot in mud slime, didn't I? This awkward silence must mean that you like each other but haven't admitted it yet."

"Tad!" Derrek admonished. "You're going to have to work on keeping those kinds of perceptive observations to yourself."

"Okay."

Azsla chuckled. She couldn't help it. The kid was so insightful she'd have to watch her step around him. Then Tad shocked her by reaching over, placing his hand on her shoulder and saying, "I hated what the Firsts did to my father. It's not fair we didn't have a chance to know one another. But I'm glad he's not alone anymore."

Her throat tightened. This kid, this young son of Derrek's, had admitted his worry over his father with such refreshing honesty that she choked up. And Tad had been worrying over Derrek even while the kid had to be hurt and angry with his father for not being with him all these years. He might be young but he could obviously deal with complex emotions on a maturity level way beyond his age. If she ever had a kid, she wanted one like Tad.

And she wondered why it was so much easier to admit to herself that she could love the boy, but not the man?

Because she couldn't have Derrek.

Yet the more time she spent with him, the more she wanted to know him better. But she couldn't afford to soften.

She couldn't allow her emotions to overwhelm her training and her good sense. It mattered not that she had switched sides. If he ever knew what she truly was, he'd consider her a monster. Sweet *Vigo,* the man had been mindwiped by her people and lost his family because of Firsts.

When her emotions got out of hand, as they were right now, she still had to cage her *Quait.* As much as she wanted to fit in, the fact remained that when Derrek had kissed her, she'd had difficulty confining her *Quait.* Like a wild animal that had been caged too long, the desire to dominate had pounded for freedom. Just as she'd yearned to see, hear, feel, touch, and smell, she ached to use her *Quait.*

The theory that she would become accustomed to doing without her primal sixth sense, that she would become used to the lack of *Quait,* wasn't working. Instead, the opposite seemed true. The tighter she caged the beast, the more it wanted out. And yet, strangely, she was becoming even better at confining the beast.

As frustration at her situation ripped through her, she calmed herself with a breathing exercise. When she again paid attention to the conversation, Derrek and Tad were discussing how to get to Tish, if she'd fight them, and why she'd felt obligated to stay with her mother when she'd obviously wanted to come with them.

As they walked to Tad's room, Azsla allowed the conversation to flow around her and soothe her. It had been too long since she'd been part of a family. Too long since she'd belonged anywhere.

Now that she'd finally found a place she might be able to call home, an asteroid was about to crash into one of Zor's oceans. And if the flooding and tidal waves didn't immediately kill those left behind, the flying debris that exploded into space and re-entered would burn all remaining life. She thought of the children playing in the streets, the shopkeepers, the families that had settled on Zor, and felt terrible. Guilty that she would survive.

In space the quarters were bound to be tight, crowded. Hiding her abilities was going to become more difficult. Especially if she stayed around Derrek and Tad. The two of them evoked too much feeling. Feelings she couldn't afford to wallow in.

But she was going with them. To a place where no First would be welcomed, among people who would despise her if they learned of her abilities.

She worried about Derrek finding out about her secret, sensing he would not only be shocked, but feel as though she'd betrayed him—perhaps even worse than his first wife had done when she'd abandoned him.

Azsla didn't really have much choice. By not going back to work at the Space Ministry where the *tranqed* Firsts could contact her, she'd likely missed the last ride home to Rama. And staying behind on Zor was a death sentence.

So she would go to the asteroids with Derrek Archer.

The idea should have upset her more than it did. And she recognized not only that she was trapped, but that her feelings for Derrek had evolved to another level.

Defining that level was impossible, yet interesting. Intriguing.

16

Derrek and Azsla accompanied Tad to a room down the hall from the master bedroom. While Tad checked out the vidscreen, ate a few cookies with a glass of milk, and settled into his new surroundings, Derrek linked in to Sauren about the evacuation plans. As he'd expected, Sauren was doing everything that could be done and promised to let Derrek know if he required any help. Ships with employees and their families along with equipment were making a mass exodus. it was only a matter of time before someone noticed and word of Katadama got out.

Tad might be a bright, curious, adventuresome boy, but this was the first time he'd ever been away from home. Azsla tried to make him comfortable, but Derrek sensed that he was missing his family and trying not to show it. Derrek handed Tad a com link for personal use. "Call home whenever you like."

Tad sighed with relief. "You aren't worried that I'll tell them you're going back for Tish?"

"I'll trust you until you prove yourself untrustworthy." At Derrek's statement Azsla winced, making Derrek wonder if he'd stated his position too baldly, but Tad seemed to get it, his eyes shining brightly. Derrek squeezed his thin shoulder, determined to make the transition as easy for the kid as possible. When Tad offered him a happy grin, Derrek warmed in wonder. Did every parent think their offspring brilliant?

He hadn't known the kid but a few hours and he already knew he'd give up everything he had to keep Tad safe. His heart swelled with love until he felt as if it was too large to fit in his ribcage. Bursting with pride over this tiny replica of himself, he told himself to enjoy this moment together.

"Goodnight, son." He gave Tad a quick hug, ruffled his hair and smiled at him.

"Night, Dad." Tad seemed a bit embarrassed at the open display of affection but he lay on his pillow with a brave grin.

Derrek and Azsla strode from Tad's room and he took Azsla's hand. She glanced sideways at him. "Were you that inquisitive at his age?"

"I'm afraid not. I was a slave, working in a coal mine and too busy trying to stay alive to pursue normal boy things. However, I like to think that if I'd lived on Zor, I would have been just like him."

"He's a great kid."

Derrek sighed. "I wonder if he's so smart and perceptive, despite Poli's parenting or because of it."

"Maybe a little of both."

"Will you go back with me tomorrow to get Tish?"

Derrek asked. "I hate to make you party to a kidnapping, but I'm clueless when it comes to teenage girls. However, I'm not clueless when it comes to women," he teased, his voice tempered with interest.

Azsla arched an eyebrow. "Really?"

Derrek's tone turned husky. "You were wonderful today. Thank you."

"That's not a bad start," she offered. "A girl always likes to hear compliments."

From the time he'd gone after his kids, she hadn't interfered or offered an opinion except when asked. In comparison with Poli, who made things difficult, Azsla had eased the situation. Now he was seeing Azsla in another light, as not just a partner, not just a sexual fantasy, but as a real, living, and very attractive woman. A woman who just might be interested in him.

And no way was he letting this opportunity pass. Not after that kiss, or the vision. Since the moment he'd seen her, she'd fascinated and intrigued him and the attraction on his part had been fierce, immediate and held him in a tight grip of yearning. Azsla already felt like part of him, and he ached to make it so. "How about you come back to my room for a drink and I'll thank you properly?"

"Sounds good. A drink, maybe a few kisses. But that's it," she warned.

"Whatever you say." He heard her terms and would abide by them if she insisted. But he wouldn't be a red-blooded Zoran male if he didn't make a play for more. Derrek might not have had to go out of his way to seduce a woman for a very long time, since there was no shortage of females who put the moves on him, but he hadn't forgotten how to pursue a woman. "However, I'm not going to make it easy for you to leave tonight."

At his words, her eyes dilated. Her nostrils flared. "One drink."

"You haven't even tasted my offering yet." He linked his arm through hers and led her down the hall to his suite, thinking he'd been spending too much time working, too much time alone. "Did I ever tell you one of my many lines of work was bartending?"

"Back on Rama?"

He should his head. "On Zor. It was my first job."

"Did you make good tips?"

He grinned and opened the door to his suite. "Oh, yeah. Those healthy tips paid for *Beta One*'s repair. She was a retrofit of a crashed Raman vessel."

Derrek slipped behind the bar, thankful for his private area. He had room in here to sleep, work, or entertain; outside his quarters he had servants who would have been happy to cough up anything he requested, but he liked having Azsla to himself, mixing her a drink by his own hand. He watched as she kicked off her shoes and curled her elegant legs beneath her on the couch. He dimmed the lights, put on soft music, and handed her the beverage.

She held up the soft aqua concoction to the light. "What's in it?"

"Blue rum. A shot of tart *haola* berries, a twist of citrus, and a dash of mint stirred over cubed sweet meringue."

She sniffed, her nostrils wrinkling at the corners of her cute-shaped nose. "It smells delicious."

He enjoyed watching the way she savored the look of

the drink and the scent of it before tasting. He sat beside her and placed an arm over her shoulder. "Go ahead. Try it."

She didn't shrug out from beneath his arm. In fact, she almost snuggled into him. Azsla tilted the glass and sipped, her eyes watching his over the rim of her glass. "Mmm. For a drink this good, I would have left you a great tip."

He tried and failed not to stare at her glossy lips or the tip of her tongue as it swirled over her bottom lip for a second taste. Despite her earlier words, from the signals she was sending out, hot sparks that heated his core, she appeared inclined to stay for more than a drink.

"Glad you like it. Watch out for the—"

"Kick." She gave him a wry look. "Wow. That's powerful magic."

"Yeah, it's stronger than it looks."

"Like you."

She thought him strong? At the compliment his blood went south. "I do my best, but it's difficult to keep in shape in space. Taylo's working on artificial gravity but has yet to—"

Amusement lit her eyes. "I was talking about inner strength. Not many men have accomplished what you have and to think you made all this possible," she gestured to the luxurious suite, "and accomplished it after a mindwipe tells me you have hidden strengths."

She sipped some more, her expression thoughtful. "The kick is smooth, sleek, and surprisingly sneaky." She laid back her head onto his shoulder, her hair cascading over his arm, her scent invading his lungs.

He leaned into her hair and inhaled. "Sweet *Vigo,* you smell good and I'll bet you taste even better."

He held his breath, wondering if she'd retreat. But she didn't. She remained snuggled against him, her breath on his neck, her thigh nestled to his, her breast a light pressure against his chest. As much as he wanted to kiss her, he prolonged the moment. He'd found her in space, a refugee from the same world as he. And ever since that first moment, the connection between them seemed to be deepening.

Almost as if she were his fate. Her summer to his winter. Her light to his darkness. He hadn't really been living, only existing, until now. In the business world he was a success, but his personal life had been nonexistent. He'd feared to love again. Feared loving and losing.

But Azsla was changing and healing him, making him reach out for a full life again.

One kiss would not be enough. Just as one night would not be enough. One lifetime might not even be enough. He didn't understand why he was so certain she was his woman to love, or why it was his time to love, but he was absolutely convinced that Azsla belonged with him.

He leaned forward to kiss her and his com beeped. He ignored it and pressed his lips to hers. Her lips were supple, silky, soft. Best of all she welcomed him, sliding her arms around his neck, parting her lips.

The beeping grew louder.

"Should you get that?" she murmured.

"Yes." But he ignored the summons and kissed her again.

She leaned closer, her chest molding against his. "But suppose it's Tad or Tish?"

He glanced at the sender ID. "It's Sauren." He flicked on the speaker. "Can it wait?"

"Not really. Bad timing?"

"The worst."

"I'll give you an hour."

"Make it two."

"One and a half. Best I can do, boss man. I also sent a shuttle to pick up Cade, Shara, and their children. He'll meet us on Alpha One."

"Thanks." Derrek clicked off the link and tugged her across his lap until his arm curved around her back. "Now where was I?"

"You were trying to convince me that you're a good kisser," she practically purred as she slid her hands up the sides of his head and combed her fingers through his hair.

"I am a good kisser," he insisted.

"Uh-huh."

"In fact, I'm so good that you aren't leaving after just one kiss."

"Is that a threat?" Her eyes glowed as she tugged his lips to hers.

"No threats. A promise." He shifted one arm under her legs and stood, lifting her as easily as if there were no gravity. Then he carried her to the bed. "We might as well be comfortable."

"I only agreed to—"

He didn't want to hear her put restraints on him, so he cut off her words with a kiss as he took her to the bed.

Somehow, he managed to carry her, then place her on the goose-down mattress without once releasing her delicious mouth.

But the moment her back touched the mattress, she bolted upright, placed her feet on the floor. "I just said one drink."

To stop her from leaving, he placed a hand on her tense shoulder. For one moment he saw anxiety in her eyes. And her reaction confused him, set alarm signals ringing. Back on Rama, slaves didn't have a lot of joy in their lives. Sex was one of the primary ways slaves had to take the edge off their misery. It was how they connected with one another. Sex was casual and easy. Her saying no, didn't make sense. And his suspicion was too close to the surface to control the hard edge in his voice. "What's the big deal?"

At his tone, she flinched but kept her cool. "I thought being a free woman gave me a choice."

"But isn't it your choice to enjoy? Why are you resisting me when you want me?" He expected her to deny wanting him. She didn't, confusing him even more.

She stared at him, her face blank. When she didn't come up with an answer, he recognized her indecision. Releasing her shoulder, he gave her a micronbit of opportunity to go. But she stayed, and he leaned in again, very lightly nudged her nose with his, until their lips met again.

Then she was pulling him down. Close. Closer. Kissing him deeply. Frantically. She might have been holding back before . . . but no longer.

As if reading his desires, she started to unfasten his

shirt buttons. Then impatient, she yanked it off. Buttons popped. He didn't mind. How could he when she was running her fingers over his flesh, teasing his shoulders with her bare palms? And all the while her tongue teased his, urged him to take. Take. Take.

Derrek never moved this fast. He liked the warm-up before lovemaking. He enjoyed long, slow kisses and tender words. He liked looking forward to what they could offer one another. But with Azsla he needed to know her all at once. Craved to taste and touch and smell her delicious scent.

He nibbled a path down her slender neck and enjoyed the way she arched into him, pleased that she hadn't stopped his progress after the one kiss she'd previously said she'd allow. He kissed a trail over her collar bone and dipped toward her breasts.

He couldn't recall ever wanting a woman so much. Right now he couldn't even recall any others. Azsla filled his senses and his thoughts. And all of it was good. "God, you're beautiful."

She breathed out a sigh, her hands busy roving over his back, urging him faster. "You aren't so bad yourself. Except . . ."

"Except?" He lifted his head and nuzzled her ear.

"You're taking way too long to remove my clothes."

He chuckled. "Always happy to oblige." He really wanted to slow down. To tease off her clothes, item by item. But when he lifted the hem of her blouse, she took matters into her own hands and shrugged out of her shirt, her bra, her slacks and panties, tossing them all onto the floor until she was totally open for him to touch wherever he wished.

Then she turned onto her side and frowned. "Your turn."

"Let me look at you." All golden skin, except for her tight pink nipples, she was feminine, her muscles emphasizing her neat shape, her clean lines, her awesome curves. "Your body pleases me. You please me."

She tugged at the closure of his pants. "My turn."

"Are you always so impatient?"

"Actually I can't remember since it's been so long."

"Then let me make this good for you." He placed his hand over hers and stopped her, surprised to find her fingers trembling. Pleased that she wanted so badly, that she wanted *him* so badly, his pulse raced.

She drew in a deep breath through her nose and released it slowly as if to regain a measure of control. But he didn't want her in control. There would be none of that. He wanted her wild and needy and melting.

He ached to give and then give more. Yet, the waiting would increase her female pleasure. "I want our first time to be memorable."

"Fine." She didn't sound happy, and, obviously reluctant, she relaxed her hand on his slacks, but he could tell it was difficult for her by the fierce pulse in her neck. And how she lay back stiff, watchful. "Do what you wish."

Ever so gently, he brushed the pads of his fingertips over her nipples. "Tell me how this feels."

"Fine."

He was beginning to hate the word "fine." Something wasn't quite right. She was trembling, clearly wanting him. Was she so annoyed that he'd slowed them down that she couldn't let it go? "Tell me what you like best," he murmured.

"I want more kisses."

"Then more kisses you shall have." He kissed the hollow of her hips, her flat stomach, her breasts. And his hands caressed the insides of her slender thighs, strong thighs. She threaded her hands through his hair, tugged his head up to her breasts, parted her legs to give his hands roving room.

And he kept thinking. Too fast. Much too fast.

Why was she rushing him? Did she fear the pleasure he could give? But if that was the case, why wasn't she backing away instead of urging him on?

With her scent in his lungs, thinking became difficult. His blood roared through his veins, heating him. Tension gathered in his loins and he ached with the blood hammering, a pulsating drum beat that made it almost impossible to ignore his own rhythm of need. "I love the feel of your skin. Your softness over firm flesh reminds me that although you look sweet enough to eat, you're strong."

"Must you talk?"

He smiled at her eagerness. "I like strong. I didn't know that until I met you," he crooned, "but a strong woman is a sexy woman and you are very, very sexy."

She guided his mouth to her breast and as he took her nipple into his mouth, she moaned. "You feel too good."

"No such thing."

"Way too good."

"Uh-huh."

"I mean it, Derrek. You can't keep doing that. My head is spinning."

"Uh-huh."

"Sweet *Vigo*." She panted. "Where . . . did . . . you learn to do . . . ah . . . that with your tongue?"

"Wait until I lick and swirl it between your legs."

"If you . . . I'll melt."

"Exactly." And he followed through, tasted her core, and as he pleasured her, she almost arched off the bed with a muffled scream.

But he didn't stop. He couldn't. Especially since he planned to push her into another spasm of pleasure and then another.

"Please. I need you inside me now."

"Okay." He started to roll from her to remove his slacks. But her fingers beat him to the job and suddenly were tearing at him, frantic, needy, wanting.

Within moments he'd settled his hips between her legs and was about to plunge into her heat. Suddenly she rolled, taking him with her. He ended up on his back with her on top. She tossed her hair over her shoulders, grinned and straddled him.

Heat encased him. Her heat. So hot, so warm. She was riding him, pumping. "Slow down, sugar. Or, I'll . . . be done before we . . ."

She gyrated faster, grinding into him, paying no attention to his words.

"Come on, babe. Easy now." He reached for her hips

to slow her rhythm. But his arms didn't obey his mind. He couldn't move them from his sides.

Sweet *Vigo*. What the frip?

He was immobilized.

Paralyzed.

Helpless.

And she was lifting up and down, pounding, the pressure, taking, giving, until his thoughts spun wildly. She was riding him, totally in control.

And he couldn't move. Couldn't caress her. Couldn't pump his hips and meet her rhythm.

His blood roared. He was on the verge of explosion, waiting for her to ride him harder, longer.

He craved to buck his hips, to touch her breasts. But his mind no longer managed his body.

Oh. God. She was dominating him.

Usurping his will.

On Rama he'd spent years submitting to Firsts. He understood exactly what was happening to him, recognized the loss of muscle control, the helplessness. But how could this be happening on Zor? With Azsla?

Holy hell. If his mind wasn't spinning. If his body wasn't hot, hard and heavy with need, he would have realized sooner that no one could do what she did—except a First.

Reaching down, she cupped his balls, massaged, tugged, teased, the sensations exquisite. So his mind might be shriveling in horror, but his body was pumping to go. And he fired into her. Exploded in a tremendous wave of physical pleasure.

Even as he orgasmed, his mind screamed. Why had she lied to him? She was a First. The enemy.

And God help him, he'd believed he'd loved her.

DERREK'S LAST SPASM had taken Azsla over the edge once more and as the lingering pleasure ebbed and she could once again think, she realized how stupid she'd been. When Derrek had asked her why she was resisting, she hadn't had an answer that wouldn't blow her cover. And because she did like him, she had sent out signals she *was* interested. So she hadn't had one good reason to refuse.

Talk about mistakes. She'd just made the biggest one of her life. In the scheme of things, if her mistake had been classified as a tidal wave, it would have flooded a continent. If it had been a volcanic explosion, the eruption would have shot ash halfway around the planet. And if it had been a Zoran quake, it would have ripped the planet in two.

She'd been an idiot. No smarter than a slave after a mindwipe. And the damage couldn't be undone.

She'd let him seduce her, arrogantly believing she could control her *Quait*. And when she'd felt the beast slipping free of the chains, she'd stupidly hurried him instead of stopping him.

But by then it had been too late. The multiple orgasms he'd given her hadn't allowed her to maintain control of her abilities and she'd lost it. Usurped his will.

She had to be the biggest ignoramus of all time. He'd been so giving. And in return she'd dominated him.

As she drew huge gasps into her lungs, she didn't want to open her eyes, didn't want to face the disgust she knew would be on his face.

He shook her off him, like a dog shedding water, with no care or caution. She rolled across the bed, feeling fury radiating off his flesh, burning her like a thousand red-hot knife blades.

She risked a look, then wished she hadn't. Muscles bunched, eyes narrowed, lips stern, he yanked on his pants, folded his arms across his chest. And said nothing.

His accusing stare said it all.

"I'm so sorry."

"Sorry you lied to me or sorry I found out?" He kept his tone low and soft, reminding her of an angry *jibiqe* before it bit the head off its prey.

"Both." She was shaking inside, sick about what had happened, what she had ruined. He was making her feel even worse, looking at her as if he'd stepped in slug slime and now had to scrape the offal from his boots.

Knowing she should try to explain, she raised her chin, looked into his bleak eyes, and wrapped a sheet around her. "I didn't mean to . . . lose control."

"You're a Raman spy, aren't you?"

"*Was* a spy. I committed treason when I saved my crew and warned you about the *tranqed* Firsts."

"More likely it was your way to gain our trust."

"It was both," she admitted, done with the lies but sick at what she'd messed up . . . a new start, with a man she admired. She should never have gotten so cocky that she thought she could control herself during the most intimate of pleasures. But she'd found him appealing, charming and attractive, and it had been so long since she'd mated. "But I chose to stay with you . . . instead of going back home."

"No doubt your superiors wanted to know what we were up to."

"They did." He had that part right. "But I never reported my findings."

"At the Space Ministry?"

"Yes. I was trained, among other things, as a weapons specialist. I was sent to see if Zor had the ability to retaliate after a Raman attack. At the time, I didn't know Rama planned to wipe out the entire planet by lobbing an asteroid at it."

"The Ramans changed that asteroid's orbit? Why should I believe you?"

"Because I'm telling the truth." She ignored his sarcastic glare, the dark brooding scowl, the intimidating set of his shoulders. A cold chunk of ice lodged in her gut and fear shivered down her spine. For the moment, she managed to ignore the tears that ached for release. She would not break down . . . at least not in front of him. "I might be able to help you stop that asteroid."

"How?" He spat the word like a bullet, as if he hoped to shoot her dead.

"You haven't been listening. I'm a weapons specialist. That means if you intend to blow it up, I might be able to rig a tactonic bomb if you can find me some tactonic material. Since no slaves were allowed to study tactonic physics, you need me. So if you're thinking of leaving me behind, you'd best reconsider."

"I don't need a fripping First on my ship, around my children or in my life."

"You aren't the only one who has suffered, you know. My parents were murdered during the slave rebellion that you're so proud of. I saw them die. I saw them torn limb from limb and I vowed that no other child would ever have to watch such a terrible thing."

His eyes didn't soften. He didn't give any encouragement other than to remain there speaking to her and firing his questions. "The Corps trained you to hide your *Quait*?" he asked, his tone cynical.

"I'm not perfect at it."

"You lose control . . . ?"

"When I'm emotional."

He glared at her. "If you believe staying on Zor means dying, you'll be very emotional. I suppose I can't stop you from coming onto my ship. Not with your *Quait* handy."

"Actually you can stop me any time you wish. All you have to do . . ."

"Yes?"

She straightened her back. "Is kill me."

He rolled his eyes. "And how can I kill you if you control my will?"

"Am I controlling you now?" she pointed out the obvious.

"If I tried to kill you, you'd become emotional. Your self-defense mechanism would go into overdrive."

"There are long distance weapons. Poisons. Rifles. In your ship, you could easily trap me in an airlock and eject me. I am alone. I have to sleep. No one watches my back. You'll have plenty of opportunities to kill me, should you wish to do so."

"Damn, you're cold."

Actually, she was freezing and hurt by his insult. Just because she could point out facts didn't mean that she had no feelings. But she pushed that down, too, knowing she couldn't function if she allowed any more pain to seep in.

"I didn't ask to be like I am. I was born with *Quait,* just as you were born with muscles that can violate those weaker than you. You lose your balance and your muscles flex. If you get angry and swing your fist, you have the ability to injure others. That's what happens to me with my *Quait.*"

"It's not the same thing."

"No, it's not." Sadness swept her into a melancholy moment. All her life she'd been fighting for a cause. To ensure other children didn't lose their parents. To ensure there would be no more rebellions. To ensure there would be peace. Instead, while earning the wrath of her own people as well as Derrek's, she'd found herself at ground zero of a killer asteroid. Perhaps she should have stayed with her own kind, but it was too late. She'd made her choice. Weary of fighting, she still wished for peace. For a shot at a normal life. Was that so much to ask for?

His eyes burned into hers. "You stand for everything I hate."

"I know."

"You can't even promise you won't use your *Quait* again, can you?"

She shrugged. "This is my first slip-up in many years. But no, I can no more guarantee I won't use my *Quait* than you can guarantee you won't use your muscles to protect yourself when threatened."

"You weren't being threatened."

"I'm trying to make you understand how instinctive it is for me to use my *Quait*. For all I know, it might happen every time I make love—not that I expect you to test that theory."

"That's for damn sure."

She'd expected his blunt words, his withdrawal, and his anger, but wasn't prepared for the deep pain that felt like she'd been hammered from the inside out, or the cold ball of nausea in her gut that almost made her wish he'd never found her sleeping pod. Because sleeping away eternity was better than suffering through his loathing.

If it was in her power she would undo her error. She would have kissed him once and left. But going back was impossible. She'd have to live or die with the choice she'd made.

And she had only herself to blame.

17

⊛

Derrek's com link beeped and he appreciated the interruption that gave him an excuse to cut out of his conversation with Azsla without looking like a coward. From the moment he'd realized what Azsla was, a First, he'd broken into a cold sweat. "Sauren, I'm on the way."

"Wait a sec." Azsla spoke almost hesitantly.

"Or what?" He spun around and glared at her, ignoring that every word he spoke seemed to hit her like a punch to the jaw. Ignoring the stark hurt in her eyes, ignoring the disappointment and pain, he couldn't hold back all his rage. She'd misled him from the first moment they'd met and now he needed to get away from her before he exploded with her betrayal, a self-indulgence he couldn't afford, not when the backlash of her retaliation was an unknown factor. Somehow he managed to keep his tone civil, albeit curt. "You going to stop me?"

"No one can stop you from your own stupidity."

How dare she talk to him like that? Apparently, now that her secret was out, she didn't have to be courteous and he'd finally see the real Azsla, who was no doubt arrogant, cold, and self-serving.

He placed his hands on his hips to keep himself from slamming his fist into a wall. "My stupidity?"

"Yes." She dropped the sheet, picked up her clothes

and dressed. "Or do you have so many tactonic experts on Zor that you can refuse my help?"

Help? She'd probably use those tactonics to speed the weapon on its journey.

But she was right about one thing. They had no tactonic experts on Zor. The Ramans had made certain their slaves never had access to powerful weapons research. And once the slaves escaped to Zor, they'd focused primarily on building a home, not fighting their former masters. Another mistake.

"How do I know you won't be trying to destroy us?" he asked, curious to hear how she would defend herself. He should have known better.

She didn't defend, she attacked. "How do I know you won't shoot me the first chance you get?" she countered in a tight tone as she buttoned her blouse.

He spun on his heel. "Do whatever you wish." He obviously couldn't stop her. But should he try? The idea hammered him like a hundred-ton weight. As angry as he was, he was no cold-blooded killer. Deep down he suspected in the heat of the moment he could kill to defend the lives of friends or family, but to plan her murder and carry it out while she slept? The idea sickened him.

Besides, a tiny part of him wanted to believe her. He didn't just have a vision. Now they'd mated. He knew her taste, her scent, her touch. And damn, they'd been good together. Every cell in him ached to believe her. Could she possibly be telling the truth? Was he a fool for considering that she might actually be willing to help them?

Did he want to believe her for personal reasons?

Yes.

But that didn't mean—

Oh, for pity's sake. The voice in his head was back. *I am not just a voice. My name is Pepko.*

Find someone else to annoy.

The alien ignored him. *Go with your heart.*

Get out of my head.

I can't right now. At least admit you love her.

Not any more, I don't, and I don't have time for you.

The alien's telepathic thought hardened. *Make time, or there will be nothing else. Only death.*

Are you threatening me? Derrek asked.

Nothing so mundane. I'm stating facts. You need the woman to stop Katadama from colliding with Zor.

Derrek had a flipping alien in his head and a traitorous First in his bed. He had to be out of his mind. If he was the only person Zor had to save the planet from disaster, then *Vigo* help them all.

Frustration sizzled through Derrek's veins. *If you're so all-knowing, why don't you do something to help?*

I am helping.

"How?" he asked aloud.

"Did you say something?" Azsla asked as she walked beside him.

He shook his head.

You need to stop questioning your feelings. The woman has the knowledge you seek.

She's the enemy. She steals free will. She is a damn First.

So what?

You don't know what she's capable of.
Neither do you.
I've seen plenty. She's just like the rest of them.
That's where you're wrong. You need her.

The alien repeated Azsla's own words. Furious that it seemed as if they were ganging up on him, Derrek strode down the hall and descended with Azsla to his control room, where Sauren and Taylo Misa, linked in by vidscreen, waited for him.

Too energized with anger to take the seat at the head of the conference table, Derrek stood behind his chair, his hands gripping the cushioned back. Azsla didn't look at him and quietly took a seat opposite Sauren.

Sauren nodded to Azsla. "Your crew left for the safety of the asteroid mines a few micronbits ago."

"Thank you," she said to Sauren, and then to Derrek, "Thank you both."

She appeared to have genuine feelings for her crew, mere slaves, and Derrek wondered if it was an act. Then Sauren turned to him. "Cade and his family are safely onboard a ship and heading out of the system."

"The others?" Derrek asked.

"We can save all our people and their families, but not too many others. We simply can't get enough craft here in time."

"What's Katadama's status?" Derrek leaned into the vidscreen, praying the brilliant engineer, Taylo, had a solution, and would distract him from Azsla, who seemed to have drawn a shield around herself. An impenetrable shield so tight that he couldn't venture to guess her thoughts. With her face stoic, her eyes narrowed and detached, she'd shut down on him, icing him out.

Taylo, a strapping man with dark blue eyes and a neatly trimmed mustache and goatee stared at Derrek through the monitor from across the solar system. "We have several choices. Our astronomers have now used sensors to render a more precise picture. After Katadama swings around the sun, it'll be on a dead collision course with Zor."

The prediction was no surprise, especially if the Ramans had planned to take out the entire planet. But Derrek finally admitted to himself that he'd been hoping Katadama would turn on its own and that action would be unnecessary. His last grasp for an easy solution dissolved, leaving him with the bitter truth. They needed to find a way to change the asteroid's course or blow it up. If they failed, hundreds of thousands of people, *his people,* would perish.

Derrek's fingers dug into the seat back, probably leaving permanent indentations. "What are our options?"

"I've considered how to deal with the problem from several angles," Taylo said. "If we'd had more time, we could have focused solar collectors to concentrate sunlight on the asteroid and vaporize enough material to alter its course. But it could take years for sunlight to redirect Katadama and we don't have years."

"Let's limit this discussion to practical options." Derrek understood Taylo liked to be thorough, but he'd never gotten the man to understand he didn't need to hear discarded theories. He liked the pertinent details boiled down to their essence.

"Sorry, boss man. There aren't any practical solutions," Sauren said, his face grim.

"The limited advance notice is an absolutely critical factor," Taylo continued. "We don't have time to paint the asteroid or cover it with glass beads—both approaches would make the surface more reflective and increase the thermal reactive forces produced when sunlight radiates off the surface."

Frustrated, Derrek really didn't want to hear more theories that wouldn't work. "Please, don't tell me what we can't do."

As usual, Taylo ignored his suggestion. If the man weren't so brilliant, Derrek wouldn't put up with what amounted to insubordination. However, he considered himself lucky to employ Taylo at any price. And if part of that price was listening to discounted theories, he'd suffer through it.

Taylo was in lecture mode. "If we had time to launch a probe to study the structure of the incoming Katadama, our task would be easier. Because not all asteroids are solid. Some are porous, others collections of rock, gravel, and dust held loosely together by gravity."

"Since we don't have time for leisurely study, how about we blow it up?" Derrek asked.

"A small bomb won't work and although I've found a pure source of tactonium, we don't have anyone with knowledge of tactonics."

"But suppose we did?" he pressed, refusing to look at Azsla, refusing to believe she was their only hope.

"A tactonic bomb's not a great solution, either. If Katadama is brittle, an explosion would likely generate many pieces, which could multiply the threat by creating smaller but still lethal rocks."

"What else is possible?" Derrek asked.

"There's the dock and push approach, where a spaceship lands on the asteroid and uses thrusters to push it in another direction, but we don't have a way to dock a ship to the asteroid."

Derrek understood the problem as soon as Taylo explained. Every ship needed a dock to lock it in place. With no planetary gravity, if one turned on the propulsion system, the ship would just fly away. Katadama would keep on its original path.

"If Katadama isn't brittle, could we blow it up?" Azsla asked, ignoring Derrek's scowl.

He would have thought she'd have the sense to read his mood, to realize anything she said would not be welcome. He could hardly bear to look at her. Azsla's actions could not only destroy *him,* she was one of the enemy seeking to obliterate this world.

If she hadn't been a First, he'd have barred her from this meeting. But he didn't have the power to stop her from doing whatever she wished. If he tried, she could invade his mind, steal his will and then he'd be totally helpless. At least for the moment, she was allowing him the appearance of autonomy. Although what he was planning to do, he didn't know.

"Assuming we had tactonium and someone with the skill to make it blow, then maybe we could save Zor. I'll spare you the scientific details," Taylo said, "but understand from what we know and guess about the asteroid's mass, density, size, porosity and composition, our only chance might be to send down an emergency pod, drill into the crust, plant the tactonic bomb and blow it up before Katadama reaches a critical distance from Zor. That way the debris won't strike our atmosphere."

"But?" Derrek prodded, sensing there was more.

"The discussion is pointless. We don't have an expert in tactonics—"

"Yes. We do. The only question is whether we can trust her." Derrek speared Azsla with a look.

"What's that supposed to mean?" Sauren asked, looking from one to the other.

Azsla raised a supercilious eyebrow, clearly expecting Derrek to speak. Before he could do so, a tech ran into the room with a message. "Boss man, I hate to interrupt, but you need to see this."

"What?" Derrek held out his hand for the hand-held vidscreen and hit play. A news broadcast was coming in live from the capital. Derrek backed the broadcast up to the beginning and a newscaster, her face flushed and her voice frightened, reported, "Raman Firsts have invaded Zor, landing in the suburb of Latonia." Sweet *Vigo,* his ex-wife and Tish lived in Latonia and his tight gut told him it wasn't a coincidence. Immediately, he tried to open a link to Tish. Got nothing. Tried another to Poli. Again nothing. The news report continued. "Troops are storming the streets and Zorans are being rounded up. Shots have been heard and the body count is rumored to be in the hundreds. Tomar appears to be the First in charge of the invasion and—"

"Tomar?" His aggression here was no coincidence.

That same First had battled with him over Azsla and her crew. If he'd known then she was a First, he would gladly have sent her to Tomar. But now Tomar was making their confrontation personal. "Sauren, how long until we must leave Zor?"

"The asteroid's mass is difficult to determine. It seems to be made up of a material with which we are unfamiliar. Taylo says to be safe we should leave within a day. Two at most."

"I should have plenty of time to go get Tish. Get my hovercraft fueled and loaded." Derrek strode to a cabinet, unlocked it, and started piling ammunition on the conference room table. Tish. He should have forced her to accompany him yesterday and now it might be too late. She was still young. Innocent. Little more than a child. But if those soldiers got a hold of her . . . Firsts loved to play with young girls her age. If they saw her curvy body and . . . he had to swallow hard to stop the churning acid rising into his throat. He couldn't do her any good if he couldn't squash his fear.

Easy.

Tish needed him thinking on all drives. She needed him calm. Careful. Logical. But how could he think straight when every cell in his body was urging him to run out the door, floor the hovercraft, and swoop down for a rescue?

"Where are you going?" Sauren asked.

"After my daughter." He didn't know how but he was going to find her and bring her to safety. "Tish is right in the middle of a war."

Sauren placed a hand on Derrek's shoulder. "Did it ever occur to you that's exactly what Tomar wants?"

"What do you mean?"

"Maybe he attacked Latonia because he expects you to come in and try to stop him."

"Then he better be ready, because I'm not going to disappoint him."

"Think. If Katadama can be stopped, you're the most likely candidate to do it. What better way to ensure the asteroid crashes into Zor than to kidnap your daughter and capture or kill you?"

"You think I'm walking into a trap?" Derrek asked.

"Yes." Azsla, Sauren, and Taylo all answered at once.

Derrek hesitated, his heart pounding too fast. He hadn't thought ahead. How could he when he was so worried about Tish? But that was probably exactly what Tomar wanted. To keep Derrek off balance. Fearing for his daughter's life. "I can't leave her. I won't."

"No one is saying you should," Azsla muttered. "But to go charging in is foolish."

"If I wait, she could die." If she wasn't dead already, but he didn't say it aloud, as if it might jinx her.

"Let's not jump to conclusions." Sauren flipped on a satellite feed and zoomed in on Poli, Mavinor, and Tish's home. "So far, they look safe enough."

"Pull back," Derrek ordered, wanting to scout out the general neighborhood, a series of homes clustered together amid a wooded area.

"There." Sauren focused on a burning house, zoomed closer and picked up several soldiers moving door to door, as if searching for someone in particular. Someone tried to run out the back, then fell as if shot, and didn't move again.

Derrek hoisted the gun onto his shoulder. "They'll reach Tish in less than an hour. Time enough for me to hover in, rescue them and—"

"You'll be shot down." Azsla frowned at him. "A sneak attack on foot would stand a better chance of success. Land in that clearing," she pointed. "Use that track of trees for cover and when you hit the street, blend with the populace so they won't target you as anyone special."

Derrek scowled at her. She was making sense. And yet, how could he trust one word that came out of those beautiful lying lips?

He looked to Sauren and his friend nodded. Finally Derrek agreed. "All right. I'll go in by hovercraft and finish on foot."

Azsla touched his arm, then jerked back as if realizing what she'd done. "Do you have a secret entrance out of here? Can you drive a less conspicuous hovercraft than the one you brought me here in?" Azsla threw questions at him and his suspicions grew. Why would she ask about secret entrances unless she was still spying?

The cooler head of Sauren put the pieces together. "You think if they went after Tish to get to Derrek that they're watching her house?"

"Tomar's smart. Tricky. If he's set a trap, going in covertly might be the only chance of succeeding."

"You sound like you admire him," Derrek accused, then recalled the First had tried to kill her while she was on board *Beta Five*. "Did Tomar know you were on my ship when he fired at us?"

"He's military. I trained in the Corps. And the two forces don't always communicate."

"A slave was in the Corps?" Sauren's eyes flashed to Azsla, full of questions.

"We don't have time for this." Derrek cut off any response she might make and spoke directly to Sauren. "When Tad wakes up, don't let him out of the building and explain to him what's happened."

"I'm going with you." Sauren picked up a weapon from the stash.

"No. I am." Azsla pushed back from the table and stood, her gaze defiant. "I know the enemy better than you do and have learned ways to counter their pursuit."

Sauren looked from one to the other and waited for Derrek to make up his mind and issue instructions. Since he didn't know she was a First and could possibly counter Derrek falling prey to another First's *Quait,* no wonder he looked confused. But Derrek understood all too well, and he didn't like it that he needed her.

"Would you please excuse us?" Derrek said to Sauren and Taylo. After his friend left and the vidscreen went dark, he faced down Azsla. "You can protect me from another First's *Quait*?"

She bit her lower lip, then raised her chin. "Yes."

"But you have to place me under your will?"

"Yes. For your own protection." She raised her hands, palms up, in entreaty. "Your decision."

His daughter's life might depend on this decision. But he didn't have to make it now. The idea of volunteering to yield his will to hers violated everything he was and stood for. Free will.

And she didn't have to ask. She could take away his autonomy any time she wished. The fact that she had said it was his decision only gave him the appearance of control, didn't it? Because any time she disagreed, she could overpower him. That's why his scalp had broken into a cold sweat, that's why when he pushed down his rage, he felt numb. Or as if he'd been clubbed on the head. The true horror of what she could so easily do would overwhelm him if he stopped and thought about it for very long.

Perhaps if he'd never been a slave, never had his mindwiped, he might accept her explanation. But he was . . . made from his experiences. Bad experiences. Life-altering ones. And acted accordingly to defend himself.

So he didn't trust her. Would never trust her.

Yet, he couldn't afford to throw her offer back in her face, either. Because, one, he might need her help to rescue Tish. And two, if he left Azsla behind and he annoyed her by his decision, she might stop him from leaving, too. Derrek had to place Tish's safety before his own preference—which was never to see Azsla again. To ship her back to her people. To forget their lovemaking . . . hah. What had occurred between them in the bedroom really scalded and burned straight to his core. He'd mated with a flipping First.

And now he needed her help.

"All right." He opened his link to Sauren. "Azsla's with me. Have you heard how Taylo's coming with the tactonium?"

"He says he has it under control."

"Good." The best thing about wealth was that it allowed him to work with top-notch people he trusted. If anyone could figure out how to make a tactonium bomb it was Taylo. "Keep us informed of the invasion status. If you reach Poli or Tish link us up. And try to worm more intel out of Laurie and tap into . . ." He could no longer speak freely in front of Azsla. And she didn't need to know his connections. "Tap into any other sources we have."

"Understood."

Sauren was a good man. He could take care of the entire operation without detailed instructions, allowing Derrek to put his efforts into rescuing his daughter. If only he could forget Azsla's First status.

But trying not to think about her *Quait* was like trying not to think about the asteroid bearing down on them. Both were threatening. Potentially lethal. And needed to be handled with the utmost care for fear of explosion.

Although Azsla had kept herself together with very minor hitches, he figured her behavior since he'd learned the truth was a closer look at her real character. He should have realized that no underfirst had such a healthy, toned body. He should have known the Ramans wouldn't allow anyone to escape. It had happened once during the revolution, but then they'd shut down the portal and it wouldn't happen again. Not in a hundred years. Not in a thousand or ten thousand. Firsts hadn't attained and maintained their positions of superiority without intelligence, wariness, and ruthlessness.

Derrek picked up several belts of ammunition and said nothing when Azsla did the same and then reached for a weapon. Although his instinct was to knock it from her hand, he knew better. Slavery had taught him to think first, and to act very cautiously.

She had no difficulty keeping pace with his long strides through the basement to an underground entrance. While he hated showing her even one escape route, he had others. And it made sense to take every precaution. He could rebuild the house if necessary. He couldn't ever replace Tish.

They exited the tunnel into a large parking facility. Bypassing his elegant and recognizable hovercraft for a less showy vehicle, he lifted the canopy and slid into the seat of a model he used when his was in the shop. "Hang on," he warned her, and gunned the engine.

The hovercraft might appear ordinary on the outside, but inside she was all high-tech engine, with motors tuned by the best mechanics in the business. The machine roared to life and he floored it, skidding through the garage door opening, knowing every second might count.

In the darkness, the engine purred. Azsla didn't chatter, having the good sense not to irritate him further and allow him to adjust to her status—if such a thing was possible.

The night seemed peaceful until he gained altitude and spied orange flames shooting into the black sky in the Latonia District. They hadn't much time. The fire would spread quickly in the dry air and he doubted emergency vehicles came out during an invasion. Now it was a toss-up if the flames or the soldiers would harm his daughter first. While he was supposed to land in secret in the woods, he now wondered if they trekked in, if Tish's bedroom would be up in a blaze before he reached it.

Putting off a final landing spot decision until later, he focused on taking advantage of every wind current. Sensing he could pick up a tail wind, he adjusted his vector, while maintaining sight of the burning city.

While he flew, Azsla programmed the route into the nav system. "We need to find the clearing to land and . . ." She looked over her shoulder. "We've picked up a tail. Three hovercrafts."

"Tomar's people?"

She shook her head. "I don't think so. Looks like Zoran military. We need to lose them."

"Yeah." He still hadn't decided if Laurie was a conspirator or a *tranqed* First, but either way he was dangerous. Derrek couldn't land in secret with three military hovercrafts lighting him up. Swerving right around a skyscraper, then left over a lake, he went for altitude and less drag. Luckily this early in the morning darkness, he didn't have to worry about traffic.

With his superior speed, they soon appeared to have the sky to themselves as they left the military far behind.

But the radar in front of Azsla sent warning beeps. "We've lost the Zorans, but I'm spotting lots of hovercraft heading right at us."

He figured those who got out of the city were fleeing and again tried to open a link to his ex or Tish, but they still didn't answer. "I'm taking us higher. Do Firsts have jamming abilities?"

"I don't know. I was only privy to the equipment necessary to my mission's success. But if your com unit is down, I'd have to say yes. Can you still reach Sauren?"

Derrek tried, but couldn't complete that link. Damn it. "We're on our own."

Derrek fumed. He had the government militia behind him and Tomar before him, and a woman at his back whom he didn't trust. Not exactly the ideal combat situation. But he would make do. Just like always.

He prayed Mavinor had had the sense to make Tish and Poli flee at the very first hint of trouble. But he'd experienced just yesterday how stubborn Poli and his daughter could be. Then again, they weren't half as stubborn as the woman with him.

Azsla had inserted herself into this mission and he didn't know why. Even if she acted the perfect partner and watched his back, he still wouldn't trust her. Because she might simply be waiting to report, to inform the others of his plans. Yet he had to risk taking her with him. Taylo could build the tactonium bomb to blow up the asteroid, but he required Azsla's technical expertise on key details.

If she helped, he'd suspect her of treachery. Ditto if she didn't. Talk about a lose–lose situation.

But with Tish's life at risk, Derrek did his best to relegate his bitterness toward Azsla to the back of his mind. When a house up ahead burst into flames, he veered around it and when he looked back, he saw no sign of Laurie's military guys.

"They've dropped off the radar," Azsla confirmed.

Now all he had to do was outwit the invading Firsts, save his daughter, escape from Zor, and stop a killer asteroid.

One thing at a time.

18

❂

Azsla might not have insisted on coming along if she'd known he intended to drive like a maniac. Derrek didn't appear to notice the vibrations rocking up through the seat hard enough to rattle her teeth. In her opinion they were lucky the hovercraft didn't shake apart, but he seemed unfazed by the fast turns, the hard angles, the tight corners that had her gripping the dash to avoid sliding out of her seat.

Despite her fear of crashing into a building or tree, she divided her attention between the radar, the flames, and the hovercraft heading their way. Most of the radar pings were from vehicles either too slow or too small to provide anything more than transportation to fleeing civilians. But some of the faster ships sported light armor and cannon blasters. She kept a close eye on one particular formation that never veered from a path straight at them.

"How much farther?" she shouted at Derrek, to be heard over the noise of the rushing air and the screaming engines.

"I'd like to get closer."

Right now they were flying over dense forest, the few clearings that might have been landing sites passing by blurrily. If he flew for much longer, they'd hit housing structures, grass parks, and pavement, losing the natural cover of the trees that would hide their landing. "We should set down now. If you wait any longer we'll lose a shot at taking cover on the ground."

"I see the perfect landing spot. Hang on tight. We're ditching hard."

He didn't exaggerate. Hovercrafts usually glided, but their owners didn't cut off the engines before the craft stopped moving. Oh . . . God. What was he thinking?

Her stomach swooped. And they fell.

They landed in a bone-jarring crunch on what she assumed was a grassy plain, but then water sprayed out from under them. He'd found some kind of shallow lake and the fluid cushioned them or they might not have remained conscious. As it was, every muscle in her body throbbed and she was certain she'd have an assortment of bruises. Her head ached from a bang. Wiping a trickle of blood away from her eye, she applied pressure to plug the wound and stop the bleeding.

Derrek had a jagged cut on one arm and a raw patch of skin on the other, where he'd skinned it on the door. After popping the canopy, he jumped overboard, sloshing up to his thighs in lake water clogged with brown and greenish vines.

"Stay there," he ordered, his tone quiet. "I'll beach the hovercraft in those trees."

"Why didn't you just drive onto the bank?" she asked,

grumpy that he'd shut down the engine before they'd landed for no damn reason that she could discern.

"Couldn't. The engine died."

She swallowed down a swear word. "If that had happened when we'd been higher in the air, we'd be dead." Under the circumstances, the only reason they were still alive was due to his piloting skills.

"If we'd been higher, we could have glided down," he disagreed, not taking credit for saving them. "The problem was we were halfway between flight and landing, and it's very odd, but we don't have time to investigate. You okay?" he asked.

"What do you mean it's odd?" She jumped out of the craft and helped push it beneath the trees.

"The failure rate isn't high on any hovercraft. And I pay top-notch mechanics good credit to keep my machines in the best shape." He frowned, looked at her with suspicion. "Sabotage is always a possibility."

"I was with you the entire time."

"I was driving."

And therefore not paying attention to her. "Don't you dare accuse me." She scowled back at him, already irritated that whenever something went wrong, he was automatically going to blame her. "I wouldn't have gotten in a machine or sabotaged a machine I was flying in, would I?"

"Probably not," he admitted, albeit grudgingly.

She snorted and rolled her eyes at the sky, letting him know with her body language that she thought his idea ludicrous. Using her annoyance to energize her walk through the thick vines and eager to be out of the water, she finally tromped into mud, then onto solid ground and peered up at the sky. "They'll find the hovercraft without much effort."

He grinned. "I hope so." Then he picked up a tree branch and bashed in the hull.

"What are you doing?"

He put a wrench to the engine, loosened a hose and some bolts until fuel leaked. Then he pulled wires out and connected them with a vicious twist.

She had to give it to Derrek, he thought fast on his feet. "Suppose someone innocent finds . . . your trap?"

"Why would a slave fleeing a Raman invasion stop to examine a craft with a hole so obviously unfixable in the side? Although they are desperate, they couldn't hope to use it for escape—"

"Point taken." She really had to start thinking differently. These people were terrified of Firsts, horrified by the possibility of becoming slaves again. And no Zoran would stop to examine the hovercraft . . . not with their freedom at stake.

She slung the blaster over her shoulder, hitched the ammo to her belt, and headed southwest over uneven ground, taking the lead, but Derrek soon caught up until they strode side by side. They skirted around clumps of thick underbrush and kept to the tall trees to avoid being spotted from the air.

Despite the rough terrain, Derrek set a fast pace with an easy stride that she suspected he could maintain for hours. When she'd left Rama, she'd been in good physical shape, too. However, the journey in space and the lack of gravity with little exercise had weakened her muscles, and she hadn't quite recovered her full stamina.

But she refused to slow him down. If she had to take twice as many strides as he did with his longer legs, she wouldn't complain. Because what she had to do next . . . was going to be difficult for them both. And she didn't know how to approach the delicate subject.

They zigzagged for cover through an open field and then into another wooded area, following either animal paths or human ones. Moonlight helped light the way, allowing her to consider the problem. She needed to put Derrek under her *Quait*. If she didn't, it would leave him vulnerable to another First's will. That was the way *Quait* worked. Whoever grabbed a slave first had the best hold.

But she couldn't let Tomar capture him.

Do it.

Sweet Vigo. Not yet, she argued with her own conscience.

Coward.

She was a coward. She knew she was. Derrek was already furious with her. One wrong move, like making a suggestion that he submit to her will and he'd . . . She couldn't imagine how he'd react to her suggestion, but it wouldn't be good. Yet, if she said nothing, both he and his daughter could die.

Derrek pulled up on the edge of the woods and peered into a neighborhood filled with burning houses. In the wind, flames jumped from rooftop to rooftop, burning, destroying. Wind gusts had been blowing the smoke in the opposite direction, but now it whirled back on itself and the reek sickened her. After just a few whiffs, she almost gagged at the odor of burning flesh and wished she could close her ears to the sounds of distant screams, cries of horror, and shouts of rage that blended with the crackle of houses burning. Many roofs had already caved, the famished flames moving on with nightmarish speed. Smoke blanketed the night sky, hellish sparks warning them that their clothing or hair could catch fire if they moved downwind of the flames.

They'd stumbled from the woods straight into the hostile invasion. Dead bodies littered the lawns. Armed soldiers stalked the sidewalks and stray canines barked, then fled in terror.

She tugged Derrek back. "Don't let them see you."

"We have to get to Tish."

"How far away do you think she is?" Azsla asked, pleased when Derrek moved back into the trees.

"Another three blocks. Maybe four."

"We have to sneak around the edges."

"Can't." He pointed to soldiers striding through the smoke. "The fire's spreading and they look like an advance unit. Tomar may be right behind them."

"What do you suggest?" she asked.

"We run for it."

She shook her head. "That's not going to—"

Derrek started to move out. "We have no choice. I must—"

"Hey, you." A First raised his weapon at Derrek.

Oh . . . God.

In a split second he'd be cannon fried. Or under the First's *Quait*. Both options were unacceptable. Terrifying.

Azsia raised her weapon and pointed it at Derrek's back. At the same time she placed him under her *Quait*. She had no time to think about how betrayed he'd feel or if he'd ever forgive her. She had to do this. Pretend she was one of them. "I'm taking him to Tomar," she said with authority.

"How did you get here? Who are you?" The First peered at her through the smoke.

At his questions, her heart skidded in her chest. She couldn't blow this. She had to act as independent and superior as a First. With a First, the best defense was usually to take an authoritative and offensive posture. "You never saw me. Understood?"

"You're Corps, aren't you?" he asked, his eyes still wary but he lowered his blaster and backed away to let them pass. "You're going the wrong way. Tomar is behind us."

"Not any more, he isn't." She bluffed, hoping he'd believe she possessed superior knowledge and praying he'd take the bait. Again, she nudged Derrek with her gun, making him walk in front of her with her *Quait*. And then she strode right past the First, who'd passed on orders to his squad to let them through.

Azsla knew Derrek must be seething, but she didn't risk explaining. Instead, she screamed at him. "Move, slave. The longer you make Tomar wait, the worse it will be for you. I said run." And she made Derrek run, then sprinted after him, praying she was running them in the right direction, worried that the guard she'd intimidated might yet call Tomar on his com unit and learn she should be stopped.

Any second she expected to feel a blast between her shoulder blades. But apparently, like most soldiers, he didn't want to bother his superiors. They sprinted around burning houses without being fired on, and finally they left the troops behind.

The smoke cleared until they could draw some much needed fresh oxygen into their starved lungs. She relaxed her *Quait* and wearily braced for Derrek's outrage.

But he didn't shout. He didn't even give her a stiff and angry attitude. Instead he eyed her with something that looked like respect.

Perhaps smoke had gotten into her eyes? Or she was misreading him?

"If there wasn't a chance of being spotted by a First, I'd hug you right now."

Hug her? He wasn't acting at all like she'd expected. Her mouth gaped open foolishly and she snapped it shut. "You aren't upset that I deliberately used my *Quait*. That I usurped your will?"

His next words appeared to come with difficulty, but he spoke clearly. "I . . . thank you. You probably saved my life back there."

"Our lives," she corrected him, relieved that he'd understood why she'd had to use her *Quait*. "Tomar considers me a traitor."

Soldiers broke through the smoke behind them. She pointed the gun at him, continuing their charade, using her *Quait* very lightly this time and allowing him the option to speak. "Let's go. How much farther?"

"Another block, I think."

"You don't know?"

"I was only here one time. And between the flames and the smoke, it's hard to tell one house from the next."

"If we find them, what's the plan to get out of here?" she asked. Because no way were Poli or Mavinor up for even a five-micronbit run. She doubted the woman even owned a pair of running shoes.

"We steal a hovercraft and fly out."

"Have you seen one?"

"I'm looking."

"Is the com still down?" she asked.

"Yes."

Behind them they heard a giant explosion. It could have been anything, a fuel depot, a military vessel crashing, but she suspected Derrek's hovercraft had just exploded, taking out a few Firsts. Hoping that might distract the Ramans and buy them a little time, they hurried down the block.

Flames hadn't reached this series of homes, but the place had an abandoned look. Anyone who could get out had probably already left. If people remained, they were holed up behind locked doors. But with the flames spreading this way, fleeing was the only intelligent option.

"There it is." Derrek pointed and raced up to the front door of the house they'd visited yesterday. He pounded with his fist. "It's Derrek. Let me in."

"Go away," Poli yelled. "You'll lead the Ramans straight to us."

Obviously in no mood to negotiate, Derrek kicked in the door. They entered to find Tish in sleeping clothes and running barefooted down the stairs, her eyes wide with fear. Mavinor stood in his night shirt, blinking as if he'd just awakened.

Poli in a night dress brandished a broom at Derrek. "What the hell do you think you're doing?"

"I've come to take Tish to safety. I'll take you too, but we need to leave now. Firsts are two blocks away and they are burning down everything in sight."

"You broke my front door." Eyes wide in shock and fear, Poli seemed totally incapable of facing the danger.

"I'll buy you a new door." Derrek lunged up the stairs to Tish and hugged her. "Sweetie, I know you love your mom, but—"

"I know. She's not good in emergencies," Tish answered and handed her father the knife she'd been holding. "I can't leave her. Please. Don't make me leave her."

Azsla's heart went out to Tish. She recalled how much she'd missed her own mother and in spite of Poli's ridiculous attitude, she didn't want Tish to go through the grief she'd suffered after her parents' deaths.

"We're all going," Derrek told his daughter. "Now go put on clothes and some flat shoes."

Azsla could see Derrek was torn between seeing that Tish dressed and convincing his wife to accompany them. Since Azsla didn't want anything to do with Poli, she volunteered, "I'll help Tish get ready." She hurried up the stairs and left Derrek to deal with his shallow ex-wife.

The girl looked from her father to her mother, who seemed to have frozen in place. Then her frightened gaze moved on to stare out the open front door at the approaching flames.

"It's going to be all right." Azsla placed a hand on her shoulder and helped guide her back upstairs. "Come on, Tish. We have to hurry."

Tish seemed to break out of her trance, spun around and took the stairs two at a time. Behind them, Azsla could hear Poli and Derrek arguing and knew she'd gotten the better end of the deal. When they reached Tish's room, she was shocked to see that the girl already had a bag packed, clothes laid out.

Tish dressed and tied on flat, comfortable-looking shoes, her practicality surprising Azsla, but Tad had said she was smart. While she obviously loved fashion, she had a pragmatic side she must have gotten from her father.

Tish picked up her bag, then stepped back into the hall. She opened a closet and lifted out a backpack. "I put some stuff for Mom in here."

Azsla slipped the backpack over her shoulder. "That was good thinking. Does she have any shoes—"

"—that she can walk in?" Tish sighed. "I'm afraid not."

As Azsla turned in the dark hallway, out of the corner of her eye, she saw the slightest movement, a dark mass among gray shadows. Without hesitation, she thrust Tish behind her. There was no time to go for her sheathed knife or her personal blaster or the weapon Derrek had given her. She barely had time to block the *tranqed* First soldier's knife hand slamming toward her throat. Fear and adrenaline made her fast and strong.

She slammed her attacker's wrist and his knife flew across the floor. Counterstriking, her hand rigid, she employed her stiff fingers like a knife, ramming them straight into a soft spot in the throat. Her opponent gurgled and died.

"Oh . . . God. Oh, my God. Oh God." Tish gasped.

Azsla spun around. "You okay?"

"Is he dead?"

"I hope so." Azsla realized she sounded harsh and that the girl was in shock. She gentled her voice. "He was trying to kill us. I had no choice."

Tish got herself together. Fast. "Don't tell Mom. She'll freak."

"All right. We keep this between us." Azsla agreed, not wanting to mention it to Derrek either. As she checked the other rooms, but found no one else inside, her thoughts raced. Derrek already considered her a monstrosity due to her *Quait*. She didn't need him to know how easily she could kill with her bare hands. But danger was closer than they'd thought. They had to leave soon. While Tomar may have sent in only one man as part of the advance, more would be on the way.

Tish and Azsla returned downstairs and saw that Mavinor had dressed, too. Poli clung to his arm, tears running down her face. "I'm not leaving."

"We don't have time for this." Derrek looked at Azsla. "Convince her for me."

Sweet *Vigo*. While Tomar and Derrek knew of her First status, no one else here did. Was Derrek asking her to use her *Quait* on Poli? Or did he simply mean for Azsla to convince her like one woman to another?

"Poli. The flames are spreading. If you stay here, you'll burn up."

"Think of the hideous scars," Tish added, looking out the window as if fearing another immediate attack.

Poli frowned at her. "You think I'm vain."

"Oh, for the love of *Vigo*." Derrek picked up Poli, tossed her over his shoulder and headed out the front door. The woman screamed and pounded her fists on Derrek's back. Mavinor and Tish followed and Azsla brought up the rear, glad Poli didn't know about the attack upstairs, even more pleased that she hadn't revealed her status to Poli, but wondering if Derrek was now disappointed in her.

Soldiers down the street began a door-to-door search. To avoid them, Derrek headed around the back of the house and toward the tree line. "You have a hovercraft in the shed?"

Tish shook her head. "It's in the shop for a tune-up."

Of course it was. That would have been too easy. When they'd reached the trees behind the house and had gone a few hundred yards, Derrek placed Poli back on her feet. "Either you walk with us . . . or you stay here and burn. If Tish didn't love you, I wouldn't have forced you to come this far. But now the choice is yours."

Poli sniffled and flung herself into Mavinor's arms. "Don't let him talk to me like that."

Mavinor and Derrek exchanged a long look as Mavinor patted her shoulder. "Now, dear. I know you're upset, but we're alive."

"I can't leave all my beautiful things behind."

Azsla slung the backpack full of Poli's belongings

at her feet. "Tish packed for you." She didn't want to be seen carrying the bag in case she had to pretend these people were her prisoners again. Firsts didn't lug, tote, or carry since they had slaves to work for them.

"Mom. Please. I'm scared and I need you to go with us," Tish said in a little girl voice.

Azsla shot her a look of surprise and Tish winked at her. The teenager was conning her mom. And from the look on Poli's face, it was actually working. Azsla's respect for Tish increased. She'd been attacked, witnessed a killing, been forced from her home and the neighborhood was burning around them, yet except for the short burst of panic back at the house, she'd kept her cool, acting far more mature than her mother.

Poli lifted her chin. "Of course you need me."

"This way." Derrek headed deeper into the woods. "I want to circle back and try to move upwind of those flames."

"How far . . ." Poli started to ask but then her voice trailed off as if she didn't want to know.

Azsla hefted the gun and again Derrek took point. With three people between them, they didn't speak to one another. However, when Azsla picked up the sound of faint screams, Derrek headed them farther away from the battle, deeper into the forest, until there was only the faint tinge of smoke, no sign of flames, and the scent of pine surrounding them.

Although the Zorans had colonized the planet, they lived close to one another in tiny communities around large cities. Between towns there remained lots of open land that had yet to be cultivated or developed. Several different kinds of wild animals could be dangerous in this terrain, especially mountain cats and wolves. As the population increased, if Katadama didn't crash into Zor, the empty parts would eventually disappear and the wildlife would move farther from civilization.

For the moment, the woods appeared untamed and nonthreatening, untouched by human hand, and she hoped it would remain that way. Azsla suspected the woodland creatures were spooked by the fire and at least they had the good sense to flee. As birds perched in the trees suddenly flew straight up, she wished she could do the same. Trudging over land was slow and dangerous. But right now, they had no other choice.

Derrek tried his com link again, and Azsla expected it to remain dead. But they must have walked out of jamming range. Sauren's voice came through clear and loud. "Derrek. I've just now picked up your GPS."

"Ramans have a jamming device. We're on foot. Can you send a hovercraft to extract us?"

"Pres Laurie has grounded all hovercraft for the duration of the invasion."

Azsla fervently wished she knew if the President of Zor was a *tranqed* First. If he was, wouldn't he have evacuated? Or had he stayed behind to help Tomar search for her and Derrek?

"What's his rationale for that stupidity?" Derrek asked, his voice tight.

"He claims if the only hovercrafts flying are Raman, then he can shoot them down."

"That's ridiculous. Whoever heard of giving up the high ground? Or the sky?"

"You want us to try and get through to you anyway?" Sauren asked, and Azsla marveled at how these people would break rules for one another, even defying their own leaders. Perhaps since they'd lived under tyranny, they didn't respect leadership—no matter whose it was. Or perhaps they valued freedom so highly they only grudgingly gave it up.

"Stay put. But if you can intercept any Raman communications that would be helpful."

"Sorry. They must have a new encryption program."

Derrek changed the subject. "How's Tad?"

"Still sleeping. Hopefully you'll be back before he wakes up."

"That's not likely, so fill him in. I want to keep this conversation short—in case Tomar can track us through the link."

"Understood."

Derrek cut the link. They were still on their own—with no help coming. Azsla wouldn't have minded the trek if Poli would just stop whining. Azsla had always liked the woods. Learning survival skills had been a favorite part of her training and when she picked up the sound of trickling water, she suggested they stop for a rest and to drink.

Poli had long since emptied the thermos Tish had packed back at the house. She leaned against a tree and folded her arms. "That water isn't clean."

"We have never found harmful organisms in running water," Mavinor told her, sipping from the creek's bank. "Poli, please come and drink something. It's fine."

"I only drink filtered."

Whatever. Azsla kneeled and sipped from the creek, appreciating the cool liquid. The only problem with Poli not drinking was that her body would shut down that much sooner and then they'd have to carry her.

Tish, bless her, had confiscated the empty thermos her mother had tossed away. She secretly filled it with water, then pretended to find it in her pack. "Here, Mom. I brought you another filtered from home," the kid lied without batting an eyelash.

Azsla had to turn away to hide her grin as Poli finally conceded to drink. One problem solved. But another followed. A bigger problem.

In the distance Azsla picked up the sound of barking canines. At first, it didn't worry her, but as the barks increased in volume she looked at Derrek. "Those dogs might be tracking us."

"That's the dumbest thing I've ever heard," Poli said.

Azsla ignored her. "They're following our scent. We need to walk in the creek."

"Water will ruin my shoes," Poli wailed.

Azsla was ready to leave her behind. Or shoot her. But even she was shocked when gentle, quiet Mavinor slapped her across the cheek. "Get in the water, Poli. We can't carry you. And I'm not losing you."

"You hit me." Poli reached up in shock and touched her cheek. "You slapped me."

"Into the water. Now."

"But—"

He raised his hand as if to slap her again.

"All right. I'm going. I'm going. There's no need to be a bully."

They trudged in the creek for an hour. Several times Azsla moved ahead and left the creek, then returned in her own footsteps to the water, hoping to lay down a false scent for the dogs.

Thankfully Poli had stopped whining. Probably because she was too short of breath to speak. Whatever the reason, Azsla was grateful.

But from the volume, she could tell the dogs were drawing closer. Finally Azsla moved ahead to speak quietly to Derrek. "I'm going back and I'll meet up with you later."

"Why would you—?"

"To set a trap. They're gaining on us."

"I'll go with you."

She shook her head. "Your daughter needs you."

"I'll be fine," Tish spoke up. "Mom, Mavinor, and I will keep walking and you can catch up." She thrust an empty canteen into his hands. "Take it."

Derrek took the canteen but looked torn between going with Azsla or staying with the others. "Tish, you and Mavinor keep your Mom moving in this direction at a steady pace." He pointed to the night sky. "See that star. The one that has a reddish cast? Follow it as it moves across the sky. That should keep you upwind of the fires. Don't go too fast or Poli will tire."

"I'm right here. I can hear you."

Tish gave Derrek a hug. And oddly, Derrek's daughter squeezed Azsla, too. "Be careful."

19

Derrek and Azsla headed back down the stream. Automatically, he refilled the canteen, knowing they might not always have readily available water to drink. But his mind wandered as he appreciated the way Azsla moved through the water—as easily as if she trod on land. What was it about her that captivated him? He not only couldn't stop staring, he marveled at her strength and stamina. She hadn't once complained about her icy wet feet or Poli's ridiculous behavior and slow pace. Any woman as tough as Azsla would have surprised him, but her behavior, a First's behavior, shocked him right down to his soul.

He'd once seen a First suffer a paper cut, blame a slave for the sharp edge and order the slave to be whipped. He'd seen a slave's hand lopped off because of a rough spot on a shoe that caused a blister. Firsts did not tolerate pain. Any pain. Those who suffered at all made certain their slaves paid. And while he was shocked by Azsla's patience and unruffled tolerance of the harsh environment, he was even more curious about the hard thump he'd heard back at the house, and this was his first opportunity to ask about it.

"When you and Tish were upstairs, did either of you trip and fall?"

She rubbed her temple as if she were stalling. "Why do you ask?"

"I heard an odd sound. It must have been you and Tish packing."

"It wasn't that." She hesitated and every muscle in her body seemed to draw tight. She straightened her back, raised her chin and squared her shoulders as if bracing for battle or preparing for insults or anger. Her reaction was very un-Firstlike because most Firsts never got to her stage of aggravation. They'd have vented long before now.

She spoke quietly, with more than a hint of frustration in her tone. "You won't like what I'm going to tell you, but I'm done lying."

"What happened upstairs? Did you and Tish get into it?"

At his accusation her eyes filled with pain, then hardened and went flat. "One of Tomar's soldiers broke into the house."

"What?" Of all the scenarios running through his head, that wasn't one of them. He'd been expecting her to say she'd bullied Tish into dressing or had been rude or had said something inappropriate. But they'd been attacked. "Why didn't you call for help?"

"There wasn't time. Afterwards, Tish asked me to remain quiet so as not to upset her mother."

"You didn't think it pertinent to tell me about a First in the house? Suppose he'd called for help or attacked—"

"I killed him." Azsla spoke flatly, with absolutely no intonation.

Oddly, he believed her and yet as he thought back on the incident, he recalled no sounds of blaster fire to back up her statement. "I didn't hear any shots."

She spoke softly, as if she had to force out every word. "I didn't use my blaster."

"Your bare hands?" He looked in shock at her slender hands with her delicate wrists and figured she must have quite a bit of skill that she hadn't wanted to admit to, then raised his gaze to meet hers. "The Corps trained you in weapons and for combat?"

She just nodded.

He'd always known that Firsts had secret squads of elite soldiers. But he'd never imagined they were made up of both men and women. He'd figured they killed with their *Quait*. But obviously she'd gone through a much more difficult life than he'd suspected. "Every First I've ever known was spoiled, self-indulgent, egotistical."

"And you are insulting me because . . . ?"

"You are not like the other Firsts I have known."

She cocked her head and raised a brow. "Every person's unique."

Unique? That had to be the understatement of the century. Azsla was like no First he'd ever met or heard of, and he realized her independent nature had likely isolated her from her own kind in ways too many to quantify. She might actually fit in here better than on Rama.

"I would have bet a salt-studded asteroid that no First could have as much self-control as you do. You must have spent months training."

"Years."

He asked the question that had been gnawing at his guts. Was she for real? "So are you simply pretending to be different from your kind? Or are you different deep down?"

She released a long sigh. "Are you asking if my behavior is an act?"

"Yes."

"And if I'm acting, then why should you believe me?"

She had a point. If she was acting, she'd continue to do so. The fact that she'd pointed it out was either a smart move to throw him off . . . or genuine frustration that he didn't believe her. But then, who would? She was full of mysteries and secrets and yet, she was certainly the most interesting woman he'd ever met.

Expression stoic, Azsla looked over her shoulder and threaded her way around a few rocks. Most people would have stepped on them, but that might have left a track of mud, and he realized her survival skills dirtside surpassed his own.

Of one thing he was certain, she was proud of her skills, of what she'd learned. He could see it in her body language. And yet, just for a *micronbit,* he'd seen vulnerability in her eyes, too.

She spoke softly now, but he didn't miss the *diamondite* thread that revealed her resolute core. "Since you won't believe my words, perhaps you should judge me by my actions."

That wouldn't necessarily work. She could very well appear to be on his side right up until the moment she turned and betrayed them all. Not that he was going to admit that doubt out loud.

Still, he felt as if he should attempt to justify his position. "Look, on Alpha One I have a pet feline. I expect her to purr when I feed her because that's what cats do. And from my experience Firsts—"

"Are narcissistic sons of bitches with no feelings for anyone except themselves."

"Now you get it."

"So does every cat purr when you pet it?"

He really was trying to understand her. "So why *are* you different? What kind of First learns survival skills, killing skills? You can issue mental blows to force other slaves to obey your every whim, including dirty bloodletting and killing, so why would you work to learn all the physical stuff?"

"What? You aren't going to accuse me of enjoying the kill with my bare hands?" Her sarcasm was fierce, biting, and revealed her hurt. "I told you. During the rebellion slaves murdered my parents. I didn't want other kids to lose—"

"You sure it wasn't that *you* sought revenge?"

"Maybe. What difference does it make?" she snapped.

"I just wondered if you'd admit it." He placed a hand on her shoulder and she stopped walking and turned. "But you couldn't go through with the revenge, could you? All those years of training made you . . . independent. More like us."

She ripped away from him and marched through the creek, shoulders tense. "I am nothing like you."

Here he was coming to believe they might actually have a chance, and she was throwing his understanding back in his face. He swatted a bug, missed, and followed her. "How are you so different?"

"Because every micronbit of every day, I have to weigh what I want against what is right. You don't understand *Quait* from my side. It's like learning to put candy in your mouth, but ignoring the sweetness. It's like opening your eyes and disregarding color. I have to keep my *Quait* bottled inside."

"You make it sound . . . painful."

"It's more exhausting than hurtful. Because using my *Quait* is as natural to me as breathing." Her voice dropped and her tone was raw. "I hadn't used my power in over a decade . . . not until we made love. The pleasure you gave me made it impossible to keep the *Quait* inside."

She'd told him that before but he hadn't understood, not really. He'd been too angry to think through what she'd tried to tell him. "You can't make love without dominating?"

She didn't answer, but the look of anguish in her eyes did it for her. Her shoulders trembled. "And now I've thrown in my lot with slaves who will despise me if they learn what I am. My future . . . doesn't look real good right now."

Damn. He'd been so caught up in the idea that she'd betrayed him with her lies and secrets, he'd never once considered things from her point of view. She'd left Firsts like herself, with the power to enslave others, and the only home she knew, to throw in her lot with former slaves who would despise her sixth sense—just because she had it—even if she used it only for good or in private. She'd never fit in anywhere.

"I'm sorry."

She turned, saw his face and her eyes narrowed. "I don't want your flipping pity."

He had no answer. So he said nothing. Just watched her twist and turn through the water, her strong legs eating up the distance even as she was careful not to dislodge a loose branch or overturn a rock. And her hurt tore at him. He didn't want her feelings to get to him. But that didn't matter. From the moment he'd seen her, he'd wanted her, and he'd never understood his reaction, or what about her made him drop his normal barriers.

Since the Corps had trained her from early childhood, she'd no doubt mastered many skills. But until now, he'd never considered what that training had done to her, how it had molded her. He suspected she was a loner by necessity more than by nature and recalled how easily she'd befriended Tish and Tad. How her crew had admired her, enough for one of them to give his life for her. How she worked well in a team.

Apparently, the enforced loneliness and the repression of her *Quait* had helped form her character, her independent personality. Her courage to abandon the known world of Rama for the uncertainty of Zor held an appeal he couldn't deny.

She stopped before a log they'd climbed over earlier and eyed it for a few moments. "Here. We'll build the trap between these branches, where our pursuers will cross over like we did."

"What can I do?" He didn't hesitate to make the offer.

For now, she was helping. That didn't mean she'd always be on his side, but for now it was enough. Had to be enough.

"Make sure to keep your feet in the water so you don't leave any tracks," she instructed, "and try not to splash the rocks. The water may not dry before they arrive and we want no evidence of our passing by."

With her knife, she cut branches of a thickness to match his thumb's diameter, slicing so low at their roots that no one would notice she'd disturbed the plants. Then she prepared a trap, setting the sharp branches into the mud, below the water line. Finally, she sliced the back of a thick branch, making a tempting handhold. The dogs would leap safely past the handhold, but whoever climbed over the log would likely grab the branch, and already weakened, it would snap, causing the person to teeter and fall onto her sharpened stakes.

"That won't kill anyone," he whispered.

She gave him a chastising look. "Killing is not my intent. An injury will serve our purposes better. They'll have to call for help or carry out the injured person or split up. Any of those scenarios will delay them and better our chances, even if they only slow to look for additional traps."

The sound of dogs barking increased in volume. "You done?" he asked, wondering how she felt about taking the life of Tomar's man. If she was upset, she hid it well. But then again, she was good at hiding things.

"All set. Let's go back."

Derrek admitted to himself that her behavior, sometimes so hard and determined, floored him. Yet he couldn't help being glad that she had killed the First—without her skill, his daughter might be a hostage. Or dead.

But he knew firsthand that Firsts were disdainful, haughty, cruel, and useless. Worst of all, they thought of themselves before all others. And he abhorred them with every atom of his being.

He couldn't trust Azsla. Sure, she appeared to be helping him now. But he simply could not bring himself to believe that she didn't have an ulterior motive. That eventually she would betray them all.

And fearing that ultimate betrayal, he sought to protect himself against relying on her, or relaxing, or even so much as letting down his guard. It was that simple. He had choices here.

Derrek and Azsla caught up to the others much sooner than he'd expected. Apparently after they left, Poli had decided she'd walked far enough and needed a rest. Azsla simply kept walking ahead and left Derrek to deal with them. He didn't blame her for putting as much distance between herself and his ex as she could.

"We need to keep going," Derrek told them. "Rest time is over."

"Oh, stop." Poli wearily raised her head. "We aren't employees who have to jump at your every command."

"Do whatever you wish." Derrek held out his hand to Tish and helped her to her feet.

"That's all you ever wanted from me—your children," Poli accused, her voice bitter.

The tension, the responsibility slid from over Derrek's shoulders. He'd had enough of Poli himself. He'd never been able to understand why he'd spent so many years feeling that he'd let her down. And quite frankly he now wondered if he would have stayed with her—if he hadn't suffered through the mindwipe. Surely she must have changed since he'd been attracted to her, because he now saw very little in her to like.

He'd assumed that she'd found him unworthy. He'd also assumed that the ensuing years must have changed her, but perhaps she wasn't so changed after all. Maybe there had been conflict in their marriage that his brother hadn't known about.

And he was done arguing. "Poli, you and Mavinor do as you like. But Tish is coming with me."

Mavinor didn't give Poli time to respond. He tugged her to her feet. "We're all going."

Derrek kept Tish by his side and strode to Azsla, who had waited for them. If she'd overheard the conversation, she didn't show it. Instead she guided them around another trap. This time she'd rigged a neck-high vine to trip and release a stone that would swing from an overhead branch into the unlucky victim—again missing the dogs.

"That's way clever," Tish said, clearly impressed. "Could you teach me how to do that?"

"Great." Poli glared at Azsla. "Teach her how to kill people. That will get her far in life."

"Better she should learn to pick out the most fashionable pair of shoes?" Derrek muttered.

Azsla raised her hand over her mouth to hide her grin.

Poli sighed. "Well, I can see you know one hell of a lot about raising a teenage girl."

Derrek let the subject drop. He found he no longer cared what Poli thought. The woman was vain, empty-headed, and her beauty left him cold. He needed to put the past behind him. And he found that he'd be glad to. From now on he intended to look toward the future, or what remained of it after Katadama struck Zor. While he would make certain his children were safe, most Zorans would die. But those that made it to the asteroids would go on—and he intended to be part of the rebuilding efforts.

And after they recovered, they would prepare better for the next attack—this time knowing the Ramans would keep returning until every one of their former slaves was dead or recaptured. The effort the Ramans had put into ruining this planet for all Zorans was well planned, vicious, and telling. Hopefully Taylo and Azsla's plan to make a tactonium bomb to blow up the asteroid was coming along on schedule.

Meanwhile, he would do what needed to be done to survive. If that meant he had to keep his friends close and his enemy closer, that's exactly what he would do.

They made good time as the stream bottom changed from larger rocks and mud to smaller stones and sand. No doubt thanks to Azsla's traps, they seemed to be staying ahead of the Ramans—at least as far as he could tell from the sounds of barking dogs.

When Azsla stopped and put her finger to her lips, he listened hard. But he only picked up the breeze ruffling the leaves, a bird's caw, the incessant hum of flying insects, and a *frong* chirping.

When she drew her blaster, he followed suit. What

danger had she picked up ahead? Moving forward, he shielded Tish with his body and strained to see through the dense forest brush.

Azsla motioned for them to get down. And that's when he heard the distant roar of a hovercraft. While they crouched still as rocks beneath the trees, the chances of them being spotted from the air weren't that high. But their pursuers were starting to gain on them, the barking growing in volume.

Yet, if they advanced, the searchers in the air might spot them. Azsla motioned them to one side of the creek and pointed to a cave. "Let's go," she whispered.

"What about our tracks?" he whispered back.

"Can't be helped. If that hovercraft spots us, we've got big trouble. It's got cannon blasters."

They hurried to the cave and she tossed a few rocks into it to make sure no living animals occupied it before leading them inside. He had to duck his head at the entrance and around a bend, but then the cave widened. Tall enough and wide enough to house them all, the cave had been used before. Judging by the skeletal remains, animals had brought their prey here for a meal.

"I'm going to cover our tracks and scout ahead," Azsla told them. "Meanwhile, you can rest."

"She's leaving us here to die," Poli wailed.

Azsla didn't answer, but slipped from the cave. Derrek went with her. She broke off a tree branch and smoothed it across the ground, covering up a heel print in one spot, a full print in another.

"What about our scent?" he asked.

Azsla shooed him back toward the cave. "See if Poli

or Tish packed any perfume or hair spray. I'll use the scents to confuse the dogs."

Derrek did as she asked and returned with *pepperite*. "Will this work?"

Azsla grinned. "It's perfect. Thanks. Did Tish happen to say why she packed it?"

"Sniffing it helps prevent a cold."

"An herbal remedy. Hmm. I'll have to try sometime." Azsla carefully took the *pepperite*, opened the container and shook a few flakes into her open palm. Then she dusted the bits over their tracks, backing down to the water. There she used a more liberal portion, no doubt trying to hide the telltale scent where they'd left the water. Then careful to save the rest, she twisted the cap shut and handed it back.

"Come on. Let's go steal us a hovercraft."

He hurried to catch up as she headed upstream. "Did I hear you right? You want to steal a Raman hovercraft?"

"Yeah. We let them see you in a clearing. While they're coming after you, I steal the hovercraft."

"And you fly away and leave me there to die." He fisted his hands on his hips, challenging her.

"Are you going to hold me personally accountable for every bad thing a First ever did to you?"

"That wouldn't be fair."

"Life ain't fair, boss man." She used the affectionate nickname his employees had given him, wondering if he'd realized that in this new world his wealth gave him privileges that most could only dream about. And while he tried to be a fair boss, he knew most of his people worked as hard as he did for just a tiny portion of the rewards.

"You'd be better bait," he finally said. "Once they get a look at you, they'll—"

"Shoot me on sight?"

"Want you for their very own."

"Yeah, their very own prisoner." She trudged through the creek. "But your idea to switch roles won't work. I'm afraid you'll have to be the bait."

"Why?"

"Because I know how to fly a Raman hovercraft."

"I'm a fast learner."

She rolled her eyes at the sky. "I'm not betting my life on you figuring out the operational codes. Besides, if you think I'd fly off and leave you . . . where would I go? Don't forget I need your sorry ass to get me off Zor before it explodes."

There was no missing her disdain, as if she would have preferred to go it alone. And to his annoyance, he felt his anger receding and the camaraderie they'd shared returning.

What was it about her that made him like her in spite of the fact she was a First? His responses had made no sense since the moment they'd met. Then after the vision of them making love in the ice cave . . . but ever since they'd made love for real, he couldn't blame the alien in his head. Or could he?

Was it an accident that Azsla and Pepko had shown up around the same time? Had the Firsts allied themselves with other aliens about whom the Zorans knew nothing? Since Pepko had admitted that he didn't have a body, for all Derrek knew, the aliens and Firsts could have been communicating on a daily basis back on Rama for tens of thousands of years.

Pepko interrupted his thoughts. *Now that's a fanciful notion. However, my kind haven't been planetbound in several millennia.*

So your showing up at the same time as Azsla was co-incidence?

I arrived when the time was right.

You didn't answer my question.

Right now, you need to befriend this woman. She has knowledge you require to stop Katadama.

You trust her? Derrek asked, curious about the alien's thought processes.

Trust is not my concern.

Why are we your concern? Aren't we boring to you?

On the contrary. I find primitive life forms a pleasant diversion. Pepko's thoughts might be a bit strange, but amusement came through.

We amuse you? Derrek didn't like the idea. *So why are you bothering me? What is it you want?*

Pepko didn't answer. Derrek didn't know if the being was still inside his head or not, but he seemed to have gone as suddenly as he'd arrived. Perhaps, he'd decided to pop into someone else's head and annoy them.

But with the forest clearing up ahead, and Azsla slowing and pointing to a parked hovercraft, he was grateful Pepko had departed. As he looked around and spied the Raman hovercraft, Derrek's hopes escalated. Perhaps he wouldn't have to be bait after all, since the vehicle was already dirtside—a lucky break for them.

Azsla took her cannon blaster from its holster and sank to the ground on her belly. He did the same. For the next half-hour she didn't move, didn't say a word, just studied the group of men who appeared to be busy with the hovercraft.

They filled it with fuel from tanks. Then two men checked the gauges while another spoke on his vidlink. Too far away from the Ramans to hear their conversation, he had the impression they were waiting for orders, although the discussion could have been general chitchat.

Azsla tapped his shoulder and motioned for Derrek to circle to the right as she edged left. With their com links set to the same channel, she could signal him to attack, so they could coordinate their moves and take out the three men from opposite sides of the clearing at the same time. The danger was that a stray shot could strike the hovercraft, leaving them still stranded, and their location outed.

Derrek crawled forward on his stomach, using his elbows to pull him through the rough grasses. He kept his head down, yet tried to keep track of Azsla's progress. She was moving as quickly as he was, as if she'd practiced belly crawling for years.

When he stopped again to judge direction and distance, he took advantage of a toppled tree for coverage. Peering out from behind the log, he searched first for Azsla. But he couldn't find her in the grass. So he moved his gaze to the two men who'd been fueling the hovercraft.

That's when he spied her. Upright and still, she'd molded herself to a tree. And when one of the Ramans stepped toward her to answer a call of nature, Derrek raised his weapon, prepared to shoot.

Only he didn't have a good angle. The hovercraft and trees blocked his shot. His pulse sped as the man headed directly toward the spot where Azsla hid.

Sweet *Vigo*. Another step and he would see her. Derrek ached to risk a shot but made himself wait.

At the moment the enemy saw her, the First stiffened in obvious shock. It was the last move he ever made. Derrek held his breath. Before he could fire, with a slashing strike and a glint of blade, Azsla cut his throat, then broke the man's fall and eased him to the ground. She'd struck in lethal silence and Derrek's heart had jammed up his throat before relief let him breathe once again.

Her attack had been swift, violent, practiced. And after she faded back into the woods, although he knew her location, he still couldn't spot her. Damn, she knew her stuff.

And she was a killer.

No, he corrected, she was a soldier. This was war. Even if he couldn't be sure what side she was on.

Derrek shoved the thought aside and focused on getting to the Raman First on his side of the camp, a man standing with his back to Derrek, the com link raised to his ear. Derrek would only have one chance to take out this enemy.

If he failed, the First would grab him with his *Quait* and if that happened, Derrek was a goner. He wouldn't be able to move, might even be forced to kill himself or Azsla. In peacetime Firsts were ruthless, but in war, he imagined they would only be worse.

Too bad Azsla couldn't protect him with her *Quait*. But to adapt to the situation, he required free will.

So in spite of his hurry to crawl the last few body lengths across the field, he had to go slowly, silently. Sweat beaded on his brow and he blinked it away, but he could do nothing about the perspiration pooling under his arms and trickling down his back.

Derrek had never killed a First. He'd never killed anyone. His fear that he'd fail, combined with his anger that he was less equipped to kill than Azsla, left a bitter taste in his mouth.

But he would not let his family down. Not his daughter, who was terrified, or his son, who was waiting for him to save the day. Not even his ex and her husband, who needed him to get off this planet whether they wanted to admit it or not.

The easiest way to take out the First would be with his cannon blaster. But once he fired, the other First would capture him in his *Quait*.

So Derrek had to move silently, stealthily, and hope he didn't crack a stray branch to alert them. He wished he could see Azsla. He wished he knew how close she was to her second target. He wished she'd risked a signal through the com link but he also feared being overheard. Losing just a precious micronbit could get them killed. Most of all, he wished he could be certain there were only two Firsts still alive in the clearing, because the craft had enough room for four and Azsla had only killed one.

He also worried about Azsla. Besides planning to kill two men to his one, she was putting her life in peril to help him and his family. The least he could do was follow through.

The First on the com link ended his conversation. He dropped his arm to his side. And reached for his blaster.

He'd either seen the dead man. Or Azsla.

Derrek couldn't wait any longer. He took the shot.

20

❋

Azsla heard the hum of Derrek's cannon blaster and swore. She'd hoped to get the drop on her target before he had any warning. Now she had to alter her plan. She reached to seize Derrek in her *Quait* and found herself a micronbit too late. Her target had grabbed him, which meant Derrek could be used against her. Instead of one enemy now stalking her, she had two. And she had no doubt the First would attempt to place Derrek in a compromising position where Azsla had to shoot him in order to take down the First.

She shot at the First and missed his heart. But the com unit dropped from his hand. He screamed in pain and held his arm to his chest, but she sensed another attack coming at her. From Derrek. The First had him in his *Quait*.

She adjusted her blaster to stun, aimed, then fired at Derrek who was just rising to his feet. He dropped to the ground unconscious. Now she had only one man to worry about—the First. But he'd disappeared into the tree line.

Should she follow him or stay with Derrek? She'd never had to make such a difficult decision, one that tore at her, clawed at her. She'd just stunned Derrek. He'd awaken in pain, blame her for betraying him. If she wasn't here to explain . . . he'd think the worst. However, as much as she hated to leave Derrek unconscious and unable to defend himself, she couldn't leave the First out there. He might reconnect with a unit and bring back help, or if he had a second weapon, he might simply wait and shoot down the hovercraft if she and Derrek attempted to escape in it.

With a heavy heart, she slipped into the forest and began to track the First. In the waning moonlight, she picked up the telltale sign of smashed grasses where the First's feet had left their marks. Clearly unskilled in the woods, he'd fled at a dead run, breaking branches that left a trail easy to follow.

She'd hoped to at least stay near Derrek, but now that would be impossible. There was no telling when the First would stop running, but she couldn't let him escape. Azsla took off after him and settled into a pace that, not so long ago, she could have kept up for hours. However, she hadn't ever recovered properly from her ordeal in space. Her muscles still weren't quite accustomed to planetary gravity, making her run much harder than it should have been.

It didn't help that she hadn't eaten in hours or that she hadn't drunk enough water during the night, either. Or that the rising sun and every step that took her away from Derrek made her feel as if she were abandoning him forever. She could only hope that the First in front of her wasn't accustomed to thinking independently and would tire quickly. Because almost always, a man could run faster than a woman. Their bodies possessed more muscular strength.

She could make up for her lack of speed only by resting less. Adrenaline helped speed her through the first few miles. Occasionally she heard her prey crashing through underbrush. He could set up an ambush behind a tree, a fallen log or make use of any of a half-dozen natural inclines for cover. But she couldn't slow down too much or she'd lose him. And as dawn brightened the sky, she worried about the passing hours.

She really wanted to get back to Derrek. The idea of leaving him on the ground where he couldn't defend himself against hungry wild animals sped her tired legs almost as much as the certainty that if he awakened before she returned, he'd believe she'd betrayed him. She was wondering if she should give up and turn around when she spied a straight shape. In nature, nothing was perfectly straight. Although she couldn't identify the object, that linear abnormality set off internal alarm signals.

At the hiss of the cannon blaster's trigger, she dived for cover. The singe of blaster fire burned her bicep.

Ignoring the pain, she scrambled behind a broken stump, realizing the First had her pinned down. With the sunlight lighting the clearing, she was an easy target. While she'd been thinking about Derrek, the First had chosen his spot well. Around her, there were few trees. If she moved from behind the stump, he'd have clear shots at her.

Azsla swore softly. She was going to have to wait out the entire day until it was dark again to make a move. And by then, Derrek would have been awake for quite some time.

Would Derrek understand why she'd shot him? Even if he did, that wouldn't make the painful awakening of his nerve endings any more pleasant to bear. Compared with the burn on her arm, what he'd endure would be agonizing.

Just to see if the First was still there, Azsla tossed a rock and heard the zing of blaster fire. He wasn't going anywhere.

Neither was she.

DERREK REGAINED CONSCIOUSNESS in slow stages. He noted that everything hurt. His fingertips, his toes, and every nerve ending in between. The worst was the pain behind his eyes, as if someone had shorted out his vision with a stabbing hot poker.

Disinclined even to attempt to open his eyelids, he took short stiff breaths, the rise and fall of his chest painful. Unfortunately, he couldn't stop breathing. On the other hand, he had no reason to even try to do more.

He'd been stunned.

This wasn't the first time, so he recognized the sensation, knew that his body would completely recover with time. Trying to speed recovery only delayed the process. So he held perfectly still, then recalled Azsla had shot him to stop the First from using Derrek against her.

Had she survived?

Bracing against optic pain, he forced open his eyes.

Bright daylight and the overhead sun told him he was well into the next day. From his position in the grass he couldn't see her. He listened and heard nothing but the wind. No voices. No breathing. No one puttering at the hovercraft.

It was as if he were totally alone, with a five hundred ton hammer banging his skull from the inside out. He knew instinctively that Azsla wouldn't have left him, if for no other reason than she needed his help to get off Zor. So either she was lying there injured, stunned, or dead, or she'd been taken prisoner. None of the options pleased him.

Although he knew the pain would be excruciating, Derrek had to know if she was still alive. He shoved one hand into the ground, clutching the grass, and pushed himself into a sitting position. Thousands of white-hot nerves burned as if he'd dropped into boiling lava. He took one look around the clearing but didn't see her before the blackness closed in on him and he passed out again.

When Derrek next awakened, the sun had moved in the sky, indicating several hours had passed. It was now late afternoon. His mouth was dry, his tongue swollen. Desperate for water, he reached for his canteen, fumbled with the top and finally gulped fluid, spilling some down his shirt in his haste.

But his parched throat eased and he forced himself to sip slowly. While the pain lingered in his nerves, it was down to a manageable level.

He sat up slowly and with a sinking hardness in his gut saw that Azsla was nowhere to be seen. Neither was the other First.

Derrek tried to link with Azsla on his com, annoyed that he hadn't thought past the pain enough to use it sooner. He didn't speak, just clicked it twice and waited for an answering click.

He got nothing.

Shoving to his feet, he tried again, hoping his height would send the signal farther. He didn't have much hope, so he was shocked to hear an answering click.

Was he imagining things?

Again he clicked, and this time he heard her whisper, "Derrek."

"Where are you?" he whispered.

"Tomar has me trapped."

"Tomar?"

"I got one look at his scarred face before I dived behind a tree. I'm waiting for sunset to escape."

"I'll come—"

"No. You're weak after that nerve blast. Stay with the hovercraft." She cut off the link, no doubt fearing he'd gotten a lock on her signal and would come after her.

Derrek sighed and linked to Sauren. "Azsla just sent me a com. Can you locate her?"

"Sure, boss man."

He appreciated that Sauren didn't ask questions. Within micronbits Sauren had beamed Derrek her satellite locator position. "Thanks. I'll be home soon."

"The sooner the better."

No kidding. "Understood."

"Word about Katadama has leaked out into the general populace. People are panicking."

"Understood."

Derrek could only imagine the chaos back in the cities. Everyone would be desperate to make it off-world. He was glad that his people and their families would be safe, but a heavy weight pressed on his heart for the rest who wouldn't survive. They'd all come here to make a new life, a better life as free people. There had been no guarantees but they'd all worked hard to build a new world. To have the Ramans ruin Zor in one deadly blow was too much to bear.

Although he knew that Sauren would protect *Beta Five* from rioters, just as Taylo would keep working on a plan to destroy Katadama, their efforts might not be enough. Derrek had no idea where they would find enough food and air and housing for the people who'd gone to the asteroids. Somehow . . . they would make do. But for all of them, the future looked dim.

At least Derrek could rely on Sauren and Taylo and that eased his mind a bit. He couldn't think about saving the world just yet, not until his daughter and Azsla were safe. However, knowing that Sauren was in charge back at the base left Derrek free to think about what he must do next. Estimating he might just make it to Azsla's location before dark, he drank the rest of his water, preferring to carry it inside him than have it weigh him down, and confiscated extra provisions from the dead.

Perhaps he could fly the hovercraft to her. He climbed inside, but the keys were gone. A quick check in the pockets of the dead men revealed that neither of them had the keys, either. So Derrek had no choice but to proceed on foot.

Derrek now had two reasons to go after the First. To save Azsla and to recover the keys.

The water he'd drunk had helped to revive Derrek, but his body still hadn't settled down. Running was going to pound his already raw nerves, but there was no help for it. That hovercraft was the best way to take his daughter to safety and he needed the keys. Besides, no way was he leaving Azsla behind.

He would have gone after any member of his team. Despite the fact that she was a First, she deserved to be treated as well as anyone else who'd helped him. And he couldn't leave her pinned down to die. Not when Taylo might need her tactonic knowledge to build a device to blow Katadama to pieces before it crashed into Zor. Not when just the idea of her dying made him tremble.

He shouldn't have taken her with him, but at the time he'd just learned she was a First and didn't trust her out of his sight. He'd also been thinking about saving his children, and hadn't realized how dangerous this mission would become.

Bringing her with him might have been a mistake. One he had to rectify. Derrek had to find her and hoped his weakness was only due to the aftereffects of the stunner and not to hypothermia or dehydration. Because not only was his body rickety, he wasn't thinking clearly, either. Only focused concentration and discipline stopped him from running full tilt into the forest.

Forcing himself to think, he picked up a cannon blaster and some ammo and draped it over his chest, then spied a pair of binoculars and took those, too. He marked the clearing in his mind and into his com link so he could find his way back, then with every beat of his heart urging him to run, run, run, he headed for Azsla. Teeth gritted against the pain, he set off at a painful lope, determined to conserve his energy.

He set his com to vibrate every quarter hour to take his bearings. With sweat pouring off him, he'd dehydrate and weaken without fluids and reminded himself to keep a sharp lookout for any sign of water. He lucked out twice during his afternoon run, refilling his water supply from small streams. Still, the precious liquid only made the journey possible. Between the heat, the pain in his every joint, and his fear for Azsla, the run was more nightmare than disciplined trek.

Derrek ran for miles, stopping only occasionally to drink and to check his direction. As the sun began to set, he finally closed in on the open meadow. Wearily, he dropped to the ground and finished at a crawl, careful to remain behind bushes, his energy depleted, but his resolve to save her just as determined as when he'd awakened.

Careful not to let the dying sun reflect off the binocular lenses and give away his position, he found Azsla easily enough. She was pinned behind a stump in the center of the meadow, with no nearby cover.

He recalled her saying she would sneak away at night, but barring the thickest fog or the blackest night, the First would pick her off the moment she broke from cover. Tonight the sky was clear, the moon bright and shiny. Talk about underestimating the danger. If she came out from behind that stump, she'd be fried.

To help her, Derrek had to find Tomar, then sneak up on him and take him out before the other man sensed his presence and immobilized him with his *Quait*. And he needed to do it all before Azsla made a move that would likely get her killed.

To save her, he might need to ask her to use her *Quait* on him again. But she might refuse. She'd already told him she'd be fine, and he feared if he contacted her that she'd send him away and try to escape alone—which in his opinion would be a death sentence, for him, for Tish, and for Azsla. And he couldn't argue with her for fear of giving away his position.

So he shaded his binoculars from the moonlight and searched the underbrush for the First. He saw boulders, dense berry thickets with spiked vines, and dead underbrush between green split-leaf plants. Finally he found the First. He sat propped against a tree, his weapon resting in the crotch of two branches and aimed at Azsla.

Derrek raised the binoculars until he could see the First's scarred face. Tomar. He'd never seen the First before, but like all his kind, he was tall and fit, with a haughty sneer on his lips that shot a chill down Derrek's spine. He'd forgotten how intimidating that natural-born superiority could be—a superiority that suggested that anyone who inconvenienced him would be reduced to slime.

Derrek had only one advantage—Tomar didn't know Derrek was here. If Derrek wanted to keep his presence a surprise, he had to move silently, slowly.

Retreating on his belly until he was certain he was out of Tomar's sight, Derrek focused on one movement at a time. After he'd gone far enough, he spread mud on his face and arms to help camouflage his flesh. But the entire time he prepared, he couldn't help but wonder why Tomar hadn't called for assistance. Probably, he either wanted the pleasure of the kill himself, or he was so egotistical, he figured he required no help.

Muscles screaming, Derrek circled in a slow crawl until he came up on Tomar's back. But the First had his back to a large tree trunk, and again Derrek didn't have a shot. If he moved to one side, he'd risk the other man picking him up in his peripheral vision.

As the moon began to rise, flying, biting bugs descended. The mud protected Derrek but Tomar kept swatting. Finally the man stood with clear impatience and taunted Azsla, "You might as well come out and let me shoot you, you're only putting off the inevitable."

"You want me? Come out of hiding and get me," Azsla shouted back.

Derrek prayed the taunting would continue, distract Tomar as well as cover any noise he might make. He was now close enough, if only the man would step from behind the tree. But he didn't.

Tomar was too smart for that. He maintained his position, pulling out a water bottle to quench his thirst. "If you come out now, I promise your death will be quick."

"I like breathing just fine. Thank you very much."

"You should have thought of that before you turned traitor."

Reminding Derrek how easily sound carried, Azsla's sigh wafted all the way across the clearing. "I have done nothing that will hurt Ramans."

"You're insane from that crackpot Corps training," Tomar roared, obviously having learned about her secret mission since their last encounter in space. "You didn't just fail to report on Zoran weapons status, you helped slaves escape."

"What difference does that make? You intended to execute them. Freeing them hurt no one."

"You insulted our way of life. Encouraged unrest. Those slaves were to be an example of what happens to radical extremists."

"Slavery is wrong."

Derrek inched closer. A few more feet and he could haul himself upright, reach around the tree, and slit Tomar's throat with his knife.

But at the sudden roar of a hovercraft overhead, one he hadn't heard sneak up on them during the shouting match, he realized time had run out. If he waited another moment, Tomar's reinforcements would arrive. Taking on one First was almost impossible. Taking on more than one was suicidal.

Derrek lunged. He must have made a noise, or moved too slowly. Tomar shifted slightly and Derrek's knife sliced the First's cheek, instead of his neck. Blood spurted but not enough. He'd missed a critical artery.

But worst of all, Derrek's greatest fear slammed down on him. As the man roared with pain and rage, Tomar's *Quait* seized Derrek, freezing him.

Totally helpless, Derrek could not move. Couldn't defend himself. Couldn't call out or speak. The horror of failing, of being unable to die fighting or trying to defend himself set into his bones with a clawing fury.

Derrek expected the First to fry him. Or torture him slowly. Either way he was dead. He'd failed Tish and Azsla. Tad would grow up without a father.

Dying right now was so damn inconvenient. He'd just reconnected with his children and now he'd lose them before he really got to know them. He'd never see them grow into adulthood. Never see them meet their mates. Never learn if Azsla was truly friend or foe.

He was done. His best hope . . . was a swift death.

Derrek heard a blast, and braced for great pain and oblivion.

But he felt nothing.

No pain.

No burns.

It was Tomar who dropped to the ground, dead. And Derrek was obviously freed of his *Quait*.

Shocked, he looked up to see Azsla running toward him, her blaster smoking. His mind began once again to function and take in details. Put together what had happened.

Azsla had shot Tomar. Saved Derrek's life.

But with the roar of the hovercraft flying down, there was no time to speak, never mind say thanks. They had mere seconds to flee before they'd be fired on. As Azsla sprinted to him, Derrek reached into Tomar's shirt, seized the keys to the hovercraft and stuffed them into his pocket.

Then Azsla was grabbing his hand and tugging him toward cover. Together they raced into the forest, ducked behind dense foliage, and kept running. On Rama the hovercrafts had heat sensors that wouldn't have let them hide. But here she'd seen two Raman hovercrafts, the damaged one with the hole in its side and Tomar's, and the equipment was bare bones due to the huge expense of transporting equipment from one planet to another.

As they forced their way through the underbrush, branches whipping their faces and tearing at their clothes, they heard confusion behind them. The hovercraft engine died. Men shouted. An enraged voice that sounded like Tomar's ordered his flunkies to find and execute them.

"I thought you'd killed him." Derrek frowned, realizing that when Tomar had dropped to the ground, he must only have been unconscious. Not dead as he'd assumed.

"You were too close, so I had to stun him. Couldn't risk you being hit by blaster fire."

The blaster wouldn't hurt a First as much as it had Derrek. Firsts were stronger and recovered more quickly. But doubts about Azsla again began to haunt him. Why hadn't she killed Tomar after he'd taken the keys? Had she been so eager to get away that she'd forgotten she'd only stunned Tomar? Or was her plan more devious? Her explanation made sense, but he still wondered if she was telling the truth.

She'd saved him from certain death, he reminded himself. Or had she?

When she'd joined him over the unconscious First's body, she'd had ample opportunity to finish off Tomar. And he already knew she wasn't squeamish about killing. If she'd known Tomar wasn't dead, why hadn't she taken the kill shot? Or suggest Derrek do it?

Of course, they had been in a hurry to escape the hovercraft. But still . . . had Azsla and Tomar set up an elaborate ruse so that Derrek would now implicitly trust her?

They sped through the forest without speaking, saving their breath for running. Twice they stopped for water and for him to check their course. But neither time was good for an in-depth analysis of what had just occurred or why.

An hour later, when they'd finally made it back to the hovercraft, Derrek had just about tapped out his physical limits. Even so, he cautiously looked around the clearing where they'd found the hovercraft to ensure it wasn't a First trap before nearing the abandoned vehicle.

Worn out from the stunner blast and the long run, he didn't hesitate to hand Azsla the keys. He was in no shape to fly. Sweating had left him salt depleted, and he also needed food and rest to recover from his ordeal.

While they seemed to have put enough distance between Tomar's men and themselves to escape, he suddenly heard canines barking. Apparently, those Firsts who had been chasing them from the burning houses had followed their trail through the forest and creeks and were getting close.

Praying Tish was still hidden and okay, he used his last remaining strength to pull himself into the hovercraft's passenger seat. Azsla scooted next to him and popped the key into the ignition. She turned it.

But the motor didn't roar to life.

"Frip," Azsla swore.

If he'd had any adrenaline left, his pulse might have sped. Wearily, he raised his head to the gauges. "We out of fuel?"

"We've got half a tank." Savagely, she twisted the key again, but nothing happened, except she uttered another curse. "I'll check the battery leads."

She slid out and poked under the hood while he hoisted his blaster toward the barking dogs. He couldn't see them yet, but from the intensity of their deep growls and yapping barks, their masters couldn't be far away.

"Battery's fine." Azsla picked up a branch. Hefting it over her shoulder, she strode to the rear.

He frowned as she stopped beside the engine. "What are you doing?"

"Giving the fripping engine block some encouragement."

Before he could say a word to stop her, she swung the branch at the engine. At the loud clang the dogs barked louder and he winced.

"Try the key," she gasped, looking over her shoulder at the dogs bolting through the clearing. They had mere micronbits until the dogs—and the Firsts—reached them.

He stunned the lead dog, then twisted the key. "Nothing."

The frenzied dogs kept advancing, their jaws flecked with foam, their teeth glistening. A First broke out of the forest.

Derrek ordered his muscles to prepare to leap clear and make a run for it. But despite his mind willing him to move, his muscles didn't obey. He was like a runner who'd pushed way past his endurance level, his stamina totally gone, his body shut down.

Azsla swung the branch again. He flipped the key and held his breath.

This time the engine turned, caught. He revved the motor, careful not to flood it with too much fuel. With a grin, Azsla leaped back into the craft just ahead of the jaw-snapping dogs. She gunned the engine and swerved away from the furious animals.

Firsts shot at them. Most went wide. But one or two blasts pinged off the hull, and he prayed to *Vigo* they'd struck nothing vital.

"Get us the hell out of here," he ordered and then felt foolish for shouting as she gave it full throttle. The acceleration felt wonderful and even as the speed pressed him into the seat, a weight lifted from his chest. He wasn't dead. He might yet reach his daughter and get her out of this mess.

Hang on, Tish. I'm almost there.

Air gusted behind them and blew back the dogs. As the hovercraft picked up speed and rose into the air, Derrek peppered the edge of the clearing with blaster fire to ensure the Firsts dived for cover instead of taking more easy shots at them.

Finally airborne, they were safe. At least for the moment.

"Taylo wouldn't let you within a parsec of his engines if he saw how you'd started this one," Derrek teased.

Azsla chuckled. "These old rust buckets need the occasional kick in the ass." She punched coordinates into the nav system. "We're heading back for Tish?"

He nodded. "I'd rather maintain com silence until we're almost right on top of her—just in case anyone's trying to listen."

But he was worried. They were hours later than he'd expected when he'd set off. And if the dogs had almost caught up with them, it meant the Firsts had gone past the cave where he'd left his daughter. Was she still safe? Had he made the right decision to leave her? Or would he return with the hovercraft, meant to carry Tish to safety, only to find her captured? Or worse?

Derrek had no idea what he would find back at the cave and tried not to second guess his decision to leave her behind with her mother and step-father. But he had a sense of time rushing by, hours lost that he could never get back.

Every moment he'd spent looking for the hovercraft, and then rescuing Azsla, had delayed them from escaping Zor, flying into space, and trying to stop the asteroid. And now, every micronbit of flight time to reach the cave took an eternity.

Was Tish okay? Had she remained hidden or had the Firsts found her? He needed all his discipline not to break radio silence. When Azsla finally set them down in a clearing within a short walk of the cave, she turned to switch off the engine, but he placed his hand over hers.

"Keep her hot."

She shook her head. "Someone could steal her if I leave it running with the key in the ignition."

"Please stay here and guard the hovercraft. I'll go get them and be back within micronbits."

"All right." Azsla removed her hand from the key and drew her weapon. "But hurry."

Like she needed to tell him that.

Then she grabbed his shirt, made a fist, and drew him close. He thought she meant to tell him something. But her eyes dilated slightly and her nostrils flared. She kissed his mouth, surprising him. "For luck."

"Thanks." He hopped down and loped toward the cave. Although he didn't dwell on that kiss or her reason for giving it, she'd lifted his spirits and energized him as he strode toward the cave.

"Tish," he called out. If she'd stayed here, she'd have heard the hovercraft, but she'd believe more Firsts had driven it and were still searching for her. She'd be hiding. "It's Derrek. Your father."

He couldn't hear an answer. Saw no movement in the cave.

"Tish!" His heart hammered as he prayed to *Vigo* and sprinted into the cave.

Dreading he might find bodies, hoping Tish would round the bend and race into his arms, he sped deeper into the darkness. Flipping on his com light to see the dark rocks and the uneven dirt floor, he searched for any sign of Tish.

But it was empty.

Tish, Poli, and Mavinor were gone.

21

✷

Azsla felt like a duck, squatting in a puddle, with a hunting party about to shoot her from all sides. The bright moonlight left her no place to hide. With the engine running, she couldn't even hear if anyone was sneaking up through the forest trees. Beyond her open clearing, she couldn't see past the thick underbrush.

Worse, since stopping, she'd spied a fuel leak spurting out on the ground. Apparently one or more of the shots fired at them had struck the tank. The fuel gauge showed they just might have enough juice to fly to the spaceport if they left soon.

Derrek hadn't been gone long, but it seemed like forever. Her burned arm hurt and she tried to ignore the pain. Keeping her blaster ready and her eyes on the dark forest's edges, she glanced only occasionally at the cave where Derrek had disappeared. So it took a moment for her to spot the movement above the cave—a tree branch shaking as if in a strong wind. Someone was up there, but in the darkness she couldn't guess if it was a bird or a Raman First.

Azsla hailed Derrek over the con. "Danger, above you. Outside the cave." She clicked off quickly, praying he'd heed her warning and hoping no one had had time to home in on the signal.

He clicked a "got it."

Now Azsla had three things to watch: the cave from which Derrek was slowly emerging, sticking close to a rock wall for cover, the person hidden above him, and the clearing's perimeter.

She found herself holding her breath, her fingers tightening on the trigger. Suddenly Derrek stepped away from the wall and held out his arms to the tree. Someone, Tish, dropped from the branch and into his embrace.

He led her toward the hovercraft, their steps increasing in pace to a full run. Azsla readied the vehicle for immediate takeoff, kicking it into gear and then holding steady.

Derrek and Tish dived in and Azsla had the craft airborne in seconds. She didn't ask what had happened to Poli and Mavinor, but concentrated on getting her night bearings as she listened to Derrek trying to calm his daughter.

"Didn't you hear me call your name?" Derrek asked.

"I must have fallen asleep," Tish admitted.

"It's fine. You were smart to hide in the tree," Derrek told her.

"We have to find Mom and Mavinor," Tish half-demanded, half-whined.

"How did you become separated?" Derrek asked, using the binoculars to scan the forest below.

"A search party came by. They didn't find us in the cave, but Mom was sure they'd eventually return, search the cave, and find us. She insisted on leaving and I couldn't stop her."

"Of course you couldn't." Derrek's voice was calm and reassuring, but his expression told another story.

Azsla didn't think he liked the role reversal between his daughter and his ex-wife. It seemed like Tish had to take care of her mother.

Azsla wasn't surprised that he'd had no active role as a parent since the mindwipe, but he was good with his daughter. He treated her as if she were intelligent and an adult, supporting her judgment.

"I knew you'd come back and we could go after Mom and Mavinor. If I left, you wouldn't know what had happened."

"Let's sweep the area."

Azsla checked her gauges. "Bad news, boss man. We don't have time for detours. Our fuel tank took a hit and is leaking. Even if we fly straight to the spaceport, we're going to be flying in on fumes."

He nodded but didn't put down the binoculars. "Tish's safety comes first. Head for the spaceport and we'll keep looking."

"Dad. We can't leave them," Tish said, sniffling and trying to hold back tears.

Derrek placed a comforting arm over her shoulders. "Honey, if we crash, we can't do them or ourselves any good."

Those tears finally escaped, but Tish brushed them away, clearly determined to be brave. Azsla shook her head at Poli's foolishness and wished the woman good fortune . . . for Tish's sake.

Meanwhile she tried to conserve every drop of fuel, gaining altitude to pick up a tail wind. But the fuel gauge seemed to be dropping even faster than she'd calculated.

Azsla raised her voice to be heard over the engine's roar. "If we can't make the spaceport, do you have a backup landing site in mind?"

"My house?"

She shook her head and angled up the nose. "It's closer to us than the spaceport, but I think we'll run out of fuel before we get there, too."

"There's a park a few miles from the spaceport. I'll punch in the coordinates." Derrek took a moment to study the lit instruments, then figured out the system, pressing the buttons and bringing up a city map on the grid. He hadn't bragged when he'd said he was a fast learner.

"Dad," Tish tugged his sleeve and pointed. "There're people waving to us."

Azsla looked down to see that Tish had not exaggerated. A huge crowd milled around a blazing bonfire in the town square below. Some waved, one shot a flare gun at them, and she swerved their craft to avoid taking a hit. Those people saw a Raman hovercraft and mistakenly believed they were all Firsts.

But they also seemed out of control. Below, several fights broke out. Fistfights. A riot.

Derrek frowned. "They aren't hiding from the Ramans. Word of the asteroid must be common now."

"Mom might be down there," Tish said.

Derrek motioned Azsla to keep flying, not that she had any intention of landing, but it was good to know they agreed. Landing to save another one or two people might get them all killed, especially if the crowd swarmed.

Even Tish seemed to realize the danger because she said nothing more about her mother.

There wasn't much to say, not as the sight of the burning capital city rose on the horizon. Although the buildings made out of *granitite* didn't burn, those of wood and plaster sent out black plumes of smoke that settled over the landscape like a shroud. Even with the fire miles away, the reek of smoke reached them. Landing anywhere was going to be dangerous. Power lines were down. People were fleeing by any means possible and might attack anyone with a vehicle.

But with their fuel leak, Azsla couldn't get anywhere near those fires. By tipping up the hovercraft's nose a bit more, she found the leak slowed, which meant the fuel was coming from the front of the tank. Thank *Vigo*. They might actually buy some time. Trying not to look at the fuel gauge every two seconds, she focused on flying, trying to eke out every air mile possible.

"Maybe you could call Sauren for a pick-up?" she suggested as the engine coughed. "We've got maybe another five miles before I'll have to ditch."

Derrek opened his link. "Sauren?"

"Yeah."

"We need to hitch a ride."

"Gotcha."

Derrek clicked off. "Sauren has us on the scope. He'll send someone to get us. No need to push us to the max. Set us down wherever you see a good spot."

"Keep your eyes peeled," she requested. The grid was no good to them since it was based on pre-invasion streets that were now blocked with debris, smoking vehicles, and sometimes mob scenes. Other streets were totally empty and darkly ominous, where nothing moved.

Her people had brought this world to its knees. All this destruction and loss of life sickened her. When she'd arrived, the buildings had impressed and tweaked her imagination. Now the city burned and what these people had worked so hard to achieve was gone.

"There." She thought Derrek was pointing to a landing site, but instead he was showing her a hovercraft flying their way. From the signal lights, she recognized the craft was of Zoran design. Probably Derrek's company's design. With its sleek body and folded wings it looked like a bird of prey on the hunt.

It was their ticket out of here. All they had to do was land. Hop in and go to the spaceport. It should have been as easy as the light night breeze that swirled the smoke into tiny spinning vortexes.

Except the engine coughed once more. A piece of the fuel tank blew off, right into the fan motors. Not even the muffled explosion could cover the sound of Tish's "Oh sweet *Vigo,* save us."

Azsla preferred not to rely on godly help. Her instruments went dead. She killed the engine and wrestled with the glide controls, trying to avoid crashing into the side of a building. They were coming down too fast. Too hard. But then with a prayer, she caught an uplift and used it to slow their descent.

"Hang on," Derrek said to Tish. "Keep your head down."

Azsla wished she had the luxury of closing her eyes,

hugging Derrek and praying for the best. Instead, she used the manual navigation controls, knowing her sense of timing might make a critical difference to them walking away . . .

Gripping the fly stick, she eased the craft down. Kept the nose up. Aimed for a clear spot on a street corner.

Out of the corner of her eye, she glimpsed crowds about a block away, but they had no choice. Even if they might be mobbed, they were going down.

Wind rushed in her ears. Time seemed to slow, allowing her to make critical, split-second decisions with no hurry at all. She'd heard of great warriors who'd told of time slowing during battle, but she'd thought the tales far-fetched and preferred scientific explanation to legend. Perhaps the adrenaline surge caused her mind to work faster, sharpened the neural connections, ramping up her reflexes and making her last-micronbit adjustments possible.

She set them down with one hard thud followed by a skidding that knocked them right up the side of a building. Azsla tensed for the impact, but felt no pain. And when the building's wall didn't topple onto them, she again dared to breathe.

"Get out. Now," she ordered, worried about the yelling crowd, but more concerned over the reek of spilled and flammable fuel.

Derrek was already moving as she shut down the engines. He lifted Tish over the side and dropped her to the ground. Azsla jumped and he followed, noting that as the three of them sprinted from the hovercraft, the angry crowd poured down the street toward them. In the back of her mind, Azsla understood these Zorans thought that all three of them were Firsts. After all, they'd just crashed a Raman hovercraft into their burning city streets. While Derrek and Tish were natives, the crowd might not stop to ascertain their allegiance before tearing them limb from limb—not with the burning city in ruins around them.

People shouted, screamed. A blaster fired. Another fired back. Then the crowd surged and seemed to focus all that roiling anger on them.

Regardless of the crowd's hostility, they had no choice but to run toward it. The smell of burning fuel sped them on the way. Just as the hovercraft exploded, Derrek pulled them to the ground. Before the flying debris had floated back to the pavement, he was pulling them both up, urging them to run toward Sauren's craft, which was coming down between them and the crowd.

As if sensing their prey was about to escape, the mob surged forward, heedless of the danger of being run over by Sauren. A few threw rocks. Luckily none reached them.

Azsla didn't get it. Alone, her *Quait* wasn't powerful enough to stop them all. But if they'd all been Firsts, they could use their *Quait* to stop the crowd. If they weren't Firsts, the Zorans were attacking their own people. They must be too scared and angry to realize that she, Derrek, and Tish had nothing to do with the burning city or the asteroid. These people had lost their ability to reason, needing to take out their frustration on anyone in their path. Or maybe these scared Zorans guessed Azsla, Derrek, and Tish were about to be saved and resented their own fates.

Sauren skidded and slowed and they dived into his hovercraft as the vehicle slid sideways. He accelerated into the skid and revved the engines. Azsla straightened in her seat and peered over the side. The steady purr sounded like angel music as they left the crowd behind.

"Everyone okay?" Derrek asked, checking Tish for injuries, then his gaze doing the same number on Azsla. But no, not exactly the same.

"Your arm?"

He'd noticed her burn.

"I'm fine."

When Derrek looked at Azsla, she saw concern. And she hoped that maybe, just maybe, he might believe that she was what and who she claimed.

The wall of ice she'd built to protect herself melted and she could no longer deny that she had never stopped wanting him—even when he'd been furious, even when she thought she'd accepted that he was so turned off by her that he couldn't get past it. Deep down, she hadn't forgotten that waking dream or her hope that they might one day make that dream a reality.

"What?" he asked.

"That was fun."

Sauren frowned. "You almost died."

"But we didn't," Derrek replied with a smile, then slung an arm over Tish's shoulder. "You can see your brother soon." He turned to Sauren. "Where is Tad?"

"Safe on the ship and waiting for us to arrive."

"Good." Derrek hadn't forgotten his promise to Tish, either. "Sauren, send out several search parties to look for Poli and Mavinor. We got separated."

"That would be impossible, boss man. Every one of our people has evacuated for the asteroid mines. We are the last to leave."

"We can refuel and go back," Tish suggested and Azsla felt her pain. The ripping agony of losing family. At least the girl still had her father.

"Laurie has closed the spaceport," Sauren gave them more bad news. "He's sending troops to stop us. It's going to be difficult enough for us to get away as it is. We can't wait."

"I'm sorry." Derrek hugged Tish and she buried her face in his chest.

Tish didn't cry like last time. While Derrek did his best to console his daughter, Azsla thanked Sauren, who had stayed behind to help his boss. Another man, a lesser man, would have left while the going was good and saved his own hide. But Sauren hadn't abandoned them and Azsla was impressed by that bond of friendship between the two men. That Sauren would risk his life to save Derrek said much about the loyalty Derrek inspired in those who knew him best.

She placed a hand on Sauren's shoulder. "Waiting for us endangered your life. Thank you."

"No problem." Sauren looked fondly at Derrek as he flew toward the spaceport. "He's saved my life three times now."

"Four," Derrek contradicted. "Don't forget that fight on Asa Fee."

"I didn't ask you to jump in. I had them covered."

"That's not the way I remember it. There was this huge miner who didn't like authority figures. He and his boys ganged up on Sauren. I had to pull rank and threaten to fire them all if they came to blows."

"Doesn't count," Sauren argued.

"If you say so."

Derrek's story had given Tish time to settle and pull herself together. She seemed resigned to the situation, accepting that nothing could be done for her loved ones, at least not at the moment.

As they reached the perimeter of the spaceport, Azsla noted troop movement on the ground. Several cannon blasters were almost in position to fire at Derrek's spaceship. The former bustling facility was now devoid of any other craft. No hovercrafts, no light flitters, no military spaceships. Everyone was gone.

Anyone who could beg, buy, or steal a spot had already taken off to escape Katadama. Obviously Laurie or his generals wanted to stop Derrek's ship from leaving, even if it meant damaging it so no one else could fly out.

"Even if we manage to get into the ship and blast off, if they fire at us, we'll be toast," Azsla said.

Tish flinched and Azsla wondered if she should have kept the thought to herself. As if reading her mind, Tish straightened. "I'm almost an adult. I'll be fine."

"That's my girl," Derrek said, then frowned at the buildup of troops, tanks, and hovercraft slowly closing in a circle around the ship. "Let's worry about how to blast off later."

Sauren drove the hovercraft right up to the spaceship's bay door. Timed perfectly, the door opened and he steered inside. The door slammed shut behind them.

The huge cargo bay was stuffed with crates of dry goods, containers with provisions, pallets of food, and a variety of tools and mining equipment.

Sauren and Derrek headed for *Beta Five*'s bridge at a fast run. Azsla took Tish's hand and followed at a slower pace. She'd seen most of the ship the first time she'd been on it. As they moved through engineering, past cabins and gathering areas, it seemed more crowded now with families, supplies, and crew on board. Clearly, Sauren had taken Derrek at his word, loading everything they could carry onto it.

She prayed it wasn't too heavy to take off, but surely the engineers had weighed the cargo and knew what they were doing. Still, at the sight of caged chickens in the hallway, next to pet felines, she smiled, glad that people had been allowed to take their pets.

Tish held tight to Azsla's hand. "This is awesome. But scary."

"Your dad has the best ship I've ever seen. He'll get us out of here."

"But those troops—"

"Let's go to the bridge and watch him deal with it," Azsla suggested, leading her down the corridor and trying not to disturb the strapped and stored cargo that rose from the floor to the ceiling deck and that narrowed the corridor by half.

An announcement wafted over the com system. "Emergency takeoff. Prepare for emergency takeoff. Emergency takeoff. Emergency countdown begins now. Ten. Nine. Eight."

Azsla grabbed Tish and plastered her against a wall,

gripping a handhold, wishing they could web in, but there was no time. "Hang on."

"Seven. Six."

"What about going to the bridge?" Tish gasped.

"We won't make it."

"Five."

"Even if we run?"

"Four."

"No." Azsla showed Tish where to grip and kept a tight grasp on her as well as the handhold.

"Three. Two."

She squeezed down on Tish's hand beside the portal frame. "We may go weightless."

"One."

"Oh, my God." Tish began to shake. Or maybe it was the entire spacecraft launching into space that shook. A roar filled their ears and buffeted them. Forces from liftoff pressed them down with the weight of acceleration. Azsla's legs trembled. They should have been webbed in. But there hadn't been time. And no one in his right mind wouldn't have given people time to prepare unless they'd had no choice.

The military must be attacking, the troops firing. Nothing else would justify this kind of risk. Lifting off without preparation was highly dangerous. People could suffer broken bones, head injuries. Azsla shuddered as she recalled that children were on board.

"Blasting off."

For one second they went weightless. The cargo shifted, but the straps held. The artificial grav kicked in and everything settled—only not exactly where it had been. Chickens squawked. Babies cried. But no one screamed. Azsla had no idea how many people were housed in the cabins to either side of the hallway, but no one came out into the corridor. Perhaps they'd webbed in but she feared there might be broken necks. Death.

"Is it safe to let go?" Tish asked.

"I don't know. Let's wait a bit and see if—" Azsla swore, and kept her arms around Tish and the door frame. Something weird was happening. The engines sounded different, as if they were about to blow.

And then Azsla knew—because her hearing had sharpened, and her eyes saw everything in painful detail—that they'd entered a portal. Hyperspace increased sensation. But there were no portals this close to a planet's surface.

However, Derrek had told her once that his new ship could open a portal anytime, anywhere. Obviously, he'd created a portal to escape Zor. Because they were most definitely in hyperspace.

She started to breathe normally again and noted a crewman already heading down the corridor, checking on the occupants of each cabin. Everyone appeared to be fine.

When he neared them, he clearly recognized Azsla and Tish. "I'm supposed to take you to your cabins." He gazed at her burned arm. "You want to see the doctor."

"Thanks. I'm okay." Azsla would have preferred to go to the bridge to find out what was going on, but Tish looked wiped out, her skin pale, dark circles under her eyes. The poor kid needed a bed and sleep. Azsla would settle her in and then go hit up Derrek for news of what had just occurred.

She hadn't expected Derrek and Tad to meet them in Tish's cabin. Brother and sister hugged and exchanged news of Poli and Mavinor. They clung to one another, as if realizing they might be the last two surviving members of the family they'd known.

Derrek gestured to the cabin. "I hope you two don't mind sharing quarters. It's a little cramped—"

"This is perfect," Tish assured him with a maturity beyond her years. "So many others aren't going to live at all." Tish was obviously thinking of her mother and Mavinor. Tad was a contradiction of happy and sad. Happy to see his father and sister but regretful about the others.

"The plan is to offload civilians. Then we stop the asteroid," Derrek told them. "If we stop Katadaina, your mom should be fine."

Tish didn't say anything but Azsla wondered if she was recalling the mob scene, the burning city, the lack of social structure they'd left behind. Her mother was so ill-equipped to deal with regular life, never mind a global emergency. But Tish remained quiet, thoughtful.

"You can stop the asteroid?" Tad asked, his eyes wide with wonder.

Derrek ruffled his son's hair. "We're going to give it a try. We have plans to make, so if you two wouldn't mind—"

"Go." Tish shooed him out the door. "Tad and I have some catching up to do."

"All right. There's food in the galley," Derrek directed. "It's just down the corridor and if you need anything, use the com link."

Azsla and Derrek departed as his kids took down the bunk beds and prepared to sleep. Shutting the door firmly behind him, Derrek took a step and then stopped, his gaze locked on hers. "As I mentioned earlier, the ship is overcrowded. There's room for you to bunk in the single women's dorm . . . or you can stay with me."

At the renewed heat in his eyes, her breath caught in her throat. Apparently not only did Derrek realize he'd accepted her, he was way ahead of her, the invitation in his expression blatant.

She grinned. "I think I'd prefer the owner's quarters." Then she moved into his arms. "It has certain advantages."

"That it does." Derrek dipped his head to kiss her. "Including lots of privacy."

Heart pounding, blood racing, she leaned into him. The moment their lips touched, the kids' door opened. She would have jumped back, but Derrek kept an arm around her waist, not the least disturbed by the curiosity of his children.

"Yes?" he asked, raising an eyebrow at Tad.

"It can wait." Tish grinned, grabbed Tad, and closed the door.

Azsla laughed. "Perhaps you might want to escort me to the privacy of your quarters? That is, if you aren't needed elsewhere?"

"Sauren has everything under control."

By the satisfied look on Derrek's face, she suspected Sauren wasn't the only one who had things under control. He looked pleased. And sexy as hell. She shouldn't still want Derrek after the way he'd rejected her for being a

First, but she did. And when he locked gazes with her, the fierce gleam in his eyes gave her a flicker of hope that he might be able to forgive her.

Azsla might have a hundred questions about their heading to the asteroids, the situation on Zor, the radioactive materials needed to make a tactonic bomb to stop Katadama. But they were safe. For the moment. The mission was risky, deadly, and the chance of surviving wasn't all that great. She'd never set off a tactonic weapon. Didn't know if the ship could flee in time to escape the blast.

She didn't know if Derrek would ever get over the fact that she'd lied to him. But she didn't want to wait one more micronbit for another of Derrek's kisses.

22

Azsla had expected the owner's quarters to be larger than the cabins she'd already seen, but when Derrek opened the door, she was stunned by the huge space and luxurious decor. Talk about extravagant. She gasped at his majestic view of space, which rivaled the one on the bridge. From here she could see the hyperspace ripples that streamed by, distorting space and time. In contrast to the darkness outside, the inside of the cabin had plush white carpets and his headboard displayed holographic designs of a pinkish white planet with emerald and sapphire water. She heard the lapping waves, smelled the salt of the sea, and his large bed appeared to be under a golden sun shaded by a tiki hut.

"We would have used the quarters to save more people, but we couldn't lift off with any more payload than what's already aboard." Derrek sounded apologetic, as if he saw the space in terms of lives he could save, but obviously that hadn't been possible.

"This . . . is . . . fabulous." She wanted to swan dive into the bed but she was covered with dirt, sweat, and grease from two days in the forest. "Where's the fresher?"

"Over there." He pointed to a door. "Have you ever taken a bath in hyperspace?"

"Can't say I have. Why?" She'd taken two steps toward the fresher and stopped as he slipped open a different pocket door than where she'd been heading. At the sight of the glorious white *marbellite* tub, her lower jaw dropped. "Is that—"

"Yeah. We recycle the water. The engines keep it at my preferred temperature."

"And that would be?"

"Hot." His eyes burned into hers.

A hot bath with wet flesh and nudity might just be the ticket to making Derrek forget that she'd lied to him. "Okay, first I'm hitting the fresher. Then the tub. I wouldn't want to get that beauty dirty." She unbuttoned her stained shirt as she walked across the carpet. "Your fresher is big enough for two," she teased.

He nodded. "It is."

"I'll wash your back if you do mine."

"I'll do more than your back," he promised, his voice husky.

"I'm counting on it." And then she peeled off her shirt and bra in one move, eager to rid herself of dirt and grime and the stink of old sweat before she contaminated his pristine quarters.

When she stood naked, the dirty clothes in her hands, she didn't know where to put them since every surface was clean and shiny. He took them from her and shoved them into a wall bin. "We have auto laundry. By the time you need them, they'll be washed, dried, and pressed."

She raised an eyebrow. "That will take hours."

"Exactly." He shot her a predatory grin that made her heart shimmy. Even if the heat in his eyes hadn't told her what he was thinking, there was no disguising his arousal. Besides the obvious erection, his nostrils flared, a pulse at his neck beat double time, and his pupils dilated. Oh, yeah. Her man was all heated up and ready to go.

"If you don't hurry into that fresher, I'm going to have you right here," he growled.

His impatience didn't stop her from moving her hips from side to side a little more than necessary as she preceded him. He slipped a hand from her waist and swatted her backside. "Hurry. You little tease."

He had no idea. She laughed and wriggled beneath his touch, anticipation starting to tingle down deep. Sweet *Vigo,* she wanted him, in her arms, in her bed, in her life—for as long as it lasted even if it might be only another day.

The fresher was actually cozy, with its black tile walls, mirrored ceiling, and white floor. Although manual cleansing wasn't necessary—the sonic cleaners and blowers did the job—she wouldn't feel clean without using soap and a buff pad to scrub deeper into her skin. Derrek possessed an assortment of lotions and pads. She sniffed several before choosing a spice that reminded her of vanillan and appelites.

She cocked her head. "Do I have something you want?" she asked.

He chuckled. "Oh, yeah. You most definitely have something I want." He took the lotion from her hands. Flipped open the cap and squeezed some into his palm. After setting down the container, he rubbed his hands together and then began to lather the scent into her neck as the fresher system boosted up. "I'm going to kiss your neck, your shoulders." As he named places on her body, he massaged the soap into her skin with caresses meant to entice as much as to clean, but remained especially careful over her burned arm.

"Mmm. You sure you know exactly what you're going to get?" she teased, the reference to her domination subtle, but he picked up on it immediately.

His tone turned confident. "Actually, I do. But you don't." He slid his hands down her back.

Damn, his hands felt good, silky, yet rough. Tender but demanding. "What do you mean?" She looked over her shoulder at him. He was staring at her back, his eyes dark with passion. With the water misting over his face and emphasizing the cut of his cheekbones, he had a look of intensity about him that sent a frisson of warmth to her core.

He winked. "I'm going to do whatever I want to you."

At his words, heat spiked, hot and harsh. Her bones turned to a gel.

"I'm taking charge beginning right now." He grinned, a predatory gleam in his eyes.

"You want to be in charge until my *Quait* kicks in?" The idea excited her. Deep down in her heart, she wanted an equal partner in bed, in all things. She wanted to share and be shared. She wanted to take charge . . . or not. That meant taking turns.

"How long can you hold out?" he murmured, sending a sizzle of tension to her pleasure center. Already dampness seeped between her thighs. His hands caressed and his tone cajoled, making her want to cavort all night. Or whatever passed for night in hyperspace.

"Still . . ." She turned and leaned into him, pressing her breasts against his chest, her cheek to his heart, not quite daring to believe she could be this happy. So at peace. "Have you forgiven me? For lying to you?"

He smoothed her hair with his hand. "I understand you lied to me out of necessity and I forgive you. Now that I know your heart is good, I trust you. I never meant to hurt you and it won't happen again. I don't give my trust lightly but when I do, I give it all the way. I won't change my mind again."

He seemed to comprehend he'd hurt her, and as badly as she wanted to forgive him, it wasn't that easy. "I may need some time to wrap my mind around—"

"Take all you like." While they stood he smoothed more lotion into her back, her bottom, her thighs, the caresses soothing, yet sensual. "There's probably one more thing you should know . . ."

"Huh?"

"There's an alien in my head."

Not now, you idiot.

Huh? It was like someone was talking to her from inside her own head. In confusion she glanced at Derrek. "Did you just call me an idiot and do it telepathically?" Azsla frowned up at him.

"So you can hear Pepko, too?" he asked, clearly annoyed at the interruption.

"Pepko? Who the hell is Pepko?"

I had to communicate with her or she might assume you were crazy and refuse to mate with you.

Derrek had an alien in his head and now it was talking to her, claiming it had something to do with their lovemaking. "And what the hell business is it of yours?" Azsla asked the alien, too annoyed to be frightened, too curious to remain silent. Talk about secrets. Maybe she didn't know Derrek at all. Maybe she should back off, reevaluate.

You people are too damn stubborn for your own good. For Stars' sake. I, Pepko, had to resort to lowering his inhibition and putting fantasies in both your heads.

"You said that wasn't a fantasy," Derrek claimed. "You said it was a scene from our future."

"Would someone please tell me what's going on?" Azsla asked in growing frustration. They might die tomorrow or the next day. And she didn't want to waste time on mysteries. She wanted to hold onto Derrek and kiss him. She didn't want to discuss fantasies, she wanted to make one.

Fantasy, future vision, it doesn't matter. What matters is that you two are destined to be together.

"Why?" Azsla asked, giving up on the idea of making love until this conversation was over.

I can only prod so much.

"You didn't answer her question," Derrek growled.

Telling the future can distort it.

"Is he always so cryptic?" Azsla asked. If the being had to interrupt their lovemaking, at least he could do them the courtesy of being articulate.

"Yes, he's usually cryptic, annoying, and interfering."

I'm just doing my job.

"And that would be?" Azsla pressed, confused and aggravated. Finally Derrek had forgiven her. And she wanted to hold him, kiss him, and make love.

I'm ensuring the future. But since I'm obviously not wanted, I'm leaving.

"And don't come back." Derrek embraced her tight. "At least not any time soon."

Had Pepko really gone? She didn't know since he had no physical form. But his sudden appearance and sudden vanishing act had stirred so many questions in Azsla she didn't know what to ask first. "Where did it come from? Has it always been in your head? What does it want from me? From us?"

"He does that," Derrek said. "Just shows up and disappears."

"How rude."

Derrek chuckled and kissed her brow. "I met him

about the same time I did you. At first, I thought I was going crazy, but gradually I accepted he has some uses. Like his lowering my resistance to you. Like that fantasy of us making love . . ."

"I don't like someone interfering with our lives," Azsla said, uneasy with the idea that an alien could invade her thoughts at will. Uneasy that Pepko had changed Derrek's mind about her. Uneasy that an alien being was now in the picture.

"That would be a triple ditto for me," Derrek agreed. "The verdict is still out on Pepko's motives. Yet, while his timing tends to be inconvenient, I don't believe he's a threat. He is annoying, though. I mean, here I have you willing, naked, and heating up and he decides to pay a visit. You'd think he'd have some sense of privacy but the concept seems one he can't grasp. After living several millennia he ought to have a little patience. But no, he interrupts and then after he realizes how annoyed I am, he leaves." He shook his head and laughed. "But he always gets in the last word."

Azsla didn't want to think about the alien. She'd learned in her short lifetime that there were too few moments of pleasure, too few times to relax between the battles, and she was damned sure not going to allow a whacked-out alien to deprive her of making love to Derrek. "Let's pretend he doesn't exist. That he didn't interrupt us."

"That's fine by me." Derrek inched his hands under her breasts, lifting them, cupping them while he did delicious things to her nipples with the pads of his fingers. At the same time, he angled his head to take a kiss.

She wanted him to take. And take some more.

Even as her feelings roused, she tamped them down. Not yet. Banishing her *Quait* to a corner on her mind, she locked it down. Derrek took his time, kissing her thoroughly, and as their bodies moved into sync she wondered if he meant to have her right there in the fresher.

Thoughts whirling, blood spinning, she wouldn't have minded. But when the fresher cycle ended, Derrek picked her up and carried her to the giant tub, stepped in, and sank with her into the lovely water.

"Oh, my." A hot bath would have been a luxury dirtside, but on a spaceship, in hyperspace, every sensation elevated to the next level. Where her nerve endings might have read exciting, they now screamed thrilling. Where her heart might have sprinted, it now galloped. Where her brain might have had trouble taking everything in, she was overwhelmed. Delightfully, erotically, deliciously overwhelmed.

The heated water might have relaxed her but it also stimulated nerve endings. Deciding she needed more of Derrek's mouth, she tugged his head back to hers for another kiss. She'd never been into kissing but Derrek made kissing special. In fact, he elevated it to an art form. And Derrek's kisses whetted her appetite, increased her hunger.

Enjoying the way he took over and set the pace, she did her best to allow him to do as he wished. If that meant letting him nudge apart her thighs, or tweak her nipples or stroke her earlobe, that's what she did. The sensory overload, his lack of any discernable pattern, drove her wild.

She couldn't predict what he would touch next, or how, or if he'd fire her up with a tiny bite on her earlobe, or tease the curls between her legs. In the end, whatever he did pleased her. Pleased her so that her breath came in pants. Pleased her so that she found herself holding back her *Quait*. Holding back more than she'd ever done before.

Sweet *Vigo*. She didn't want him to stop.

So when he lifted her from the tub, her body warm, wet, and wanton, she simply pillowed her head on his chest and let him carry her to the bed.

She didn't care that she was wet or that the sheets would dampen. She could think only of the pleasure he was giving her and the gratification to come.

When Derrek snapped metal and leather cuffs over her wrists and ankles, she jerked open her eyes in surprise. She'd heard of slaves who were into bondage, but Firsts . . . well, the act was meaningless for a First since they could order their partner to release the bindings. Without hesitation, she let him have his way. After all, she could use her *Quait* to get him to free her any time she wished.

He'd attached her arms over her head, her feet to the corner bed posts. Testing the bonds, she found she had wiggle room. However, she didn't see the point. But when she expected him to come to her, he instead walked across the room and dropped the key into a metal box.

Finally, he turned to her, a look of complete triumph in his eyes, a warm smile on his lips. Fists on his slim hips that showed off his cut abdominal muscles and the sexy triangle of hair below, he looked entirely too sexy and pleased with himself.

"What have you done?"

He folded his arms across his chest. "That was the only key."

"Like I'd want someone else to unlock me."

"You still aren't getting it." He chuckled. "I can't take the key out of that box."

She lifted her head and stared at him. "What?"

"It's on a timer. Unless the ship has an emergency, I can't open the box for three hours."

She frowned at him. "When did you set this up?"

"After I learned you were a First, I ordered my chief engineer to make the change."

She peered at him. Back then, for certain he hadn't been thinking of lovemaking. He'd been thinking of imprisoning her. But she let it go. He'd forgiven her and things had changed between them.

Three hours? She tested her bonds. Her wrists were wrapped in leather, the metal cuffs tight. Her ankles the same.

Of course, she could stop him from doing anything she didn't like. Make him do anything she wanted . . . except free her. He'd taken away that option.

At the idea of how he'd shifted things in his favor, dampness creamed between her thighs. Her nipples tightened. And when he kneeled between her parted legs, she suspected she was going to have a very good time.

"I underestimated you," she admitted.

He stroked the insides of her thighs, his voice low and husky. "I'm glad you approve of my tactics."

"I didn't say that," but she grinned. "But so far, so good."

"Ah, then you see the beauty of my plan and all its ramifications?" he teased.

Ramifications? Stars. She could barely think at all. And every rational part of her was bent on tamping down her *Quait*. "What . . . are . . . you . . . saying?"

For an answer, he used his fingers, stroking, teasing, caressing. When she thought she could hold back no more, he replaced his fingers with his mouth. What he was doing was incredibly better than what she'd have directed him to do with her mind. . . . She finally got it.

His plan was wicked.

Devilish.

He was giving her so much pleasure that taking over would be a bad thing. She could never be so inventive. . . . Oh, my. Where had he learned how to . . . ah. . . .

She was holding herself back. Delaying her pleasure so he could give her more. He had her right on the edge. Yet, she knew the moment she went over she would lose control.

But if she kept it together . . . he would keep giving her more. And as much as she wanted more, she ached for release.

That's when she started tugging against the bonds. Not that it did any good. She had no choice but to take more pleasure . . . and more.

No one could last forever. But she wanted to. She wanted this moment to stretch out. She wanted to wait. She wanted to do so not only for herself but for him.

But the tension was gathering. She arched her back, lifting toward him. Aching. Yearning. Needing him inside her.

Just as the first tendrils of *Quait* escaped, he pulled back his hands and his mouth.

She gazed up at his face, fierce in concentration and forced her *Quait* into a semblance of order. Reached with the last of her strength to check her own need.

"You're tormenting me," she complained.

"I'm not done." He took her nipple between his teeth, teased the tip with his tongue.

"I can't wait . . . can't hold back . . . I'm . . ." But she could hold back. As good as he now felt, he was giving her time to recover and she didn't know whether to laugh or to cry. But then she just went with the freedom, the happiness, the absolute wonder that he brought to worshiping her body that had her bursting with an inner bliss.

"Please, Derrek. I want you inside me," she pleaded.

"Thank you for asking." He shifted between her legs.

"I'm not asking. I'm begging."

He thrust into her. And she did lose it. Yet she didn't feel so much as if she were taking control but adding her own crazed lust to his. They were moving together, pumping in a primitive dance, both physically and mentally bound, tied together until she could no longer tell where her will began and his ended. Because they desired the exact same thing.

When the ultimate explosion swept her away, she took him with her, crashing senses, heart-pounding craziness, and the wonderful swirling of emotions that couldn't be sorted or analyzed . . . only felt.

After she finally caught her breath and stirred, she realized the cuffs still held her fast. Derrek picked up his head and checked the timer.

He shot her a totally mischievous grin. "You know that box isn't going to open for another hour. I think I can put that time to good use."

She grinned. "Well, you know, I always did hate to waste time."

23

During the journey to Alpha One, Derrek's home base among the asteroid mines, Azsla consulted frequently with Taylo Misa, and found the scientist to be brilliant, thorough, and extremely helpful. After she'd drawn up the specs for the tactonics housing she'd need to stop Katadama, he'd promised to have the device ready by the time they arrived.

As they had popped out of hyperspace, Azsla surveyed the specs from the link in Derrek's cabin. Taylo had already found and mined the tactonium she'd need for the bomb. Her major worry was that Katadama's density seemed higher than any substance in their solar system.

As if the prospect that she might fail to stop Katadama wasn't enough to worry about, she had a new concern. Sauren had picked up Tomar on the nav system. He was following them, stalking them. So far he'd stayed out of weapons range, but he could open a portal and drop out of deep space right in front of them at any time. While he didn't have hyperspace technology aboard his vessel, he could tap into the machines the Ramans had established on the Zoran moon, the ones they'd been using to transport *tranqed* Raman Firsts to Zor.

First chance they got, Derrek planned to knock out those lunar systems. But dealing with Katadama had to come before anything else—even Derrek's brother Cade agreed. After Laurie had run away to a bunker on the planet to hide, Cade and his wife Shara had sent their children to safety but had returned to Zor. Cade had taken over the government—what was left of it—and was trying to restore order.

While Derrek claimed Cade was a fool, Azsla knew Derrek worried over his brother. However, if Cade lived, he'd be elected in a landslide for standing by his homeworld in a time of crisis when he could so easily have fled.

Humans are complex creatures.

As the alien thought popped into her head, she sat up quickly in Derrek's bed. "What do you want?"

Why must you assume that I want something? Pepko asked.

"Why else would you be here?" she pulled the blanket up over her nudity. Although the alien may or may not have eyes, she didn't want it leering.

Really. Corporeal form has held no interest to me for several millennia.

"You just like to hang out in my head because you are lonely?" Azsla prodded.

Humans are more willing to sacrifice themselves for those they believe they know. So I thought we should get to know one another. Hang out.

"Sacrifice ourselves?" She most certainly didn't like the sound of that.

"Humans will go to extraordinary lengths to help their friends and loved ones. It ensures the continuation of your species."

"And the point?"

"My species may be on the brink of extinction."

"I'm sorry. Are you the last one . . . what do you call yourselves?"

We go by many names. Your people will come to call us the Perceptive Ones.

Azsla shivered. It was creepy enough that the alien was in her head. But when he mentioned the future in all-knowing terms, he weirded her out.

"You should be happy that Derrek and I are together according to your plan. But you want something else from us, don't you?"

Yes.

"Wow. Almost a straightforward answer." She shoved a lock of hair from her forehead. "You going to tell me or are we going to play ten questions?"

I don't play games. I am preparing you . . . for the future.

"How?" Azsla asked, wishing Pepko wasn't so set on being cryptic. She didn't like puzzles or prophets or aliens in her head. But when he didn't answer, she found that he'd left her on edge. His talk of sacrifice had spooked her and she didn't feel the least bit prepared.

Feeling a need to escape the empty cabin, she threw off the blanket, dressed, and headed for the bridge. She found Derrek with a cup of *whai* in hand, Tad perched beside him as he explained nav controls to his son. Tish stood at Sauren's station, her eyes moving from scanner to scanner like a crew member. The fast-paced action in hyperspace seemed to agree with her and she seemed to be maturing during their journey.

In greeting, Derrek lifted his cup in Azsla's direction. "We're almost home. Go ahead, Tad, show her."

Tad punched a button and a large asteroid appeared on his vidscreen. White in color, the rock orbited Zor's sun in a cluster with many other asteroids. While Alpha One wasn't the largest, it appeared to be the most stable. It didn't spin but held its orientation in a fixed position, allowing her to see only one side. The asteroid reminded her of a foot, and the ankle curve was where Derrek had made his home. He'd set the structure into the asteroid face with giant windows that allowed him to look out into the solar system. At the heel was a landing pad with locks for his ship, and a domed tunnel led from the spaceport to his home and to Taylo's.

"Sauren's going to drop us off, then take the others to their new homes before returning to pick us up in the morning. That should give you time to go over the tactonics again with Taylo."

"We need to leave as soon as possible," she reminded him. They had only a short window of time in which to blow Katadama. To wait meant Zor might draw the pieces into the planet's gravitational pull. But if they timed it right, they should prevent any of the pieces from striking the planet.

"We're scheduled to lift off tomorrow morning."

Tad turned up his face to his father. "Dad, I want to come with you."

"Me, too," Tish added from across the bridge.

Derrek shook his head and sipped his *whai*. "It's too dangerous. I don't want you kids around radiation. You still have lots of growing up to do."

"I'm fully grown," Tish argued.

"Your mother is already unhappy with me. If I take you all into a dangerous situation, she'd never let me see you again—and with good reason." Derrek stood, ending the discussion. "Sauren, take us in."

"Aye, boss man."

Tish watch him closely and Sauren eased the controls to manual.

"Next time I might let you land us," Derrek said to Tad.

"Wow."

Derrek blanked his instruments. "Tad, work the nav equations without the vidscreen."

"Why?"

Derrek rubbed his son's shoulder. "Every good pilot can perform those calculations in his head. We can't rely on the instruments. As good as they are, they go down sometimes."

Azsla watched Alpha One grow bigger as they approached. She'd heard this asteroid had originally been Derrek's first salt mine. After he'd taken out the salt, he'd used the empty mine shafts to build his home. And his company did the same with each salt mine they emptied, creating a community of homes for his employees that was close to self-sufficient.

They created air from the chemicals they found, ditto for water. They grew food hydroponically. Yet they were dependent on Zor for medicines, plastics, machine parts, engine repairs, and a myriad of other products too numerous to count. If Katadama struck Zor, they couldn't make a permanent home in these asteroids. They'd eventually have to move on.

In the meantime, every home and facility was stuffed to the roof with people and all their belongings. Most prayed to go home. But some would stay. Some might even use the asteroids as a home base to explore outward. With Derrek's new hyperdrive, there was no limit to traveling the solar system, or the galaxy. They could go anywhere.

As Azsla surveyed the starscape, the sheer size of space boggled her mind. If there were other species out there besides Earth and Ramans and Pepko, her people had yet to meet them. But she suspected the galaxy might be teeming with life.

She could almost understand Derrek's attraction to space. Almost. As the ship closed the distance between them and Alpha One, she caught herself holding her breath. One cracked seal, one loss of pressure and they'd all be dead.

Luckily, the systems held and they set down with little fanfare, not so much as a puff of dust as the locks kicked in. Before they exited the ship, they donned space suits and although their magnetic boots kept them firmly attached to the artificial decking, Derrek still clipped everyone to a lead line.

"Dad, won't our boots hold us?" Tad protested, while Azsla marveled at the scenery. The white rocks were quartz crystals, which reflected enough sunlight that her visor automatically darkened to protect her eyes. From here she could see Zor, a sapphire and emerald jewel in the heavens. The sun shone brightly, but thousands of asteroids shaded them from direct sunlight.

She tilted up her head and felt as if she were falling. Not a good idea. Quickly she straightened and let her swimming senses reorient. Without the magnetic boots, she'd have gone floating off into space. But it still wasn't the same as real gravity. Her organs seemed to be floating around in her body, instead of resting comfortably in place.

Sauren took off in the ship. Derrek led them toward his home and answered Tad's question. "If the generator goes down and the backup fails to come on line, you could go floating off into space without a lead line."

"Has that ever happened?" Tish asked.

"Once. I lost two good men and before I listened to them die as their air ran out, I promised them that it would never happen to anyone else. So you wear the leads if you come outside or I'll lock you in the dungeon. Got it?"

"Yes, sir," Tad said, then skipped—or tried to—his exuberance impossible to keep down. "We have a dungeon? Cool. Can I see it?"

"Actually, you're going to live in it," Derrek told

them. "I figured you'd like to spread out in your own space. Tish, you'll have your own room. I hope you like plants. You'll be quartered in the hydroponic section."

Azsla caught Tish's grin of delight through her face-plate. As for Azsla, she was rooming with Derrek for their night on Alpha One—that is, if they got any sleep. She had lots of work to do and as much as she wanted to get started, she couldn't help but admire Derrek's aster-oid.

He'd spared no expense. Every system had backups. A *marbellite* wall by the entrance had the engraved names of people who had died here. It was a sobering reminder that simple mistakes could turn into critical disasters.

They entered the double-walled lock, waited for pres-sure and air to circulate, then removed and carefully hung up their space suits. Derrek slipped magnets on his shoes and handed out a pair to everyone else.

"Do we have to wear them?" Tad asked.

"Not if you promise to be careful," Derrek agreed.

Tad whooped, shoved the magnets into his pocket, and let himself float. At his smile of delight, Tish fol-lowed suit. Azsla watched them twist and turn, but both of them were stuck. They couldn't go up or down or sideways without pushing off and they'd left themselves helpless.

Derrek didn't say a word. He simply waited for them to figure it out.

"How about a hand, Dad?" Tad asked.

"What would you do if I wasn't here?" Derrek coun-tered without offering to help.

Tad took off his shoe and threw it against a wall. The

shoe bounced back and he caught it. The action moved him forward about an inch. Derrek laughed. "That might take a while. We'll leave you two to have fun."

He took Azsla's hand and led her out the lock.

"I can't believe he's just going to leave us here," Tish complained.

"He's tough," Tad defended his father, sounding proud. "Besides, we can do this, Tish. Watch." He threw his shoe and caught it again. Tish tried puffing air through her lips.

Azsla kept her voice low so the kids wouldn't hear her chuckle. "You think they'll be okay?"

"I'll check on them through the link. It may take them an hour or two to work their way to a wall, but it's a lesson they won't forget."

Derrek led her through another airlock, and they entered a crescent-shaped all-purpose room with a domed ceiling that looked carved from rock. The ceiling had to be three stories high. A spectacular window gave them a view of spinning and orbiting asteroids, the sun and several planets, including Zor. They could even see Sauren as he navigated *Beta Five* through the asteroid belt.

Inside, despite the blackness of space that could have made the room cold, couches in bright colors, lemon, tangelo, and lime green, plus multicolored throw rugs and three-dimensional sculptures kept the place lively, cheerful, and very livable. It was a room where one could relax in front of a stone fireplace—one that had no chimney and used gas for fuel—watch a huge vidscreen, or conduct a party or a business meeting at the conference table.

"The salt mine was originally this size and then we followed veins deeper into Alpha One," Derrek said. "Those veins now serve as corridors. We dug out extra space later as needed. Taylo and his wife Lasa live here full time. Lasa's agreed to look after Cade's and my kids while we're gone."

Azsla had forgotten that Cade and Shara's children were already here. They'd wanted to make sure their children would survive.

As he spoke, a diminutive white-haired lady with sparkling green eyes and a snub nose greeted them with a wide smile. Derrek made the introductions and then she asked, "Have a good trip?"

"Yes, thanks."

Lasa set a tray of fresh-baked cookies on a table and spoke over her shoulder as she departed. "I made these for the kids. Thought they might like to try their dad's favorite."

Derrek took a handful. "Thanks." Then he placed one between Azsla's lips. "Try."

The scent was strange to her, and the tan cookies had dark spots in them, but they smelled delicious. She bit into it without hesitation and the most wonderful sweet flavor spread over her tongue. "What is that?"

"Chocolate chip cookies. When Shara left Earth, she made Cade take her favorite foods through the portal. Good thing she was wealthy, because the portal closed soon after they left. However, we have a huge stockpile of chocolate, among other things." He grinned, then the smile died. "Cade and Shara should be here with us, instead of on Zor."

"If we do our job right, they should be safe," she said, then changed the subject. "Taylo and I are working on a timing device so I can set the charge, then still have time to get away. How long a lead time will I need to return to the ship and for us to depart into hyperspace?"

"Fifteen micronbits. Let's leave extra time and aim for thirty."

She shook her head. "I'd rather not set it so far in advance. The calculations need to be precise and made according to many factors, some of which change as the asteroid spins and light hits it. The longer the timer setting, the more chance of error." She helped herself to another cookie and followed Derrek down a corridor. "Where are we going?"

"I want to show you something." He led her into the master suite, decorated in golds and yellows and soft bronzes.

But the back side of Alpha One had a completely different view and the huge window took center stage. She'd heard about Alpha One's twirling water crystals but to see them actually spinning outside took her breath away. Three blue spectrum moons orbited and spun, casting an array of changing sparkles over the pristine *granitite* face of Mount Crion, a glinting mountain peak whose jagged edges framed the crystals.

"Wow." She stared into the beauty of space and

understood the appeal of living out here. "It's so beautiful. Does it ever look the same?"

"Nope. Maybe that's why you remind me of home. You're always changing."

"You make me sound flighty."

"Open-minded," he corrected her. "Since you've left Rama, you've changed sides, accepted me and my children. You really are an amazing woman . . . for a First," he teased.

"You aren't so bad yourself. But—"

"Shh." He slung an arm over her shoulder. "I'm not rushing you. And let's not talk about doubts. Not when we have to leave in the morning."

"All right." She turned to him. "You don't have an ice cave here, do you?"

"Like the one in Pepko's vision? No. Why?"

"Because he claimed it was from our future. That would indicate we live through tomorrow. That ice cave is waiting for us sometime in our future."

"Maybe the interfering alien is good for something after all."

"You think?" Azsla embraced Derrek, enjoying the solid feel of him in her arms. "Did Pepko realize that I need you and your ship to blow up Katadama and you needed me for the tactonics?"

"I don't know. He's been rather cryptic. He's never explained why we must be together, only that we must be so."

Azsla shivered and Derrek rubbed his arms over her back. "Is he playing us?"

"Probably. But I don't have any regrets. Not since he brought you to me." Derrek tightened his arms around her. "In a perfect universe, we might have found one another without Pepko's messing with my mind—"

"What do you mean?" she asked. "He used *Quait* on you?"

Derrek shook his head. "He lowered my natural inhibitions so I couldn't resist you. But don't think I don't want you. Pepko claims he can't change me, only help me see what's already in my heart."

"He's manipulated us. But why?" she asked, almost hoping the alien would speak up and recalling his chat about sacrifice. But he appeared to be gone, leaving them alone with their questions.

24

The next morning Derrek and Azsla left Alpha One. Knowing Taylo's wife would take care of his children eased Derrek's mind. If anything happened to him and Azsla, his friend's wife would treat them like her own. Although Derrek had considered dismissing his crew, he needed them. However, because of the danger of the mission, he'd asked for volunteers and had been proud when all of them—Adain, Cavin, Paycon, and Doc Falcon—had agreed to accompany him. Even Azsla's old crew had volunteered but there had been no need to endanger Micoo, Jadlan, or Rak, who'd settled in as a crew on one of his mining transports. However, he did need Azsla as a weapons specialist. Her role in setting the bomb off and destroying Katadama was vital.

Even with the crew bustling around Derrek, the bridge seemed quiet. All business. He drank a cup of *whai* and stared at the vidscreen, the silence between him and his crew easy and compatible.

Since the controls were automated, his crew simply needed to watch over the programs and override the nav system if an emergency occurred. But nothing out of the ordinary was happening now that they'd left the asteroid belt behind. Space out here was relatively empty of cosmic dust, stray meteors, or debris and *Beta Five*'s programming worked flawlessly. When they kicked into hyperdrive, Derrek left Sauren at the helm of the bridge and headed down to the cargo bay, where he found Azsla.

She was sitting on the deck, tweaking the timing device with her mini computer, a last micronbit adjustment. He recalled those same fingers running down his back last night, encouraging him to take her harder, faster, deeper. He couldn't seem to get enough of her and prayed this mission would go smoothly.

Azsla seemed calm enough now, but after they'd both fallen asleep in one another's arms, she'd awakened him in the early morning hours, a nightmare causing her to sit up with a violent gasp. He'd asked her what was wrong, but she hadn't answered, just sleepily hugged him and pretended to return to sleep.

But it had taken a long time before she'd relaxed in his arms and he still wasn't certain if she'd slept since then. Perhaps the use of tactonics haunted her as it did him. The weaponry had been tested long ago and no one living had ever set one off. However, the ancient texts describing the weapon told of destruction so massive, radiation so severe, that no one within detonation range had enough flesh and bone left to bury, never mind survive.

Derrek found the tubular-shaped missile, with its tactonium-enriched core, threatening but necessary. While the tactonics might be their last hope of saving Zor, he hated the idea that in its tiny compartment, one nudge would connect the tactonium to the reactor and start a reaction that couldn't be stopped. The timing device was not sophisticated. Once she turned on the damned thing, she had no way to turn it off.

With his thoughts focused on how he would set down on the asteroid without jarring the bomb, he didn't notice exactly when Azsla had gone so still. Too still.

She'd almost totally stopped moving. She was sitting like a statue, her eyes unseeing, her chest barely rising and falling. The eerie spike of fear he felt at her unnatural pose almost unglued him.

"What is it?" he asked, his mouth dry.

She didn't answer.

He hurried around the bomb and shook her shoulder. "Azsla?"

When she still didn't come out of her trance, his concern escalated to frantic. He had no idea what to do and hit his link to summon Doc Falcon. "I've never seen anyone so far gone who didn't have a severe injury. Should I shake her harder? Or will that harm her?"

"Don't do anything until I arrive," Doc Falcon ordered.

Derrek turned back to Azsla. "Talk to me," he begged. "Damn it. You're scaring me."

Her eyes were open. Her pulse seemed normal. But her mind . . . wasn't there.

What the hell was going on? Was she acting out some secret First ritual? Was she sick? Had her mind snapped?

Gently, he gathered her into his arms and rocked her against him. Her skin seemed a bit colder than normal, but unlike last night, she didn't hug back. She didn't respond. It was as if she had no awareness he was there.

Derrek couldn't help worrying that he'd asked too much from her. Maybe the pressure had gotten to her and she'd snapped. Maybe the idea of setting the timer on a tactonic bomb had caused her to lose it. But she'd always seemed so in control of herself during battle. As if she could deal with any emergency and keep a cool head. If this was his fault, for assuming she could handle the pressure and she'd cracked, he'd never forgive himself.

"Please. Come back to me. I need you. Azsla, please. Talk to me. Hug me. Give me some indication that you're still here with me."

She didn't move. Didn't respond.

Where was the doc?

Derrek was about to hit the com link to ask where he was, when Azsla blinked. One micronbit she'd been gone, the next she was back.

"Are you all right?" he asked.

"Define all right," she muttered with a sarcasm that relieved him.

"Are you ill?"

"Nope. Just pregnant."

"What!" Her announcement decked him. Here he'd been worrying if she was losing her mind and she came out of her trance to make an out-of-the-vacuum statement that made her sound crazy. How could she be pregnant when he'd taken precautions? He'd had his yearly anti-insemination shot. His sperm weren't able to impregnate a mate and those shots never failed. Never.

Just then Doc Falcon hurried into the cargo bay. Derrek waved him back. "She's fine."

"You're sure."

"Yes. False alarm." Derrek wanted to speak to her before asking the doctor to examine her, especially after her statement. Everyone knew pregnant women sometimes fainted . . . but she'd looked to have been in a trance.

"Whatever you say, boss man." The doc shook his head and departed.

"I'm carrying twins. Your son and daughter," Azsla insisted, a pleased smile lighting up her face.

"But—"

"Your alien friend altered your body chemistry. Apparently children are necessary." She spoke in a dreamy tone, as if she had yet to process and comprehend all she'd said.

"But—"

"Careful, dear. Don't say anything you wouldn't want our children to hear."

What did she mean? That their children could hear? They hadn't been born yet. And babies couldn't understand their conversation. She wasn't making sense. Even worse, they were on an important and dangerous mission. She should not be pregnant. The timing was—

Hi, Pop.

Hi, Dad.

"Who thought that?" Derrek leaned against the console, his knees ready to buckle, his thoughts churning like a redlining hyperdrive engine. He had to be asleep and dreaming. Nothing made sense. But he wasn't asleep. And he couldn't discount the thoughts in his head. His children had yet to be born, but they were communicating with him telepathically. But human babies didn't do that.

We've shocked him.

You think.

"Are you saying my kids are speaking to me telepathically?" he asked Azsla, so stunned he could barely force the concept into words.

Our gestation period is faster than normal.

Ready or not, we're going to be born soon.

Okay, so beings were communicating with him. But that didn't mean they were his kids or talking to him from Azsla's womb. Derrek placed his hand on Azsla's stomach. There *was* a bump in her belly, one he could have sworn hadn't been there the night before. But babies didn't grow that quickly. Had she been pregnant all along and he'd failed to notice? Not possible. He'd had his hands all over her delicious body. That bump had grown—literally overnight. "When did this happen?"

She shrugged. "I don't know. But there's more I have to tell you."

"More?" Even as he braced himself, he didn't know if his heart could take any more news.

Easy, Mom. Dad's heartbeat is elevated.

His pulse is racing. We don't want to give him a heart attack.

"Our children are telepathic?" Derrek asked, his thoughts swirling in a fog of surprise, shock, and disbelief.

"Apparently. Your alien friend . . ."

"Pepko!" Derrek shouted.

Under his hand, the babies jumped.

Don't be mad, Dad.

Yeah, Pop. Pepko did us a favor.

"He altered your DNA." Derrek's anger began to soar now that he was finally getting over the shock. "How dare he change you?"

It's necessary. Derrek recognized the mature telepathic voice of Pepko, so different from the twins. About damn time he showed up and accounted for his actions.

"Necessary? Why?" Derrek asked.

The survival of your species and ours is at stake.

"There are more of you?" Azsla asked. "Was that who I dreamed about?"

Derrek looked at Azsla's face. She had this faraway look in her eyes, as if she were recalling her vision. That's when it hit him. Her strange trance earlier when she wouldn't respond or move must have been another vision. Pepko was manipulating them.

Only a little. I nudge. You aren't doing anything you don't want to do.

"I'd call altering my children's DNA and expediting the pregnancy process a helluva lot more than a nudge."

Dad, it's going to be all right.

We like being telepathic.

"My children haven't even been born yet and they are arguing with me. It's fripping unbelievable."

"Don't swear in front of the babies, dear," Azsla instructed him in a mild tone as if she totally accepted what was going on here.

Yeah, don't curse, Dad, or you might singe our delicate ears.

You don't have ears yet, one twin teased the other.

"Enough," Azsla interrupted. "You two be quiet and let your father and me talk."

That's what you get for being fresh.

I wasn't.

Was too.

"Quiet," Derrek ordered, surprised when they actually listened. "That's better. Now give your mother and me some privacy please. Or is that impossible?"

We'll tune out, the babies both promised. And he chose to believe that meant they weren't listening. However, he wasn't certain. After all, there was no way to check. Nor was he sure if he really wanted to know. So he took them at their word.

"When did you know about the babies?" he asked Azsla.

"Last night . . . I suspected, but I wasn't sure until just a few micronbits ago when they started communicating telepathically."

She hadn't said if she wanted to be a mother, but from the pleased look in her eyes, he didn't have to hear her say the words. Her look of wonder said everything he needed to know. He'd always hoped to have more children some day, so he couldn't say he was displeased. Children would bind Azsla and him tight together. They'd be a real family.

Sweet *Vigo*. What if the children had the powers of a First? What if they could dominate him? His people?

"Do you know if our kids will be Firsts?" he asked, careful to keep his tone neutral, for Azsla's sake.

"That will depend on their salt intake. If we keep it down, they won't become like me," she sought to reassure him. And he wondered how she knew, if Pepko and the twins had given her information he wasn't privy to, then decided it didn't matter. Any former slaves could give their children too much salt and turn them into Firsts. For the moment, doing so was illegal. The escaped slaves of Zor hadn't wanted to turn into arrogant, superior Firsts. Too much power was not a good thing, at least not with humanity at this stage of evolution.

However, now he had to wonder how telepathy might alter them. If one could feel another's pain, would that stop people from abusing their powers? Derrek didn't know but just thinking about it made his head ache.

"Alert. Alert." The nav system set off a shrilling alarm. Derrek stood, about to head for the bridge, when Sauren's voice came in over his link. "We're under attack. Brace for impact."

Attack? He hadn't had time to process that he was going to be a father again, never mind the fact that he was having twins who were genetically altered and tele-pathic, and now he had a new emergency.

Sauren could handle the bridge. Derrek had a duty to protect Azsla and his yet-to-be-born babes. He kneeled, took Azsla into his arms, and braced.

Missile fire shook the ship. An explosion ripped through the hull. Automatic shields kicked in and Derrck heard Sauren give orders for his crew to make repairs.

Damage reports came in. No injuries except minor bruises and cuts. All systems were good to go. But the second cargo hold had suffered damage. The crew was making a quick inventory.

Derrek stood and took Azsla's hand. As if still dazed by her impending motherhood, she silently accompa-nied him back to the bridge. Derrek frowned at the blinking light on the vidscreen. "What is it?"

"A Raman ship. Tomar's ship." Sauren's hands flew over the monitor, calculating distances and vectors. "He jumped out of hyperspace and fired. There was no way to avoid the attack. I counterfired, but did little damage. He'll be back."

"Get us out of here. Jump through hyperspace for Katadama," Derrek ordered.

Tomar was like a hound with a scent in his nose who wouldn't give up the chase. Every time Derrek thought he'd seen the last of Tomar, the First showed up again and caused trouble. He regretted being unable to finish him off back on Zor. Now Derrek was about to set down on an asteroid, where he, Azsla, and several engineers would plant the tactonium bomb. Then they'd set a timer to delay the explosion, to give them all time to return to the ship and use the new portal device to escape the resulting blast. But now he had to worry about an attack.

"Sir," one of the crew reported in. "We've got a problem. The oxygen tanks were damaged. We only have enough left for two people to go down to the asteroid."

With Tomar ready to attack again soon, Derrek worked furiously to come up with a plan to take Azsla to safety. "Tomar knows we're heading to Katadama. We have to get there first. If we redline the engines, we can offload before Tomar's within striking distance." As he explained, he boosted the engines to the max and turned the controls back over to Sauren.

Azsla nodded, her face serene, her eyes composed. "All right. But I'm going alone."

"No." Derrek shook his head.

"We're short on oxygen. As much as I love you, I'd rather have double the amount of air than have you with me. And I can set the bomb by myself."

"You need me to drill."

"I can do it." She looked at him with a hard stare that made his stomach boil as if in acid. The moment had come where he had to trust her. If he set her down on that asteroid alone and she refused to set off the bomb, Katadama would destroy Zor as her people wanted. Tomar could stop by, pick her up, and she could return to Rama a heroine.

But she wouldn't do that. Of course she wouldn't. Derrek believed in her. But he didn't want her to go alone. Where she'd be unprotected, where he couldn't help her. In fact, to help her, he'd have to lead Tomar away from here. He hadn't had time to process how much her pregnancy meant to him, but he knew he didn't want to let her go. He had to use all his willpower to keep himself from reaching out, gathering her into his arms, and holding onto her.

And he couldn't go with her. She needed that extra oxygen.

"This is going to be tight, Azsla." He took a deep breath. They had no other choice. "Get into a space suit. Make sure to take every microunit of extra oxygen."

Her eyes calm, her face serene, she nodded as if she too understood the gravity of what they were about to do. And the consequences.

By the Stars, he didn't want to lose her. "Promise me that you won't set the timer until I'm done with Tomar and am free to swing around to pick you up."

She nodded, but he noticed how her hand dropped to her womb.

"I expect you to take good care of yourself down there." Derrek hated altering the plan. He was supposed to set down on Katadama, help her with the bomb, and then they'd leave together in *Beta Five*. Since Tomar would be determined to stop her, Derrek needed to take the battle elsewhere. With the ship, he had weapons at his disposal—weapons that would protect Azsla and their babes. But Sauren could handle the battle and Derrek would have gone with her in a heartbeat, if not for the loss of the extra oxygen.

Dear God. It was bad enough to put her life in peril, but it was just too much to risk the babes, too.

We're ready.

We were made to do this.

Maybe they should abandon the tactonic bomb and Katadama. Go home to Alpha One. Derrek didn't say the thought out loud. As much as he wanted to save his family, protect them—no matter what—he thought of the hundreds of thousands of Zorans whose lives depended on their success. They'd already been through so much. The escape from Rama. Building a new world. Even considering turning around felt like giving up. Like cowardice.

Yet, his family meant more to him than all those strangers.

There's no reason you can't have us and save them, too.

Come on, Dad. We're young but we can help.

"You aren't supposed to help," he muttered. "Sweet *Vigo*, you aren't even born yet."

"Did you say something?" Azsla asked.

"Our children don't want us to turn back," he admitted, scratching his head at how the twins could already have language skills and knowledge of their world. Obviously, they'd absorbed a lot of information quickly, and he suspected they were not only telepathic but off the charts in the smarts department. Raising those two hellions wasn't going to be easy, but he was damned certain he wanted to live long enough to try.

Azsla sounded proud and calm. "Of course they don't want to quit. They take after you that way."

"I'm not the one setting down on a fripping asteroid—"

"Language, please."

"—with a tactonic bomb tucked under my arm. I don't like it."

She folded her arms across her chest. "You were willing to let your brother and his wife risk their lives. Now it's our turn."

Derrek didn't reply. They were running short on time. Azsla had to blow Katadama while the asteroid was still far enough out of Zor's gravity well that the larger pieces wouldn't be drawn in.

In retrospect, they should have left last night. Dumped the civilians on Alpha One and gone. But he'd been exhausted and he'd wanted to settle Tad and Tish at his home. Plus he needed a good night's rest before this mission. He reminded himself that Taylo and Azsla had also required time to refine the bomb's timer. Besides, he couldn't have predicted that Tomar would follow and attack.

Again, he was wasting time he couldn't spare. On useless thoughts. On should haves and could haves. This time his thoughts were his own.

Focus.

Make a plan.

One. Keep Tomar off Azsla's back. Two. Kill the First. Three. Make sure to fly back and pick up Azsla before Katadama moved within range of Zor's gravity well. Somehow he had to buy enough time to take her to safety.

25

❂

Perhaps Azsla was already hormonal due to her pregnancy, but she paused on the asteroid, taking a few micronbits to get her bearings. She didn't know which was stranger, walking on an asteroid, her upcoming motherhood, or Derrek's trusting her. For a moment back there, she'd thought he might insist on accompanying her. But he'd kept his word. When he trusted . . . he trusted with his whole heart. He trusted her enough that he was risking all the Zorans' lives on her word. And that trust—meant everything to her and was like a shining sun deep in her soul that kept her warmed from the inside out.

In addition, the wonder of her impending motherhood had her thrilled and scared. She didn't know if she was equipped to mother telepathic children. They would be so vulnerable. Everyone had negative thoughts and her children would hear them. Would they be able to cope? To comprehend the inherent goodness in most people? To deal with the aberrant evil?

The twins would grow up so fast. They would learn everyone's secrets. . . . Coping would be a challenge.

She watched Derrek take off and pull up the space anchors. His invention, giant hooks on cables, an innovative modification of old-fashioned ship's anchors that latched onto the asteroid instead of the sea bottom, had done the job. She'd learned Derrek could be quite ingenious about a variety of things—from lovemaking to spaceship design, and he was a man well equipped to handle whatever came his way.

Too bad they hadn't had time to design a bomb that could burrow into the asteroid. For that, she'd have to drill. If only they'd had the technology to simply blast the asteroid apart by dumping the tactonics on Katadama, they'd already be done. Unfortunately, their calculations had shown that the asteroid was too dense to risk a surface detonation. Azsla must plant the bomb deep into the crust to ensure the tactonics disintegrated the entire asteroid.

So the spaceship had needed merely to hover over a flat surface and she dropped from *Beta Five* to the asteroid via her suit's jets. The lack of gravity allowed her to hold the tactonic explosives under her arm, jet out of the cargo bay, and land on the asteroid under her suit's power.

The lack of atmosphere allowed Derrek to rocket off in silence. The asteroid was barren. No people. No sign of life. No one for hundreds of thousands of miles. It was just her, her babies, and the rock that was Katadama. Yet, overhead, the awesome starscape of twinkling stars, sparkling space dust, and the Zoran sun in the distance, reminded her that although the universe was very large, she'd made a place for herself. With Derrek. And her babes. She'd found a home out here with a man she loved and respected. They were about to have a family.

Now all she had left to do was save the planet.

After losing sight of *Beta Five* and Derrek, she shoved away the feelings of loneliness. Told herself it was simply her whacked-out hormones. She had work. And an entire life waiting for her.

The asteroid looked old, worn down, and the crusty surface reminded her of a Raman desert. She really didn't understand why it came up so dense on their sensor scans and wondered about the core material and if she was going to have difficulty drilling.

"You okay?" Although Derrek was so far away that she could no longer see his ship, his voice came in warm and clear over the com link. The man could be remarkably perceptive, almost as if he knew how the isolation was getting to her. But his caring bolstered her spirit. "We're all fine."

"Don't let those babes boss you around," he teased. She found it endearing that he knew her well enough to realize that the reminder of her babes comforted her, pushed away her funk. "Remember you're the one in charge."

"You think I'm a pushover?" she shot back at him, suddenly in a much better mood and appreciative of his company.

"I refuse to answer that."

"On the grounds that I'll get even the next time I see you?" she teased.

"Exactly." His voice was once again upbeat and so was hers. They were good for one another that way. Although his protective instincts toward her and the children had clearly torn at him earlier, she'd known he would do the right thing. Derrek was a good man. The best. But as much as she enjoyed his company, he didn't need the distraction of her voice before he tangled with Tomar. "I'm a little busy right now. Talk to you later."

"Later. But just in case . . . I love you."

After he said the words, he cut the link, almost as if he feared her response. But . . . she would have told him that she loved him, too. And that wasn't just the hormones talking.

She wasn't certain when she'd fallen for him. But she wanted a future with him. Wanted to raise their children together. Grow old together.

That wouldn't happen if she didn't get down to business.

Azsla shifted the bomb lower and surveyed the area. Derrek had set her down on a level expanse. Several hundred yards away, hills rolled into bigger hills. If she could find a cave, a crack in the rock, some kind of fissure, she could set the bomb even deeper to ensure the explosion reduced the asteroid to dust particles too small to hurt Zor even if they did hit the atmosphere.

There's a cave over the next hill.

"And how would you know that?" she asked her child, uncertain which of them had communicated. So far, she couldn't tell them apart. However, this time, the mental touch was light, airy, almost pure and had seemed so very much more hesitant and childish than the voice the twins had used earlier.

We live here. Help us.

No wonder the mental touch was different. A chill went down her spine and iced her blood. The voice in her head did not belong to her babes. It sounded as if it belonged to many beings, beings who all issued the same thought. And unless they lived in space, they were here with her on the asteroid she intended to destroy.

Save us.

Azsla looked around but saw no one. "Who are you? Where are you?"

She barely considered the idea that she might be going crazy. Derrek had heard Pepko's telepathy and the babes', too. So she had no reason to doubt that other beings might be out here—no matter how unlikely that seemed. Besides, Pepko didn't have a body, hence he didn't require air.

"Answer me," she demanded. "This asteroid is going to crash into a planet and kill hundreds of thousands of intelligent beings. I must blow it up to stop that from happening."

You will kill us and yourself, too.

She didn't bother mentioning her babes and kept walking toward the hills. A dark place in the landscape beckoned, possibly the cave. "You can escape this asteroid with me. We will make room on our vessel for you and take you wherever you wish to go."

Unacceptable. We hibernate here. To leave the womb too soon is to die.

She was sorry but if the beings communicating with her really were on the asteroid and it crashed into Zor, they would all die anyway. She didn't want to be cold. But she didn't see any choice but to go on with her plan.

She'd brought drilling equipment, but if she found a deep cave, she wouldn't have to use it for as long, and her task would be so much easier. Luckily, in the weightlessness of space, she could easily carry the drill, the bomb, and the extra supply of air. So she walked toward the best possibility of uneven terrain, hoping the distance wasn't deceptive, because she had nothing to judge the scale of things, no trees, no familiar landmarks—just barren sand, packed down tight after a millennium of coasting through space.

She stuck to her mission but the idea of other beings, children, living on this asteroid still hit her hard. She didn't want to kill. Telling herself they would die anyway if this rock collided with Zor didn't make her feel any better and she trudged on with a heavy heart. Who would believe that of all the rocks in the solar system, the Firsts would have chosen one with live beings on it to hurl at Zor? It was an everlasting shame on their spirits.

Don't blow them up, Mom.

Ah, talk about hard choices. Her babes didn't understand, but she appreciated their soft hearts, their wish to do good.

"I have no choice."

There's another way. The beings' voices combined with her own children's as one. And the echo in her head stopped her forward progress.

"And what would that be?" she asked.

One moment Azsla was standing on the asteroid, the next she was inside a cave and surrounded by pulsing red light crystals. What the frip was going on now? She'd really had enough surprises for one day, maybe for a lifetime, but this vision was too fantastic not to enjoy. Above her head, millions of crystal formations rippled with reds, everything from deep burgundy to scarlet, to cherry, roses, and pinks. Just like her last waking vision, she knew this one was real . . . these details didn't come from her mind. She couldn't have thought up anything so fantastical.

Along with the pulsing red hues, sound echoed through the cavern, although it was unlike anything she'd ever heard. Part musical, part vocal, part animalistic, the thrum vibrated up from her feet, resonated through her bones, and sang through her blood. It was marvelous, relaxing, and energizing all at the same time.

"Where am I?" she asked.

In the womb.

"I don't understand."

Pepko's impatient thoughts entered her mind. *This is where my kind nurtures our young.*

"Where is this place?"

Your consciousness is now residing inside the core of the asteroid you call Katadama.

Oh . . . my God. Her thoughts raced as she put together the facts as she knew them. Pepko had come into Derrek's life at the same time she'd come on her mission. And from the start, Pepko had wanted Derrek and her to be together. Pepko had wanted Derrek to bring her here. So she would refuse to torch the asteroid. So she would save the young of his race. Pepko had been playing them . . .

If I had waited for you to arrive to plead my case, you would have been too upset by the telepathy to listen to reason, Pepko admitted.

So Pepko had prepared her for this moment by gradually teaching her to accept telepathy, visions, and aliens. Like brainwashing.

It's not brainwashing if it's true.

Even as she marveled at the stunning crystals, she wondered if everything she'd experienced had been leading to this moment. The accident in space. Her meeting Derrek. The alien's insistence they belonged together. All so Derrek would bring her here to save them.

But how? Refusing to do her job would simply kill everyone when the asteroid crashed into Zor. Yet . . . frustration tumbled in her gut and rose up her throat. Why did she have to be the one to blow up these fascinating beings?

I brought you here to save us. Not do more harm. Surely your dinky mind can understand that there might be another solution than to blow up Katadama?

Dinky mind? "For someone pleading his case, you might want to try compliments instead of insults," she muttered.

I merely speak the truth. Your minds are terribly limited.

Your minds? Was he referring to her race? Or her babes? She didn't ask but retorted with attitude. "You want me and my limited mind to save your young?"

Yes.

"If you're so superior, why don't you save them yourself?" she asked, totally annoyed with Pepko and his machinations.

Adults don't take corporeal form.

"You altered my children. That was physical."

Some of us can still manage to nudge matter as small as a chromosome. But we cannot do more.

"But your young take physical form?"

We place our young in the womb and they must incubate for ten thousand years before birth. To protect them we carefully choose asteroids with safe orbital patterns. But Ramans altered the womb's orbit. You must save them.

Aware that time was running out and that Katadama was orbiting ever closer to Zor's gravitational pull, Azsla only needed to know one thing. "Exactly what do you want me to do?"

DERREK DIDN'T UNDERSTAND why Azsla wasn't answering his com link. Maybe it was a link failure due to a blocked signal at her current location. Maybe it was a simple mechanical malfunction. Although he tried to focus on Tomar's ship closing on him in the vidscreen, part of him remained on the asteroid with her. She should be drilling by now. Communication wasn't strictly necessary. She'd be fine.

Tomar's ship hailed Derrek and he ordered Adain to ignore it. He didn't want to distract his crew from working the nav, weapons, and piloting stations by trading insults with Tomar. Besides, they'd gone beyond words. This First's mission to prevent them from blowing up Katadama was clear. He'd already fired on them several times, proving he'd do whatever it took to shoot them down.

Derrek ordered Paycon to power up the weapons and

told Cavin to raise shields. Before *Beta Five* engaged Tomar, Derrek asked Adain to made one more attempt to contact Azsla. But Adain did no better than Derrek. They got nothing but static.

26

✦

This asteroid is made up of fendiziom, Pepko told Azsla.

"Never heard of the stuff," Azsla muttered and continued to watch the crystals. The reddish light rippling across the giant cavern mesmerized her. To think life came in such a package startled and amazed and saddened her, because they were all going to die.

Fendiziom is made from material similar to a black star's.

That would explain the massive density they'd noted and couldn't account for on their instruments. "So what's your point?" Azsla prodded.

A holo pic of the asteroid in three dimensions materialized before her eyes. She could see the cavern where she seemed to be. But also the place where her body still stood, as well as the *fendiziom* that encapsulated the womb. However, the material had a much greater thickness on one side of the asteroid. And beyond it, she saw a blinking green X.

Plant the bomb where you see the green X. It will

*redirect the asteroid away from Zor. The fendiziom will
protect our young from the explosion.*

Was his suggestion feasible? Excitement caused her
thoughts to spin like a wash cycle. Would it work?
Would the dense substance protect them? Would the
force of the bomb be enough to turn the asteroid's direction away from Zor? "I need to calculate the forces."

That's been done.

She'd have to rely on his equations. Without a computer, she couldn't do the math. But since Pepko was
just as eager to save his young as she was to save the Zorans, she saw no reason to distrust his motives. Still . . .
she hesitated. The blinking green X was in tough terrain.
Craggy. She didn't know if she could reach the area in
time. Or if Derrek could hover there to pick her up before the bomb exploded.

"End this vision. Put me back in my body," she demanded.

In the space of a heartbeat, her mind transported from
the cave and returned to the asteroid's surface. She
checked the time. Walking wouldn't cut it. Running
wouldn't either. If she wanted to do as Pepko suggested,
make it to the denser *fendiziom*, she'd have to use her
space suit's jets.

She hit the com link. "Derrek."

"Where have you been?" His tone was gruff and curt
as if he had his hands full.

"There are millions of baby Pepkos in the asteroid's
core. Instead of dead center, Pepko wants me to set the
bomb off to one side to redirect the blast and steer
Katadama away from Zor."

"Will that work?"

"He says it will. But, to get to the right location in time I have to use my suit's jets." Through the link, she heard *Beta Five*'s weapons fire and her heart tightened into a knot. Derrek was under attack and she shouldn't be disturbing him. She should have made the decision herself but had wanted his take. She'd also wanted to hear his voice one more time—in case she jetted off the asteroid.

Despite the danger, his voice remained calm, albeit curt. "It's your call."

"You may not be able to hover over the terrain I'm heading into."

"If necessary, I'll jet down in my suit to pick you up. Just be careful with the jets. You have no backup. If you sail off the asteroid into space—"

"I know. And I love you, too."

Knowing she must stop stalling and act, she cut the link, took a strong hold of the bomb, turned on the suit's jets, and flew toward the asteroid's far horizon. Beneath her, the terrain changed from flat and compact, to hilly and jagged. Flying was the only way to go, but landing was going to be tricky.

Sweat beaded on her face and she couldn't wipe it away or even turn up the suit's AC for fear of missing the landing spot. A quick check of her gauges showed her jet fuel was about out. She needed to land soon and peered ahead for a good spot to set down.

She wanted smooth and flat, but steep and craggy seemed her only options. If she waited too long, she'd have no way to land and risked coasting off into space.

So after sending a swift prayer to *Vigo,* Azsla changed her direction and headed straight for the surface. And then, as the fuel ran out, she swore.

She wouldn't float off the asteroid, but she was coming in too hard, too fast and with the mass from the bomb, the landing might break her legs.

Her knees bent, her arm clutching the bomb tight so she wouldn't drop it, she braced for impact. Without gravity, a hard landing could also bounce the bomb back into space and she'd have no way to retrieve it.

But the same thing could happen to her. She hit the ground, absorbing the landing force with her legs, and then scrambled for a handhold, crusty dirt, a rock, anything to keep her connected to the asteroid. Seizing the lip of a crater formation almost tore her arm from her shoulder—at least, that's what it felt like, as pain shot from her fingertips to her neck. But she now stood on spot X. With a groan of pain, she held firm and steadied the bomb and drilling equipment.

With no time to look around, she slung the bomb and its pack onto her back, removed the drill from its container, and looked for a fissure. Finding one, she pushed into it, crawled down the incline, and found herself in a cave that descended even deeper into the asteroid. She might only be changing Katadama's orbital vector instead of blowing it up, but she still needed the blast to give the rock a good kick. That meant embedding the bomb firmly.

She scanned the inside of the cave for the hardest rock source she could find. According to her instruments, the dark spots seemed the densest. Gritting her teeth, she set the bit into the black stuff, wedged her feet into cracked rocks for leverage and began to drill.

DERREK LOCKED ONTO Tomar's ship and Sauren fired a blaster burst. At the same time, his own warning alarm sounded. Tomar's ship had a lock on *Beta Five*. Knowing they were about to be toast, Derrek shot out chaff, jammed the aft thrusters into overdrive, and ignored his whining engines.

Tomar's ship took a direct hit, disintegrating in a ball of fire that flashed across the black sky. Finally the First was off their tail. And would never bother a free Zoran again.

But Derrek and his crew had no time to celebrate. They still had to deal with Tomar's last effort to kill them all: Before his ship exploded, Tomar had sent five cannon blasts directly at them. Derrek employed every trick he knew to evade disaster.

Cavin used the nav system to slip past the first two blasts. Derrek opened a hole into hyperspace to dispose of shots three and four. But the fifth had their number and Sauren couldn't shake the lock.

"Alert. Alert. Brace for impact." Already webbed in, Derrek glanced at the monitor. Despite their best efforts, a full load of cannon blast was flying straight at *Beta Five*. Unless the chaff fooled the heat-seeking blaster's sensors, they were roasted meat.

"Come on. Turn." Benet cut out all nonemergency systems, poured more juice into the engines. If they could buy another few micronbits . . . they might—

An explosion rocked the ship, snapping back

Derrek's head so hard he blacked out for a few micron-bits. When he opened his eyes, smoke was pouring from several stations and a fire roared out of engineering. Ignoring a cut over his eye that bled down his cheek, Derrek unwebbed and put out the fire. Sauren and Adain slapped emergency patches on the hull breach before going to Benet and Cavin and helping them back to their feet.

Pressure and air were holding. Life support was failing but remained sufficient to keep the crew warm and would supply enough recycled air for a few days.

Adain reported. "Communications are still up."

Benet hugged his station. "Boss man. The engine's blowing circuits, but we can repair them with spare parts."

"How long will it take?" Derrek asked.

Benet checked his monitor and paled. "Sorry, boss man. Repairing the engines before Azsla runs out of air . . . isn't possible."

Derrek refused to accept the answer. "She took a double pack of air."

"It'll take a full day to repair those circuits. Maybe we can cut it in half if we blow every safety precaution and bust our butts. But that . . ."

Wouldn't be enough. Azsla would still run out of air before they returned. She had to set the bomb off within the next thirty minutes or miss the window to blow Katadama.

"Derrek? You still there?" Azsla's voice came through the com, bright and cheerful.

"Yeah." He hated to give her the bad news. But had

no choice. "Tomar's dead—but his last shot fried *Beta Five*'s engine circuits."

"How long to make the repairs?"

"We'll do our best."

He had to. Even as he spoke, he hurried to the cargo bay to drum up the spare circuits and oversee the repairs.

"I can't wait. I'll miss the window." Her voice was calm, collected as if she was accepting . . . what he'd just told her and was working out the full ramifications. Her next words confirmed his growing suspicions. "I'm setting the timer and hoping for the best."

His knees buckled and he slumped in an entryway. Sweet *Vigo*. He was going to lose her . . . and the best part of him would die with her. "If you set the blast to go off, I won't be able to reach you in time."

"Ramans did this. And I'm one of them. But even if my people had had nothing to do with creating this disaster, I can't let all your people die when I can save them. And it's not just the Zorans, the aliens in this asteroid will die, too, if I don't do something. Besides, waiting for you won't do me any good, I'll run out of air before you arrive." She paused and he heard scraping as if she were crawling or digging as she spoke. "This asteroid has really dense rock. Maybe I can hide from the blast. Maybe you'll finish those repairs sooner than you think."

He doubted she could hide from a tactonic weapon. The radiation, the blast kick, and the damage would be fierce. Flesh and blood didn't stand a chance against weapons like that. Derrek's heart squeezed down so hard he couldn't breathe, couldn't speak. Azsla was going to die in the blast she created. And he couldn't help her.

She was going to sacrifice herself for the good of his people. And to think he'd once doubted her. Tears trailed down his cheeks. Despite Pepko, regardless of the fact that she was a First, she was his life mate. The Ramans and their mindwipe had cost him his family and now the Ramans were going to take away his future. If only they had another ship to send out this far into the solar system, but *Beta Five* was the only Zoran vessel with hyperspace technology modifications. No one else could fly here fast enough to be of any use. No one else would come to save her.

And he could do nothing. Nothing.

She and his babies were going to die in a tactonic blast. He would lose them all. Tears choked down his throat and a sob of frustration welled in his chest.

"Derrek. I'm sorry," she spoke softly as if knowing that living without her was going to be harder for him than dying by her side. "I have to do this."

"I know." He heard the certainty in her voice. And hated her courage. Why couldn't she do the cowardly thing, conserve her air and wait until he got back. Maybe he'd make it in time.

Why couldn't she try to save herself and their children? For a moment, he thought about trying to talk her out of it but then shame washed over him. In her place he would have made the same choice. And she had the right to choose the manner of her death. Giving her life to save others was the better way out. But he'd never thought that her leaving him would feel as if acid whips flayed him from the inside out. He could barely speak. "I'm so sorry."

"Remember the good times, okay—hey," she paused, "maybe I'm not going to die after all." She suddenly sounded cheerful, excited.

Had she changed her mind? He didn't think so and believed she was referring to something else. "What are you saying?"

"Remember the vision Pepko told us was from our future?"

As if he could ever forget. Her naked on the furs. Her breath steaming from her full lips. Her arms held out to him, beckoning . . . "The vision of us making love in the ice cave?" he asked, shoving to his feet.

"Yes. Since we've never found that cave, it's part of our future. That means I have to live long enough to be there with you."

Derrek knew she was trying to cheer him. He could poke more holes in her theory than he had in his ship. Pepko may have lied. Or they could have many alternate futures. Or it could be a dream. But for her sake, he agreed. "After you set that timer, you get away fast and find a good place to hide. I'll be there . . . soon."

"All right. Promise me something," she asked, slightly out of breath from her exertions.

"Anything." He expected her to ask him to see to her will, or to remember her on a certain day every year if she didn't make it.

"Keep your kids with you for a while. Get to know them. Poli's had them long enough. It's your turn now."

With a lump in his throat, he promised and hurried to the cargo bay, thinking she was a goner. If the blast didn't shred her to atoms, the lack of air would kill her. Yet she was thinking of him and his children.

The optimist in him hoped for the impossible. Because even the slimmest margin of hope was better than the gaping black abyss of the alternative: losing her forever.

Sweet *Vigo*. He was going to work like a maniac—if only to stave off the black thoughts roaring through his head.

27

✦

Azsla finished drilling, but kept the equipment, hoping to use it later to dig herself a hidey hole. She placed the bomb into the snug hole she'd drilled, pleased with the tight fit. Then she collected her gear— and with a deep breath of resolve, set the timer on her wrist at the same moment she depressed the one on the bomb.

With the bomb set to go off, she backed out fast, scraping elbows, knees, and banging her forehead against the inside of her helmet. Although she'd told Derrek she could ride out the blast, she suspected her chances of survival were infinitesimal. However, doing anything, even retreating at a crawl, was better than giving up and sitting around waiting for the blast to take her out.

Navigating the narrow tunnel took longer than she'd have thought, but she still had several minutes until detonation. Finally, she reached a large chamber and could turn around. When she faced the stars at the end of the tunnel, she started to plan her next move.

Trouble was, once she could stand again, she couldn't travel fast enough to escape the blast, never mind the aftershocks that were certain to follow. Her only hope was to find the biggest pile of *fendiziom* available and hide behind it.

Or under it, her baby suggested.

Mom, there's an ancient tunnel and air, the other twin added. *Hurry. Hurry. Hurry.*

"A tunnel? Air?" How could her unborn children know about an ancient tunnel?

We learned of the primeval secret from the alien young. Hurry, Mom.

She stood outside the cave, glad to be upright. "I can't hurry until you tell me which direction to go."

She has a point. Although her twins had yet to be born and didn't yet have names, she was beginning to recognize their mental voices. One was more earnest, the other more sarcastic.

"Where's the tunnel?" she asked.

Look to your right.

She realized her fetuses couldn't see from inside the womb but needed her eyes to take in the view for them, needed her brain to register what she saw. Then they took those images from her mind, processed them, and compared them with the alien's images. Micronbits ticked away and she took the opportunity to breathe deeply and take a short rest.

Thirty degrees to your right.

Thirty-two. Aim for that triple peak.

Azsla didn't hesitate. She bunched her thighs and leaped into space. With no gravity, she had to aim for a point in the asteroid's terrain that would eventually stop her flight. If she chose a place too far away, her mass would be too great for her muscles to stop her. If she stopped too soon, she'd waste time. So she soared, then bounced down, grabbed a handhold to recover, then aimed once more and relaunched. The method was clumsy, the risk was enormous—but so was failing to get to safety in time. She couldn't survive the blast in the open. It remained to be seen if she could survive at all.

So she kept going. She clung to the drill, launched, grabbed and landed, aimed and relaunched. She didn't concern herself with air usage and kept tight hold of her determination. With the continual launching and landing, her muscles burned. Once she missed her handhold and tumbled, somersaulting and skidding. If her suit tore, she was done. Ditto for her air hose. Or if she broke a bone.

Her frantic, frenzied scramble bordered on desperate and she feared the twins would suffer.

We're fine.

We like spinning.

A little to the right.

She leaped and checked her timer. "Eighty micron-bits."

Almost there.

See that iron deposit. Looks like rust.

"I see it." Her eyes picked out the reddish stain amid the gray rock.

That would be the bull's-eye. The door should be to the right of that huge boulder.

"I'm on it." She clenched the drill, landed and skid-ded to a halt, throwing up dust that spun in her lamp-light's beam.

Azsla clawed at the door with her gloved fingers, and then a screwdriver, but couldn't find any leverage. With-out hesitating, she readied the drill. As much as she wanted to set the speed to high, if she broke the bit, she had no time for a repair job.

Her timer flashed sixty micronbits.

Mom, move the bit to the right and up twenty degrees.

Azsla redirected her efforts, leaning into the drill as hard as she dared. And tried not to think about how her child knew what was inside the metal door. A door no one had used for ten thousand years. Which meant they couldn't grab it out of her memory. Or anyone else's either, except maybe Pepko's.

Fifty micronbits.

She felt the metal giving beneath the drill, rammed the bit through, jammed it at an angle to catch the teeth in the door, and yanked backwards. The door opened so easily she flew onto her butt. Shoving to her feet, she bounded through the door, slamming it behind her.

Forty micronbits.

Run to the right. There's a vertical shaft. Take it down.

Azsla lumbered down the narrow hall, unable to maintain an easy gait. She kept hitting her helmet, and finally turned her body parallel to the floor, belly down, and used her feet on the walls to propel forward. When she reached the shaft, she took hold of the ceiling, aimed her feet down. And shoved.

Thirty micronbits.

"How far down does this go?"

To the core.

Twenty micronbits.

As she fell, Azsla caught the overtone of worry in her babes' thoughts. "What is it?"

Ten.

We need the young to allow us entrance.

They are being stubborn.

Azsla understood that opening the door to save her would risk all the young inside. "We can't jeopardize their lives. There are many of them. Few of us. Although I love you both dearly . . . we cannot place our own—"

Five.

Pepko's mature thoughts broke in. *The double airlock will open for Azsla and her kin. Your destiny is tied to ours.*

Her babes' relief and joy and jubilation flooded through her.

No sooner had the emotions shot through her, than she heard the clang of metal opening below her feet. She slipped past the door and it snapped closed, entombing her alive. A second door opened and closed after she passed through. Shortly thereafter, she landed lightly, a cushion of air softening her landing.

Remove your helmet. The air is safe for you to breathe here, Pepko told her.

Azsla did as he suggested, conserving the oxygen she had left in her tanks and looking around. She was inside the cave with the shimmering red crystals. The young were all radiating one color now, bright scarlet. An air stream set her down gently, her feet touching the cave's bottom with no more force than if she'd stood up from a chair.

Four micronbits.

"Thank you. Pepko, would you please tell Derrek that I'm alive?"

Two.

That would be unnecessary interference.

One.

The blast would have knocked her off her feet, but more air shot out to stabilize her. Azsla found herself holding her breath as the cave seemed to flex under her, around her, over her. The crystals brightened to a fiery red, making her wonder if this was the end, that the womb was about to cave. A few rocks rumbled. The entire asteroid shook.

The very air inside vibrated.

The crystals wailed in terror.

Azsla's hands curled protectively around her womb. She'd done everything she could. Would her efforts be enough? Had the blast changed Katadama's orbit enough to prevent it from crashing into Zor? Would the asteroid hold together and protect the young? Would she and her babes survive?

The shaking increased. Part of the ceiling caved, and the crystals in that area screamed, and then went silent. She couldn't go to them. The asteroid shook so much that all she could do was scrunch against a wall, pull her knees to her chest, and place her head down to protect her own babes.

There was nothing left to do but pray to *Vigo* that they would all survive—the crystal young, the Zorans, and Azsla and her babies were now in the hands of powers greater than their own.

28

Heart heavy, Derrek repaired *Beta Five*'s engines, replacing the damaged circuits deep in the ship's belly. Meanwhile reports came in from Sauren on the bridge. "The tactonic explosion on Katadama altered the asteroid's course. Zor and everyone on that planet are going to be fine."

"How bad was the explosion?" Derrek asked, hoping that there might still be a piece big enough for Azsla to have hidden on. However, she'd long since run out of air. Right now, he wanted to recover her body and take her home to Alpha One to honor in a death ceremony.

"One third of the asteroid disintegrated. The bigger pieces will eventually leave our solar system, while the majority will likely join our asteroid belt. But none except the tiniest pieces will fall to Zor. You saved the world, Derrek."

Not him. Her. "Azsla did it. Have you heard anything . . . ?

"I'm sorry." Sauren's tone was one of solemn sadness. Derrek knew his friend believed Azsla was gone. "Even if she went into a sleep-trance and managed her air—if she was still there during the blast, she couldn't have survived. We should go home."

"We will—after I search for her body. I have to look." Worn out, physically and emotionally, Derrek shook his head, knowing that if there was any hope Sauren would have given it to him. Still in shock, he hadn't yet felt the full measure of his grief—but it was coming. And it would hit hard. "I promised her that I would go back for my children. But I can't leave without . . . looking for her."

"I understand."

"She planned to use the drill to dig. Maybe—" He couldn't even say the words—words that sounded hopeless.

"The top layers of Katadama are gone. The entire asteroid is radioactive. Be careful. Tish and Tad need you."

"Send them a message. Give them my love." Derrek shut down the link, his throat tight with sorrow. He still felt so connected to Azsla he had difficulty believing she was really gone. Was it really possible she was no more?

Any moment he expected her to link in but the com remained silent.

Still . . . she was so resourceful, maybe she had found a cave, a hole, a place to avoid the radiation. As he mourned, Derrek drove home the last circuit board and Benet tested his engines. They coughed, then flared to life.

Without hesitation, Derrek ordered Sauren to rev the hyperdrive and set course for Katadama in her new path through the stars. The journey took less than an hour. Breaking out of hyperspace, from the bridge, Derrek surveyed the massive damage, the blackened rock, the red-hot lava. The blast had shorn off one entire end of the asteroid and the burnt rust now looked charred. The hills and rough terrain had melted to slag.

His instruments told him that the molten lava formed a layer twenty feet thick. No one could have survived in a cave or by digging a hole. She was gone.

He slumped into his station, heart squeezing into a heavy fist. His children would never be born, never mind grow up. Tish and Tad would never meet the twins. He and Azsla would never—

Dad, is that you?

"Pepko, don't toy with me," Derrek growled.

Dad, it's us. We made it. So did Mom.

Derrek raised his head, and narrowed his eyes at the asteroid. Pepko might be condescending but he'd never been cruel. Was it really possible that Azsla and his babies had survived? There was no fripping way. Had he finally lost it? Was he imagining voices in his head? He was almost afraid to hope.

He cleared his throat of tears. "Where are you?"

Sauren eyed him strangely. So did his crew. Derrek paid no attention. If the babies were alive—so was Azsla.

We're in the asteroid's core. The Perceptive Ones built this place with a tunnel into the center. We're safe and ready to be picked up. We'll come to you. You ready to catch us?

"Oh, sweet *Vigo*." Derrek jumped up from his station. "Azsla's alive. She found an air pocket in the core. And she's coming. Sauren, get us closer."

"Derrek. Nothing has come in over the link. I see no sign of Azsla. Maybe you need to see Doc Falcon," Sauren gently suggested.

"I'm not crazy." He laughed, his heart expanding with joy. "She's alive. I haven't lost it." Derrek had never told Sauren about Pepko, about Azsla's pregnancy or the twins' telepathy. And any explanation now would make him sound as if he'd really gone off the deep end of the vortex. So he didn't bother to explain. "Train all our sensors on the asteroid. And prepare a suit for me to jet into space."

"But—"

"Just do it."

WHEN THE ASTEROID stopped shaking, Azsla un-curled her body and crawled over to the crystals that had fallen. They still glowed a pale pink, but clearly, they weren't going to survive much longer on their own.

Gently, she smoothed away the rock particles that had fallen on them, her hope rising as their color deepened yet another shade. Very carefully, she slid her hands under the crystals, found them a new spot in the *fendiziom* and transplanted them as if she were repotting a plant.

Although she had no idea if they would live, her actions brought her solace. At least if the young didn't make it, they would die among their own kind.

It took her a while to move all the broken crystals and then she took a break, sipping water through a straw in her suit. Hunger pains began to gnaw at her gut, and she broke out an energy bar. Since she'd been trained in tactonics, she already knew the condition on the surface. Massive radiation. Rocks reduced to molten lava. She was trapped here.

Yet, knowing Derrek would return kept her going. Although her link wouldn't work through the core and the radiation, her twins assured her they could contact Derrek when he came in range. However, escaping the core was a major problem. If the ancient doors still worked after the blast, opening them would allow radiation to enter and that would kill the crystals.

Radiation won't harm us, Pepko told her.

"You're certain?" she asked.

Human, how can you still doubt me after all we've been through together? His words might have been sardonic, but his tone was gentle. *We owe you a great debt for risking your life to redirect Katadama. You saved our young by avoiding the crash into Zor.*

"You saved my twins by opening the doors. I'd say we're even. And I thank you in kind."

That's where you underestimate your actions. You saved hundreds. We saved three. And we owe you a boon.

"Your thanks are more than enough."

Azsla felt a warmth in her womb. An odd heat that she couldn't explain and didn't understand.

I have given your children the location of a world. A world of ancient machines that still work. Machines that will eliminate sickness and allow your kind to increase your life span by a factor of ten.

Azsla didn't know what to say. She knew Pepko meant well, but she wasn't certain she wanted her children to go off and explore other planets. Space travel was dangerous.

It's exciting.

Think of the adventure, Mom.

"Now see what you've done?" Azsla sighed, knowing it would be many years before her children would fly off and leave her—that is, if they lived long enough to grow up. She still had no idea how they would escape the core.

Your life mate is here. When you are ready, launch yourself through the shaft and the double hatches will open for you.

"How?"

It's a fail-safe mechanism built in case they ever needed to make repairs.

"But they don't have bodies. How can they—"

Other races build things for them. Mom, you need to go.

"What about the lava crust?"

The fendiziom tunnel will protect us.

Azsla didn't hesitate. Derrek was up there. The twins had been right. Of course he'd come back for her even if it had seemed hopeless.

Derrek was here. Waiting for her. Although she doubted she could make it to the surface, she was going to try.

She replaced her helmet and headed straight to the vertical tunnel, her way out past the lava crust. Bending her knees, she thrust hard, then placed her arms by her sides and let her speed build. Making it past the hot layers without burning up was probably impossible, even if the *fendiziom* tunnel walls held back the lava, but she had no choice. Staying below meant dying from lack of water and food.

At least this end would be quick—for both her and the twins.

But then the air—air that had cushioned her fall—boosted her, accelerating her speed beyond anything her muscles could have done. Like a projectile, she rocketed past the heat and the radiation, her speed so great she barely noticed a temperature change. She rocketed into space, soaring toward *Beta Five* and Derrek—who had no difficulty jetting out to meet her.

The blast had burned her com link. But words weren't necessary. He embraced her, space suit to space suit—a thoroughly ridiculous and unsatisfying hug. Nevertheless, tears of joy escaped her eyes. When he held her tight and jetted them all to safety, she could barely believe they'd succeeded. They were all going to live. Their children were going to be born. They were all going to have a future—albeit one altered by Pepko.

29

✵

Derrek had insisted on throwing a celebration party on Alpha One and it seemed as if every one of his hundreds of employees had crowded into the hydroponics facility—the largest area under one roof. The tanks had been pushed aside, and Tish's things sat in a corner. Tables laden with food and drink, live music, and balloons floating from the roof lent a festive air to the party atmosphere.

Azsla helped herself to a soy sandwich and a glass of milk. She seemed to be eating nonstop these days. And was packing on the weight.

We're growing babes.

We need nutrition.

Azsla smiled. The twins always had that effect on her and she looked forward to their birth—which wouldn't be long at the rate they were growing. But they weren't the only family here.

Cade and Shara had flown in from Zor and Derrek's brother was filling him in on the rebuilding process. Laurie had resigned. While they might never know if he'd collaborated with Firsts, he was incompetent and now out of office. Azsla had hoped to stand quietly in a corner, observing from a distance, but that had been impossible. It seemed as though every single citizen felt bound to thank her for her efforts. While she appreciated their heartfelt thanks, she felt like a fraud. Because if they'd known she was a First, her reception would have been quite different. In fact, she suspected no one would have come to the party at all.

Among so many strangers it was good to see Micoo again. When she approached Azsla in a skirt, dressed as a female, Azsla had grinned in delight. Especially when she'd noticed the pleasure in Jadlan's eyes as he escorted Micoo over to Azsla. The two women hugged. Azsla laughed and stepped back. "Let me look at you."

"She's beautiful, don't you think?" Jadlan asked.

"Looks like you have an admirer," Azsla teased and Micoo blushed happily.

"Derrek's foreman has put us on the same crew," Micoo told her.

They didn't talk more because Rak joined them, gave Azsla's forearm a hearty shake, then glanced at Azsla's swollen belly. "You haven't wasted any time starting a family. When are you due?"

Azsla shrugged. "We don't know." Keeping quiet about the Perceptive Ones had been impossible, especially when people saw how quickly her babes were growing. She might be giving birth inside a month.

Tish and Tad wriggled through the adults. Tish grinned, leaned forward, and whispered in Azsla's ear. "Poli and Mavinor are okay. They made it."

"That's great."

"And Mom's agreed to let us stay for a long visit. Since Dad said he'd pay for engineering school, she won't fight it."

"Even better," Azsla agreed.

Tad tugged Azsla's hand. "Dad wants you to join him over there."

Azsla nodded her good-byes and let Tad lead her through the crowded room. She saw Derrek on the dais. He looked stunning in a white shirt and dark gray pants. But it was his warm twinkling eyes that made her feel special, as if she were the only woman in the room—certainly the only one he was interested in. He held out his hand and she waddled awkwardly toward him, not minding her swollen belly.

When she stood beside him, he kissed her full on the mouth—in front of everyone. Azsla tried to draw away. *Vigo,* she loved Derrek, but they were in public. Yet, as he kissed her, she forgot the audience. He was everything she wanted in a man, sharp, innovative, loyal, and most of all kind. He'd even gotten over his own prejudice against her being a First. As they kissed, people stopped their own conversations. A few of the miners hooted. Azsla drew back but Derrek tucked his arm around her and she noted he held a microphone.

"Speech. Speech." The miners clapped and demanded, stomping their boots and creating an uproar.

Derrek waited for the ruckus to die down and Azsla tried to leave, but he kept her beside him. "I'd like to make a toast to my life mate and the mother of my twins." He raised his glass and the audience cheered.

Once again Derrek waited for the noise to die down before he continued. "While all of you know that Azsla risked her life—and the lives of our children—to save all free Zorans, what you don't know is that Azsla is not merely the warm and beautiful woman that I love. Like most women she has secrets and I'm going to share one of them with you now, my friends."

At his words, Azsla tensed, her gut churning. Her *Quait* rose as her emotions tugged like a wild canine against a leash. Mustering control, she tamped down her *Quait*, but this time she didn't have to stomp as hard. Reining in was easier than ever before and with wonder, she realized she had help. The twins were aiding her. She didn't know how, but their life forces were adding to her own. While they might still be babies, their powers were strong, and her *Quait* easily curled and lay down without a whisper.

"Azsla came to Zor as a spy," Derrek told the crowd. "But when she saw our way was just, when she saw what free men could do, she changed sides. My friends, Azsla is a First." Derrek said the words with pride, his eyes daring anyone to defy him. "Unlike us—slaves who ran away to be free—Azsla was already free. She gave up a life of privilege and took on our cause. And then she risked her life to save us all."

The miners went silent. Murmurs rippled through their amazement and then someone in the back started to applaud. For a moment that lone person's claps echoed and then another joined in. Then another. The sounds of approval echoed through the room and through her soul.

She'd never expected these people to accept her for herself. She'd never thought they could accept a First as one of them. But as the crowd surged forward to praise her, she realized that she might have been a First, but Derrek had set her free. She would no longer have to live a double life, pretending to be what she was not.

If she slipped up, and she might, it wouldn't be so bad. Her secret was out—and that meant she didn't have the burden of being perfect. Derrek had just bravely done her the biggest favor of all. He'd accepted her and asked his people to do the same and they'd responded with surprising warmth. Heart hammering with happiness, she turned to him. "You couldn't have given me a better gift. 'Thank you' doesn't seem enough. I love you, boss man."

Derrek gathered her into his arms, his cheek against hers, his lips by her ear. "You're certain you love me?"

"Yeah."

"Enough to live in space?"

"Of course. I'm waiting for you to find us that ice cave," she teased.

All right, Mom.

That means you're coming with us to explore that new planet that the Perceptive Ones told us how to find?

"Did I say that?" she murmured, willing to explore the entire universe with Derrek and her children if that's what they wanted.

Derrek chuckled. "I believe you did agree. But I think we should discuss family matters later." Derrek kissed her again. And this time Azsla didn't care who was watching or cheering. She was exactly where she wanted to be, with whom she wanted to be. With her children and Derrek, surrounded by love.

Turn the page for a preview of

Dancing
With Fire

SUSAN KEARNEY

▼

Coming in July 2008

tor paranormal romance

A TOR PAPERBACK

ISBN-13: 978-0-7653-5845-5   ISBN-10: 0-7653-5845-X

Damn, the woman had moves.

Stunned and awed, Sawyer Scott peered through the sheer curtains into Kaylin Danner's dance studio. Ignoring the hot Florida sunshine baking his neck while he stood on the sidewalk, he watched, riveted by Kaylin's shapely silhouette.

The pink door of the dance studio and the radical music of Goldfrapp was out of his element, but Sawyer would have given up dinners for a week to watch her dance all evening. In fact, Kaylin's erotic and undulating movements, like thread pulling from a silk cocoon, had so seduced him that he'd almost forgotten he'd come to her school about business.

And forgetting business wasn't like him at all. During the last ten years, while Sawyer had earned doctorates in chemistry and physics at MIT, he'd rarely been distracted from his goal of running a manufacturing plant with Kaylin's father, Dr. Henry Danner. Set on having the satisfaction of being an innovator and entrepreneur, he'd turned down a big offer from a petrochemical company to work with Henry. And they'd made remarkable progress. In fact, they were on the verge of a breakthrough. Sawyer had never regretted his dedication, a dedication that meant he'd been doing little more than studying, researching, and dreaming about oil. Yet now, seeing Kaylin dance, he had no doubt she'd be invading his thoughts as easily as she'd distracted him from his objective.

Sawyer had no idea what kind of dancing Kaylin was performing but was fairly certain it wasn't the classical ballet she taught the neighborhood children. No way. These moves were as complex as they were mesmerizing.

But he wasn't here to watch a private performance or to enroll as a student in her class. He was here on business. Sawyer forced himself to knock on the door. But Kaylin didn't stop dancing.

"Probably can't hear over the drumbeat," he muttered.

Taking a deep breath, Sawyer opened the door and stepped from warm and humid to sultry and steamy. Kaylin wore a black sports bra and matching yoga pants that sat low on her hips and flared wide at the ankles. Her feet were bare, her hair in a messy knot at the back of her head. However, her clothing, or lack of it, had nothing to do with his breath whistling out of his lungs. Her body ebbed and flowed like a wave, the rhythm provocative, the beat primal. The effect she had on him was druglike, tantalizing, like a whitecap swelling, breaking, sweeping him under.

From outside the studio, the full impact of her skill hadn't been as apparent. Her stomach muscles, emphasized by a slick gleam of sweat, shimmered and flexed as she spun a complete rotation. As she twirled, she caught sight of him and went still. If he hadn't been watching closely, he wouldn't have seen her bristle, her nostrils flare, her lips tighten, her eyes narrow—just a bit. Then she flicked off the music, picked up a towel and draped it around her graceful neck, and raised an imperious eyebrow.

Dabbing her face with the towel, she shot him a you-better-have-a-damn-good-reason-for-invading-my-space look. "Yes?"

"That dance . . . wow." He could tell by her expression she wasn't sure whether to take his words as a compliment. She bit her lower lip, the confidence and the sensuality of the dance hidden, replaced by invisible armor she'd wrapped around her rigid frame. She appeared as unhappy as he'd be if a stranger intruded on one of his experiments. Uncertain if he'd offended her, he combed his fingers through his hair. "Sorry. I didn't mean to come in uninvited. I knocked. You didn't hear. Those moves you do . . . that's not classical ballet, is it?"

Kaylin chuckled, her green eyes brightening, her lips breaking into a wide and playful grin. In that one moment, her barriers shredded and her inner self shone through. "That was tribal belly dance. An experiment."

"If you want my opinion"—and he wasn't sure she did—"your experiment's an unqualified success."

"Thanks, but as you aren't a dance critic . . . What are you doing here?"

She hadn't taken long to redirect his personal comments. She did it smoothly, giving him a gently brushoff. He had to give her credit. Kaylin Danner was outwardly consistent. Her tribal dancing—a wild aberration in her normally staid character—had shocked and intrigued him into forgetting his latest quadratic equation. To his frustration, the Kaylin he'd occasionally seen around her father's business had returned, the one who was a master at keeping Sawyer at an emotional distance. "I'm looking for your father."

She frowned. "Isn't he at the lab?"

Twenty-five years ago Henry Danner had built his lab, a nine-thousand-square-foot steel building on the one-acre lot next door to the house he'd inherited from his grandparents. Back then, building and zoning hadn't existed and the industrial building in the middle of the neighborhood had been grandfathered in, allowing Henry to work legally on his inventions literally in his own backyard. Although Kaylin's studio shared land with her family's home and stood about a hundred yards behind her father's laboratory, Sawyer hadn't been here before.

Since Henry had promised to make Sawyer a partner in an exciting new business, they'd stayed busy at the lab. Lately, their experiments had appeared promising and Sawyer had just returned to Tampa after an interesting consultation with researchers at the University of Michigan. With technology growing exponentially, Sawyer and Henry couldn't afford not to stay apprised of the latest developments.

"Your father didn't answer the phone or my knock." Sawyer pulled a key from his pocket and held it up. "My key didn't work and he didn't answer his cell. I heard your music, and thought you might know where he is. So I came over. Why'd he change the locks?"

"He upgraded security." Kaylin went from uptight to thoughtful. "You were gone last week, right?"

"Yeah. Why?" Sawyer was surprised she'd noticed his absence. Kaylin didn't come over to the lab much, if ever. She preferred her dancing. According to Henry, she'd been all set to head for New York and ply her talents on Broadway four years ago. Then her mother, Danielle, had died and Kaylin had given up a serious boyfriend and her dreams. She'd stayed home to raise her younger sisters and undoubtedly to pick up the slack. Henry, who would be the first to admit he was a better inventor than businessman, needed Kaylin's help to pay the bills. Though with Sawyer on board, that was about to change.

Still, he'd understood why Kaylin was so prickly. As much as he admired her loyalty to her family, he thought it a shame that she'd given up her ambitions to stay home and teach ballet to five-year-olds. Anyone who could move like she did should be sharing her talent with the world.

"Would you like a glass of water?" Kaylin asked, then headed toward an alcove she used as her studio's office.

The apricot-painted walls showed off framed pictures of her students as well as posters of famous ballet stars from the New York City and Moscow ballets. A pair of pink toe shoes hung from ribbons on a hook, signed by some ballerina whose name he couldn't read. She opened the minifridge beside her desk, and removed a pitcher of water, poured two glasses, and handed him one.

She sighed. "Dad told me this morning he has the biodiesel formula all worked out. He was waiting for you to get back to fire up the plant's reactor. But after class when I walked my students to their parents' cars, I heard the generator go on. I assumed you were with him. You think he started without you?"

"I doubt it. It takes both of us to make fuel. He was probably just warming up the power." However, the generator hadn't been on when Sawyer had discovered his key didn't work. He hoped the power wasn't on the fritz.

Kaylin's shoulders slumped as she let down her guard again, allowing him to see her concern. "Dad's been working too hard. Sometimes to relax, he sits by my mother's rosebushes. Did you check out the backyard?"

Kaylin stood, pulled open the sheer curtains so they could both peer out the window. Sawyer's gaze swept over the lot that Kaylin's students' parents used for parking. Spiked grass with Mexican heather, blooming yellow, pink, and orange zinnias, and variegated ginger decorated the yard. The children and their folks were long gone. But Henry wasn't there.

His gaze swept over the Danners' back porch, a cozy deck with a potted pink grapefruit tree and hanging baskets of white and pink orchids. Their mutt, Randy, lay curled and lazy on a lounger cushion, sunbathing in a beam of Florida sunlight that filtered between palm fronds. The grass needed mowing and the orange trees required pruning, but the ferns beneath the moss-laden granddaddy oaks shone green and healthy. A swift perusal of the fading olive-colored paint along with the curling shingles and sagging shutters of the family's two-story home reminded Sawyer the house needed repairs to squeak through another hurricane season. He didn't see Henry anywhere.

Kaylin went to her big yellow purse on a hook by her desk and pulled out a key. "Let's see if he's in the lab." As she lifted the purse, an airline ticket fell out.

"Going somewhere?" he asked.

"Maybe." Her jaw clenched. A muscle in her neck tightened, and she picked up the ticket and replaced it in her purse.

"Maybe? But you've already bought the ticket." His eyebrows rose in surprise. Kaylin helped support the family with her dance studio. She was practical, full of common sense and managed the family checkbook like a seasoned accountant and financial planner. And she never, ever went anywhere. Not to the beach with friends. Not over to Disney or Universal Studios for a day trip. Certainly not anywhere that required air travel. It was so out of character for her to buy an airline ticket, never mind one that she wasn't certain she'd use, that Sawyer's curiosity was piqued. And from the flush of color in her cheeks, she didn't want to talk.

"I haven't—"

One moment she was placing her purse strap onto her

shoulder and speaking, the next a thunderous roar rocked them. The glass panes of her studio's windows shattered. Sawyer yanked her to the floor with him and caught a glimpse outside. Of a fiery inferno.

"Oh, God," he breathed.

The lab had exploded.